A CHRISTMAS COLLECTION

'tis the damn Season

ERIN A. KING • CHRISTINA MITCHELL •
MEIKA USHER • LIZ ZERKEL

PIGASUS PEN PUBLISHING

Created with Vellum

ONE BLIZZARD.
FOUR CANCELED FLIGHTS.
'TIS THE DAMN SEASON.

HERE COMES SANTA CLAUS by ERIN A. KING

Zoe Monroe hasn't seen her younger sister on their shared Christmas Eve birthday in five years. When a blizzard strands her at the airport on December 23rd, it looks like this year will be no different. Fortunately, a sexy stranger in a Santa suit offers to share the last available hotel room with her. While he's not who she'd planned to spend her Christmas with, she can't deny that he jingles her bells. Maybe this year, she'll make sure she ends up on Santa's naughty list…

MISS YOU LIKE CHRISTMAS by CHRISTINA MITCHELL

The only thing Gabriel Tilki wants for Christmas is for it to be over. What used to be the security guard's favorite time of year now just makes his heart ache. But a winter storm and a chance encounter with a charming, disheveled mental health influencer might just be what he needs to get his Christmas back. And maybe in return, he can give her the Christmas she's never had.

WONDERLAND by MEIKA USHER

A road trip with a hot stranger was NOT on Jane Archer's Christmas list this year. But when a massive blizzard shuts down airports across the entire Midwest, how else is she supposed to get home for the holidays? As the miles pass beneath the wheels of their tiny rental car, Jane begins to wonder if this brash, bold woman in the driver's seat isn't exactly what she wanted for Christmas...

A MERRY LITTLE CHRISTMAS by LIZ ZERKEL

Mae Thompson needs some Christmas magic. As if losing her job right before the holidays wasn't bad enough, a Midwestern blizzard strands her in the wrong city with the very man who annoyed her for the entire flight. And the entire cab ride to her hotel. And at the hotel. Since the universe keeps throwing Mae and Lon together, they stop fighting it—and each other—and decide to make this a Christmas to remember.

here comes santa claus

ERIN A. KING

For Kevin, who always lets me have all the frosting roses

CHAPTER 1

Zoe Monroe heaved a sigh as she collapsed into an empty seat at gate A7, blowing her mid-length blonde hair out of her face. She glanced around at her fellow fliers—tired-looking businesspeople; parents at the end of their patience with holiday traveling with their toddlers; a starry-eyed couple snuggling together, the woman glancing down at the diamond twinkling on her left hand—and was glad she was, for once, on this side of the gate.

She pulled the mini bottle of peppermint schnapps out of her purse and popped the top off the grande white mocha she had bought at the airport coffee shop. She poured in half the mini bottle, stared at the coffee for a beat, then dumped the rest in. *Merry Christmas to me,* she thought, snapping the lid back on the drink and stuffing the now-empty schnapps bottle back into her purse.

This was the first Christmas in five years that she hadn't had to work. The first Christmas in five years that her family hadn't had to celebrate early or late to accommodate her schedule.

Her first year as a flight attendant, she'd known she'd have to work all the holidays. She was young then, barely twenty-one, bright-eyed and thrilled to have found a job that would let her travel the world after her failed attempt at college. She hadn't even minded that "the world" would be limited to domestic flights until she was able to make the move to an international airline. There was so much of the United States she hadn't seen, she figured anything that got her out of her tiny Nebraska hometown was worth working holidays. She'd had visions of herself standing next to the Grand Canyon, dipping her toes in both the Atlantic and Pacific oceans, eating lobster rolls in Maine...but in five years she had mostly seen the insides of hotel bars and the highways that ran near the various airports across the country.

She'd gotten to go to a few cool places, of course. She'd ordered a latte at the original Starbucks (after waiting in an obscenely long line of fellow tourists doing the same). Visited the Museum of Modern Art. Toured the Biltmore. And she could have switched airlines, but she'd have been starting at the bottom of the pecking order again, and after watching her teenage sister Lydia's face as she tried to pretend like celebrating Christmas—and their shared Christmas Eve birthday—on November 12th or February 8th or whatever was no big deal, she couldn't bring herself to do it. Maybe now that she'd finally earned a Christmas off, she could start looking for something new.

Zoe took another long pull from her boozy-minty coffee, letting her gaze wander the airport. At the gate across the aisle, a white man in a Santa costume chatted with some kids. She watched as one of the kids' moms said something to him, and he nodded, lifting the child onto his lap for a photo. The fabric of Santa's sleeve pulled taut across his bicep; it looked like Santa worked out. She let her gaze drift to Santa's face, chatting with the little boy he had just posed for a picture with. It was hard to tell specifics with the beard and wig, but he appeared to be young for a Santa—under thirty—and the way the corners of his eyes crinkled when he laughed at something the little boy said, she wouldn't be surprised if he was good-looking underneath the plasticky white hair.

As if he felt her staring, Santa looked across the aisle and made eye contact with her. Zoe's stomach flip-flopped and she felt a zing of electric desire shoot through her as his ice-blue eyes locked onto hers.

Yeah. Under the beard, Santa was *hot.* She was sure of it.

Zoe ripped her gaze back to the coffee cup in her hands, fiddling with the cardboard sleeve as though it was the most important thing in the world. Her face heated with the knowledge that Hot Santa had just caught her ogling him, and she felt certain that he knew that that was exactly what she was doing.

Her phone buzzed with a text, and she pulled it out of her coat pocket, grateful for a legitimate distraction. It was from her roommate Gina. "*Blizzard coming in fast. What time is your flight again?*"

Zoe tapped her answer out on the phone's screen. "*1:30.*"

Gina's response came quickly. "*I hope it holds out so you don't miss your trip.*"

Shit. This couldn't be happening. This was the first time she had won a bid to have Christmas off in *five years,* her sister was counting on her to be home, her parents had even bought her a plane ticket so she wouldn't risk not being able to get a flight home as a non-rev. She slumped against the seat and shoved her phone back into the pocket of her parka, squeezing her eyes shut. "Fuck," she muttered under her breath. "Fuck, fuck, *fuck.*"

"Well, that's not very family-friendly," said a voice next to her. Zoe opened her eyes to see Hot Santa, blue eyes twinkling, grinning at her. She glared at him, and he shrugged. "I'm just saying. Lots of kids around. Grandmas. That cat."

He pointed to a soft-sided pet carrier at the feet of a middle-aged woman nearby. "That cat looks offended."

"It's a cat, and it's in a carrier," she muttered. "I don't think I'm the one offending it."

"That's probably true," Hot Santa said, his tone far more agreeable than it had any right to be given her own crankitude. "I came over because I thought we had a moment there a second ago and I was hoping to chat you up, but I'm sensing the moment has passed and you'd prefer if I just disappeared."

She stared at him. "You're Santa."

He looked down at himself. "Sometimes."

"I don't want to be chatted up by Santa."

"Fair enough," he replied, standing. "Merry Christmas." Hot Santa handed her a candy cane, tossing a wave over his shoulder as he retreated to his own gate.

You were just an asshole to Santa Claus, Zoe's brain said. *Hot Santa Claus, at that. What sort of monster are you?*

The sort who, it appeared, would not be going home for Christmas for the fifth year in a row.

Zoe's stomach churned as she stared down at the coffee still clutched in her hands, her red-and-gold fingernails a bright contrast against the white paper cup. Maybe the storm would bypass them. Or at least hold off long enough for her plane to get away from the airport. She would not be able to handle letting her family down yet again.

Her phone buzzed again in her pocket, and she dug it back out. "*Happy birthday eve!*" Lydia had sent a picture of herself, long blonde hair in a messy ponytail and gray eyes big with excitement, holding up a cupcake—lemon, which only she and Zoe liked, and which their mother dutifully made a half dozen of every year just for them.

Zoe closed her texts and pulled up a video call with Lydia. "What's up?" her sister said around a mouthful of cupcake when she answered.

"You'd better not eat all of those," Zoe admonished. "Put half of them aside for me right now."

"Mm, sorry, we're all out of Tupperware, guess you're just gonna have to fly here faster if you want to have any left," Lydia told her, licking frosting off her thumb.

"Yeah," Zoe mumbled, "about that. Turns out there's a big blizzard coming through. Looks like I may be delayed."

"Delayed is fine," Lydia replied, "canceled is not fine. Don't get canceled."

"Well, I won't if I can help it," she assured her. "But it's really not up to me. Is Mom or Dad there?"

"Yeah." The video shook as Lydia walked from the kitchen to the living room. "Hey Mom, Zoe wants you."

"Hi, honey," her mother said after Lydia passed the phone over. She had never liked video chatting, and turned the camera around so Zoe was still looking at her sister, who began making faces at her.

"Hi, Mom." Zoe filled her in on the blizzard and likely delay. "So I guess I'll keep you posted, but it's not looking good for me getting there on time."

"What about driving? Is there any chance you could outrun the storm?"

"I doubt it. Gina dropped me off so I don't have a car here. Plus it's like a thirteen-hour drive, it doesn't make any more sense to drive than it does to just wait it out."

"That's fine. Just let us know what's going on as you find out, okay, sweetie?"

"Will do, Mom. Go ahead and give me back to Lyds. I love you."

"Love you too, Zoe Belle." Her mother handed the phone back to Lydia, who flashed a quick peace sign before unceremoniously hanging up on her.

She wandered over to the window. The snow had begun to fall, and while it didn't look like much now, it was going to start coming down harder and faster soon. She sidled up to the counter. “Are we looking at just a delay, or a full-on cancellation?” she asked the desk attendant, whose crisp blue uniform and short, carefully-gelled black hair was at odds with the stressed expression they wore.

They shook their head. “Hard to say. I’m about to announce the delay, but I wouldn’t be surprised if we end up canceling.” The attendant turned away, picking up the receiver to make the announcement. The PA system garbled their voice, but not so much that the dozens of passengers at the gate couldn’t understand that their plans had just been royally fucked. A collective groan went up all around the gate.

She stared out the window again. What to do? Assume the flight would be canceled, and try to find a way back to her apartment? Try to get a hotel room nearby before everyone else in the airport had the same thought and there were none available? Or hold out hope for a simple delay and risk not having a place to sleep tonight if the tides turned and she was stranded after all?

Optimism was the way to go, she decided. She never chose optimism, but this was the first Christmas in years that she was able to be home for, and she wasn’t going to give up on it. She would manifest a Christmas-birthday miracle for herself, and the storm would bypass them, and she would be on a plane to the Omaha airport before dinnertime.

Returning to her seat, she glanced across to where she had last seen Hot Santa. He had disappeared, taking his biceps and his blue eyes with him into the ether. *Good riddance,* Zoe thought. The last thing she needed while trying to stop a storm by sheer force of will was the distraction of a cocky, sexy Santa Claus.

CHAPTER 2

"May I have your attention, please. Cortana flight 2237 has been canceled due to the impending weather. We apologize for the inconvenience, but the safety of our passengers and flight crew is our priority..."

Welp. That was the last time Zoe was ever going to choose optimism. She was going to miss Christmas. Again. She was going to miss her and Lydia's birthday. *Again.*

Text receipt tones pinged, phones rang, people ranted into their cells about the massive inconvenience they were facing, and through it all, she just sat and stared at her hands.

She couldn't bring herself to call her family yet. She didn't want to do it with all these people around, because she knew she would cry, and she didn't want an entire airport's worth of people to see her break down.

She glanced across the aisle against her better judgment. Hot Santa had not returned since he had disappeared around forty-five minutes ago. Which was probably a blessing. She *really* didn't want Hot Santa to see her cry. She was an ugly crier, all blotchy and gross, and the only thing worse than Hot Santa thinking of her as the cranky asshole who yelled at him for saying hi was to have him think of her as the snot-covered, red-faced asshole who yelled at him.

The airport was providing cots for stranded patrons to sleep on while the storm raged outside, but Zoe didn't want to stay at the airport. She wanted to go home, and if she couldn't go home to her family, she'd go home to the beige apartment she and Gina had never gotten around to decorating. It was a boring apartment, but it was hers, and right now she just wanted to curl up in bed with her weighted blanket and *Labyrinth*—not exactly a holiday movie, but the cinematic comfort food her soul was craving at the moment.

Zoe trudged to the taxi area outside the airport, but there weren't any taxis. She opened up her ride share app, but it crashed before it finished loading. She tried again with the same result. "Asshole app," she growled at her phone, trying a third time, knowing full well that it wouldn't load. Which, of course, it didn't. "You suck."

There was, as far as she could figure, only one option. The closest hotel was about a half mile away, and it would be far better than sleeping on a cot in the airport.

Hoisting her purse onto her shoulder and pulling the hood of her coat up, she stepped out into the swirling snow, dragging her suitcase behind her.

❄

By the time she reached the hotel, Zoe was soaking wet, chilled to her bones, aching from the weight of her shoulder bag, and angrier than she had probably ever been.

This was such bullshit. This was *Christmas*. Tomorrow was her *birthday*, and her *little sister's* birthday, and she wasn't going to be able to be there for any of it. She couldn't help but feel that the universe had a vendetta against her for some reason.

"What the hell did I ever do to you?" she muttered under

her breath as she let her bag slide off her shoulder and land on the floor with a wet *schlop*. "Stupid universe. Stupid snow. Stupid Christmas." She made her way over to the concierge desk, manned by a short Black girl with gorgeous long box braids and a round face. She already looked apologetic, her dark eyes wide behind her tortoiseshell glasses.

Zoe sighed, defeated before she'd even begun. "You don't have a room, do you?"

"I'm so sorry," the concierge said, and she did sound legitimately sorry. "Someone just booked the last one."

"Are you sure?" Zoe asked, feeling the flush of panic begin to creep up her neck, climbing toward her face. What was she going to do if she couldn't get a room? She really, really did not want to make the cold, wet trip back to the airport only to wake up on her birthday unshowered, on a cot with a flat pillow and a scratchy blanket, surrounded by hundreds of other people who were also unshowered and poorly rested. "There's got to be something. I can crash out on one of those little loveseats over there, those look cozy. I'm not picky, I swear. I just…this was going to be my first Christmas with my family in five years and now I don't get to see them and I just could really use a break." She was begging, and she knew it was not a good look, but she just could not handle one more setback in her life right now.

"I'm so sorry," the girl said again.

"I don't suppose there's a room here containing a hot single man who'd be willing to let a pathetic girl shack up with him in exchange for some under-the-shirt action?"

"I'm so sorry," the concierge said a third time. Zoe was beginning to suspect the girl was actually a robot whose speech program was in need of an update.

"I mean, it's a tempting offer," a male voice said from behind her. She turned around to find Hot Santa standing by the elevators, halfway de-Santafied. He was in his late twenties, with a duffel bag over one shoulder and dark hair rumpled from being smooshed under the fur-trimmed red hat dangling from his fingers. The plastic wig and beard he'd worn at the airport peeked out from a pocket, and his blue eyes twinkled with mischief. Twinkled. Like he was actually Santa Claus, not just a frat boy doing some kind of weird airport cosplay.

Zoe turned back to the desk robot. "Any other hot single men? Or even averagely-attractive ones? Hell, I'll settle for 'knows how to use deodorant and isn't a Republican', and I'm even willing to budge on one of those." She could handle some body odor for a night if it meant not having to trek back to the airport, where she was sure she'd encounter a wide variety of human stenches anyway.

Hot Santa strode over and leaned on the counter as the desk robot blinked, her already large eyes widening even further, giving her the look of a frightened owl. "Um, um, I —I'm—"

"So sorry," Zoe finished the sentence for her. "Yeah. I figured. It was worth a shot, though."

"It really doesn't matter to me one way or the other," Hot Santa said, settling the red velvet cap back on his head. "But if you were serious about needing a place to crash, I was serious about letting you." He held up his hands, palms out, as Zoe opened her mouth to reply. "I know you were joking about the under-shirt stuff. I wouldn't expect anything but over-the-shirt."

Zoe shot him a look. The same sort of look someone would give a kitten that had just brought them a decapitated bird for the fourth day in a row and was now hacking up a hairball. A look that said, "You were so cute, then you were annoying, and now I mostly hate you."

He put his hands down. "Okay, so only you get to make the jokes. Got it. Has it occurred to you that being so cranky might not be the way to get a stranger to offer you their extra bed?"

She bent down and gathered up her backpack, slinging the strap over her shoulder and turning toward the lobby doors with her wheeled suitcase in tow. "Okay, welp, back to the airport I go."

He reached out and touched her shoulder as she stalked past him. "Hey, I'm sorry. Honestly, if you want to crash in my room, you can. I don't need two beds, there's no reason for you to hike all the way back to the airport in this mess. You can pretend I'm not even there. I won't make any more jokes, I'll wear extra deodorant, and I'll even show you my Facebook page to prove I voted for Hillary, if you want."

"Um," said the girl behind the desk, but they both ignored her.

"Why would you do that?" Zoe asked him, one eyebrow raised suspiciously. "You don't know me. Why would you give me your extra bed?"

"Um," the girl said again, and once again the word disappeared unnoticed into the stale, dry air of the hotel lobby.

"Call it a Christmas miracle," he said. "It's ridiculous for half the room to not even be used when there are people, like you, who need a place to crash."

"I'm paying you for half the room," she told him. "No boob stuff, just Venmo. Also, I'm doing a location share and sending your picture to my friends and family in case you turn out to be an axe murderer." She held up her phone. "Say cheese."

"Cheese," he replied, smiling amiably as she snapped a photo of him. He gestured toward the elevators. "After you."

She stared at him for a moment longer, then hefted her bag higher on her shoulder and walked past him to the elevator that was opening to let another woman off. As he followed behind her, the desk clerk called after them, "Um, I'm so sorry, but there's—"

Zoe turned toward her, but the elevators closed, cutting

her off. Probably it hadn't been that important, she figured, and if it was, the girl could call up to the room.

She turned her attention back to her phone. "*Hotels are all booked, am sharing a room with a generous stranger,*" she texted Gina and Lydia. "*If he murders me, show this pic to police. His name is—*"

"Hey, uh, what's your name?" She couldn't call him Hot Santa in her "in case I go missing" text.

"Guy. Guy Cameron. I live in Detroit, I'm a pediatric nurse at Children's, and I promise I am not going to murder, dismember, or otherwise harm you."

She narrowed her eyes, returning to her text. "That's exactly what a dismembering axe murderer would say." She tapped out Guy's information and hit send, immediately seeing Gina emphasize the photo, while Lydia responded with "*hes hot*".

The elevator door opened, depositing them onto the fourth floor. Zoe trailed behind Guy as he led the way to room 417 and slid the keycard into the door, pushing it open. She was responding to Gina's borderline pornographic responses to Guy's picture, reminding her friend that her teenaged sister was also on the text and to keep it in her pants, and bumped into Guy's back when he stopped halfway into the room. "Uh, ow?" She glanced back down at her phone. The run-in had resulted in her fat-fingering the response of "*please remember we had a child*" instead of the intended "*please remember we have a child in this thread.*"

"Sorry," he said, still standing in the doorway. "It's just that there's only one bed, and I thought there were two."

"I'm sorry, did you say there's only one bed?" She peered around him to see that, yes, there was indeed a single king-sized bed in the middle of the room. "They didn't tell you when you booked the room that it was a single-bed situation?"

"No." He finally stepped into the room and she followed.

Maybe there was a pull-out sofa, or a cot, or even an air mattress tucked into a corner that they couldn't see from the doorway.

But no. Just the one bed, a chair and desk, and an armchair. TV on the entertainment stand across from the bed, mini-fridge next to it with a coffee pot on top. But no second bed. No pull-out couch. No air mattress. Not so much as a sleeping bag.

Zoe marched over to the phone by the side of the bed and picked up the receiver, jabbing her finger at the button to call the front desk. "Front desk," said the voice on the other end.

"Hi, this is Zoe Monroe up in four-seventeen. I was just downstairs, begging you for a room, and a guy who swears he's not an axe murderer offered to let me crash with him?"

"Yes, ma'am."

"You didn't tell us there's only one bed in here."

"I'm so sorry," the front desk robot girl said, and Zoe closed her eyes and gritted her teeth against the urge to scream. "I tried to, but you both left for the elevators before I could."

"Okay," Zoe said, keeping her voice as even as she could, "so we just need to be switched into a room with two beds."

"I'm so sorry, there are no other available rooms."

"I know, that's how I ended up in this situation to begin with. But surely there's someone who is in a room with two beds who doesn't need two beds, and you can switch us?"

"I'm so sorry, I'm afraid that's not going to be possible. All of the other guests are already settled into their rooms, we can't just tell them they need to leave. We don't have any other rooms that haven't been checked into yet."

This was it. This was the last of Zoe's rapidly dwindling supply of patience, dissolving into a buzz in her bloodstream that threatened to launch her through the ceiling. "Do you at least have, like, a cot, or something?"

"I'm so sorry." The concierge paused. "I can, um, send up a complimentary bottle of wine for the inconvenience…?"

As suddenly as it had come on, the desire to burn everything to the ground left Zoe, and she sat down heavily on the edge of the bed. "Whatever. Fine. Just…can you see if you can scrounge up some extra pillows and blankets?"

"Certainly, Ms. Montrose." The girl hung up before Zoe could correct her—not that she really cared at this point. What did it matter what the AI in a meatsuit running the desk thought her last name was, when she was about to have to build herself a bed on the floor out of spare blankets and complimentary cheap wine?

"Let me guess." Guy had been standing just inside the foyer of the room, watching her talk to the clerk. "She's so sorry, but there are no other rooms available?"

"So sorry," Zoe agreed. "But we get a complimentary bottle of wine for the inconvenience."

"Well, that's nice of them," he said. "It'll be easier for you to axe-murder me if I'm drunk."

"I thought you were going to axe-murder me," she said, suppressing the grin that threatened to splash itself across her face. She wasn't done being mad at the situation and she wasn't sure she trusted him. She didn't want to—or at least, not until she was done being mad at everything.

"We can flip a coin," he offered. "Heads, I murder you; tails, you murder me?"

"How about heads, you sleep on the floor; tails, I do?"

He cocked his head, considering this. "It's certainly a less messy suggestion."

"Somewhat more comfortable, too, probably."

Guy dug into his pocket and pulled out a quarter. "All right, then. But first—we're sharing a room and about to flip for the bed, I feel like I should know your name."

Zoe was pretty sure she had said her name on the phone —in fact, she knew she had, because the girl on the other end later called her the wrong name. "I just told the desk chick my name."

"But you haven't told me."

"But you heard me tell her."

"How do I know you gave her your real name?"

"How do you know I'll give *you* my real name?"

He flipped the coin back and forth across his knuckles. "I guess I don't. But humor me. Play by the nice rules society has created for us. What should I call you?"

She heaved an exaggerated sigh. "Zoe."

"There, was that so hard?" She glared at him. "All right, flipping the coin. Heads or tails? Who's sleeping on the floor tonight?" He tossed the quarter and caught it, slapping it down on the back of his other hand and holding it out for her to see.

"Tails. I'm on the floor." She felt herself deflate. This was the way it should be, she knew. She was the invader here. He deserved the bed. But boy, that bed sure did look comfortable after a long-ass day of waiting and snow-hiking.

He shook his head, dark hair flopping into his eyes. "Nope. Sorry. I can't let you be the one to sleep on the floor."

"The coin hath spoken."

"I just don't feel good about making you sleep on the floor. It feels unchivalrous."

"Well, it's your room, so I'm not making *you* sleep on the floor. Especially not after the coin flipped tails." A knock at the door interrupted the argument. Guy, who was closest to it, answered, and after a moment he returned to the main part of the room with a single flat pillow and a small stack of white sheets. "Tell me," Zoe said, "that that is not what they sent up in response to my request for extra pillows and blankets."

"Indeed it is. But look," He tossed the bedding onto the bed and held up something about the size of a toothpaste tube. "They also sent us our free wine." He handed her the single-serving plastic bottle of chardonnay. “I’m not sure we can drink it all in one sitting.”

“I’m gonna need more than fifty cents’ worth of cheap chardonnay if I’m sleeping on the floor with a couple of sheets and a pillow made of cardboard,” she muttered, crossing the room and unwrapping the plastic film from the flimsy plastic cups sitting next to the coffee station. “And it’s fucking December and there’s a damn blizzard happening, do they not know that you need a red wine for a December blizzard? Heathens.” She cracked the screw-top of the wine and let the liquid glug out into the two small cups. Turning to hand one to Guy, she paused. “What?”

He appeared to be trying very hard not to laugh. “Nothing.”

“What?” she said again, narrowing her eyes at him.

“It’s just…you’re so grumpy.”

She shoved the wine at him and downed her own cup in a single swallow. It was, as she had suspected, terrible. Wincing at the sour taste, she chucked the bottle into the trash can with more force than was strictly necessary. “Do I not have the right to be grumpy? I’m stranded at an airport hotel two days before the first Christmas I was supposed to spend with my family in five years, and the hotel couldn’t even send up a blanket, and their idea of a consolation prize is half a cup of bad wine, and I don’t even have a room of my own and wouldn’t have had any place to sleep at all if you weren’t so *fucking nice*.” The tears that had been threatening to fall all afternoon finally broke, cascading down her face as she swiped angrily at them.

He tossed his Santa hat, beard, and wig onto the bed. “I’ll be right back,” he said, and disappeared into the hallway, leaving her alone to put herself back together.

She blew her nose, then rinsed her face in the bathroom, realizing when she looked in the mirror that she was still wearing her damp parka. She draped it over the chair in the corner of the room, debated taking off her wet boots, and decided not to because it didn't feel right to make herself at home in Guy's room when he wasn't even there.

She sat in the chair and checked her phone, but all she had missed was a male stripper-themed GIF dance-off between Gina and Lydia. She clicked the screen off and tossed the phone down on the side table just as the door opened.

Guy entered the room holding a full-sized bottle of pinot noir and two wine glasses aloft. "I come bearing provisions."

"Oh, thank god," she said. "Let me guess, they're out of extra pillows and blankets, though?"

He nodded. "They're so sorry."

For whatever reason, that was the thing that broke her. She snorted a laugh, and her giggles soon turned to full-on guffaws, tears of mirth brimming in her eyes. Guy just stood watching for a moment, bemused, before opening the wine and pouring two glasses. "If I hand this to you, are you just going to slosh it everywhere?"

"Probably!" she howled, reaching out her hand anyway. He raised an eyebrow and set the glass on the table next to her. She wiped at her eyes, willing herself to calm down, and after a few moments she was able to pick up the wine glass without spilling it. She took a sip, her laughter ebbing away as the wine slid down her throat. "Oh, God. This has really been a shitshow of a day." For the first time since they had entered the room, she looked directly at him. "Thank you, by the way. I'm not sure I said it yet, and even if I did I was probably an asshole about it. I really appreciate you letting me crash here tonight. You absolutely didn't have to do that."

"You're welcome." He raised his own glass and downed half of it, his eyes bulging as he coughed. "Oh, wow. That's, um, not a chugging drink, huh."

She snickered. "Not much of a wine drinker, I guess?"

"I'm more of a beer guy," he admitted, setting the glass

down on the nightstand. He surveyed the bed. "I'm going to make a suggestion and I don't know how you'll feel about it, but if you aren't into it that's totally fine."

"O…kay…"

"I think we have enough pillows," he began, lifting the corner of one, "that we could build a pillow fence down the middle of the bed, if you're okay with sharing."

Zoe eyed the pile of pillows. Two king-sized, three extra regular-sized ones for decoration (inasmuch as plain white-cased pillows could serve as decoration), and a throw pillow that matched the gray-and-black color scheme of the room. Her gaze slid to the paltry stack of spare sheets and the single pathetic-looking pillow that housekeeping had brought up. If she slept on the floor with that, she may as well have stayed at the airport—at least then she'd have a cot.

"Okay," she said, her voice firm with her decision. "A pillow fence down the middle does sound better than a couple of sheets on the floor."

His shoulders sagged with relief and a lopsided grin appeared on his face. "Thank goodness. I really didn't want to keep arguing about who was going to sleep on the floor. I don't think anybody was going to win that one."

"Oh, no, I'd have won," she said. "But I'm also glad we don't have to argue about it." She pulled back the comforter and began to stuff pillows underneath it. The barrier stretched almost to the foot of the king-sized bed; she surveyed her work, tugging the bedding straight again over the mound of pillows. They'd be able to kick each other if they really wanted to, with that gap by the foot of the bed, but a king-sized bed was pretty big so it should be easy enough to pretend she was alone. Unless—"You don't snore, do you?"

He considered this. "I don't think so. Do you?"

She shook her head. "I do sometimes talk in my sleep, but

just, like, a word or two, and it's not a super regular occurrence."

They both stared at the bed for an uncomfortable moment longer. "Should we—" she began, right as he said, "Is it too early to—" Laughing awkwardly, she gestured for him to continue.

"I just," he said, the tips of his ears turning pink, "it seems really early to go to bed, but I'm kind of tired after being at the airport all day."

"I am too," she said, grateful that he'd had the same thought she had. "And my jeans are still wet from walking over here in the snow. We should at least change clothes."

"I'd be lying if I said I wasn't ready to not be wearing this," he admitted, gesturing at the Santa suit. "It stopped being comfortable a few hours ago."

"Do I even want to know why you were wearing a Santa suit at the airport to begin with?"

"I had it from playing Santa at the hospital, and I thought it would bring some holiday magic to families that were traveling with little kids."

"Did it work, do you think?"

His face scrunched up and he tilted his head in a "so-so" motion. "The kids seemed to like it. I think most of the parents were a little weirded out."

"Imagine that." She turned to heft her suitcase onto the bed and when she looked up again, he had removed the fuzzy red jacket. The white t-shirt he wore underneath affirmed her earlier suspicion that this Santa did indeed work out. The thin cotton pulled across the muscles of his back when he bent down to retrieve his own suitcase, and she allowed herself a moment to appreciate the sight before forcing her eyes back to her own bag.

"Maybe we can find a movie to watch," she said, attempting to distract herself from the appreciative tingles his lack of jacket was creating in her nether region, "or I have some trashy celebrity gossip magazines we can read, or there's always TikTok to scroll."

Guy nodded, toeing his shoes off and kicking them into the corner. "That sounds good. I do love a good 'Celebs Are Just Like Us' story."

"I like the 'Who Wore It Better' ones, myself," she said, unzipping her suitcase and sifting through the contents.

She had brought two pairs of pajamas: a pair of black shorts and a gray t-shirt with her would-be alma mater's name printed on it; and a light blue flannel set printed with cartoon penguins.

The penguins were meant to be worn tomorrow night—every year she bought matching Christmas pajamas for herself and Lydia and gave them to her sister on the morning of December 24 (or, recently, whatever the day before their official Christmas celebration was). They would then wear them on Christmas Eve night, their special matching birthday Christmas jammies, while they opened their birthday presents and ate cake.

But something told Zoe she wouldn't be home tomorrow night to eat cake with her sister in matching penguin pajamas, and her feet and legs were still cold from being in damp socks and jeans for so long. Still, though, she wasn't going to wear her birthday pajamas until her birthday, because they were special, to be shared with Lydia. Not worn in front of a stranger. So she grabbed the shorts and t-shirt, a pair of fuzzy socks, and her toiletry bag and disappeared into the bathroom to change.

When she padded out of the bathroom a few minutes later after calling out to confirm he was decent, her face was scrubbed clean and her teeth were brushed, and her blonde hair was looped on her head in a topknot. She'd done what she could to make herself look as bedtime-cute as possible without looking like she was trying too hard. She didn't want him thinking she wanted to get his attention. Because she didn't. But she'd be lying if she didn't admit to herself that she found him attractive. She couldn't let herself not put in at least the bare minimum amount of effort to look a little bit cute.

Guy was folding the clothes he'd been wearing into a neat little pile. His own pajamas were gray sweatpants and a fitted black t-shirt, and Zoe willed her gaze not to drop below his waist. Everyone knew that gray sweats were lingerie for the male body. He could have been in his underwear and she'd have found it less arousing.

He tucked the pile of clothing into his duffel bag and flopped onto his side of the bed. Zoe sat on her side a little more carefully, leaning back against the non-barrier pillow and tucking her legs under the comforter. The line of pillows between them seemed very small when she glanced over at him, sprawled out on top of the covers. What sort of defense was a pillow against the pull of the gray sweatpants? Zoe wished she'd packed some cuter pajamas.

Not that it mattered. Because the pillows were there for a reason, and there was still a not-zero chance he was an axe murderer. And she really didn't want to be the girl who fucked the axe murderer.

"Is that where you went to school?" Guy asked, pointing at her University of Nebraska shirt.

She glanced down, her hand coming up to rub at the letters printed across her chest. "Sort of. I only stayed a year. Turns out I'm not the college type."

"How's that?"

"I partied too much and ended up on academic probation," she admitted, feeling an embarrassed flush heat her skin. "Bringing my grades up would have taken more effort and commitment than I cared to put in, so I decided to go straight into working instead. Managed to get a job as a flight attendant for Cortana, and that was that." She usually didn't care what people thought of her when they learned she had dropped out of school, and he didn't seem to be judging her, but she didn't want to continue this line of conversation, so she changed the subject. "So, what're you in the mood for? TV, book, social media, or 'Who Wore It Better'?"

"I have to be honest, I've never actually read a gossip magazine."

"They're terrible," she admitted, "but I love them." She swung her legs out of the bed and fetched the magazines from her purse. "Here, try this one. It's usually a little less tabloid-y. It's a good gateway." Guy took the proffered magazine and Zoe slid back under the covers, cracking open her own reading material.

She was gazing at red-carpet photos from an action movie premiere when she became acutely aware of the fact that Guy smelled good. Like, really good. Like a sexy campfire, or thunder, or something.

She shoved the thought aside and turned the page. Her eyes drifted over photos of some singer she didn't recognize, walking her dog in the rain.

Guy shifted, that fire-and-rain scent wafting over again. She turned another page, forcing herself to focus on the list of quotes from celebrities about their favorite guilty pleasures. One aging starlet announced that her favorite guilty pleasure was cursing, while a young TV actress said that hers was pasta.

"These are not guilty pleasures," Zoe muttered.

"Hm?" Guy looked up from his own magazine.

She showed him the page. "Pasta is not a guilty pleasure."

"I guess it is if you're on a really strict diet and exercise program."

"Even then, the term guilty pleasure implies you feel bad for indulging. No one should feel bad for eating spaghetti," Zoe insisted. "If she said her guilty pleasure was eating an entire key lime pie in a single sitting, okay, maybe. But a bowl of macaroni making you feel guilty is just sad. I feel bad for her."

"Eating an entire pie would make a person feel a lot of things, probably," he mused. "Like nauseated. Regretful. All-powerful."

"Any of those," she agreed, stifling a huge yawn that came out of nowhere. "Wow. Sorry."

He closed his magazine and tossed it aside, covering a yawn of his own with one hand. "I think I'm magazined out. Is it bedtime?"

She checked the time on her phone and groaned. "It's not even eight. How is that possible?"

"It's been a long day. I vote for bedtime. Okay by you if I turn this light off? You can leave yours on, if you want."

"No, that's fine." He clicked off the light on his side of the bed and hunkered down under the covers. She added his discarded magazine to her own stack and put them on her nightstand before turning out her own light. The room plunged into the odd darkness that only hotel rooms possess—bits of light from the parking lot streetlamps eking around the edges of the blackout curtains, joining the glow of the clock on Guy's side of the bed in an unfamiliar shadow-color. She could hear people moving around in the hallway, doors opening and closing in the distance, the low murmur of voices down the hall. "Good night," she said, her eyelids already beginning to droop with exhaustion from the day. She was only half aware she had said it, and for a moment was confused when he replied, "Good night, Zoe," before she remembered the sound of her own voice from a moment before. She burrowed into the blankets, closed her eyes fully, and fell into sleep.

CHAPTER 3

The bathroom was steamy from her shower as Zoe towel-dried her hair, her reflection obscured by the fog on the mirror. She cracked the door open to let some of the moisture out, and the sound of Christmas music trickled in through the opening. "Here comes Santa Claus, here comes Santa Claus..." She hummed along, running a comb through her shoulder-length waves and doing a little shimmy in time with the music.

The door opened further and there stood Guy, decked out head to toe in his Santa outfit. "Hey."

"Hey," she replied. "You can have the shower, if you want it. I'm done." She slipped past him but he caught her by the waist, the plastic hair of his beard tickling her shoulder as he pulled her close.

"The shower isn't what I want," he said, leaning down to kiss her.

Zoe swam back into a vague sense of awareness, rolling onto her side. She'd been sleeping poorly all night, moving from one missed-Christmas stress dream to another, and was so tired from it that she could barely drag herself into consciousness enough to reposition before she slipped back under the haze of sleep, finding herself once again in the company of Santa-Guy.

They were in the bedroom now, and Guy was wearing only the Santa hat and pants. The towel Zoe had been wrapped in had been replaced with his fuzzy red coat, open in the front and baring her to him. She sat on the bed, arching her back so her naked breasts pushed out towards him. "You wanted something," she reminded him, sliding off the mattress and sinking to her knees in front of him as she tugged at the red pants until they pooled at his feet. He was thick and hard, velvet-smooth, and her tongue darted out to run along his length. He made a strangled sound and buried his hands in her hair, urging her on as she took him into her mouth.

The dream shifted, and now she was straddling him, grinding her hips against his, his cock buried inside her. He grabbed the lapels of her coat, pulling her down into a kiss that tasted of peppermint and wine, and it was snowing inside the room, but she wasn't cold. She kept moving against him, feeling her orgasm building, the white fur along the edge of his Santa hat soft against her forehead as they kissed, his tongue stroking into her mouth as as hers had stroked along his shaft moments before. The snow was cold but her jacket was warm, and his hand cupped her ass as he urged her toward release, guiding her against him, her nipples grazing his chest as he thrust up into her, hitting the exact right spot—

A door slammed somewhere in the distance, jolting her awake. Her eyes flew open to see Guy, still asleep, inches from her face. She shot backwards on instinct, dislodging his hand from where it was resting on her hip. She had thrown her leg over the pillow barrier in her sleep, bringing herself entirely too close to him, and now she eased out of the bed, the almost-orgasm from her dream still pounding in her blood and between her legs.

Standing in the half-dark, she checked the time on her phone. 6:43— way too fucking early but she was wide awake, and knew she wouldn't be able to go back to sleep after all that.

She glanced over at Guy, still asleep and blissfully

unaware of the discomfort she was experiencing. His hair was messy from sleep, but in a way that looked almost intentional, and the shadow of a beard darkening his jaw added an appealing roughness to his pretty-boy features. Zoe's thoughts flickered to the feel of that stubble against her bare skin moments before, and her innermost muscles tightened at the memory.

Nope, she thought, forcing the image away. *Nope nope nope.* She scurried into the bathroom, leaving all thoughts of beard scruff and hot naked Santas in the bed where they belonged.

Safely hidden in the bathroom, she turned on the light and looked into the mirror. *Yikes.* Her hair had gone into full Medusa mode, the topknot sliding down and to the side while wavy tendrils escaped every which way including straight up. She pulled the scrunchie out and scraped her hair back into submission, knotting it back on top of her head where it belonged before taking care of her other morning needs.

When she was looking a bit more presentable and feeling minty-fresh, she returned to the bedroom, where Guy was now sitting up in bed, turning the lamp on his nightstand on. "Sorry, did I wake you up?" she said softly.

"It's fine," he replied. "Just scared me for a second. I forgot there was someone else here and I thought maybe there was a deranged psychopath brushing their teeth."

"Well, I do like to have my dental hygiene handled before I disembowel my victims," she said.

"That's considerate of you," he replied, swinging his legs out of bed. "At least they don't have to get disemboweled *and* smell morning breath. Speaking of..." He scooted past her, rummaged in his suitcase for a moment, and headed into the bathroom. A moment later, she heard the shower turn on.

Zoe went to the small single-cup coffee maker by the TV and began to brew a cup of coffee for herself and one for

Guy. When he emerged from the bathroom, smelling like hotel shampoo, cedar, and fresh air, and wearing jeans and a gray henley that made his blue eyes pop, she had to remind herself to breathe.

"I made coffee. If you want it." She held out the paper cup, a zing shooting up her arm straight to her belly when his fingers brushed hers as he took it from her. She shoved the memory of the dream-version of those fingers twisting in her hair as she dropped to her knees away. "It's, uh, hot." *Duh, Captain Obvious.*

The corner of his lips lifted. "Thanks." He sat back down on the bed, setting his coffee on the nightstand, and she reached for her suitcase, grabbing items at random.

"I'm gonna go shower," she announced, a little too loudly, and scrambled for the bathroom, locking the door behind her. It was still steamy from his shower, and smelled like him—cologne, aftershave, whatever it was, she was dizzy with the scent. She rubbed a clear circle in the mirror, looking her reflection in the eye. "Do not," she whispered fiercely to herself, "get any ideas." She turned on the shower and stripped off her pajamas, folding them to probably wear again that night—unless she caved and wore her Christmas Eve penguins even without Lydia. She stepped under the spray, wetting her hair and enjoying the feeling of the water waking up her senses. Her logical senses. Not the illogical ones that had been awakened overnight by her stupid, traitorous subconscious.

Taking a washcloth from the shelf next to the shower, she wet it and paused, her hand halfway to the bar of soap. Which Guy had used. Why did it seem weird to use the same bar of soap he had used?

Because against her better judgment, she was picturing him running the bar over his body, that's why.

There was a wet washcloth in the shower, so clearly the soap had not made the journey across all of his skin, but now that she'd had the thought, she couldn't shake it. She tried to distract her mind as she rubbed the bar onto the washcloth and the washcloth over her own body, but nothing was really working to kill the image of Guy soaping his chest and arms and…lower.

"Dammit," she muttered. "I'm not gonna fuck Hot Santa. I'm *not*."

Even if it was looking like it was going to take an awful lot of willpower to stop herself.

CHAPTER 4

When she emerged from the bathroom wearing black leggings and a white tunic sweater, a comb in her hand working the knots out of her hair, Guy was looking at something on his phone, the open room service menu sitting on the bed next to him. Zoe felt her shoulders slump as she registered what he was doing. "Oh, balls. I forgot to charge my phone last night. I bet it's dead." She dug through her purse and pulled out a charging cable, then picked up the phone from the nightstand. "Two whole percent. That's actually surprising."

Guy watched her plug it in, the screen lighting up. "Do you need to use mine?"

She shook her head, returning to her combing as she glanced at the clock. 7:32. "No, it's too early to call home. I'll let it charge for a bit." She picked up her coffee cup and took a cautious sip. It was still too hot, and it was both too weak and too acidic. She put it back down and sat on the bed. "Can I buy you breakfast as a thank you for letting me crash and not making my skin into a coat?"

"Where do you live that you are so convinced you're

going to be gruesomely murdered?" he wondered with a laugh.

"Detroit," she replied. "But it's really just that I listen to a lot of true crime podcasts."

"Maybe you should stop," he suggested, grinning when she held up a middle finger at him. "But yes, you can buy me breakfast. Do you want to order room service or wait till the restaurant is open?"

"What time will that be?"

"Ten-thirty. But they start room service at six-thirty, and there's a continental breakfast till ten."

She made a face. "I'd much rather have a hot breakfast than eat stale cereal with a plastic spoon."

"Agreed." He picked up the menu, and she caught a whiff of that woods-and-storms scent again as they both bent their heads to look at it. It should be illegal to smell that good. "What do you want?"

She pretended to peruse the menu, knowing full well what she was getting already, but wanting to stay close enough to sniff him just a little longer. It was a bad idea, maybe a little creepy, and went firmly against her determination not to get tangled up in sexy feelings about him, but she couldn't help it. He smelled *so good*. Finally, she pointed to the breakfast platter with bacon, eggs, toast, and hash browns. "This, with coffee. Maybe the restaurant coffee is better than this stuff." She glared at the steaming cup of acid-water sitting on the nightstand.

He picked up the phone and placed her order, then requested the oatmeal with berries and nuts for himself, with an orange juice. "Very healthy," she commented when he hung up. "I hope you're not going to judge me for eating every bite of grease and starch on my plate."

He shrugged. "I like oatmeal. And I'm banking on you getting full and not eating all of your bacon so I can finish it."

She shook her head, her damp waves sticking to her cheeks. "Nuh-uh. Not happening."

"Then I'll just have to steal some when you're not looking. You've gotta blink sometime."

"I've been a *Doctor Who* fan since I was fifteen," she said, opening her eyes wide and pinning her gaze on him. "I know how to not blink."

"I don't know what that means, but you look scary, and I promise not to steal your bacon if you stop looking at me like that."

"You don't know 'Blink'?" she asked. "We're gonna have to fix that."

"If I agree to whatever 'Blink' is, do I get a piece of bacon?"

She did her best to ignore the puppy-dog eyes he was giving her, but she was only human. "Fine. One piece." Fishing her laptop out of her backpack, she settled on the bed, indicating that he should do the same. "Now sit your butt down and let me introduce you to my Gallifreyan boyfriend."

❄

Two hours later, they had finished eating and watched the 'Blink' episode of *Doctor Who*, then gone back and watched the first episode of the ninth series.

"'Blink' was way better," Guy said, finishing the last swallow of his orange juice from breakfast. "But I did like that one, too. It's kind of cheesy, but it was fun. I'd watch more."

"I feel like I've done my due diligence as a Whovian, converting a new nerd." Zoe closed the laptop and plugged it in to charge. "So. Tell me about you."

"What do you want to know?" He lounged back on the bed, bunching pillows behind his back.

"Literally anything. You said you work at Children's, so you must live in the area?" She spun the desk chair she was sitting in around to look at him.

"Yep."

"...so why didn't you go back home instead of getting a hotel room?"

"My roommate gave me a ride to the airport so I didn't have a car. And I was hoping that maybe the snow wouldn't last so long and it would be easier to get back to the airport from here than from my apartment."

"Yeah, same. Were you headed to see family?"

"My dad. My parents live in Florida, where I grew up. My dad isn't handling my mom getting remarried too well, so I was going to go do the bachelor Christmas thing with him." He sighed, holding up his phone. "I keep checking the weather and my flight app, hoping things will change and my flight can get rescheduled, but it's still snowing."

"I mean." She pointed out the window. "Yeah."

He sat up, tossing the phone aside. "You know what? Let's go play in it."

Zoe glanced out the window again, then back at him. "Seriously? There's like four feet of snow out there."

"It's not four feet," he scoffed. "And I never got to play in the snow growing up. I didn't have snow ever until I was twenty-four and moved here."

"And now you have it from November until April," she pointed out. "That doesn't give you your fill?"

"Come on," he said, standing and crossing to his duffel bag, beginning to pull clothes from it. "We're stuck here, so let's make it worthwhile. Let's go build a snow fort and find some kids to have a snowball fight with."

She turned the chair so she could face him fully. "First of all," she said, "I don't have any snow gear, and I'm betting you don't either, seeing as you were traveling to Florida. And second, no kids are going to be outside playing in snow as deep as they are tall."

"It's not that deep," he insisted. "And the hotel has laundry service, we'll go play for a little bit and then send our clothes to dry off. Come on. What else are we gonna do? *Doctor Who* is fun and all, but I need a break."

"We can watch something else," Zoe said, grabbing the remote and flicking over to the channel guide. "Look, there's a *Die Hard* marathon." She clicked the channel over just in time to see the elevator doors open to the words "Now I have a machine gun ho-ho-ho" scrawled on a dead man's shirt. "And it's still on the first one, we've got lots of good action movie time left!"

Guy pulled on a sweatshirt. "You can stay in if you want to, but I'm going to go throw snowballs and capture the magic of my lost youth."

Before Zoe could respond, her phone rang. She picked it up, gesturing for Guy to stay quiet before swiping to answer the video call. "Hey, Lyds."

"Oh good, you're alive," Lydia said.

Guy snorted behind her, and Zoe turned around and shot him a stink eye. He grinned cheerfully and waved at Lydia. "So am I, we both win."

"He's even hotter on video," Lydia told her.

"Shut up," Zoe muttered as Guy smirked and returned to his suitcase.

"Anyway, I was just calling to say happy birthday," Lydia continued. "Mom got a family cake with frosting roses and if you don't come home tonight I'm gonna eat them *all* and you won't be able to do a damn thing about it, so you should probably come home."

"Happy birthday to you too, and don't you dare eat all the flowers off that cake or I will make a banner out of every pair of underwear you own and hang it across the front of your school." Zoe told her, turning her back on Guy, who was watching her out of the corner of his eye and not even pretending to be subtle about it. "I'm hoping maybe they'll clear things out enough that I can get home for at least a little bit before my vacation is up and I have to go back to work."

"That would be good," Lydia said. "Oh, Mom also made birthday sprinkle waffles for breakfast. I put some in the freezer for you in case you can come home."

"Thanks, kiddo," Zoe said, a lump rising in her throat. "I had zero waffles today and let me tell you what a bummer that was. Although I did have bacon."

"So did I. She made cinnamon whipped cream, too, but we ate it all."

"Why do you hate me?" Zoe groaned, and her sister giggled.

A few minutes and a number of good-natured insults later, they hung up, and Guy looked over at her. "Happy birthday, I guess? Do I dare ask how old?"

Zoe shrugged, embarrassed. "Twenty-six. It's a weird thing to announce to the stranger you're sharing a hotel room with that it's your birthday."

"And your sister's birthday?"

She nodded. "Exactly ten years apart. What are the odds, right?"

"Sounds like you two are close," he said, sitting on the bed.

She nodded, fiddling with the sound switch on her phone, clicking it off and back on again. "We are. My parents had trouble getting pregnant with me, so we always thought I was going to be an only child, which only made me desperately want a sibling. Lydia was a surprise, and she's the best thing that ever happened to us." She looked up at him, and he was watching her intently, listening. She didn't know why she was telling him this, except that she was suddenly aching from missing her family and somehow talking distracted her from the bruised feeling behind the lump in her throat.

"She seems like a pretty cool kid, based on that limited interaction."

"She is. She's wickedly smart, and so funny, and she's a volleyball star and does all this humanitarian stuff with her club at school. She's almost certainly going to get scholarships to a bunch of amazing colleges, and then she'll go become a doctor or something and save babies and puppies from certain death. Unlike her older sister, who still hasn't paid off the student loans for the year of college she failed out of." He opened his mouth to say something, but she cut him off, embarrassed to have laid her shortcomings out in front of him once more. "I don't know why I told you all that. I'm rambling. Let's go build a snow fort."

"Zoe—"

"No, you're right, it'll be fun. And when we come back, maybe we can watch some *Die Hard*."

❄

"Wow," Guy said, looking around. Snowflakes drifted through the air still, but it had calmed down considerably since the previous evening's whiteout conditions. "There's a lot more snow than I realized."

Zoe, shivering in her less-than-adequate-for-the-weather jeans and sneakers (the only shoes she had packed besides the low-heeled black ankle boots of the night before), squinted at the dim sunlight bouncing off the frozen wasteland surrounding them. "I mean. It's Michigan. In the middle of a blizzard. How long did you say you've lived here, Florida Man?"

"Long enough that I am not surprised by the snow itself, Birthday Girl," he retorted, kicking snow in her direction. She dodged, but it was half-hearted, as his kick hadn't had any power behind it. "It's that I'm not used to seeing this much without anything plowed or turned into a snowman or peed on by the neighbor's dog. It's impressive. And beautiful."

Surveying the hotel parking lot, with cars buried past the tops of their tires and a Chili's across the street, looking sad and lonely with its lights off, she thought that they had different definitions of "beautiful". A bunch of minivans and a chain restaurant didn't scream "winter wonderland" to her.

She turned to tell him this, but stopped before the words left her lips. He was gazing around at the icy powder, flakes caught in his dark hair and on his eyelashes, looking for all the world like what he was seeing was actual magic.

"Yeah," she said softly. "Beautiful." Because he was. He really, really was.

Thwap! Something hit Zoe in the back, and she turned to see a couple of kids giggling as they peered around a silver Subaru. "Got you!" they called out, ducking back behind the car. She could hear them giggling, presumably replenishing their snowball supply for a second attack.

"Oh, it's *on*," she growled, scooping up handfuls of her own snow and packing them into a sphere. It was great snowball snow, just wet enough to pack but not so much that it formed a ball of ice. No, these were Christmas movie snowballs, the light kind that would burst into a shower of powder upon making contact with their target. "I don't care if you're all, like, twelve. You are going *down*."

Suddenly, snowballs sailed through the air from behind her, raining down on the tweens, who scattered from the Subaru to take cover behind other cars. Zoe turned to see Guy packing and throwing snowballs faster than she'd have thought humanly possible. "What?" he asked, letting another snowball fly.

"How are you throwing those so fast?" she asked.

He shrugged, scooping up another handful of snow. "I played baseball in high school and college."

Another snowball hit Zoe, this time in the side of the

thigh. She looked to her left to see her attacker duck behind the hotel's sign. She readied her snowball, and as the kid peeked over the top of the sign to see if she was looking at him, she threw it as hard as she could, shrieking with glee when it caught him on the side of the head, pouring cold snow into the neck of his coat. "Yippee-ki-yay, motherfucker!" she hollered, pumping her fist.

"Zoe," Guy laughed, "I don't think you can scream 'motherfucker' at a kid!"

"I was not screaming, I was quoting," she replied primly. "And anyway, that kid deserved it. He got me first."

"Okay, well, they're all going to keep getting us if we keep standing out in the open like this," he pointed out as he ducked another snow bomb lobbed by one of the brat pack. He grabbed her hand and tugged her toward the cars parked to his right. "We need to find some cover, and we're not going to have time to build a fort, so we'll have to make do with what's available. Do you want the truck, or the Camry?"

She considered briefly. "The truck. We can climb into the bed of it and hide, then bomb them from above. They'll never expect it."

He looked dubious as he slipped behind the truck, tugging her with him. "I don't know, that seems like a really good way to get cornered."

"It'll be perfect."

"There's no way they won't see us climbing up there."

He had a point. She popped her head up just enough to see inside the bed of the pickup. "Damn. You're right. Plus it's totally full of snow. We'll drown if we get in there." She turned back to Guy, who was adding to the small pile of snowballs he'd already made. "Okay. So that plan won't work. What's Plan B?"

He snorted a laugh. "I'm not entirely sure we really had a Plan A, but it's your birthday, so I'll let you pretend." Before she could lodge a protest, he continued. "I think Plan B is that we hide behind this truck and throw snowballs at those kids."

Her shoulders slumped, but she crouched beside him and began to pack snowballs together. "It's not very exciting, but I guess there's something to be said for simplicity."

At that moment, three snowballs pelted them, one hitting her in the back of the head, another in the small of her back, and the third catching Guy right in the side of his face. He shook his head, which didn't do much to clear the snow from his eyelashes but it must have done enough because before Zoe knew what was happening, he had scooped up an armload of snowballs and taken off after their attackers, flinging snow and yelling barely intelligible movie quotes about freedom and war and Sparta, peppered with whoops and cheers whenever one of his projectiles made contact. She scrambled to gather her own ammo, and took off after him, her sneakered feet sliding in the snow.

She couldn't see any of the kids, so she ducked back between two cars, creeping behind one of them to peek between it and the next one. Nothing. She slunk behind that one, and as she poked her head around its tail lights, she saw a navy blue coat and a bright red knitted beanie.

Bingo.

She let a snowball fly, catching the kid in the shoulder, then chucked another one as they turned with a yelp of surprise. This one got the teenager square in the chest, but as Zoe pulled her arm back to throw another one, a barrage of snowballs rained down on her.

She'd been tricked.

In spite of her own earlier plan to attack from above, she hadn't thought to look up. Six or seven kids sat on top of nearby minivans and SUVs, discharging frozen orbs at her one after another. She tried to return fire, but there were too many of them, and she had to keep her head down to avoid being pelted in the face. She dropped her armful of snow, shielding her face and head as she called out, “I surrender! I surrender!”

The kids must not have been able to hear her, or perhaps they were so caught up in the battle that they weren’t paying attention, because the snowballs just kept coming. Zoe made a break for the hotel entrance, and Guy appeared seemingly out of nowhere, holding his coat up behind her shoulders as a shield and guiding her to the door.

Inside, she stamped her feet and brushed at her jeans, clearing off as much snow as she could. “I can’t believe we lost!”

“We were completely outnumbered,” he reminded her. “There were like twenty of them. There was no way we were gonna win.”

“Still,” she grumbled, “we should have been able to outsmart them. They’re just kids.”

“Who probably play way more first-person shooter games than either of us.”

Instead of replying, she shivered, her teeth chattering. “I’m freezing.”

“Yeah. Let’s go back up to the room and get dry clothes on.” He guided her toward the elevator with a hand on her back, which normally would have annoyed her—she did not need to be *guided* anywhere—but she was too cold to care at this point.

By the time they reached the room, she was completely miserable. Her toes and fingers, which moments ago had been too frozen to feel how cold they were, had begun to thaw painfully, and she sniffled as her nose began to run. Every cell in her body was screaming for warmth.

“Go hop in the shower,” he told her. “You look frozen.”

Perhaps a bigger person would have protested, insisted he go first, at least pretended to put up a fight. But Zoe, soaked to the skin in melted snow, was not a bigger person, and she gratefully accepted his offer.

She stood under the spray, the warm water stinging her chilled skin, until finally she turned off the shower lest she use up all the hot water and leave none for Guy. Teeth still chattering, she wrapped herself in a towel only to realize that she had entered the bathroom without dry clothes. She cracked the door open. "Hey, Guy? Are you going to want to shower?"

"Yeah," he said, his voice sounding strained. "I'm freezing."

"I forgot to bring my clothes in, so if it won't weird you out for me to come out in a towel, I'll get dressed out there while you're in here."

"That's fine." He appeared from around the corner, a bundle of clothing clutched in his hands and his jaw tight against the bone-deep chill threatening to make his own teeth knock together. She stepped aside to let him past, thinking of nothing but her warm flannel penguin pajamas and the fluffy duvet on the bed.

When he emerged from the bathroom, clad in those gray sweatpants and a long-sleeved black t-shirt, she was buried deep in the covers, still shivering in spite of the flannel pajamas and the thick hotel bathrobe she'd pulled on over them, although the tremors had subsided a bit. "That is a glorious idea," he said, diving into the bed beside her. They sat, both shaking with cold and with the blankets pulled up to their chins for a few minutes until Zoe let out an exasperated grumble.

"This is ridiculous. How am I still cold? I used to play outside in the snow for hours as a kid and I never got this cold."

"Yeah, but you probably dressed appropriately. Not jeans and sneakers." He climbed out of bed and shrugged on his Santa coat. "I should have brought a sweatshirt or something."

"You know there are bathrobes in the closet, right?"

"Yeah, but this is softer."

"Is it? It looks itchy."

"You're just jealous that you don't have a cool Santa suit."

"Yes, that's exactly it," she deadpanned. "If only I could be as cool as you."

Climbing back under the covers, he plunked the Santa hat on her head. "Here. Now you're *almost* as cool as me."

"My life is complete." Another shiver ran through her, and she tugged the hat down over her ears. "Except I want cheap mac and cheese. This kind of post-snow chill calls for mac and cheese from the blue box, that's what I always ate for lunch on snow days growing up. With red grapes, and marshmallows for dessert."

"That's extremely specific," he laughed, sliding down so he could burrow under the covers more.

"I don't know why that's what I always had, but we always had those things on hand and I guess I just created a tradition for myself." She smiled, remembering when she was younger and would come in from playing outside and start a pot of water boiling, dancing from foot to foot to warm herself up.

"Well, I'm not sure we can get you blue box mac and cheese, but if we tell the kitchen it's your birthday maybe they can scrounge up some fancy macaroni for you."

She groaned. "I don't wanna think about my stupid birthday."

"Why do you say it's stupid? You aren't one of those women who laments getting older and wishes she could stay seventeen forever, are you?"

She scrunched her nose up. "God, no. I just always miss Lydia when I'm not home for our birthday."

"How much younger is she?"

"Ten years. When I was little I used to pretend I had a twin sister named Lydia, because I read the name in a book and thought it was the most beautiful name I'd ever heard. That's why my parents named her Lydia."

“That’s sweet.”

“They were going to call her Audrey, but then she showed up early, on my birthday, and I told them her name was Lydia and they just went with it.” She paused, thinking back over what he’d told her earlier about his parents. “I’m guessing you’re an only child?”

“Yeah,” he said, turning to look at her. His damp hair curled across his forehead and she almost reached out to push it out of his eyes, but stopped herself. They might be having a getting-to-know-you chat, but pushing his hair off his face was a step too far. “I always wanted a sibling though. Was it weird having one so much younger? Feels like it would almost feel like still not having one. By the time she was old enough to really interact or play or anything you’d have been in, what, middle school?”

“Yeah. It was kind of weird. But she was enough younger that when she wanted to tag along with me when I did stuff it wasn’t annoying so much as it was cute.” Zoe toyed with the fuzzy pom-pom on the Santa hat as she spoke. Her thoughts flashed back to her dream from that morning, and she pulled the hat off, stuffing it under the covers where she could forget about it and the butterflies that had started to flit around in her belly at the memory of her lips wrapped around dream-Guy’s arousal. “Enough about me. You said you’re a pediatric nurse? That’s gotta be a tough job, what made you get into that line of work?”

“I like kids, and I’m good with them. And I like helping people.”

“The hours must suck.”

“Sometimes. No more than your job, though. Were you supposed to be working yesterday?”

“No, I finally won a bid to have Christmas off. My first Christmas off since I started the job, and I didn’t even get to have it.” She felt impotent rage well up inside her at the unfairness of it, and forced the threatening tears down. One spilled over anyway, and she blinked furiously. "Sorry. You're missing your Christmas too, and you're not crying about it."

"It's okay," he told her, reaching out a hand and brushing the tear away. His thumb was warm against her cheek in spite of the chill she knew they both still felt, and she felt the heat of it shoot straight to her toes. "You're allowed to be upset. It's a really unfair situation."

His voice was soft, and his hand was still cupping her cheek, and before she even realized she was doing it, she leaned toward him, her eyes closing. He moved to meet her halfway, but just before their lips touched, a loud knocking sound split the air. They sprang apart, their eyes popping open.

"Housekeeping!"

"Uh," Guy called out, "uh, no thank you! We're, uh, we're good!"

"You don't need anything? More coffee, shampoo, cups?"

"Shit," Zoe whispered, "we probably do need those things."

"Wait here," he said, climbing out of bed and going to the door. She could hear the murmured exchange between Guy and the housekeeper, and then Guy came back into the room carrying a pile of assorted toiletries, plastic cups, and coffee-pod packets. He dumped them on the TV stand and climbed back into the bed, looking expectantly at Zoe, whose stomach chose that moment to let out a growl that would shame the angriest tiger. He let out a bark of laughter and reached for the phone.

"Or not," he said, dialing the number for room service and requesting two mac and cheeses, two side salads, a bottle of red wine, and a slice of chocolate cake. Hanging up, he said, "I hope chocolate is okay. It's all that was on the menu."

"Chocolate is more than okay, but you didn't look at the menu," she said.

"I did while you were showering earlier. Trying to

distract myself from the cold." His own stomach let out a grumble—paltry in comparison to her own, but still insistent. He ignored it. "I also called to see if they could do a birthday candle, but they told me there's no fire allowed in the rooms."

"Makes sense. That was nice of you to think of, though. Thanks." She was truly touched that he'd thought of it, and she gave him a genuine smile.

"It's your birthday," he replied, "you have to have candles to blow out. Except apparently you're not allowed to. But don't worry, I have a plan. In the meantime..." He reached across her and grabbed the remote off her nightstand, and the only thing that stopped her from grabbing him and finishing what housekeeping had interrupted was the rumble her stomach let out again.

She stared down at it as he clicked on the TV. "I ate a huge breakfast," she said to her abdomen. "How are you making these sounds? How can you possibly be hungry again?"

"You ran around in the snow for like half an hour and then spent the next forty-five minutes trying to warm up from the inside out. Bet you burned a lot of energy doing all that." Guy was gazing intently at the TV as he flipped channels. "Here we go. *Die Hard*. Just for you, Birthday Girl."

An hour later, their food was delivered. By that point, both of them were so ravenous that they fell upon their pasta like lions devouring a gazelle, inhaling the food so quickly they barely tasted it.

"I'm sure the kitchen is slammed," Guy said in between bites of gooey, cheesy noodles, "but an hour for macaroni, salad, and cake seems a bit excessive."

"No kidding," Zoe agreed. "Unless they baked and frosted the cake after we ordered, there's really no excuse."

"Speaking of cake, I think I saw a holiday baking thing on the tv menu. Can we take a break from *Die Hard*? I'm gonna be in a full-fledged food coma here soon and I'll need something without a plot I have to follow."

"Solid point." She picked up the remote from where he had left it on the pillow fence earlier and changed the channel. "Also speaking of cake, you realize you only got one piece. Do you not like cake, or is this like the bacon situation where you think I'm gonna share and then you end up sad because I won't?"

"I still can't believe you wouldn't let me have a single bite unless I watched your nerd show."

"You liked the nerd show."

He nodded gravely. "You are correct, I did. And yes, if you offer me a bite of cake I will accept it. But I don't really do sweets, so a whole piece to myself would be way too much."

"Oh man. I love sweets. Gimme all the baked goods." She tossed the remote back down after finding the correct channel and scooped up another forkful of macaroni. "We always have these chocolate crinkle cookies my aunt makes, with crushed-up peppermints sprinkled on top. They're amazing. It's not Christmas until I've eaten one of Aunt Tina's peppermint-chocolate cookies."

"Now see, that's a nice Christmas tradition," he said with a chuckle. "My mom always makes watermelon mojitos, and insists they're Christmassy because watermelon is red and green. She also makes them for literally every other holiday, though, so they're not exactly a Christmas-specific tradition, but there's something about drinking a watermelon mojito out of a snowman mug that just feels like Christmas to me."

She giggled, picturing it. "I love that."

He pointed to the TV, where the baking show host was unveiling the intricate gingerbread house the contestants were supposed to replicate. "Now that, that's like fairy-tale Christmas shit. Nobody really makes stuff like that, right? Homemade Christmas cookies are one thing, but that's a lot for anyone who isn't a professional pastry chef."

"You're asking the wrong person. We're a slice-and-bake family, except for Tina's one cookie recipe." She tipped her head back onto the pillow. "I think I might actually be done eating. I'm so full."

"You haven't eaten your cake."

She groaned, pulling a pillow-fence pillow over her face. "I can't. Too full. No more food."

"You have to blow out your candles! Or, well, your not-candles."

"Later," she promised. "Right now I just need to be in a food coma."

"I suppose I can agree to that." He stood up and began clearing their dishes, waving her away when she tried to help. "It's your birthday. Birthday girls don't clean up."

"I'll agree to that," she said, happily snuggling down into the bed. She replaced the barrier pillow she had stolen, pausing only briefly to consider *not* replacing it. After all, they had almost kissed earlier and at this point she really had no reason to believe he was going to dismember her. All signs pointed to *Zoe's gonna bang Hot Santa*.

But, she told herself, she was full to her eyeballs with macaroni, and was feeling decidedly unsexy as a result. It was not banging time.

Yet.

CHAPTER 5

It was dark. Not dark-dark, but significantly darker than it had been. Zoe reached blearily for her phone, almost dropping it when she realized it was 7:00. She glanced at the TV, still on the cooking channel, and then over at Guy, asleep on the other side of the bed.

How had they slept the whole second half of the day away? This was some jet lag-style bullshit, and she did not approve. She wasn't supposed to accidentally take a five-hour nap. She was never going to be able to fall asleep for real tonight after this.

She slid out of bed and dipped into the bathroom for some water, being as quiet as she could to avoid waking Guy, but he was awake anyway when she came back out into the bedroom. "Damn, you're a light sleeper," she told him, and he shrugged.

"You get used to being on half-alert when you work in a hospital," he replied.

"Do you learn to fall asleep easily too?" she asked, dropping back down onto the bed. "Because I could use some tips on how to sleep at night after sleeping all day."

"You're the flight attendant, shouldn't you be telling me how to combat jet lag?"

"I can tell you how to *avoid* jet lag, by not sleeping when the sun is out even if your body says it's bedtime. But clearly I'm bad at following my own advice." She sighed, turning her head to glance out the window at the streetlamp-bright parking lot. "But then, I guess the sun didn't really come out today, did it? No wonder my body is confused. Too many carbs and no sunshine makes Zoe a sleepy zombie, apparently."

Guy disappeared into the bathroom and came back out with his own drink. "And you didn't even finish your carbs," he reminded her. "You still have to eat your cake."

"Oh, yeah." She had forgotten about the cake, which was a testament to exactly how much macaroni she had eaten. She was not normally one to forget about cake. "I'm gonna call Lydia and make her blow out the candles with me."

She muted the cooking channel and grabbed her phone while he retrieved the slice of cake from under its room-service dome and sat down next to her on the bed.

"Hey," Lydia said when she picked up.

"Hey yourself," Zoe replied. "Go get yourself some cake, it's candles time."

"Don't have to tell me twice!" Lydia dropped the phone, leaving Zoe and Guy staring up at the ceiling of Zoe's parents' living room. The phone jostled a moment, and then Zoe's dad peered down at them from an unflattering angle.

"Happy birthday, Kitten," he said, smiling at the screen, his familiar salt-and-pepper hair and round face causing another pang of missing her family to squeeze at her chest. "Who's that, is that that might-be-a-serial killer you're shacked up with?"

Zoe rolled her eyes at him, but couldn't help her grin. "Yes, this is Guy. In addition to being not-a-murderer, he's promised me not-candles for my birthday cake."

"Is that Zoe?" A woman's voice floated in from offscreen, and a moment later Zoe's mom appeared next to her husband, taller than he was and blonde just like her daughters. "Happy birthday! Still snowed in?"

Zoe nodded. "Still snowed in," she confirmed. "We're doing long-distance birthday candles."

"I was wondering why your dad was using Lydia's phone." Her mom craned her neck to see something, presumably Lydia in the kitchen. "Lydia, are you cutting the cake before candles?"

"I'm putting candles in my piece." Lydia's voice was barely audible. "I'm coming back in there."

"You'd better be bringing cake for us too," her father called.

"I am!"

Zoe glanced over her shoulder at Guy, who was observing all this with a smile. Turning back to the phone, she called out, "You'd better not be piling all the frosting roses on your plate, Lydia Audrey."

"Oh, she absolutely is," their mother assured her. "She's putting every single one on, and you know she'll only eat half of them and then have to stop because she feels sick."

"You'd better save the ones she doesn't eat for me," Zoe reminded her. "It's the only thing I want for my birthday."

"And here I thought you wanted to be home for your birthday," her dad said with a look of mock indignation.

"Okay, fine," she laughed, "it's one of only two things I want for my birthday."

Lydia waltzed back into the room with a long grill lighter under her arm and holding three plates, two of which held normal-sized pieces of cake. The third plate may have held a normal-sized piece of cake or it may not have had any cake on it at all—it was impossible to tell because the entire surface was covered in frosting flowers. A small pink candle poked out of the pile of sugary goo.

"My flowers!" Zoe moaned, and Lydia scooped one up with her finger and stuck it into her own mouth, loudly humming her appreciation for its deliciousness at the camera. "I hope you get coal in your stocking."

"Lydia, you're going to be sick," their mother admonished, but Lydia looked unrepentant as she licked frosting off her fingers.

"I'm lighting the candle," their father announced, taking the lighter from Lydia and clicking it on.

"That's my cue," Guy said, turning the flashlight app on his phone on and holding it over the slice of cake on Zoe's plate.

"Seriously? That's my birthday candle?" She was sort of impressed at his ingenuity, but she wasn't going to tell him that. She could tell he was proud of himself, and suspected if she stroked his ego on top of it she would create a monster.

Before he could say anything, Lydia's candle was lit and her parents had begun to sing. Lydia joined in, singing to Zoe, and Zoe and Guy added their voices to the mix. Guy was a terrible singer, which was somehow adorable, and Zoe felt the same stirrings low in her belly that housekeeping had interrupted before their nap. Which was stupid. A man being unable to carry a tune should not be turning her on, especially while she was on a video chat with her parents, of all people.

And yet, here she was. Charmed and horny.

She didn't have any more time to muse on this, however, because the song ended and Lydia blew out her candle. Zoe waited for Guy to turn off the phone light, but he didn't. She raised her eyebrows at him, and he raised his right back. "You have to blow it out," he said.

"I…the flashlight?"

"The candle." She stared at him, confused, and he pointed to the phone. "Make a wish and blow out your birthday candle."

"This is ridiculous."

"Birthday wishes don't come true if you don't blow out the candle," he pointed out.

She rolled her eyes and he wiggled the phone at her. She let out a short, mock-annoyed sigh and screwed her eyes shut, pretending to make a wish. In the back of her mind, the sentence, "I wish you would kiss me" floated by, but she only half-registered that she'd thought it before she blew on the phone, ending the charade. He clicked off the light and dropped the phone into his lap so he could applaud. "Good job, Birthday Girl. May your wish come true."

Zoe's parents and Lydia also clapped. "What'd you wish for?" Lydia asked, shoveling a huge forkful of frosting into her mouth.

"She can't tell you," Guy and Zoe's mom said in unison. "Ugh, I don't know how you can do that," her mom added, watching Lydia lift another glob of yellow and green frosting to her lips. "Way too much frosting."

"Speaking of frosting, I'm going to go eat my own cake," Zoe told her family. "I hope I'll see you guys tomorrow. I'll keep you posted on what's happening with the weather."

They said their goodbyes and hung up, and Zoe glanced at Guy to find him eyeing her cake. "You still think I'm gonna share that, don't you?"

"I'm hoping," he said, giving her the same big sappy cartoon-dog eyes he'd given her over the bacon that morning.

"Fine. If you promise to stop making that face, I will share," she promised, "but the first bite is for the birthday girl."

"That's only fair."

She forked up a bite of cake, making sure to include as much frosting as possible, and slid it between her lips. She had not expected hotel room service cake that had sat under a metal dome for hours to be much more than passingly edible, and she was surprised to discover that it was still moist, and the frosting was still the perfect consistency. "Oh, wow. That's really good." She took a second bite, and Guy reached out and stopped her hand as she went for a third.

"Hey, now. Leave a bite for the not-a-murderer you're shacked up with." He tugged gently on her wrist, and she allowed him to guide her hand to his mouth. His eyes closed in bliss as he chewed, and she couldn't help but stare at him. She'd never seen anyone enjoy a bite of cake this much.

"Wishing you'd gotten your own?" she asked, bemused.

"Yes." He opened his eyes and looked from the plate to her. "Don't suppose you'd be willing to share the rest…?"

"And here I thought you didn't like sweets." She grinned and pushed the plate toward him. "Knock yourself out." He took another bite, then offered the fork to her again. She shook her head, enjoying watching him savor the chocolate. His eyebrow lifted, his head cocked to the side, and he did a little zoomy airplane motion with the forkful of cake. It would have been patronizing if it hadn't been so ridiculous, and she burst out laughing before leaning toward him and taking the proffered bite into her mouth.

"Oops, you've got frosting…" He reached out and swiped his thumb against her lower lip, and before she even realized she was doing it, her hand caught his wrist and her tongue darted out to lick the chocolate off. Guy's entire body went still, his blue eyes darkening as he watched her.

She could bail out of this. Release his hand, move away, let him finish the cake. Pretend that her licking frosting off his fingers had been a goofy reaction to his silly airplane schtick. They could go back to watching TV with a pile of pillows between them, like nothing had ever happened.

She could.

But she didn't want to.

And so, instead of releasing his hand, she held onto it, her tongue running along the soft pad of his thumb, her eyes locked on his. Her lips closed around the digit, and he swallowed, his own lips parting as he said her name, so softly she could have been imagining it. She let go of his wrist, reaching out to run her fingers across the stubble on his jaw. That was all the signal he needed to close the gap between them, his mouth finding hers and fitting to it so perfectly that she wondered for the briefest of moments why she had ever thought she should resist this, before his tongue slid against hers and all rational thought left her brain.

Her fingers clutched at the cotton of his t-shirt, pulling him down to her as she lay back on the pile of pillows that had been meant to keep them separate. He fumbled for the plate, which was still on the bed between them, and just barely managed to transfer it to the nightstand without dumping cake all over the floor or breaking their kiss. "Impressive," she breathed against his lips, and she felt his smile before he moved, trailing kisses down the soft skin on the side of her neck.

She flattened her hands on his chest and ran them across his shoulders, exploring him as his mouth dipped into the V of her penguin pajamas to kiss along the hollow of her collarbone, his fingers coming to the top button. "Okay if I undo this?" She nodded, and he flicked the button open before moving to the next one. "What about this one?"

"If you're going to ask me about every single button, we should just turn the TV back on and forget this whole thing," she said, and he chuckled, his breath warm against the skin of her throat.

"Noted," he said, his hand pushing the fabric aside so he could nip at the soft spot where her neck and shoulder met. She sucked in a breath, and he did it again in the same spot on the other side, his thumb grazing her nipple through her clothes as his hand skated down to the next button, and she arched her back into his touch. He opened the shirt slowly, as though she was the final gift to be unwrapped on Christmas morning and he wanted to make it last. The fabric parted to reveal the white tank top she had put on underneath, back when she was still trying to convince herself she wasn't going to sleep with him and therefore needed as many barriers as she could get. "Well, that's just not fair."

She laughed softly, sitting up and letting the flannel top fall off her shoulders before reaching for the hem of his t-shirt and tugging it up, tracing her fingers lightly along his stomach. He sucked in a breath, and she inched his shirt higher, leaning in to kiss along his stomach as she revealed his torso bit by bit, his muscles rigid under her touch as he held himself still, relishing in the attention she was paying his body while at the same time clearly holding himself back from pinning her to the mattress. Putting him out of his misery, she pulled his shirt the rest of the way off, then lay back, pulling him down into another kiss.

His palm was warm on her shoulder as he slipped the tank's spaghetti strap off it, then did the same on the other side. She was dizzy with the taste of him by the time he slid a hand up under the stretchy cotton of her shirt, his fingers just barely brushing the underside of her breast, skimming across her skin and driving her wild. Grabbing for his hand, she tried to make him move higher, touch her harder, do *something* more than what he was doing, but he resisted, his hand sliding back down to her hip.

Two could play this game. She trailed her own fingers over his chest, circling but never quite touching his nipples, and then teased along the edge of his waistband, slipping just her fingertips under the elastic. He did the same to her, his touch making her shiver. She pressed her chest against his, desperate for more sensation than the soft, teasing caresses they had been trading, and she deepened the kiss. A moan escaped her lips, and he pulled away, leaving her confused for a moment before she realized that he was pulling her tank top over her head. She raised herself up to make it easier for him, and then his mouth was on her right breast, his thumb grazing the left one, and she lost herself in the sensation, nothing existing but his lips on her skin, until he moved lower and pulled the flannel penguin pants off, tossing them aside to join the rest of her clothing on the floor. His bare shoulder brushed against her inner thigh as he bent back down to her, and it was somehow one of the most erotic things she had ever experienced. Which was absurd; a shoulder touching a thigh should not be getting this sort of reaction from her. But before she was able to spend too much time thinking about it, Guy's thumb traced over the fabric of her underwear, teasing the most sensitive part of her, and she forgot about everything except his touch. "Oh, god." His thumb slipped under the elastic, finding her clit and circling it as his mouth returned to her breast. She gasped as his teeth grazed her nipple, almost giving her what she'd been aching for. He did it again, harder this time, and her breath caught. She tangled her fingers in his hair, holding him there as he nipped at her again and withdrew his hand from between her legs to draw the pale blue fabric of her underwear down.

As her legs came free from the garment, he nudged them apart, baring her to him. She was wet with need, and he drew a finger along the seam of her center, sliding it inside her. Her hips bucked against his hand as a second finger slipped into her and he bent his head, his tongue flicking gently against her clit before flattening to press against it. His fingers moved in time with his tongue, curling and sliding, flicking and pressing, and Zoe's head fell back against the bed as she gave herself over to the glorious pressure he was creating inside her. His free hand reached up to pinch her nipple, bringing her higher, higher, and she could feel the break on the horizon when he suddenly withdrew his finger and took his mouth off of her.

"What are you…? No, don't stop!" she gasped, reaching a

hand out to pull him back. Guy chuckled and leaned over her again, catching her mouth as he ground his hips against hers. She fumbled at his sweatpants, desperate to remove the final barrier to the orgasm she had been so close to.

He helped her shove the pants and his boxer briefs off and she wrapped her hand around his length, eliciting an intake of air and an under-his-breath "Oh, fuck." She moved her hand, experimenting with different speeds and pressure, and his hips bucked against her palm. "This is going to be over pretty fast if you keep that up," he whispered, his eyes closed and his forehead against her neck.

She grinned, taking her hand away, and he looked up at her, his eyes narrowed. "I didn't mean you should stop." That made her laugh fully, and he joined her, their amusement giving way to more murmurs of pleasure as their hands found one another again, his bringing her back to the precipice and hers guiding him there too.

"Condom," she breathed, needing to feel him inside her, and he stilled in her arms.

"Shit." He let his head drop to her shoulder, his sweat-damp hair tickling her neck. "I wasn't expecting—I don't think I have…fuck."

She pushed against his chest, rolling him off of her. "I do." She leaned over the side of the bed, reaching for her purse on the chair by the window, and rummaged for the strip of "you never know when you might need one" condoms she kept in one of the inner pockets. "Lucky you," she said, turning back to him with a grin. "Flight attendants are trained to be prepared for any emergency."

"Thank god for that," Guy said as she straddled him, ripping the packet open. She allowed herself a moment to admire him, stroking her hand up and down his shaft a few times before unrolling the condom over it. She hovered her hips over his and moved against him. His erection twitched with excitement against her slickness but she didn't sink down onto it just yet. Instead, she bent to press her lips to his again, kissing him deeply until his fingers tightened on her waist and he let out a low growl. "I don't want to be pushy," he said, his voice strained, "but if you don't stop teasing me I'm going to have to take the reins here."

She lifted an eyebrow, challenging him, and he flipped her onto her back, pinning her wrists over her head and nudging her thighs apart with his own. His tongue parted her lips again as he lined himself up with her entrance, pressing forward and burying himself deep inside her with one slow, deliberate thrust that lit up every cell in her body. Just as slowly, he withdrew, leaving her feeling empty and needy until he plunged forward again, his pace adjusting according to her breathy sounds of affirmation until he found a pace that hit exactly the right spot at exactly the right rhythm. The pressure built inside her as she gasped "oh" and "yes" and "more" and "harder" until she didn't even know what she was saying. She pulled her hands free from his to glide them over his arms, his back, his chest with no real purpose or focus; she just wanted to touch him, to feel his solid body against hers as proof that this was real, this was actually happening, this was not some dream she was going to wake up from unsatisfied and aching with unmet need.

He hooked an arm under one of her knees, allowing him to drive into her harder and deeper. She kept one hand on his shoulder to anchor herself and let the other drift down between her own legs, stroking herself closer to the crescendo building inside her. The delicious pressure swelled, enveloping her in a tingling warmth as she broke apart, waves of pleasure thrumming through her from her toes to her ears.

"You're beautiful when you come," he whispered, releasing her leg so she could wrap it around his waist and pull him closer. Body still buzzing with the aftershocks of her orgasm, she hooked her other leg around him too, and caught his face in her hands to bring his lips back to hers. He cupped a hand around the back of her neck as they moved against each other, foreheads touching, the tempo of his thrusts growing uneven as he neared his own climax. When his breath rushed out in a groan of ecstasy and his hips pressed hard against hers, his cock pulsing inside her, she held him close, their fingers intertwined as they both waited for their pulses to slow and their breathing to return to normal. The sparkling feeling of her orgasm still skated over her skin when he raised a hand to brush her hair out of her face and press a kiss to her temple before shifting his weight off of her, rolling to his side to dispose of the condom. Turning back to her and wrapping an arm around her, he pulled her close. As she drifted off to sleep, the little spoon to his big one, it crossed her mind that maybe this blizzard hadn't been the worst thing to happen after all.

CHAPTER 6

Something rattled by Zoe's head, and she sat up with a start, her eyes darting around the room and her heart pounding. The rattling noise came again, and she grabbed for her phone, vibrating against the wood of the nightstand in the darkness and reminding her of when her mom used to shake a can of pennies at the family dog when he was being naughty.

Guy propped himself on an elbow, squinting at her as she blinked down at the screen. "What's up?"

"My airline app just sent a notification that my flight's been rescheduled. Check your phone, I bet yours is too."

He reached for the phone on his own nightstand. "Yep. New flight at eight-fifteen tonight."

"Damn. Mine's at twelve-twenty." She clicked through the app to check in virtually and confirm her seat, then flopped back against the pillows. "It's only a little after seven. I guess I could go back to sleep for a bit, but I don't think I can. I'm gonna go ahead and get up." She threw back the covers, and Guy reached over and clicked on his bedside light, making her grab the sheet and cover her naked body; not that he hadn't already seen her naked—hell, he'd been inside her a few hours ago—but somehow this felt different. "You don't have to get up, you should go back to sleep."

"It's okay, I'm up," he said, grabbing her around the waist and pulling her to him.

"I can see that." She placed a hand on the blanket, where it tented over his groin, and smirked. All her shyness from a moment ago was gone, knowing he wanted her to stay in bed with him, knowing he was hard and ready, and she let the sheet fall away from where she had clutched it to her chest.

"Minx," he growled, catching a nipple between his teeth and making her inhale sharply at the bright ache the motion caused. Her hand slipped under the blanket to wrap around him. His hips moved under her touch and he made an incoherent sound of appreciation.

She leaned down and whispered in his ear, "I'll be right back."

"No, where are you going? Don't go."

"Right back," she promised. She hated to hit pause on what they were doing, but nature was calling. Loudly.

She took care of business in the bathroom as quickly as she could, swishing some of the complimentary mouthwash as she washed her hands. Guy was sitting up when she returned to the bedroom. "Good idea. You're a practical woman, Miss Monroe. I like that about you." He stood and walked to the bathroom, completely comfortable in his nudity. She certainly wasn't complaining; he had a great ass.

The pillow barrier was still in the bed, though now it was more a random scattering of pillows than anything resembling a fortress. She crawled back under the covers and began pulling pillows out from the blankets, tossing them on the floor, when she caught a flash of red between the sheets and unearthed Guy's Santa hat. She had forgotten she'd stuffed it under the blankets yesterday. Inspiration hitting her, she put the hat on and arranged herself on the bed in a come-hither pose.

The bathroom door opened and Guy came out with his cock still standing at attention. He paused, taking in the sight of her, spread out on the bed wearing nothing but his Santa hat, and his eyes grew so wide so half feared they'd roll right out of his head. "Merry Christmas to me," he said, prowling across the mattress and pushing her thighs apart. He buried his face between them, licking into her once before kissing along her stomach from hip bone to hip bone. She reached up and removed the hat, settling it onto his head.

He quirked an eyebrow at her, the tip of one finger teasing her entrance. "I don't want to judge your turn-ons, but really? Santa does it for you?"

"Just one particular Santa." She raised her hips to encourage him to continue, and he grinned wickedly before closing his mouth over her clit and sliding two fingers deep into her. Zoe's head dropped onto the pillow, and she lost herself in the sensation of his mouth and hands on her most sensitive spots, his morning beard scraping her skin while the pom-pom on the hat tickled along the same path in a delicious contrast. His mouth kept a consistent pressure, the flat of his tongue sliding over the swollen bud as his fingers pressed into her and brought her closer, closer…until she reached the precipice and tipped over the edge, spiraling into blinding white bliss.

A few moments later, when she had gone contentedly limp, Guy crawled up her body to kiss her, tasting of mouthwash and sex. She sighed and shifted so she was lying on her side facing him. "I no longer want to get up."

"You don't have to," he said. He pulled the blanket up over them and wrapped his arms around her. "You can go back to sleep for a bit. We've got time."

"What about you?" She cuddled closer, his hard-on pressed against her stomach.

"I'm perfectly fine just like this."

She gazed up at him, his blue eyes dark with want, and

she traced a finger along the edge of the hat he still wore. "I don't need to sleep," she said, betraying her own words with a yawn.

He kissed her forehead, a sweetly chaste gesture considering where he'd been kissing her moments before. "Sleep. I'm happy just to hold you."

She felt a swell of affection for him even as her eyes fluttered closed, the aftereffects of her orgasm carrying her away. To think that two days ago she had been annoyed when he approached her at the airport, and now here they were, falling asleep in one another's arms. He was a good person, she thought to herself as sleep pulled her under. Kind and funny and caring. And she wasn't ready to say goodbye just yet.

❄

An hour later, Zoe drifted back into consciousness, her head still on Guy's shoulder and his arms still holding her tight to him. She looked up at him to discover he was still wearing the Santa hat. She chuckled, and he stirred, his own eyes opening to find her giggling at him. "What's so funny?"

"You're still Santa."

"It's still Christmas, of course I'm still Santa." He stretched, glancing over at his phone on the nightstand and tapping the screen to check the time. "Eight-forty-three. What time was your flight rescheduled for again? Twelve something?"

"Yeah, twelve-twenty." She traced little circles on his bare chest with her fingers. "Probably I should get up and shower and go find some breakfast."

"You've got some time."

"You just want me to stay naked in bed, don't you?"

"Can you blame me?"

She huffed a laugh at that, reaching her face up to kiss

him. "Trust me, I'd love to. But I suspect the airport will be a zoo, and that's assuming I can get a car or something to take me there. I might have to walk again."

"We'll find you a car or a shuttle or something. If the airport is open again, the roads are probably clear enough for cars." He sat up, letting the sheets pool around his waist. "You know. I should probably shower too."

Looking back over her shoulder as she pushed the covers off her legs, Zoe raised an eyebrow. "Are you angling for an invitation to join me?"

"I would never," he said, a hand to his chest in mock shock. "But since you asked, yes, I'd love to." He jumped from the bed and disappeared into the bathroom. She heard the shower turn on and followed the sound, finding Guy at the sink putting toothpaste on his toothbrush while the water heated. She joined him, and he skimmed a hand down her side as they stood naked in front of the mirror, brushing their teeth together like they'd done it a thousand times. It was both completely comfortable and a little weird; but then, this whole being-held-hostage-by-a-blizzard experience had been weird and also far easier than it had any right to be, and every bit of that was thanks to the man standing next to her.

In the shower, hot water cascading around them, she dropped to her knees and showed him exactly how much she appreciated everything he'd done for her these past few days.

CHAPTER 7

"You didn't have to come with me," Zoe told Guy for the umpteenth time that morning as they walked through the terminal to security. "I'm good. You could have stayed and had a proper breakfast and not a stale bagel while you stood in the cold waiting for a cab to take you to the airport eight hours earlier than you need to be here just to drop me off."

"I know," he said again, "but we had to check out, and what else am I going to do while I wait? May as well hang out and people-watch."

Zoe dodged a texting teenager who wasn't looking where they were going. "I mean, don't get me wrong, it's super sweet of you. I just think you might not be thinking straight. Your brain is sex-addled. You'll regret this around noon when you realize you still have another eight hours till your flight and airport chairs aren't comfortable."

"I may be addled, but it was well worth it," he said, shooting her a pointed look. She grinned, looking down at her boots. He reached over and tucked a strand of hair behind her ear. "Besides, as you have repeatedly pointed out, I have a lot of time to kill. I can take a nap while I wait to un-addle my brain. Got a nice cushy pillow and everything." He patted the duffel bag over his shoulder, which was somewhat more full now than it had been before. He had crammed his Santa beard and pants into it this morning, filling up any extra space that had been there when he'd been wearing the ridiculous outfit two days ago. The coat wouldn't fit, so he was wearing that over his jeans and white thermal henley, and got some curious glances as they walked.

"I still can't believe you decided to dress up like Santa at the airport," she said. "Such a bizarre impulse."

He shrugged, making the bag slip. He hoisted it back up onto his shoulder as he said, "I thought it would be charming and whimsical." Grabbing for her hand, he shot her a lopsided grin. "Plus, I thought maybe I could find a cute girl who'd be willing to sit on my lap. At least that part worked."

"Gross, you perv," she laughed, but didn't pull away. His fingers were warm in hers, and a pulse of regret squeezed her chest at the knowledge that soon she'd be getting on a plane and leaving him behind.

They reached security, which Zoe was able to bypass with her work credentials, but Guy was going to have to suffer through. "I can go through with you," she said. "It's only fair, you got here early for me."

He shook his head. "Absolutely not. No one should have to suffer through security if they don't have to. Plus you'd probably miss your flight."

"I'd take you through the employee line if I could."

"I know." He pulled her toward him, threading his fingers into her hair and gazing down at her with those striking blue eyes. That shade had become her favorite color over the past few days. "I had a really great time with you. Thanks for making a pretty unfortunate situation a whole lot better."

"Me too," she told him. Her eyes stung, but she refused to cry. Crying would be stupid. They lived in the same city, for

Pete's sake, it's not like they'd never see each other again. "Thanks for my birthday candle."

"I hope your wish comes true."

"It already did." She went up on her tiptoes and pressed her lips to his, holding on tight to the lapels of his Santa jacket. His hand came around her lower back, the other still tangled in her hair, holding her to him as he returned the kiss. When he released her, she stepped back and forced herself to take a deep breath. "You should get in line, I guess. Not that you don't have plenty of time to waste standing around."

"Hey, my time is valuable," he said. "Those TikToks aren't gonna watch themselves."

She reached into her purse and pulled out the magazines from the first night. That night felt like eons ago, she thought as she held the glossy pages out to him. "In case you reach the end of the internet before your flight."

He smiled as he took them, his eyes crinkling at the corners. "I guess I did bail out before I figured out who wore it best. Thanks."

She grabbed the handle of her suitcase. "All right, off I go, I guess. Bye, Hot Santa."

"Bye, Zoe. Tell your family Merry Christmas from me."

"I will." Offering him a last smile, she turned and headed off to the employee security line. It wasn't until she was at her gate, standing in line to board, that she realized she hadn't paid him back for her half of the room. She pulled out her phone to ask for his Venmo and a second realization hit her.

They hadn't exchanged numbers.

Her heart sank, and she checked the time. There was no way she could get back to security and find him before she had to board; she probably couldn't even get to his gate at the other end of the terminal. And he might not even be there even if she could.

We live in the same city, she reminded herself again. *I know where he works. I'll find him when I get back.*

She didn't like it, but she'd have to live with it. There wasn't really any other option.

The tears that had been pricking her eyes since the security line finally won the battle, spilling down her cheeks. She had done a lot of crying the past couple of days for someone who wasn't much of a crier. She swiped at her face with the sleeve of her black hoodie as she approached the gate, boarding pass at the ready. She was holding out her hand to scan it when she heard Guy shout her name.

"Zoe!"

She turned, but didn't see him. *You're losing it,* she told herself. *Hearing things.*

"Zoe!" his voice called out again, and this time, she did see him—dodging people and suitcases, Santa coat flapping and duffel bag bouncing against his side as he dashed through the terminal toward her gate. He skidded to a stop as she stepped out of the line, her boarding pass forgotten. "I didn't get your number," he gasped, dropping his duffel bag at his feet. "The security line was so long I was afraid I'd be too late, so I ran. But I needed to get your number. I can't let you just disappear after the past few days."

She reached both hands out to touch him. It hadn't been that long since she'd seen him—an hour, maybe—but she needed to feel him, to prove to herself that he was really there, that he had run the entire length of the airport just to get her number. Because he wasn't ready to let her go yet, either.

Giddy laughter bubbled up in her, spilling over as she hugged him. "I didn't realize until it was too late that I didn't have your number, so I was just going to stalk you at work when I got back."

"Spoken like a true axe murderer," he said, sweeping her into a dizzying kiss. People all around them began to clap and whistle, and they broke apart, self-conscious and grinning. "Give me your phone, Birthday Girl."

"It's not my birthday anymore," she said as she handed it over. "You're gonna have to find a new nickname."

"You'll always be Birthday Girl to me," he said, sending a text to himself before handing the phone back to her.

She glanced down at the screen. An eggplant emoji. "Classy."

"I try." He reached into his jacket pocket and pulled his Santa hat out, dropping it on her head. "Merry Christmas. Call me when you land?"

"Yeah." The line was almost nonexistent now; the rest of the passengers had almost finished boarding. "I have to go. I don't want to. But I have to."

"Go. There's frosting roses waiting for you in Nebraska. I'll be here when you get back, and I'll take you out for a proper date. A grown-up-sized bottle of wine, and an actual table to eat off of, and chairs, and everything."

"Be still, my heart." She touched his cheek. "Merry Christmas, Hot Santa. I'll call you in a bit."

The other passengers cheered again when she boarded the plane. Her face was hot with embarrassment but she was unable to wipe the dopey, lovesick grin off her face as she found a spot for her suitcase in the overhead bin and squeezed into her window seat. She rubbed the soft pompom on the Santa hat against her cheek, opening up Guy's text and breathing a soft laugh at the emoji as she saved his contact information.

As the plane began to taxi, Zoe closed her eyes, her limbs buzzing with the giddiness of new love. She was excited to see her family, but she had to admit that she was actually glad she'd gotten stranded. She and Lydia could wear their penguin pajamas tonight, only one day late, and eat their sprinkle waffles in the morning, and it would barely be any different than if she'd gotten there on time.

And maybe, she thought, next year she'd be sitting next to Guy on her flight home, instead of leaving him behind. They could eat frosting roses and wear Santa hats and sure, it would probably be in October or March or something, but who cared? It didn't matter when she celebrated, as long as she was with the people she cared about. Mom. Dad. Lydia. And Santa.

A grin spread across her face as the plane lifted into the sky.

Definitely Santa.

THE END

1

1.

ACKNOWLEDGMENTS

First and foremost, a never-ending series of thank yous to my husband Kevin, who is my biggest fan and staunchest supporter. I love you even more than I love frosting roses.

Thank you also to my girls, Lorelai and Kaylee, who have put up with a lot of "I'll be there in a minute"s and "Can you make yourself dinner?"s over the years when I've been on a roll with my writing and haven't wanted to pause lest I lose my train of thought. You two take it all in stride and seeing how excited you were for me when I told you I not only finished, but was publishing, this book was very heartwarming. Moon and stars, unicorns and rainbows.

To my parents, Ron and Susan, who have also always supported me, whether I was saying I was going to write a book, or fling myself over logs on horseback at almost 40, or major in theatre.

My Yes Do girls (Christina, Meika, and Liz) for the many re-reads, edits, TikToks, memes, vent sessions, and laughs. Y'all are the best and there's no one else I'd rather share this with.

My Wet Hot American Moon Juice fam (Alex, Daniel, James, Kyle, Mason, Morgan, Raeanna, and Tracy), who will never not yes-and me into producing something, even if that something is a list of every bagel flavor at Panera just to hit my word count or a podcast with a ridiculous concept and an even more ridiculous name.

Lyssa Kay Adams and Alyssa Alexander, thank you so much for boosting this book in your newsletters and other writer spaces. Y'all are lovely people and wonderful friends, and it's pretty cool to have such talented writers in our corner saying people should read our words.

My Rachel Lawson Eventing barn family, thank you for being my home away from home. You have shown me and my kids the importance of hard work, loving what you do, and committing to your dreams. Every single one of you is my hero and role model and I want to be just like you when I grow up.

And finally, thank you to you, the reader, for picking up this book and getting to know Zoe and Guy with me. I love these two goofballs and I hope you did, too. Merry Christmas!

ABOUT ERIN

ERIN A. KING writes contemporary love stories with a heavy sprinkling of humor and heat. She also co-hosts several podcasts on The Scavengers Network and lends her voice to many audio fiction podcasts. When she's not at the keyboard or behind the mic, she can be found walking her dogs, riding her horse, or drinking far too much coffee. She lives in Virginia with her ever-supportive husband and two daughters—one a competitive gymnast, the other an adorable agent of chaos. You can find her on most social media platforms as @unabashedlyerin.

miss you like christmas
CHRISTINA MITCHELL

For all the magical bitches

CHAPTER 1

Christmas music blared overhead, and Gabriel Tilki sighed, pulling a sleek gray stingray from the bin of stuffed animals in the airport gift shop. He added it to his pile of assorted, overpriced things on the counter. Hopefully, his employees at the hotel would like these silly little gifts. The storm was making an already unbearable holiday weekend even worse, and they could all use some cheer that didn't come from the never-ending loop of sugary Christmas songs assaulting them from every direction.

"Do you have bras?" A silky voice cut through the din of grumpy, grounded travelers clearing the shelves of everything they could carry.

He shook his head at the odd question and picked up a snow globe from a glass display. He stared into it, a stone in his stomach. There was a black family inside. Parents. Children, putting haphazard decorations on a spindly, crooked tree, boxes of ornaments overflowing behind them, and a kitten batting at a droopy pine bough.

The usual rush of melancholy that now came with the season tightened around him, and he put it back on the shelf.

"Is there any chance that you've got, say… underwear at

least?" That same smooth voice asked. "I'll take anything at this point. Boxers even."

"Afraid not," a perkily uninterested worker responded. "But there's some leggings and sweaters on the rack back there if you wanna take a look."

The silky voice murmured thanks, and Gabriel found himself searching through the throng for the owner. Maybe it had just been far too long since he'd felt a pique of interest in anyone, but that voice had sent a satisfying shiver through him, like the first sip of hot cocoa on an icy day. Sweet and decadent and warm. He wanted to see who it belonged to.

It didn't belong to the little old white ladies sifting through the scented soaps. Nor the exhausted-looking woman in a hijab, pulling on a huge floral rolling suitcase while she also wrestled two boisterous children from the porcelain knickknacks and the "Detroit Strong" t-shirts.

He left his stuff on the counter and wove his way between the customers. At first all he could see was a head full of intricate hair. He wasn't well-versed in the hairstyles of black women, but he was sure they were called locs or something. The night manager at the hotel had the same style of hair. Only this woman's was decorated with little gold hoops and strands of thread here and there, like golden tinsel. She was holding up a pair of green leggings with grinning snowmen on the knees.

"How desperate am I?" she said to no one.

He really should have just walked on, his curiosity reasonably assuaged, but he stepped forward instead. "No idea, but I think the shop on the other side of the airport has a better selection of clothes," he said, hoping he didn't sound like a creep.

A pair of warm amber eyes slid his way. "Are you saying that this isn't the perfect ensemble?" She held up the ugly leggings and a matching sweater. She pressed something on the sweater and the whole front lit up, red and green flashing like a gaudy holiday traffic light, illuminating her dark skin and the simple gold hoop in her nose.

"I take it back. You're not gonna do better than that."

She snorted. "Don't make me laugh. I'm mad at the world."

He ran his hands over the hangers, making them clack. He met people all day every day working in security. Drunk. Sober. Belligerent. Kind. People didn't make him nervous. But for some reason, this woman did. "My apologies," he said. "I wouldn't want to make your day better."

"Thank you for understanding," she said, a bright smile winking in and out of existence, along with a pair of dimples that mesmerized him.

He stared down at the clothes in front of him and plucked an outfit out and held it up. "This is...not as bad."

"Is that a onesie?" She rounded the rack and took it from him. At 6'3", he was used to women being a lot shorter than he was, but she was fairly tall, coming up to his chin. But she was also bundled up in a bulky winter coat, so everything else was a mystery.

"It has a hood," he said, as if that mattered.

"They lost my luggage, so...." She studied the red and white candy cane striped onesie. "It's better than the snowmen," she declared, tossing it over her arm. "It's almost my size, and I've heard horizontal stripes are *very* flattering." She grabbed another onesie from the rack and eyed his fur-lined leather jacket. "Is your flight delayed too?"

"Oh, no. I work security at the hotel across the street. I'm just picking up some stuff."

"Don't you have a gift shop there?"

"Not right now. They're doing renovations."

She grabbed a few other things from the shelf beside the clothing and turned toward the counter. "No chance that you've got a room available at that hotel, is there?"

"Not a one," he said. "With the renovations, we've got a

bunch of rooms *un*available on the garden level, so we were already booked solid before the flights were even grounded."

"Worth a shot," she said with a sigh. "Fuck this storm and fuck the holidays."

"Agreed."

He followed her to the line, which was snaking nearly out the door. He gathered up his pile of cheesy gifts and she glanced back at it. "Aw, is that a manta ray?"

"Stingray."

She laughed. "How can you tell the difference?"

"Manta rays are smarter and much bigger. No stinger in the tail. Mouth up front. The stingray's mouth is underneath and they're more aggressive. There's a museum in Chicago where you can put your hand in the water and touch stingrays. Er, cownose rays, but they're related. I took my niece there about a dozen times." He pressed his lips together to stop his babbling and the painful jab in his ribs thinking about his family.

"That sounds like a lot of fun. I love stuff like that." Balancing all the clothes in her hands, she reached over and patted the stuffed stingray. He noted that she wasn't wearing a wedding ring and, for some reason, it gave him a boost of cheer. He wondered if she'd looked down at his decidedly paler hand and noticed the same thing.

Maybe she noticed his sneaky glance, because she smiled —a lips together, mouth curled up in the corner kind of smile. He felt it like a warm weight on his chest.

"So, where were you headed?" he asked.

She hesitated and he felt guilty for going straight to something so personal. But after a moment she shook her head. "New York. Family visit." Her face scrunched up in distaste as she said, *New York*.

Clearly there was more to the story than a family visit and for some strange reason, he wanted to know that story. "So, what's your na--"

The shrill ring of his cell cut off his question. Shit. He wrestled with his stuff to answer it. Without hesitation the woman turned her already-full arms toward him and said, "Here."

He dropped everything into them and answered the phone. "Is every–"

"We've had a couple incidents, Gabe," Samantha sounded out of breath.

He rolled his eyes at the nickname. "What's going on?"

"Still haven't heard from Jake. He was supposed to be here twenty minutes ago. Got a call from Malik, and he said that traffic is at a standstill and the cabs aren't running, so he ain't coming in, unless we can get him some skis. We've got homeless people camping in the lobby and it's too cold to kick them out, but we're getting complaints from dickheads. Also, that huge crowd of grounded fliers that came looking for rooms a while ago? They were mad we didn't have any, so they went to the bar and got hammered. Reigna ran out of mid-shelf rum and whisky, so a patron threw a bowl of peanuts at her, and she threw it back. Nailed him right in the nose. Blood everywhere. I called the cops to remove him, but they're up to their eyebrows with the storm. No telling how long it's gonna be with the way the weather is going. I can handle the bar mess, but there's no one watching the door or the cameras."

"Did you call Osvaldo?"

"Yeah, but it's gonna take him an hour at least. The roads are so bad the poor guy is *walking* here."

"Shit. Well, I'll be there as quickly as I can." He gave Miss Silky Voice a regretful smile. "Sorry, I've gotta go."

A shadow of disappointment crossed her face, but she nodded. "Be safe."

That same disappointment rushed through him as he headed for the exit and called the hotel to request the shuttle.

The whole ride back, he stared straight out the window at

the blinding white snow and thought about brown high cheekbones, amber eyes, and a snarky little sense of humor. There was something intriguing about her, and he was desperate to know more--well to know anything, really. Name. Occupation. Age. What kind of toppings she liked on a pizza. The important stuff.

But their moment was gone, and he felt an achy sort of regret about it that he tried to shake off. It was just as well. She would be leaving when the storm passed, anyhow.

❄

The next ninety minutes of Gabriel's shift were a mess of ornery guests, belligerent non-guests, one furious bartender, a security staff stretched paper thin, and three noise complaints against a couple who were enjoying their bed a little too audibly for other people's comfort.

Honestly, he was jealous. It'd been a while since someone had moaned his name with such passion while slamming a headboard against the wall. And no one had ever screamed, "Give it to me, big daddy," at him either, though he wasn't sure if that was a good thing or a bad thing.

When things calmed down, he sent Samantha and Osvaldo to get themselves dinner, while he manned the security desk. He glanced at his phone, hoping for a text back from Yasmin, but as usual there was nothing. His little sister was busy with her new life in Seattle, and only sporadically responded to his texts, especially during the holidays. Just like his mom, she preferred to avoid anything that might hurt.

God, he missed them. He missed his whole and happy family. The way things used to be. The way they never would be again.

The phone on the desk rang shrilly and he answered, hoping it wasn't another complaint. "Security," he muttered, as he shoved his cell in his pocket and stared down at the camera feed, hoping there wasn't an issue he'd missed. He usually wasn't one to let his thoughts wander. A decade in the military had trained him to stay focused on the mission at hand. But for the last three years, his focus had been slipping, and the closer it got to Christmas, the worse it became.

"Hey, Gabe!"

He sighed. "I hate nicknames, Doris."

"I know. That's why I keep using them." The older woman chuckled. "I got someone here asking for you. I'm assuming it's you anyway."

His cell dinged and he fumbled for it, while he pinched the desk phone between his shoulder and his ear. "Send them over." He hung up and turned off his screen lock, but it wasn't a text from his mom or sister. Just one letting him know that there was a holiday sale at his local market.

Dammit.

"Hi, literal stranger," a plush, satiny voice said.

He looked up and his heart stuttered. The woman from the gift shop stood there, giving him a tentative smile. Melting snow dripped from her hair and shoulders.

He sat up straighter. "Um, hi--hi," he said, stumbling over the single word. "Uh, how'd you… find me?"

She shrugged. "There are only three hotels directly across from the airport and it's not like I had other things to do. Found you on the second try."

"You're leaking. Snow. I mean." He fumbled for some napkins on the desk and handed them over.

She smiled gratefully and wiped her face and jacket. Pocketing the damp paper, she stuck her hand out. "I'm Talia."

That name suited her. Warm, like the sun on beach sand. He shook her chilly hand. "Oh, uh, Gabe--Gabriel. Not Gabe. I don't like nicknames. Gabriel." Jesus Christ.

Her mouth curled into a smile. "So I shouldn't call you Gabe, then?"

"Please don't."

"Alright Gabriel-not-Gabe, I am your unofficial stalker for the evening. I have a gift for you." She leaned down and picked up a bag resting on the floor beside her. "Here you go."

"What would make you an official stalker?" He reached out and took the bag from her.

"I don't know. I think I need a license for that, or something."

Inside the bag was a familiar pile of assorted tchotchkes and stuffed animals. "I forgot all about this. I'm so sorry I stuck you with it. How much do I owe–"

She waved a hand at him. "Nothing. You don't owe me anything. It's been a long, shitty day for me, and I imagine it hasn't been much better for you. So Merry whatever. Christmahanakwanzidan. I hope your niece and your kids like that stuff."

"Oh, I don't have kids–or a partner, er..." Why did he tell her that? Who cared? "These are for my employees."

"Oh." She seemed to perk up some. "I shouldn't have assumed…"

He ran a hand over the new silver hairs mingling with the black hair at his temples. "No worries. I'm forty-two. I'm used to people thinking I have kids."

"No, that wasn't it. I wouldn't make that kind of judgment based on age. Lots of people don't have kids. I'm forty and I don't have them. I just saw stuffed animals and thought…" She laughed helplessly and threw her arms out at her sides. "I'm not my best self today and I wasn't thinking. Sorry about that."

"Nothing to be sorry about." He took a breath and released the tension from his shoulders. Seeing her just as flustered as he was made him feel a little less self-conscious.

He smiled at her. "This is the nicest thing anyone's done for me in a long time. Can I order you something to eat? We've got a great restaurant here. It has a Michelin star. Whatever that means."

She bit her lush lower lip. "Oh, that's so...Nah, it's alright. Defeats the whole good deed thing if I get something out of it." She backed away, shifting a carry-on bag high on her shoulder, as she picked up another bulging gift shop bag with the sleeve of a peppermint striped onesie sticking out of it. "Anyway, I already bought a room temperature tuna fish sandwich from a food stand, and I've got a comfy cot calling me in the terminal."

"Oof, those cots are rough."

"Yeah, I think the floor would actually be more comfortable." She took a few more steps back and gave him a wave. "Happy Christmas Eve-eve, Gabriel-not-Gabe."

One chance meeting was something he could let go of, but this felt...different. She'd wandered out in the middle of a storm to bring him a bag full of meaningless stuff, so she must have felt the same oddly acute fascination that he did. He didn't want her to go, but damned if he could find the right words to say about it, so he watched her turn away.

"Later alligator," he finally blurted out. Heat started at his jaw and spread over his whole face. He tried to keep his weird cheeseball tendencies to himself, but sometimes they just slipped out.

"After a while, crocodile," she volleyed back, laughing. Then she headed for the door. Beneath her voluminous coat and the thin scarf, she really wasn't dressed for the weather at all. It was bitterly cold outside, and she only had on soaked-through tennis shoes and leggings. With no gloves.

"Talia," he called out. "Wait."

But she was already gone. He shot up to go after her, but his two-way radio crackled to life. "Gabriel, we have a problem on the third floor. Someone's drunk and naked in the hall."

He was bone-exhausted by the time his shift was over hours later. He'd texted all his employees to check on them and most were unable to come in for their next shift. The streets were impassable, and the city declared it a state of emergency, asking people to stay off the roads if possible. It looked like he was going to have to find a place to sleep at the hotel, so he could be there to cover in the morning.

He wondered if Talia made it back to the airport safely. Would it be weird to call over there and check? He sighed. He didn't even know her last name to have them page her.

One problem at a time, he supposed. He made his way to his office to retrieve the bug out bag he carried daily. He'd never quite stopped being a boy scout or a marine on the inside. So, he always had an extra set of clothes, first aid supplies, water, MREs, and a handful of other things he might need in case of emergency.

He slung it over his shoulder and closed the office door behind him. The break room has a fairly comfortable couch in it that he could crash on. He stopped by the front desk to let the night manager know where he'd be, but she was on the phone, looking stressed.

"I can probably get you thirty blankets, but I don't know about the pillows…" Her pen clacked on the desk tunelessly. "Right. Tell Jovan he owes me big time," she said before hanging up.

"Hey, Imani," he said. "I've gotta come back and cover in the morning, so I'm gonna be sleeping in the break room. I don't know if I snore, but don't be alarmed if you hear me sawing logs."

"Hey, Cap." She looked up at him, her expression thoughtful. "I need a favor."

He eyed her warily. "What is it?"

"You've got a commercial driver's license, right?"

The lumpy couch was calling him, and he was only half paying attention to her. "Yeah?"

"Cool. Metro called and said they ran out of bedding for all the stranded passengers. They asked to borrow some of ours. Since the flights are all grounded, I let Manny go home, so now I've got no one to drive the shuttle to take the stuff over there. Can you do it?"

He wanted to say no. He was just so damned exhausted. The holidays wore him down in the best of circumstances, and these weren't the best. But there were stranded people at the airport and he could make their night a little better if he sucked it up and did this. Knowing that, he really didn't have a choice.

"Dammit," he said.

She grinned from ear to ear. "You are a lifesaver! I owe you."

He remembered Talia's words earlier. *Defeats the whole good deed thing if I get something out of it.* "You don't owe me anything."

"Still, I'll pay you back, you know I will. For now, I'll have housekeeping bring the bedding down while you go to the restaurant and order whatever you want before they close. Tell Joel to put it on the management tab."

He was too hungry to argue. At the restaurant, Joel cheerfully tossed a menu at him. "You barely made it, but in the spirit of the holidays, I will not kill you for keeping us here an extra twenty minutes."

"Your grudging kindness is all I can ask for," he said, studying the menu. His eyes skimmed past the roast beef holiday family special. The sandwiches mostly looked unappetizing. His thoughts drifted to Talia sleeping in an airport cot, eating a likely contaminated tuna sandwich if he knew anything about the food stand.

Would he see her there? Did that defeat the whole good deed thing if he got something out of it?

"Can I get two burgers and fries?" he asked. "With all the stuff on the side?" He thought for a moment. Talia ate tuna fish, but she could be pescatarian or something. "A house salad with lemon dressing. And maybe something chocolate for dessert? The lava torte thing. And uh, two sets of silverware."

Fifteen minutes later he had a bag of delicious food, but no dessert. "Sorry, Captain," Joel said. "I want to say that we're completely out of desserts, but the truth is, the chef threatened my life for even suggesting he heat up anything else." He walked to the tall tree decorating the restaurant and plucked two candy canes from it. "You can have these, though." He handed them over with a cheery smile. "For you and what I'm assuming is an incredibly hot date."

"You're the best." Gabriel gave him a cheesy wink and slid the candy into his jacket pocket before heading to the front.

Imani had pulled the shuttle up front already, and the seats were laden with piles of folded blankets and pillows. "Be slow and be safe, alright? Go to the luggage pickup area and show your security badge. They'll let you in." She looked at the bag of food. "Want me to put that in the breakroom for you?"

"Um, no. I know someone over there, so I'm gonna…"

"Gotcha gotcha." She waved him off and he found himself making the slow drive to the airport. In good weather the shuttle barely took seven minutes. It took a lot longer, with the snow coming down as hard as it was, but there were no other vehicles going into the airport or coming out of it, and it looked like they were plowing every couple hours, so it wasn't as bad as it could have been.

He pulled up to the doors, where cars would ordinarily be lined up to the road with grinning families eager to be with their loved ones. But now, it was deathly quiet.

Kinda felt familiar.

The door flew open and Donald, one of the airport security guards he knew, stood there with an exhausted smile. "Heeeey, Gabriel! How you doing, man?"

"Doing better than these folks," he said, pulling him in for a quick hug.

Donald patted him heartily on the back. "No shit. Every time I think I'm having a bad time, I try to remember that at least I'll be sleeping in the employee lounge and not on a cot in a cold-ass baggage claim."

"Speaking of feeling cold." He looked Donald over. "What's this about?" He pointed to his dark, shiny bald head.

Donald ran a hand over his dome. "Shaving my head in the winter wasn't my best idea. But this hairline was receding so far back it looked like I had on a headband. It was time."

"Middle age is coming on fast," he said with a laugh. "Lucky for you and your wife, you're still pretty."

"I am, aren't I?" Donald grinned and waved Gabriel toward the doors. "I could use your help with this, if you have a second."

Nodding, Gabriel loaded Donald up and then filled his own arms to help carry the bedding inside. All around the baggage claim were at least one hundred cots all lined in neat rows. "Why baggage claim?" he asked. "This has gotta be the coldest part of the building."

"That's why we needed the extra blankets." He shook his head. "We had two muggings, a theft, and an argument that turned into a full-blown fist fight over a charging station, of all the bullshit you could get mad about. And it all happened at the same time. We were running all over the place."

"'Tis the damned season," Gabriel murmured.

"I know, right? So, management decided that we needed to centralize everyone so it'd be easier to keep an eye on things. There's one other terminal that still has people, cuz they were already settled in for the night, but this is most of the stranded." Donald directed him to follow as he made his way to the far side of the room. "These last two rows don't have blankets or pillows. If you could…"

Nodding, he distributed the bedding to weary, angry, and sad travelers, who mostly thanked him kindly. When he finished, he was left holding one blanket. Donald walked over holding one pillow. "That's everyone taken care of, I think."

Gabriel nodded and looked around the cavernous space. He hadn't seen Talia. "Listen, there's a woman here that I—I know. I brought her some food…"

"What she look like?"

"Um, black. Tall-ish. Had um, locs with gold things in it." He paused. "Beautiful smile."

Donald gave him a knowing look. "Oh, white guy's got it bad for a sister, huh?"

"Shut up and tell me where she is, I know you know."

The other man grinned. "I do know. Go get the food."

When he came back inside, Donald walked him to the far end of the room and there she was. Sitting cross-legged on a cot, with her coat still on, holding up her phone and speaking to the screen.

As they got closer, her words carried to them. "It's been a hard day. I'm exhausted." She sniffled and wiped tears off her cheeks. "I was trying to stay positive and tough, but then I remembered that I don't have to do that. I can go ahead and wallow a little. It's healthy. So honestly, this sucks." She sighed heavily. "Anyway, I wish everyone well on this fine Christmas Eve-eve." She paused. "It's after midnight though, which technically makes it the 24th. So just a happy Christmas Eve, then. I hope you have nice warm beds and something delicious to eat." She held up a barely touched sandwich. "Remember to follow Mama Talia's advice. Care for yourself and set good boundaries. Do something kind when you feel unkind. And most importantly, keep being the absolutely glorious magical bitches I know that you can…" she trailed off and stared at him as he approached. "Hey," she said. "What are you doing here?"

"Um, I—I brought extra bedding from the hotel. For the people here. And I brought food. For you. Us, if you're okay with it." He closed his eyes and tried to rally his power of speech. "Please don't eat that sandwich. It could make you sick."

He felt a little woozy at the sight of her shiny smile. She glanced back at her phone. "Oh shit. I didn't mean to record that." She fussed with her phone for a second and then gave up. "Oh well. A little mystery for my viewers."

Donald shifted from foot to foot and dropped the remaining pillow onto her cot. "Ma'am, are you alright with this fool being here and bringing you food?"

She nodded. "I am."

He bobbed his head at her. "Alright then, I'll be over there, by the exit if you need anything. Don't let the security shirt he's wearing make you think he can get away with any shit." He pointed at his dark eyes and then pointed the same two fingers at Gabriel. "I'm watching him."

Laughing, Gabriel played with the edges of the blanket he was holding. "Um, viewers, you said?"

"Yeah, I'm sort of a…I don't even know what you'd call it. I make mental wellness videos."

"For magical bitches?"

"Exactly." She patted the space beside her.

He hesitated. "I don't think that cot was meant to hold my weight and yours."

"Oh!" She hopped off it. "We can sit on the floor. I was right, it's definitely more comfortable anyway."

She grabbed the thin blanket the airport had provided and spread it out on the floor, picnic style, while he pulled out the Styrofoam containers and handed her two of them. She peeked inside and her face lit up. "A salad sounds so good right now but french fries sound even better. This is great!"

He sat cross legged in front of her. "Burger and fries are probably a little cold."

"I'm not picky." She took a huge bite of salad, followed by some fries. "Cold fries are still fries." Her eyes went all shimmery. "Thank you. Really."

"No worries." He opened his container and his stomach growled audibly.

She reached across the space between them and patted his abdomen. "Food's comin', buddy."

He laughed. His belly felt warm where she'd touched it. Ordinarily he would have been a little self-conscious. His stomach wasn't quite as muscled and flat as it had been in his twenties or even his thirties. The Marines had kept him hard. Now that he was out, he still went to the gym and tried to keep up, but ever since he hit forty-two, things had gotten a touch softer. "You're…different," he said.

She jabbed a french fry into ketchup and nodded. "I get that a lot." She ate her food with gusto, taking huge bites of burger and then sitting back to savor it as she chewed. He liked that. He liked women who loved food and weren't self-conscious about it. "Mmm, this is so good!" She shook her head. "I can't believe you brought me dinner."

"Well, I mean, I had to eat. You had to eat. And that sandwich sounded like a hazard."

Her phone, sitting beside her, pinged several times and she reached over and silenced it. "Sorry about that."

"It's alright. Celebrities gotta interact with the little people."

She snorted. "I'm hardly a celebrity. I will say that I've been, upon occasion, a moderate viral success."

"Whoa, someone has a high opinion of themselves."

Her laugh was bright and boisterous, just like she was. Several people rolled over in their cots and shot them a glare, as though the airport wasn't a never-ending barrage of clanking and shoes and crying children anyhow.

She seemed impervious to the reactions, though. "So, Gabriel, tell me something boring about yourself."

He choked back a laugh. "Not something interesting?"

"Interesting comes with a lot of pressure. Boring is an easier place to start."

"Alright." He thought for a moment. "I was born about ten miles outside Detroit."

"Wow, that is boring as hell."

"I take my assignments seriously." He sat his burger down. "How about you?"

"I like to watch videos and streams of other people playing video games that I'm too lazy to play myself."

"You cheated. That's actually interesting."

"No, it is not!"

After that, they traded boring tidbits about themselves that got progressively less boring. He learned that, in addition to making "wellness influencer" videos, whatever those were, she was also an artist and a mental health counselor. She lived in Denver. She had three siblings, didn't care for mangos, and could memorize a commercial jingle after just one listen. Oh, and her favorite pizza topping was pineapple. That was it. Just pineapple.

Clearly, no one was perfect.

"So yeah, that's how I ended up losing that bet, and had to get my first piercing," she said. "Never bet against people smarter than you. Your turn."

"How many piercings do you have besides the one in your nose?" He handed her a candy cane from his pocket.

She lit up and unwrapped it, sliding it into her mouth and sucking. His body suddenly became very alert. "This isn't twenty questions," she said. "It's your turn to tell me something boring about you."

"But I have follow-up questions. How many? Where?"

"Nope."

He gave a heavy mock-sigh. "Fine. I have about..." he counted on his fingers. "Ten tattoos."

Her eyes roamed him, as if she could see beneath his jacket and uniform to find them all, but she kept her lips together and didn't ask about them.

"You can ask. I'm not stingy about the information like *someone* here."

"Nope," she said. "I'm not a hypocrite. I can live without my curiosity being assuaged. Can you?"

"Absolutely not. Where are your piercings?"

She covered her mouth to hide her shock of a laugh. "You're really funny."

He shook his head. "Not usually."

"Well, you're on fire tonight." She played with her phone for a moment, looking conflicted and then sat it back down with a sigh. "I'm having fun and I really hate to end this, but it's late and I'm exhausted. And freezing."

"Oh yeah, no problem." He shuffled to his feet, oddly resistant to leaving. He glanced out at the continuing downfall of snow and looked back at her. "Um, I have a proposition for you. No, not a—um, wait that's not..." He groaned and scrubbed a hand over his face.

She stared at him with amused eyes. "Well, I'm not sleeping with you, nor am I telling you where my piercings are."

"No no, not those things..." He shifted, the half-baked idea sounding worse and worse in his head. "You know what? Never mind. I was just...there's no proposition."

"You can't do that now. I won't be able to sleep. I'm too intrigued!"

He zipped up his coat. "Nope. You'll have to live without your curiosity being *assuaged*."

"Nooooo." She sat up straighter, with her legs folded

beneath her and it made him think things. Adult things. "Please," she said, her amber eyes wide.

He swallowed hard past the rush of desire suddenly choking him. "Well, it's just that it's too dangerous for me to drive home, and since I have to cover in the morning, I was going to sleep on the couch in the hotel anyhow, but it's still snowing. It's really not far to the hotel, but it's just a stressful drive back in the dark..." he trailed off.

"So you wanna sleep here. With me?" She stared at him for a long moment, as if she could see into his soul. "I don't know if I should trust you like that."

Disappointment hung over him like a winter storm cloud, but he kept his expression cheerful. "That's absolutely fair. I can head back to the hotel. Like I said, it was a dumb idea, that's why I—"

"You're not upset about it?"

"I work in security, remember? Safety is everything. You're smart not to trust some random stranger who literally gave you candy."

"True. But I didn't even hesitate to eat it. For some reason, I trust you. Even though my better judgment says I shouldn't trust anyone I just met."

"You should probably always heed your better judgment."

"Probably." She picked up her phone and toyed with it. "Are you comfortable being on camera?"

"Like in a video? I guess. Why?"

She dug into her bag and pulled out a little tripod. He watched, baffled as she sat it on the cot and attached her phone to it. After a few seconds of moving it around, she leaned it downward and sat back on the floor. "Alright, come here."

Unsure what was happening, he shifted over onto her side of the blanket, and she scooted closer until they were shoulder to shoulder. Her hair smelled sweet and slightly tropical. She held up a tiny microphone in one hand and a remote in the other. On her phone screen, the record symbol appeared over their faces.

"I have a dilemma," she said into the mic. "I've been taught that one should never take candy from strangers. But this very handsome stranger here brought me some dinner as well as candy. Now, a smarter woman would definitely not trust a man with this face." She pointed her long dark nails at him.

He stared at himself on the screen. Fair skin. Black hair. Brown eyes. Strong nose. Scruffy five o'clock shadow. He looked fine. "What's wrong with my face?"

She waved off his question. "Anyway, I'm camped out in an airport and he brought bedding to help us all out. Since he can't go home tonight, he might as well stay here. And if I share space with him, I'll be twice as warm, but I'll also be cuddling up to someone who seems very nice, but whom I don't know at all."

"All I am is warm bedding to you, aren't I?"

Her lips quirked. "Right now, yes." She returned to addressing the screen. "Please tell my viewers who you are in case you pull some shady shit on me."

He laughed and shook his head. "Hello, I'm Gabriel Tilki."

"What do you do for a living, Gabriel Tilki?"

"I'm the head of security at the hotel across the street."

"Can verify. I actually saw him at work, plus he's got the badge." She pointed at his chest. "So Gabriel, do you live in Detroit?"

She was looking at him now and she was sitting so close. He glanced at her lips and a sudden reckless urge to kiss her pushed its way past anything resembling common sense. He resisted that urge with every fiber of his being and dragged his eyes where they belonged. "No," he said slowly. "I live outside the city. It's not too far from here, when there's not a major storm anyhow. But I've been in the area for most of my life."

"Where did you live when you weren't here?"

"Wherever the Marines sent me."

"Ahhhh, that explains the posture. You sit straighter than anyone I've ever met."

"First you come for my face and now my posture? I want my candy back."

"Too late." She was still so close and for just a moment, her eyes dropped to his lips. But she seemed to think better of it as well, and turned back to the camera. "Okay, Gabriel, it's time to make a sacred oath before all my seven hundred thousand-ish followers."

"Whoa, that's a lot of followers." He took a deep breath. "But I'm ready."

"I need you to solemnly swear that you will not burgle, manhandle, or otherwise harm me or my property."

"I, Gabriel, solemnly swear that I will not do any of those things you just said."

"Be specific," she said, fighting a smile.

"I, Gabriel, solemnly swear that I will not burgle, um, grope, or otherwise harm you or your stuff."

"Close enough." She gave the camera a thumbs up. "I'll post again in the morning, so you'll know that I'm unburgled."

He watched quietly as she played the video back and did some kind of magical editing stuff to it that was beyond him, and then she posted it. "Okay, Gabriel," she said, tossing her phone aside. "Let's do this."

Together they laid out the extra bedding and made a nest. He dug into his bag and pulled out a hoodie and a t-shirt. Unbuttoning and removing his work shirt, he shivered as icy air skittered over his bare skin.

He glanced back at Talia. "Are you warm enough? I have a wool travel blanket if you're not."

She hesitated and he could feel the weight of her eyes on him, tracing the lines of his tattoos. The black bands that circled his forearm on one side and his bicep on the other. The flowers. The poems. The manta ray tattoo that spread like angel wings across his upper back. Her gaze replaced the cold air with something warm that teased over him pleasurably, like a soft hand.

"Are you really asking me that right now? Put your shirt on, sir. And then ask me again."

Laughing, he pulled the t-shirt on and then the hoodie. "Better?"

"I mean, now I can accurately gauge my temperature. I'm doing alright."

He folded his uniform shirt neatly. He'd have to wear it again when he went back to work in the morning, so best to make it look presentable. That done, he put their bags beneath the bedding with them.

She rolled onto her side so she was facing him. "Thank you again for doing all of this."

"It's not a problem." He turned so he was facing her. "Can I ask a question?"

"Go for it."

He hesitated, but his curiosity won out. "Why are you headed to New York?"

"Ah, that's...complicated."

"Sorry, I didn't mean to pry."

Her lips tilted in amusement. "Sure you did."

"Maybe I did. It just feels like there's a story there."

"Hmm." Her brow furrowed. "I'm really bad at keeping secrets, aren't I?"

"Yeah, your face is talking when you aren't."

"Stupid chatty fucking face." She sighed. "Typical shit. Blah blah blah family issues. Blah blah blah lonely holidays."

He raised his eyebrows and waited for more.

"*Fiiinnnne.*" She smiled softly and bunched the pillow up beneath her head. "I grew up in Brooklyn. My family is still there. I'm not and I like it that way. They're very..." she scrunched up her nose. "They're particular. They like things done in very specific ways and I like to do things my own way." She ran a hand through her hair. "This year, they guilted me into coming to visit because my sister had a baby. I'm not sure what's worse, being trapped here or being trapped there watching everyone pretend their lives are perfect."

"I think you *do* know the answer."

"Yeah. This is better," she said. "Every time I think I've found my center, when I'm healthy and happy, they turn up to take a little of that away." Even beneath the coat and the blankets, he could see her shoulders sag. "It was stupid to take this trip. Nothing good ever comes from spending time with people who look down on you. I've been engaging in some magical thinking and I'm convinced the storm is nature's way of telling me I should have stayed home." She frowned and shook her head. "What about you? Got anyone at home right now, missing you?"

"Is that your subtle way of asking if I'm single?"

"No. I wasn't being subtle."

He barked a laugh and someone a few cots down shushed them. He waved apologetically. "I'm single. And no family in town." He pushed aside the flicker of pain the words brought. "My mom moved three years ago, and my sister moved shortly thereafter."

"Personally, that sounds like heaven, but you sound sad about it."

"I am." He rolled onto his back. "So what's your favorite Christmas movie?"

"*Die Hard*," she said without hesitation.

"Now is that because you really think it's a Christmas movie, or do you just want to start an argument?"

"Both."

He stifled another surprised laugh. After that, the subject of family was gently set aside and they talked about their favorite movies for a while, which was nice. Eventually though, her voice got scratchy and her eyes began to droop closed.

"I'm falling out," she whispered.

"Then go to sleep."

She seemed to be considering something. "Um, are you okay with platonic cuddling?"

A thrill jittered through him. "I've been told that I'm an amazing cuddler."

"Oh, thank god. 'Cause you look warm and I like hugs." She turned away from him and pushed closer until they were spooned up, her bottom, padded as it was by the coat, pressed to him.

"Is it alright if I put my…" He wasn't sure how to describe it, so he just let his arm hover over her.

She grabbed his forearm and pulled it around her. "Oh, you're so *warrrrrrm*." A soft moan crept out of her, and he stared across the to the wall with the giant Luggage Claim sign on it, trying to not replay that moan in his head. What was wrong with him? She was a perfect stranger. A perfectly lovely stranger with a voice that caressed him, and the sweetest dimples he'd ever seen. With a filthy mouth and a sugary smile. And based on the few things she said about her family, maybe a little broken. He pulled her close and held her tight.

He knew about broken.

CHAPTER 2

Gabriel sipped his third cup of coffee and grimaced. No amount of sugar ever truly made the bitterness of coffee palatable for a sweet tooth like his. If hot cocoa would have kept him awake he'd have preferred that, but he was exhausted and sore from sleeping on the airport floor, and cocoa just didn't have the caffeine he needed.

Not that he regretted sleeping there.

He stared out the revolving doors for the hundredth time, but there was nothing to see. The storm continued, somehow worsening overnight. There was a wall of white between the hotel and the airport. Between them.

Talia had woken up while he was packing his bag and had watched him quietly. He asked her to come to the hotel and spend the day there, rather than the airport, but she said she didn't want him to feel obligated to babysit her.

He'd wanted to argue that it would have been fun if she'd come over. That he liked seeing her face. But that was the kind of thing that sounded cute in your head, but when said out loud to someone you hardly knew, it could come across as creepy.

At least she'd given him her number. They'd been texting

ridiculous memes and silly things all day. He'd even felt comfortable enough to send some god-awful cheesy dad jokes that were rewarded with rows of tearful laughing emojis.

His phone jangled in his pocket and he sat down the coffee. "An actual phone call?" he said, instead of hello. "I thought young people don't do that anymore."

"I'm hardly a young person," Talia said. "I only play one on the internet."

"They say forty is the new twenty."

"Tell that to my back. She says forty is still forty." Her yawn carried through the phone. "I'm so bored. I've read the whole internet. Tell me a joke."

"Alright, but I'm going to burn through all my best material by the end of the day at this rate." He thought for a moment. "Did you know that Norway has barcodes on their Navy vessels?"

"Oh, god. Go on. Make it awful."

"It's so when they come back to port they can...*Scandinavian*." He said the word slowly, emphasizing the syllables.

Her bright loud laugh warmed him from head to toe in a way that no coffee or cocoa ever could.

"That's the worst one yet. Have you been googling these or something?"

"Nope. Lucky for you, I've had years to workshop these gems with my niece. She's got great taste in jokes and thinks I'm hilarious. She's the only one who does, but still."

"I think you're hilarious," she said, sounding affronted.

"Well that makes two, then. My comedy career is taking off any second now." There was a sudden shout in the background and then an echoing choir of people singing a terrible pop version of a Christmas classic. "What the heck is going on?"

"Someone started a singalong to the holiday music overhead. And that's my cue to get the hell out of here." The singing faded. "Guess I'm taking you shopping with me."

"Did all that jolliness give you a craving for rampant capitalist consumerism?"

"Not so much. It just seems like my luggage isn't coming back to me. Also, holiday jolliness makes me a little itchy."

He snickered. "Are any of the shops even open?"

"Yeah, one of the gift shops is. There's a market open, and I heard someone say there's fast food too." He listened to her hum as she made her way to the shop. "Aw, Coney Island is closed. That's a bummer." She sighed. "Okay we're here. You'll be shocked to know that the snowman light up outfit has not been sold."

"Stunned. I'm stunned."

She chattered about various things, and he couldn't help the smile stretching across his face. Why did he like this woman so much?

Suddenly, she quieted, and he heard her speaking softer and away from the phone. "I'm sorry, what did you need?"

He couldn't make out what the other person was saying. But Talia said, "Oh that's so sweet. Absolutely!" There was another pause and then she gave a braying laugh. "You think so? Maybe you're right." There was more talk he couldn't hear. "It was so nice to meet you." She sighed into the phone, still laughing.

"Everything alright?" he asked.

"Yeah. It was a fan. Um, I think I just got a message from the universe."

"Do tell."

She hesitated. "Nah. The universe might want me to keep it a secret. Anyway, it's getting weird over here, so I'm taking it as a sign that I need to come see you."

"Oh yeah, you should heed that."

She laughed and it sent another spike of warmth through him.

"Seriously, though," he said. "The storm is getting worse. There are no flights going out tonight. Come on over and bring all your stuff. I'll find us a place to sleep." He couldn't guarantee that at all but sleeping beside her had been the most right thing he'd done in a long time, and he wanted to do that again. Ideally in a bed. But he'd take what he could get.

If his use of the word *us* surprised her, she didn't say so. "Is your shuttle running today?"

"Yeah, not that there's anything for him to do. But let me see what time I can get it over there."

Turned out, Khalil, the shuttle driver, was dying for a task, so he was decidedly chipper at the idea of tooling through a white-out storm to pick Talia up. "You got it, Captain!" His eyes slid slyly toward him. "Don texted me last night. Said your girl is a whole snack."

His face burned. "Um, she's um, yeah, maybe? I guess. I don't really know what that means."

Khalil shook his head and headed outside. "Well, whatever she is, I'll be back with her."

It was a painfully long half hour before he returned with Talia. She was carrying three bags from the airport shop. Her jacket was still wrapped tightly around her, and she had some inexpensive-looking gloves and a pair of knee-high galoshes. She looked adorably disheveled, and he couldn't help the smile that took over his face.

"You look like a million dollars."

"Ha," she said. "For that you get a hug." She sat her bags down and wrapped her arms around him.

He held her tight and after a moment pressed his forehead to hers. She sighed dreamily and then pulled back, looking at him with twinkling eyes.

He glanced at Khalil who was watching them curiously. Caught, he flushed. "Um, it was nice to finally meet you, Mama Talia!"

“Nice to meet you too, Khalil.”

He glanced over at Gabriel and grinned. “Definitely ho-ho-yes.”

She closed her eyes for a moment, but a smile danced all over her pretty face. “Definitely.”

With that Khalil hopped back onto the shuttle bus to park it.

“What was all that about?” Gabriel asked.

“The universe is being very talkative with me today. Don’t worry about it.” Her arms were still around him, and he found it hard to worry about anything. Her mouth twitched, as if she’d read his mind. “So…”

It was painful letting her go, but he did. And then ran a hand through his hair to keep from grabbing her and pulling her close again. “So, I thought that it’d be more comfortable to hang out in our break room. I ran it by the manager and she’s fine with it. These are unusual circumstances, so everyone is being pretty flexible.”

“It’s really nice of her. I appreciate it.”

“Are you hungry? I can take my lunch in a bit, and we can eat at the restaurant.”

“I’d love that. But is there a place where I can clean up? I want to change, and I’d murder someone for a hot shower.”

“I know the feeling,” he said. “I scrubbed my armpits in the sink when I got here. Sadly, that’s the best you’re gonna get.” His face burned as he realized precisely how unsexy that image probably was.

Her laugh was clear and chimey as a Christmas bell. “I’ll take that.”

He led her to the employee bathroom. “Okay, I’m gonna go do my rounds and I’ll meet you at the restaurant in twenty.”

Never in his career had he worked faster to get to his lunch break. He had time to stop and look in the mirror, lamenting his lack of a razor. He grew facial hair so fast he never bothered fully shaving. He usually kept his stubble long and groomed, which gave him a dangerous looking edge that worked for his job. But the scruff was a little out of control now. He sighed. At least they'd look disheveled together.

He smoothed out his wrinkled pants and headed to the restaurant. She was already seated. He took a moment and just looked at her. She was finally out of her jacket but was wearing that truly horrendous Christmas sweater with flashing lights. It didn't tell him anything about what she had going on underneath it. He knew she was rounded and curvy, but he wanted a little more inspiration for the lusty thoughts he'd been having since waking up with his morning wood pressed against her coat-covered ass.

She was on the phone with someone, her expression was grim, her gorgeous smile nowhere to be found. "I'm sorry I didn't fly out a day earlier, but I do not have the power to change the weather or go back in time. If I did, I'd be there. The storm isn't letting up—" she took a deep breath. "No, I'm not trying to ruin Zara's first Christmas. This is me telling you that it's unlikely I'm going to make it, becau—" Her eyes narrowed. "I understand that the pictures won't be perfect unless everyone is there, but you'll have to learn to live with them being *good enough*." Whatever was said, she flinched. "Right. Well, wish everyone a Merry Christmas for me. I'm really glad they're not sleeping on the airport floor." She jabbed the screen and then slammed the phone on the table.

"Hey." He sat down slowly. "You look festive."

She looked up at him, her eyes stormy. "It's a lie. I do not feel festive inside."

"Well, you lie beautifully." He drummed his fingers on the table. "I didn't mean to eavesdrop, but I heard some of that. Would you like to talk about it?"

She tilted her head and looked at him for a long moment, as if debating what to say. Right then, the waitress came to take their order. Though he was eager to hear what was going on with her, he couldn't help but notice the decisive way Talia chose her food. No dithering over what to get. He liked that. After the waitress wandered off, he raised his eyebrows and waited.

"Alright." She leaned back in her chair. "I've never been any good at telling a short story, but the condensed version is that my affluent black parents believe that we have an obligation to the world to appear perfect. To be leaders. To impress white people. I grew up with them dictating everything I could do and say. How I dressed and wore my hair. *Always represent, Talia. Never let them see you sweat. Keep your feelings to yourself, you'll make us look bad.*" She rolled her eyes. "I've never been great at following rules. I was a problem child that liked art and being silly and digging my hands in the dirt." She smirked. "My mom calls me a heathen. 'Talia, stop behaving like a heathen and cross your legs!' and 'Talia, go flat iron your hair, you look like a heathen.'"

He tried to imagine growing up like that. His family had been very different. "That sounds miserable."

She shrugged. "Coulda been worse. But I didn't have a good time, that's for sure. They churched me and smoothed me. Straightened my hair while I kicked and screamed. It's just…not who I am." The waitress brought their drinks and Talia thanked her, before sipping her hot chocolate. She closed her eyes and smiled contentedly for a moment. "My brothers and sister are just like them. *Stepfords*. Law School. Med School. Business School. Married wealthy. They live in boring neighborhoods with boring partners, and they're having kids that they're making into boring clones of themselves."

"So that's why you don't like going back?"

"Yeah. There's nothing in Prospect Heights for me, except my family's disapproval. I'm forty, unmarried, no children, and I didn't bother with grad school. So all I have in their eyes is a useless Bachelor's degree in counseling and an even more useless one in fine arts. And worst of all…" She leaned forward and he leaned forward too, mesmerized by the intensity of her eyes. "I go on the internet and tell people my actual feelings. My failures and successes. When I've been sad or frustrated. When I had to take anxiety meds. It's *disgusting. Appalling,* even."

"Being honest and sincere? How devoid of class," he said.

"Precisely. So vulgar." She lifted her mug and saluted him with it. "And if that's vulgar then I'll proudly call myself that. People have to feel things. It's toxic to pretend that everything's fine all the time. That's why I became a counselor. You don't have to wallow, but you can't push feelings aside forever. My sister is so unhappy. She married the *right guy* and has the *right house* and just had the *perfect baby* and she's wilting like a picked flower every time I speak to her. This isn't *her* life. It's like a play she's performing for my parent's approval. But I can't say anything because everyone believes that I just like to start trouble where there is none." She sighed. "I'm already sick of the sound of my own voice. Tell me about your family."

His body tensed up. As always, the words and feelings that he had got all tangled up inside and he couldn't unknot them. "Um, typical Persian family. Loving. Happy. Loud. No drama or anything."

She raised an eyebrow and said nothing, and he recognized it for what it was. A counselor making the quiet uncomfortable so the patient would fill it. He raised an eyebrow back and said nothing.

"Hmm," she finally said after what felt like a full minute of silence. "You're a vault, huh?"

"Sometimes." He drummed his fingers on the table. "So, you're a therapist?"

"Not exactly. That required more school than I wanted to bother with. I know just enough to be dangerous and no more. But I worked as a mental health counselor for years. I didn't treat big problems. I was more of a shoulder to lean on. Someone safe to talk to when things were tough."

"You didn't like it?"

"I did, but it was taxing. As an outlet I started painting these little cards with nurturing scenes on them, with affirming phrases. 'Your feelings are real and valid,' and 'You are worthy of love,' and 'You are enough.' Basic emotional care stuff. And I gave them to patients. One of them took a picture of his and put it online. People went crazy. They wanted to know where to buy them. He came in and showed me, all excited. So I started some social media accounts and began selling them, and then I made some videos and people really liked those too. It was cool to be able to affect people on a bigger scale than just individual sessions."

"And that's how Mama Talia was born."

She smiled. "Yes."

"Wow. So now you do that full time?"

"Sort of. I don't like making or selling ad space, so I have a crowdfunding thing where people pay monthly, and I give more content and individualized art. I do alright for myself. Sometimes the funding and sales take a dip. When that happens, I just teach community art classes or do wellness seminars. Those are fun."

"And that keeps the lights on?"

"Yeah. Usually. I mean, I'm not getting rich from it, not that I want to be rich. I'm not high maintenance, so it's fine. I don't like being tied down in doing just one thing anyhow, so it's nice to have that flexibility. It also takes pressure off me to perform for the camera. If I'm not feeling it, I don't do it. I'd rather be authentic and natural than force it for cash."

God, he really liked her. Her passion, her care for others. Her absolute assuredness in who she was and what she wanted to do. It was energizing.

"Anyway," she said. "Tell me about Gabriel-not-Gabe. What do you actually do here?"

"I'm the chief of security, so normally I'd be overseeing things, keeping an eye on the rest of the security staff, making the schedule, doing paperwork. I'm usually the policy police more than anything. But with the storm, and half my staff not available, I'm doing everything. Watching cameras, handling disturbances, checking on strange noises and still doing all the other stuff. It's been a long couple days."

"You poor guy," she said. "How'd you go from the Marines to security?"

"Happenstance. I went into the military to pay for college and ended up staying for a long time. But I realized I didn't want to make a life career out of it, so I got out and went to school for a while. I was getting a degree in IT Cyber Security. But I wasn't happy, and my da—" the word stuck in his throat, and he cleared it. "My dad said maybe school just isn't the right fit for me. He told me there was no harm in trying something else. So, I applied for a job in security in a department store and just worked my way from there. I like it. I've always worked with good people and the job is interesting. Every day you encounter something different, so it keeps you on your toes."

"Wow, you're lucky to have a dad who supported you in changing your trajectory. My dad would have blown a gasket if I told him I didn't want to finish my degree. He kind of did when I didn't go to grad school."

His chest tightened. "Yeah, my dad was great."

"Was?" She tilted her head. "I'm sorry. Would you like to talk about it?"

He shrugged in the way he'd become used to shrugging about it. "It's been three years. I've made peace with it."

She gave him a soft smile. "Subject change then?"

"Please."

"How has your day been?"

"Much more uneventful than yesterday."

She took a sip of her cocoa. "Because of the storm, you think?"

"No. It's odd, but for some reason people tend to behave on Christmas Eve. Not always, but often it's like the hush before the thunder. Yesterday we ended up with a full-on bar brawl. Today, so far, the worst has been a couple of noise complaints."

"But tomorrow..."

"Christmas? It'll be fine in the morning, but by the evening it'll all go to hell." He shook his head. "People start off wanting to behave and give up by dinner. And the more money they have, the earlier they give up on civility. We once had a fancy midnight Christmas wedding reception in the ballroom, and it was a total clusterfuck. Combining bougie people with the holiday, a wedding, and booze was a recipe for the cops being called at least four times. Rich people are the worst." He started to roll his eyes and then froze. "No offense..."

"None taken. I'm not rich, my family is. And rich people *are* usually the worst." She leaned back for a moment. "Though I'm curious what a bougie-ass Christmas wedding reception is like."

"Eye-searing. That's the best description. They've never met subtlety. Everything is red and green and there's so much of it. Why have one fancy tree when you can have ten? Why have a single poinsettia on the table when you can have an entire garden, coated in glitter? It's like the Grinch took that bag full of stolen decorations and chucked the whole thing into the ballroom."

Talia's laugh curled around him like a silky ribbon. "It's the glitter that pisses you off, isn't it?"

He nodded. "It gets *everywhere*. Even if you never step foot in the ballroom, you're scrubbing it off your ass for a week."

Talia was still laughing at that image when the waitress came and dropped off their sandwiches. They spent the rest of the meal telling stories and chatting about nothing.

Afterward, she wandered off to film a video and he finished the rest of his shift. Luckily, he had a few employees who lived nearby and who offered to come in and relieve him. Free of responsibility for the rest of the day and excited to spend more time with Talia, he whistled a happy tune and went looking for her.

The break room was empty. Huh. He turned to search elsewhere and walked into Imani, who was padded from the collision by arms full of bedding and towels

"Oh, sorry!" He glanced at his watch. "You're here awfully early."

"Yeah, Viv couldn't make it in so here I am, working a double." She pointed the linens at him. "I have a present for you."

"Let me get those." He took everything out of her arms. "A present for me? What is it?"

"Come on." She gestured for him to follow as she led him to the employees-only elevator.

"What are we—"

"Just hush." She took them down to the garden level, where the hotel was in the midst of renovations that had been halted by the storm. It was empty and the quiet was strange. The hall was only half wallpapered and most of the rooms didn't even have doors yet.

She led him to a room at the far end of the hall that did have a door and knocked on it before entering.

Inside, Talia sat on a bare mattress on the floor, a laptop in front of her. She looked up and smiled and his heart flipped over and sideways.

"Most of the rooms down here are basically ready to go, except for the furniture and paint." Imani said. "Oh, and doors. But those are on backorder or something." She grinned. "So, this is currently the garden level luxury suite." She grinned. "It's not much, but it's better than sleeping on the floor or on the break room couch." She patted the linens he'd taken from her. "These are for you. I already brought down the toiletries."

Warmth bloomed in his chest. "Thank you for this."

"I told you I'd pay you back for your help." She flipped her locs over her shoulder. "Merry Christmas."

"Thank you so much Imani," Talia said.

"You know I got you, girl. I can't even believe you're here. Your videos helped me through some rough times."

Talia's beautiful smile widened. "That makes me so happy."

Imani tossed some key cards on the mattress. "Just think of it as taking candy canes from a stranger." She turned toward Gabriel and winked, much to his confusion. "Anyway," she continued. "I'm out of here. Don't get into trouble."

Gabriel didn't know what to say. He tried to clear his head. "Um, I'll be here if you need any help tonight."

"Osvaldo should be able to handle things, but I'll text you if I need you." She gave them a wave. "Ho-ho-yes!" she shouted as she departed.

He swallowed and stood there, unsure what to do. His heart was pounding at the thought of actually being alone with Talia. Thoughts rushed at him. The impure kind. What would it be like to slide his hands under that horrible sweater and touch her soft skin. Would she want that?

Her mouth twitched as if she heard his thoughts. She patted the mattress and wriggled her eyebrows.

One laugh and his tension melted away. He sat the linens down and joined her. "So, you really are famous, huh?"

"Fame is so relative anymore. I really don't know what I am. But the people who have seen my videos tend to be very fervent in their appreciation for them."

"I guess so." He leaned back a little. "She's the second person to say 'Ho-ho-yes.' What's that about?"

"Heh." Talia shook her head. "Third actually. The lady at the airport while we were on the phone said it, too. I guess my followers really enjoyed meeting you and they've been trending #hohoyes all day."

"Why?"

"Because on the video of us, I put #hohoyes or #hohono in the caption. You know, about sleeping next to each other. Apparently, it's a resounding yes. Also, there's been a lot of #takecandycanesfromstrangers, so I think it's safe to say that they're shipping us."

"Sorry, I'm really not a social media guy. What does that mean?"

"It means they're rooting for us to…" She smirked. "Get to know each other."

Heat rushed to his face and he cleared his throat. "You mean they want us to…"

"Yes, sir." Her eyes twinkled with amusement. "Wait till you see what they've been saying about you and your…candy cane."

"Oh my god."

"Yeah, apparently, that's what they think I'll be saying."

He groaned. "I'm sorry, I need to go find a hole to crawl into."

"Yeah, that's what they're…"

He biffed her with a pillow before she could say anything more and she snickered. "Okay, okay, well in other news, I'm going to be anti-social for a little bit, while I finish editing this video. Do you want me to do this with my earbuds in, so you don't have to hear the same clips play over and over?"

Happy for the subject change, he shook his head. "No, I want to hear. This is interesting." He sat beside her, acutely aware of how close their bodies were while he quietly watched as she arranged the pieces of the video and enhanced things, adding little images and text.

She must have gone outside and filmed in the snow. In the video, it fell down on her, catching in her eyelashes as she talked about the melancholy of the holidays for some people and how it was alright not to feel holly and jolly. And that traditions could be broken or reclaimed and that was alright too.

His chest tightened as he listened. "I can see why people love you," he said. "This is stuff they need to hear. It's so hard when things change." A lump formed in his throat. "All the traditions that used to fill you with joy suddenly leave you empty, but everyone expects you to just carry on like the joy is still there."

She tilted her head, as if she expected him to say more, but he'd said enough. "Anyway, that video was beautiful."

Her hand covered his and gave it a squeeze before returning to the laptop and he took it as an opportunity to change the subject. "What um, do you do for Christmas?" he asked.

"You mean besides sleeping next to strange men in airports?"

"I'm not strange. But go on."

She seemed a little puzzled by the question. "Um, nothing."

"You wouldn't be putting up a tree, or wrapping gifts? None of that stuff?"

"No, I don't really...do that." She sat back. "Holidays in the Evans household were about as much fun as getting a mammogram. We didn't put up decorations ourselves, we had a service come in and put them up for us, so they'd look perfect. We had two huge trees we weren't allowed to touch. We weren't even allowed to buy each other presents. My parents gave us short lists of what to get everyone else in the family, we picked one item and then they bought them, had them professionally wrapped and delivered to whomever, on our behalf. There were horrible family holiday photos and…" She took a breath. "You get the point. It sucked. Christmas is just a holiday I've never enjoyed."

"So have you ever tried, like, reclaiming it like you said in the video?"

She made a face. "No. I think that ship has sailed." Her phone pinged and she turned off the sounds. "Here come the comments. Anyway, I've talked plenty about my family and you've dodged talking about yours every time I ask. What were your holidays like?"

Despite the jolt of anxiety her words brought, he couldn't help but laugh at her bald statement. "You don't pull any punches, do you?"

"I pull plenty. But this one is bugging me. You keep digging into me about mine and I get the feeling something in you wants to talk about yours."

"I really don't," he said. "My family was great. The holidays were fun."

"But?"

He shrugged. "I think we should focus on reclaiming the holidays for you."

She groaned and flopped down on the bed. "You know what I think?"

"I cannot begin to imagine," he said.

"I think I want to take a nap. On this comfy-ass mattress."

"Avoidance technique, Miss Evans?"

"Let's say I learned it from someone in this room."

He snorted and pulled her to her feet. "At least let me make the bed. I spent too many years in the military to sleep on bedding that's less than crisp."

They put the sheets on, and she laughed when he neatly made the corners despite there being no actual bed to tuck anything into. They climbed in and sighed contentedly at the same time.

"This is the life," she groaned.

"A mattress on the floor of an unpainted hotel room and a strange man's parts rubbing against you obscenely while we cuddle?"

"I said it, and I meant it."

Laughing, he moved closer to her back and wrapped an arm around her waist, without hesitation this time. Beneath the ugly sweater, she was soft and squishy in all the ways he liked. She shifted and her ass curved tight against him, hitting just the right spot as she moved. He gave a sharp exhalation and tightened his hold on her.

"Did you do that on purpose?" he murmured.

"No, I didn't do it on purpose!" Then she snickered. "Mostly."

Shaking his head, he held her as she fell asleep, her breathing relaxed and even. He pressed his face against the crook of her neck. Maybe it was weird, but he indulged in a small kiss right there, letting his lips linger for just a moment. She gave a contented sigh.

Sleep was more elusive for him, though. In his mind, he kept replaying everything she'd said about the holidays. There was a hurting, a raw wound in Talia when it came to Christmas. Despite his hesitance to talk about his own family, he felt bonded to her, lost with her in the fog of what Christmas could be and what it felt like now. He brushed his nose against the spot on her neck he'd kissed. Nothing could give him back what he'd had before, but maybe...maybe he could give her what she'd never had at all.

The idea wouldn't let go of him as he laid there. He started making a plan and mapping out the fastest way to do everything. Once it seemed doable, he untangled himself from her. He missed her warmth immediately, but he climbed off the mattress and pocketed a key card before sneaking out the door.

First things first, he called the airport gift shop and paid for what he wanted over the phone, then he called Khalil, who was already at the airport, probably visiting Donald, and asked if he'd pick a few things up for him.

"Ho-ho-yes," Khalil said.

Gabriel fought the heat that rushed to his cheeks, now knowing what those words meant. "I, um…okay. Thanks."

After that, he made his way to the storage room. Luckily, it was on the same floor they were, so it wasn't hard to dig through all the old stuff and find what he was looking for. He quietly brought it all to the room, and then rushed outside to get the rest from Khalil.

By the time Talia woke up, looking rested and a little bit more rumpled than before, he had a pile of boxes and bags in the room and a couple of hot chocolates in steaming to-go cups in his hands.

She sat up and rubbed her eyes. "Whatcha doing?"

"Something that might annoy you."

"Interesting." She climbed out of the covers and crawled across the bed before sprawling out on her belly, with her legs swinging in the air like a teenager. "I am looking forward to my annoyance."

"We're going to have a Christmas."

Her lip quirked and while she didn't roll her eyes, it was everything just shy of an eye roll. "Pushy. Are you a Virgo by chance?"

"Taurus."

"Hmph."

"And you're a Water sign sun. Scorpio I'm guessing, with an earth sign rising, probably Capricorn. And I suspect you've got a few Aquarius placements as well."

She shot up. "How did you know that?"

He gave her a lazy grin. "My sister Yasmin puts a lot of stock in astrology. I've sat through many lectures."

"You're an ever-surprising man. And I'll be honest. Most men? Not that surprising."

"On behalf of everyone who calls themselves a man… you're not wrong."

She shuffled off the bed. "I would be a hypocrite if I didn't indulge this little exercise, wouldn't I?"

"A massive hypocrite. The very worst kind. Like politician level."

"Oh, that's bad." She sighed heavily. "If I participate in this, do I get one of those?" She pointed toward the steaming cups of hot cocoa.

"You do."

"Fine, let's take back Christmas. But," she held up a finger. "This will require you to tell me a little about your happy holidays so I can know that I'm doing this properly."

He groaned. "Fine."

She gave a little squeak of delight at getting her way. "Tell me."

He sat heavily on the mattress. "Let's see. On Christmas Eve, we played obnoxious Christmas music."

She nodded and got on her phone. A moment later, a cheesy Christmas ballad about going home filled the room.

"Okay, now this is important. We would take our baths and then put on identical pajamas."

"You're making that up."

"I'm not. It was a thing my mom loved. The whole family did it."

She nodded thoughtfully. "Okay, next?"

"We took family photos. Just candids. And then we filled each other's stockings with joke gifts or fun ones. We didn't do the Santa thing. My parents thought it was lying to us, so they brought out the real gifts and put them under the tree. We turned on the lights, sang songs, and watched holiday movies. At midnight, we opened our presents."

Her brows drew together. "Then what did you do on Christmas Day?"

The other stuff was easy to recall. But Christmas morning

hurt like a punch to the throat. He sat for a moment, trying to push past the pain. "On Christmas morning, we make breakfast. My mom made cinnamon rolls, and my dad made kuku sabzi, which is sort of like a Persian frittata that my great-grandmother used to make. And everyone got a helper job. I cracked the eggs. Even as an adult, that was my job." He smiled, the memory so warm and vivid he could touch it. "After we ate breakfast, we'd watch Christmas cartoons and then my dad would bundle us all up and take us for our holiday walk. No matter the weather, we always took that walk. My dad—" he paused to let the emotion leak away before it came out in his voice. "My dad saw beauty in everything. He'd point out the ice on the trees and the way our breath formed shapes in the cold air. He'd say things like, 'Look, look, look, Gabriel, look at that sky. How does it make you feel?' And whatever I answered, he'd say, 'You are blessed to feel so much!'" He closed his eyes. "He made every day magical, but especially Christmas." Tears tightened his eyes. "My mother and my sister, they don't like to feel too much. They're pretty...reserved I guess, comparatively. My father was an artist and a poet. He felt everything. *I* felt everything."

"You say that in past tense. You don't feel everything, now?"

He stared at the wall. "I guess I—I don't want to, now."

She reached over and gripped his hand tight. "Alright, so what's all this stuff?"

He was relieved that she didn't push for more information than he could give at that moment. "Decorations. Lights. A tree. We're gonna put it all up."

"Well, let's start at the beginning," she said. "We have to take our baths and put on identical outfits."

"Um, we don't have identical outfits."

Her smile was wider than the Cheshire cat's. "Oh, but we do."

After her shower, Talia emerged from the bathroom and struck a pose. "What do you think?"

"Holy fu…" He stared at the red and white striped onesie she was sporting. It clung to her every full, generous curve. Especially her ass, which was quite honestly, the best gift he'd ever been blessed with. Also, he could count at least two piercings, because her nipple rings were not hidden by the stretchy thin material. None of his musings about her form had done justice to what had been under that ugly sweater. The room was suddenly a lot warmer.

"That good, huh?" She threw her head back and laughed. "I don't think I look as good as you do in yours."

"I cannot believe you bought two of these." He shifted uncomfortably in his green and white striped onesie that was far too tight for his tall, broad frame. When he left the bathroom in it, he'd been mortified. The damn thing was obscene, showing every inch of his dick and frankly, it squeezed his balls, cleaving them into a swollen camel toe. Also, it was made for someone much shorter so the whole thing only came to his mid-calves. Then, to add insult to injury, it was V-neck, which left his rather Gaston-like chest hair exposed.

She'd nearly cried from laughing though, so it was kind of worth it.

"If you buy one Christmas onesie, you're making a statement, so you might as well buy two."

"Your logic baffles me."

She grinned and dropped to the floor like a little kid. "Okay, so how the hell do we do this?"

He dumped out the lights and the various decorations. "Let's start by filling the space with tacky junk I found in the storage room."

"I love this journey for us."

They set up a lighted snowman in one corner of the room, tied a squashed wreath to the window's curtain rod, and taped loads of balding gold garland to the walls. He handed her some rumpled stockings and she hung them on hangers in the closet.

He'd also found a cheap novelty pillow in storage that made him laugh, so he tossed it onto the bed. It said, "Let it snow," but the spacing on the letters was wonky, and it looked more like 'Le tits now.'

Talia nearly snorted out her now-cold cocoa. She placed the pillow neatly in the center of the regular bed pillows to showcase it, then stood back to observe the whole room. "I can't tell if this looks awful or amazing," she said.

"The magic of Christmas makes the awful look amazing. No one would watch Christmas movies otherwise."

"When you put it that way, those tacky-ass, bougie weddings make a lot more sense."

He nodded as he pulled the limb of an artificial tree from a dusty box and held it up. "Now the *pièce de résistance*."

"That seems complicated."

"It's not." He put the pole together and showed her how to pop the branches into place and spread them out to make the tree look fuller. Soon they had a tree that looked only slightly better than Charlie Brown's droopy little pine.

She'd never decorated one before, so she kept stopping to marvel at the pretty glittery bulbs, which made him smile. They'd over-decorated, so the limbs were bowing under the weight of the lights and bulbs. He dug the angel topper out and grimaced, handing it to her.

"This girl has lived some shit," she said. The angel's curly yellow hair was ratty and smelly, her big blue eyes were pink from leaking dye, and her dress was stained nicotine yellow. Talia stretched on her tiptoes and plopped it on the tree. It tilted sideways and stayed there.

"Do you want me to fix that?" he asked.

She tilted her head the same direction the angel was leaning. "Nah. Perfection is overrated. I kind of like it like this."

They laid out the tree skirt and then he handed her a bag. "These are the presents for my employees. I've got paper and tape. Want to wrap them with me?"

"I'm really bad at wrapping gifts," she said. "It'll look like a five-year-old did it."

"That can only add to the charm." They sat cross-legged on the floor and haphazardly wrapped stuffed animals, keychains, and random other things. They splayed them out under the tree, and she sighed happily. "Now what?"

"Now we watch a movie." He glanced at his phone. "When it's over, it'll be Christmas, and then we'll open our gifts."

She bit her lip. "I don't have a gift for you."

"That's alright. Though, I do have one for you."

"What? You shouldn't have done that."

"Yeah, well I did. Don't argue with me about it. Just come here and watch a movie with me."

Giving in, she turned down the lights and they cuddled close, eating sandwiches and chocolate peppermint fudge cake from the restaurant, while they watched Die Hard on her laptop. She pointed out all the ways it very much was a Christmas movie. Afterward, they put the music back on and he made her close her eyes while he placed presents under the tree and in her stocking.

She dug her hand into the stocking first and pulled out a folded piece of paper. "What is this?"

"Stockings are for simple joys," he said.

Looking at him with suspicion she unfolded the paper and stared down at it unblinking. "'Why did the doctor warn the dad not to eat Christmas tree decorations?'" She flipped the paper over. "'He didn't want him to catch tinsel-itis.'" Her groan could probably be heard on the next floor of the hotel. "This is the worst pun I've ever read."

"You're welcome," he said cheerfully.

Her laugh was clear and warm. She folded the paper carefully and put it in her bag. "Thank you. I'm keeping this horrible joke forever."

He reached under the tree and pulled out the gift he was actually nervous about and put it in her hands.

"It's heavy!" Scraping her teeth over her lower lip, she unwrapped it quickly, choosing not to savor the moment, but to get right to it. He liked that. She threw the paper aside and stared at the snow globe, her smile wavering. "Oh," she said softly.

The black family inside were smiling and happy as they decorated a spindly tree. The tiny kitty played with a tree limb. Ornaments spilled out over the floor, and no one seemed concerned about it. "This is what you deserved to have," he said.

She stroked her fingers over the cool glass of the globe. "I don't..." She flipped it over and spun the little latch to make tinny Christmas music play. Snow fluttered down around the family when she flipped it upright and sat it down. "This is so..." She turned and threw herself into his arms.

He held her as she sniffled against his neck, tears dampening his awful onesie. "What are we doing here, Gabriel?" she whispered.

"I don't know. Something stupid."

She gave a soft huff of a laugh, her breath tickling the side of his neck. After a moment, she pulled back and studied him with shining eyes. The heat in her gaze curled inside of him like fireplace smoke. He slid his hands into her locs and pulled her against him, closing most of the distance, but leaving some room for her to decide. She didn't hesitate, thank god. Her lips met his, and it was as if every light on the tree brightened.

Swaying, they kissed through a handful of sweetly melancholy Christmas songs, in the glow of an endless circuit of red, green, and white lights that chased each other around the unpainted walls of the room.

Her mouth tasted like peppermint and home. Like he'd always belonged there. He tilted his head to deepen the kiss and she groaned deep in her throat and stood taller, meeting his pressure and his intensity. There was no more gentle sweetness to it after that. Just greedy, frenzied desire. She nipped his lower lip and sucked on it and his whole body caught fire. His hands roamed her, stroking from her waist, down to that gorgeous full ass, gripping it and grinding her against his hardening cock.

Without breaking the kiss, he pulled her down on top of him as he landed on the mattress. She moaned and arched her back, giving him more to hold onto as she fumbled with the buttons of her onesie.

"Wait," he said.

She froze, her eyes dark with desire. "What is it?"

"I just don't want you to think that I expected anything here. Or that I did any of this to get you into bed. We don't have to…"

She nodded and unbuttoned her onesie, spreading it open to expose gloriously heavy breasts, with gold bars through her dark nipples. She raised an eyebrow.

"If you're sure," he said. Faster than he'd ever moved, he had one breast in his mouth, sucking and pulling on her nipple. The bar gave him an easy target to work with. She made deep and breathy sounds of pleasure as he worked the other nipple with his fingers, tugging on her piercing.

She pushed him back and eagerly undid the buttons of his outfit. Shoving it open, she stared at his chest fully on display. He touched the crisp dark hair she was looking at. "Um, I'm Persian so…"

She threw her head back and laughed. "I'm into it. Show me more."

He nodded and rolled her onto her back, more than

happy to remove the stupid onesie. In a few short jerks, he was naked. She made a rumbling sound of pleasure as she ran her fingers over the tattoos on his shoulders and arms and down his abdomen, tracing their way lower and lower, until she had his cock firmly in her hand. He gave a rather tragic moan of pleasure. It had been a long time.

"Ooh, I like that," she said. She rocked forward and kissed his neck, sucking gently on his skin as she stroked him.

"One of us—oh god don't stop—one of us is wearing too much clothing," he grunted.

"Mmm, you have disparate desires. I can stop touching you and undress or I can keep my clothes on and touch you."

"No, you can do both, I believe in you." Laughing, he reached down and began awkwardly pulling the tight fabric down her mouth-watering hips.

She sat up on her knees, not letting go of him as she tried to shimmy out of it with only one hand to assist. "I want you to know that I'd be naked right now if you'd let me stop holding your dick."

"I have zero regrets," he said, watching her breasts sway as she struggled to remove the onesie.

He leaned forward to help her onto her back and pulled the onesie off her, leaving her naked and the sexiest woman he'd ever had in his arms. "Fuck," he ground out. He ran the palm of his hand over her breasts and her soft round stomach and down to the tempting V between her legs. He pressed his hand to it, and she gasped and arched into his palm. Oooh, she was pierced there, too.

He leaned down and gave searing suctioning kisses to her thighs, getting closer and closer to those delicate lips. He hovered over them and paused. "Is this alright?" he asked.

"Completely fine, sir." He could hear the smile in her voice, and it only stoked the fire in him.

"Do you want to direct me, or let me freestyle?"

Her laugh shook her body in the most sensual way. "I'm curious to see how you do with improvisation."

"I think you'll be pleased with my ability to wing it," he said. With that, he put her legs on his broad shoulders. He kissed her there first, gently and slowly, before using his hands to open her up so he could give her the Christmas gift she truly deserved.

Fuck, she tasted good. It had been a while but clearly, he still had the skills. Soon she was writhing beneath him, her moans so loud and delicious. He reached up with both hands and tugged on her nipples while he licked and sucked her pierced clit, trying to pay attention to what she liked. He was definitely in the right spot when her silky, thick thighs clamped over his ears and her hands dug into his hair, tugging to hold him in place.

"Gabriel," she breathed out. "Oh god!" Her abdomen tightened and then so did the rest of her, and she jerked, arching into his mouth. He stayed there, letting her ride the orgasm out on his tongue. Finally, she dropped her hips back to the bed, groaning.

He sat up and ran his hands along her waist as he trailed his sticky tongue up to her nipples and gave them some more love before making his way to her mouth. He paused and she grabbed his head and pulled him down for a kiss, sucking the taste of herself from him.

"Fuck me now," she said. "Pretty please."

He pressed his forehead to hers. His body was aching and needy. "I can't. I don't have any condoms."

She gave him a knowing smile. "Front pocket of my bag."

He scrambled over to the other side of the bed and reached into the pocket, pulling out a pack of condoms with a tag on it from one of the airport shops. He raised an eyebrow. "Did you have plans to seduce me, Miss Evans?"

"Yes. And clearly it worked."

"It sure as hell did." He tore open the box and pulled out a packet. With quick fingers, he tore it open and rolled the condom on.

She watched with heated eyes and scrambled onto her knees, lifting her ass into the air, showing him how she wanted it. His mouth watered and the condom was forgotten as he buried his face in her from behind and ate her pussy all over again.

"Oh my god," she cried out, arching toward his mouth. He gripped her ass so hard he'd probably leave bruises, but god, he wanted to leave a bruise or two. Just a mark to show he'd made an impression. Based on her nearly screaming into the pillow, he had. But some proof would be nice too.

She shoved her hands against the wall and pushed back, demanding more. He sucked her clit until his own head was spinning and he was tighter than a drum. She came with a sharp cry and fell onto the bed. Without waiting any longer, he slid into her. She was wet and accommodating, stretching to let him in. She just felt so good. So right.

He gently tugged on her locs. “Can I pull your hair?”

"You'd better," she said, her voice husky and strained.

He wrapped her locs around his fist and yanked hard and she arched up and released a stream of delicious obscenities as he gave a thrust. Her guttural wail sent chills of desire up his back, raising the hairs on his neck and sending pleasure pings everywhere. "That's so good, baby," he whispered in her ear as he pumped inside of her. "Make more noise for me."

Soon she surpassed the cries she'd made earlier. He'd have felt bad for the people in the next room if there'd been any, but there weren't. He pounded into her in ways he'd never done before with anyone. He was a big guy and he always tried to be careful, but she didn't want careful, and it was beyond exciting.

Even more so, because she wasn't careful with him either. Eventually she was on top, bouncing up and down, biting his shoulder, digging her long, dark nails into his chest, nearly drawing blood as she rode him hard.

When he came, it burst like the first rays of sunlight on cold snow. Sharp and exhilarating and beautiful. A moment later, she cried out and collapsed on top of him, shuddering. He wrapped his arms around her and kissed her all the way through her orgasm, wanting to taste every bit of her pleasure.

She made a purring sort of sound as she tried to roll off him, but he held her tight, keeping her chest pressed to his. "Don't go yet," he said. "I like you here."

"Aren't you squished?"

"Not at all." He kissed her neck and shoulder, and she relaxed on top of him. They stayed like that for a little while. Bodies still connected, fingertips skating over muscles and curves, tender kisses pressed to damp skin.

Finally, she sat up and he let go, enjoying the way her body jiggled and swayed as she stretched. He quickly removed the condom and threw it away. Then he turned back and ran a hand over her stomach, splaying it against her dark skin, loving the contrast between them. He reached up and cupped her soft breasts with both hands, the weight resting on his palms.

A soft moan escaped her, and he grinned as he sat up and ran his tongue in the valley between them before pulling one nipple into his eager mouth. Her hands dug into his hair, and she gasped. "You can't possibly be ready to come again."

"I don't really need to come again." He pulled back and wriggled his eyebrows at her. "But you do." With that he flipped her onto her back, and she laughed as he began exploring all her softness.

"Tell me a terrible joke," she said, as he kissed his way across her softly padded rib cage.

He thought for a moment. "Okay. Why was the candy cane so expensive?"

She shook her head. "No idea."

"It was in…" He paused for dramatic effect. "Mint condition."

First, she groaned and then she cackled. Finally, she took a deep breath, still snickering. "Alright. That did it for me. I'm definitely ready to go again."

"Oddly enough," he said, looking down at his now half-risen cock. "So am I."

CHAPTER 3

The next morning, Gabriel watched the Christmas lights glide over Talia's skin, making patterns for him to kiss and touch. She sighed contentedly, her own hands tracing the muscles of his chest. They'd been up for a while. The sun had made a slow trek from the horizon to the sky, casting the snow outside the window in vibrant, glittering light.

"So, what are your plans today?" she asked.

"As long as the employees I spoke to last night show up, I'm off work and have no plans."

"Oh good." She stretched like a happy house cat. "Let's have breakfast and then do everything we did last night, again."

"Do I have to wear the onesie again?"

"Did you wear it last night?"

He groaned. "Yes."

"Put it back on then."

He laughed and rolled over top of her, kissing her until she had no more orders to give. After a while, he sat up. "I have something special for you."

She gave him a skeptical look and glanced at his crotch. "Is that what you're calling him down there?"

"No. I call him Moderate Gabriel."

Her laugh was like light on a frozen lake. "Most guys would have gone with 'Big Gabriel' or even, 'Lil' Gabriel.'

"Yeah no. One is too arrogant, and one isn't arrogant enough. Moderate Gabriel and I do good work."

"This is true. The work was top-notch," she said. "But you already gave me amazing gifts last night."

"It's not a gift, really." He reached under the tree and came back with a headband with deer antlers on it in one hand, and a light-up Santa hat in the other. "Take your pick."

"Well, obviously I want the antlers."

"Obviously." He sat them on her head and plopped the Santa hat on his. "Get dressed, we're giving out presents. Then we'll have breakfast."

He grabbed the t-shirt and sweats from his bugout bag and wore them over his onesie; not eager for his employees to see Moderate Gabriel bulging out of the striped fabric.

They passed out the ridiculous gifts. Samantha held her necklace with a tiny cupcake on it close to her heart. Her husband was a baker, and he knew she'd love it. Imani, who was packing up to go home, giggled with glee at the "head bitch in charge" keyring he'd found for her.

After that, they made their way to the restaurant's Christmas breakfast buffet. People were lined up to make omelets and waffles. They grabbed plates and made their way down the line. At the omelet station, Talia smiled brightly at the chef. "I'd love a cheese omelet, but do you think my friend here could crack the eggs? He always cracks the eggs on Christmas Day."

The chef shrugged. "Sure. But if you get shells all over my omelet maker, you're scrubbin' it."

Gabriel swallowed and shook his head at her. "You really listen to everything, don't you?"

She grinned and gestured toward the eggs. He grabbed three from the bowl and with years of practice, broke them one-handed.

The chef grunted his surprise. "Nicely done."

Warmth slipped through him like silk at her murmured agreement. But a wave of melancholy tinged it and he tried to push that aside.

Once the omelet was done, they made their way to the fruit and sweet pastries and then found a cozy table toward the back of the restaurant, close to the fireplace, where they could see the flames licking at the wood and hear it crackling. They clinked their hot cocoa mugs together and toasted the holidays.

After eating and paying, he sighed, strangely happy and sad at the same time. It felt like the warmth of the holidays, all the ways it used to be, but still wasn't.

"Do you want to take a Christmas walk?" she asked.

He hesitated. It was something he hadn't done since he lost his dad. But he wanted every minute with her he could get, so he nodded. He followed her back to the room, where they bundled up and she put on her tall galoshes. She slid her hand into his, their fingers intertwining as they made their way out the back door. The sun was warm, and the snow was still falling, though it was less of a brick wall and more of a gentle flurry, floating down to catch in their eyelashes.

They walked quietly for a while, making their way through the thick, slick snow. He didn't feel any awkwardness at the silence. It felt so full of something real and gentle. He squeezed her hand tighter.

She squeezed back and gave him a cautious smile. "Talk to me."

"I—I don't want to bum you out."

"I can manage my own emotions. Tell me what's on your mind."

There was so much, it was overwhelming to even

consider talking about. But she'd been right. There was a part of him that was pushing at the edges of his resistance, desperate to talk about it.

"Three years ago on Christmas morning, my dad passed away." The memory was a painful blur of ambulances and tears. "His favorite day of the year. After that, my family just...stopped celebrating it." He hesitated and she stood still, as if waiting for him to find his emotional footing. "After he was gone, my mom, she didn't really want to deal with messy emotions. That's just how she is. I love her and she's a great mom. She and my dad were so good together, because he had the big emotions, she had the reason. But without him, she changed." He stared at the ground. "She married someone less than a year after he passed away."

"That must have been hard."

"You would think not, since I'm a grown man, but it *was* hard. It felt like she betrayed him. Us. She and her new husband moved out of state. She didn't want the house anymore. So I bought it. Then right after, my sister decided to move to Seattle."

"Along with your niece."

"Yeah. My dad died and then everyone else just walked away and started new lives."

"Leaving you alone to pick up the pieces."

"And I've tried. I've tried so hard." The food he'd eaten sat like a lump in his stomach. "I've tried to move on. I go to work. I come home to the house we grew up in and it's empty and all I want is my family back. I want my Christmases back." He took a shuddering breath. "My dad always loved to look at the sky. Especially when it snowed. And for three years, I've felt like I couldn't look up at it." He felt the sting of tears and he did everything he could to end that before it began.

"Gabriel, I know nothing can ever feel the same as what you had with your father. And grief has its own timetable. It can't be rushed or brushed away. But I think..." She took a breath. "If he was even half the person you say he was, your dad would want you to feel your grief, but he'd also want you to find your joy again. You can do both. I promise you can."

"I'm not sure I'm capable of that."

"You are. But it starts here." She gestured toward the sky. "Look up."

He shook his head. It seemed small, but it was too much to ask.

"You deserve to live in this world, not just survive it. You gave me Christmas, but you need it too. Look up."

Something cold and brittle fractured in his chest. He knew she was right. He'd been sleepwalking. Avoiding the holidays and relationships and anything that reminded him of loss, afraid to let his always outsized emotions run free.

It took so long, his eyes slowly moving across the horizon and up to the sky. The dazzling blue hurt to look at, but he looked anyway, tracing the clouds and the snowflakes and the rays of the sun beaming down.

"How does the sky make you feel?" she asked softly.

"It makes me feel..." He swallowed the pain and the love that flowed through him, remembering his father's bold smile. His soft voice. Scalding tears flowed from Gabriel's eyes and for the first time since the funeral, he let them go. "I feel broken. Like pieces of me are gone and I'll never get them back." A sob tore through him. "I miss my dad, Talia."

She pressed her warm hands to his jaw. "It sucks that when you have the kind of heart that loves so big, like yours does, it means you hurt big, too," she said softly. "But your dad was right. You're blessed to feel so much. You truly are." Then she quietly held him tight, while he cried his heart out for all that he didn't have anymore. And the longer her arms were around him, the more aware he became of what he *could* have.

For three years he'd been holding his breath, but with her,

he could release it. He could breathe out what was lost and breathe in something new.

She reached up and wiped away his tears with her gloved fingers and he kissed that hand, before pulling her closer and kissing her lips until they were both breathless.

Her phone buzzed in the pocket of her jacket, and she pulled away. "Got a text. Sorry."

"Go ahead."

She stared at the screen and didn't speak for a moment. Moving slowly, she slid it back in her pocket, but she didn't look at him. Instead, her gaze seemed lost in the snow between her feet. "My flight's been rescheduled," she said finally.

He felt the weight of ice dropping from his chest to his stomach. He'd known it was coming. That this was temporary. Like a blooming flower that couldn't help but wither when you plucked it from the ground.

What could he say? He couldn't ask her to stay there, in a strange city for someone she barely knew. To leave her life behind. And he couldn't see himself leaving his own life behind. His family home. It hurt too much to consider.

The whole way back to the hotel, he tried to convince himself that it was going to be alright. His time with her had been special and had begun to heal something broken within him. Maybe that's just what it was always meant to be. Hopefully, maybe he'd healed something within her too.

Back in the room, they silently made their way to the bed. Their clothes came off layer by layer, until they were both laid bare. This time, when he slid inside of her, it was slow and tinged with heartache. And when she climbed on top of him, her slow, sweet grind felt like heaven and hell at once.

Afterward, they took the tree down and packed everything away. She changed into leggings and that hideous light up sweater that had made him laugh every time he saw it. But now, he didn't have much laughter left.

"I'll walk you over," he said. "If you want." The words croaked from his throat.

"I'd like that."

They made their way across the street, where traffic had resumed, and life was beginning to emerge. People were walking around, yelling at their kids to be careful in the snow. The spell of quiet and peace had been broken and the noise brought reality with it.

The line to TSA security was long and she held back from joining it. "Gabriel?"

He stroked her dark locs. "Hmm?"

She shook her head and didn't finish the thought. Instead, she stood straighter and kissed him. With her arms wrapped around his neck, they held each other far too tight, neither willing to let go first.

The warmth of her arms thawed the cold that had been living inside of him the last few years. This was rare. Beautiful and special. He'd never met anyone like her, and yet, he barely knew her. He didn't know her favorite color or which side of the bed she preferred. If she always ate breakfast or if she was one of those people who drank shakes and went jogging before sunrise. Did she hate sitcoms and slapstick comedy the way he did? Was she a messy painter, leaving splatters everywhere, or was she careful and meticulous?

There was so much he didn't know. So much he wanted to know.

And yet, what little he did know felt like enough. It felt like everything. Like she was…his person. The gentle reason to his big emotions. He'd waited forty-two years to find her, just to have her for two days.

"Thank you for everything," she murmured.

"I think you did more for me than I did for you."

"How do you even quantify that?" she asked.

"Well, one of us cried like an infant today and it wasn't you."

She laughed against his neck. "Tell me a joke."

He racked his brain for a good one. "Who is Santa's favorite pop star?"

"No idea."

"Beyon-sleigh."

She shook her head. "That's the worst one yet."

"Oh, I've got so many more."

Her sniffle was loud and final as she released him. He felt a shiver as the cold air replaced the warmth of her arms. Her cheeks were shiny with tracks of tears. "I don't like saying goodbye. So, merry Christmahanakwanzidan, Gabriel-not-Gabe," she said.

"Merry…all the stuff you just said."

With that, she turned and pulled her carry-on bag over her shoulder and got in line. He stayed and watched her run her bag through the scanner and get scanned herself. On the other side, she slid her shoes back on and looked around.

"Zoe!" Suddenly a man came racing through the departure hall, running as if his life depended on it. He wore some kind of red… Santa coat as he barreled around people. "Zoe!" he called again. Everyone cranked their heads to see what was going on as the man rushed to a terminal.

Gabriel glanced at Talia, who was watching the whole thing with amused eyes. He grabbed his phone and texted her. *What did I tell you? Christmas makes everyone nuts. Even Santa.*

She reached for her buzzing phone, and he knew the moment she read it, because he could hear her cackle of laughter above the din of the security area. She looked around. When her gaze landed on him, she pressed her fingers to her lips and blew him a kiss.

And like the cheese ball he was, he caught it and blew it back. She laughed in that way that felt like the sun shining just on him, before turning and heading for her gate. He watched as she disappeared from his sight and likely from his life.

He cried the whole way home.

CHAPTER 4

For four days, Gabriel got up every morning and looked at the sky. He would record himself and send the videos to Talia.

She got up every morning and did the same for him.

Her time at her family's home was just as miserable as she'd expected. But she said he made it better by sending her horrible jokes.

It is amazing how cleansing a bad joke can be, she texted.

Thinking about that, he sent horrible ones to his mom and sister, who both texted back laughing emojis. He took it as an invitation to call them and for once, they answered. He didn't get heavy and talk about feelings, but they managed to catch up, and laugh with each other. It felt a little like having a family again. It wasn't a lot, but it was a start.

Two days before New Year's Eve, he texted Talia. *I'm making cinnamon rolls. Bet you wish you were here.*

Hmm, she typed. *If you'd told me you knew how to make cinnamon rolls I'd have probably stayed.*

He snorted. *A man wants to be wanted for more than his rolls.*

She sent him a row of laughing emojis. A moment later she texted again. *Hey, I have a dumb question.*

Your questions are never dumb.

His phone pinged a moment later. *What's in your dad's kuku sabzi?*

His heart twisted painfully and happily at the same time. He hadn't realized how much worse his grief had been when he felt like he couldn't talk about his dad. Just having her mention him so openly made it feel like his dad wasn't a sad memory to be erased, but a beautiful vibrant piece of himself that still existed, even if it wasn't in the exact same configuration it'd been when he was alive.

He knew the hurt, the big chasm in his life, would always be there. But now, there was hope too.

Smiling, he sent her the recipe.

That next night, after work, he ate a cinnamon roll and laid on his couch, feeling a raw kind of happy, and wishing Talia was there. A new year was coming, and he wanted to spend it with her. But she was on her way back to Denver. She'd decreed her punishment was over and she was bailing a day early from her family's judgment.

Wanting to hear her voice, he made his way to her social media. He hadn't watched any of her videos because, oddly enough, it felt like an invasion of privacy. Those were hers. But now he was desperate for her voice. He watched bunches of them before clicking on the one she'd made with him. Their faces were squished close together and he couldn't figure out where he was supposed to look, but when she looked at him and when he looked at her, the sparks were brighter than a bonfire. His heart squeezed painfully. The comments were full of dirty jokes and encouragement for Talia to sleep beside him and do more than that. There were tons of funny hashtags there as well. #candyfromstrangersisthebestcandy, #candycaneigetyournumber, and of course, #hohoyes.

There were also gushing compliments about his appearance, which he was both embarrassed and flattered by.

Apparently, he and Talia were both "snacks," and he was a "zaddy." He didn't know what that meant, and he was too scared to Google it.

He looked for another video. She'd been silent for a while after her winter holiday one, but it looked like she'd posted the night before. He clicked on it.

She was sitting in a huge fancy kitchen. Must have been her parents' house. She looked tired and sad. "Happy New Year's Eve-eve. I know I look like crap; you don't need to tell me in the comments. My family has kindly told me every hour on the hour." She sighed. "I'm doing something different today. I'm going to cook something and we're going to talk."

One by one, she raised up the ingredients. Eggs. Cilantro, parsley, dill, leeks. Oh.

He sat up and watched closer. "I've already washed and trimmed the herbs. Onto the leeks." She set about dicing them. "This is going to get extra personal today. Um, I wanted to do some research into kuku sabzi before making this video and I ended up on some site with Persian terms of endearment. There was one…" She looked up at the ceiling. "Delbar-am. It means, the one who stole my heart. Isn't that beautiful?"

There was a warm weight in his chest as he watched her work. He'd heard that endearment his whole life. His mother would laugh when his father called her that. "You're so dramatic, Karim." But her eyes would sparkle with happiness and every once in a while, she'd kiss him on the cheek and say it back.

Talia dropped the leeks into a hot pan with oil. They sizzled pleasantly. "Have you ever met someone, and the connection was so strong, so right, that it literally only took a moment to feel like you've known them forever?"

The weight in his chest shifted.

While the leeks softened, she chopped the rest of the herbs. She rocked her knife back and forth, making fast work of them. It was clear she knew her way around the kitchen. "I think I had the chance for something...special. And I walked away. I got on a stupid plane and went somewhere I didn't want to go, leaving the first place I *wanted* to stay in a long time."

His heart twisted as a tear trekked down her cheek. "I think I made a mistake. It's never hurt so much to say goodbye to someone." She worked quietly and methodically while she considered her words. "In some ways, I feel like I'm too old to feel this way. Like yeah, it's not that hard. Just tell him I want to do the long-distance thing. Or whatever. But I don't want that. I want...Well, what I want isn't logical or even smart." She shook her head. "Maybe I'm just being all-or-nothing. Should I call him and talk to him about it? If I did, what would I say? 'Hey, I kinda, sorta accidentally fell for you. Mind if I move in?'"

He gripped the phone hard and tried to catch hold of the breath that was rushing out of his body.

The kuku crisped, and she peeked under the pan lid to check on it. "That's insane, right? I cannot do that. I'm just going to go home tonight and try to get a grip." She shook her head. "I'll be back when this is done cooking." There was a funny little break with intermission music playing. When she returned to the screen, she was holding a platter of perfectly cut kuku sabzi. It looked heavenly. His dad would have been impressed.

"Yup. This is delicious," she said as she took a bite. "This is...something I didn't even know existed, but now that I know, how can I live my life without it? I'll have to make it again. I'll have to..." She gave a sad laugh, her shoulders sagging. "I really do need to get a grip." With that, she told her viewers to care for themselves and to set good boundaries. To be kind when they didn't feel kind. And to keep being glorious, magical bitches.

His heart pounded violently in his chest, bashing into his ribs as if it could escape and make its way to Talia. He closed the app on his phone and sat up. None of this made sense. What they felt. Like she said, it wasn't logical or smart. Yet, as irrational as it was, he missed her. He missed her so much. He…

He loved her.

And she loved him.

It was crazy. It was stupid. But neither of those things made it any less true. Why had they both let this beautiful thing go? They hadn't even talked about trying to do it long-distance. Maybe because neither of them wanted that. His emotions didn't always make room for middle ground. For safety. He didn't want to just try something for a while in case it might work. He knew in his soul it would. He wanted her in his arms every night, and he could have her there. But he'd have to give up his comfort. He'd have to walk away from his family home full of old memories, in order to breathe in the new ones he so desperately wanted.

He checked his watch. She was on her way back to Denver, but she'd told him roughly where she lived. Before he had a chance to overthink it, he packed a bag and requested a last-minute flight for the morning. It cost a fortune but what the hell, he didn't take vacations or spend much, so he had a hefty savings account.

All night, his heart pounded like crazy. He barely slept. He texted Talia a single bad joke, but she didn't respond.

Driving to the airport, he felt slightly unstable, but also warm and soft. Blanketed in the feeling that his dad would have cheered him on. He would have loved Talia too, and would have called her Gabriel's delbar-am. But in some ways she already felt like more than the one who *held* his heart. She was his atashe del-am. The very *fire* of his heart.

The airport was back to being what it had always been. Loud, bustling, people coming and going, hearts breaking or souls connecting. He breathed in the life of it. The life he'd forgotten existed.

Unsure what to do with the hour he had until his flight, he wandered to the gift shop. The shelves had finally been restocked and the selection of cheesy souvenirs was back to what it had been before the storm. He poked through the stuffed animals and the snow globes, remembering Talia's amber eyes glistening when she opened her gift. Smiling, he ran his hands over the clothing rack full of ugly, discounted holiday sweaters.

"Can I interest you in some candy?" A silky voice, warm as a cup of cocoa wrapped around him.

He spun and stared, his heart thumping so loud it drowned out the lingering remnants of holiday music still spilling from the overhead speakers.

Talia stood there in her bulky winter coat, her dusky cheeks ever so slightly flushed a rich plum, her familiar pleather bag slung over her shoulder.

She was holding out a candy cane.

His insides fluttered like snowflakes in a soft breeze. He had no idea why she was there and not in Denver, and he probably should have asked questions, but he didn't want to ask a damned thing. He grabbed her and pulled her into his arms. She held him tight, and he pressed kisses to her forehead and her temples.

"Well, hello to you, too." Laughing she pulled back and stared up at him. "Are you playing hooky from work?"

"No. I was, um..." He held up his bag. "I was coming to see you."

A little smile hovered at the corners of her lips. "To see me? In Denver?"

"Yeah. I—" On his way to the airport, he had thought of lots of words to say when he saw her. Romantic ones, silly ones. The options were overwhelming. But now that she was there, standing in front of him, he forgot anything he'd planned. "Talia, I missed the fuck out of you, and I wanted to be with you at midnight tonight. And the next night. And maybe a few more nights. All of them, actually. All the nights. I know that's dramatic. I'm dramatic. And cheesy. But I—"

She kissed him hard and pulled back, her eyes shimmering. "Are you serious?"

"Yeah, I'm serious."

"Well, I missed the fuck out of you too," she said, breathlessly. "Here I was, thinking I would be the dramatic one, but you are killing my drama queen vibe."

"You can't take my crown away." He pulled her close and slipped a hand into her hair, pulling her toward him. He teased her lips with his, before giving her a slow, soft kiss that left them both shaking, not with desire but with something far more beautiful.

He pressed a finger under her chin and tilted her face toward his. "Look, I don't care what we do or where we go. I just...I want to be where you are."

She chewed on her lower lip. "Are we crazy?"

"I think you know the answer to that." He grabbed her bag and slung it over his other shoulder. "It's a solid ho-ho-yes. Now, come on."

"But your ticket..."

"Screw it. I'll postpone my flight for when we travel back to Denver. To live. Or to move your stuff here. Whatever you want." They made their way to the desk to do just that, and afterward, she kissed him until his knees shook.

He gripped her hand, turning it to press his lips to her palm before he threaded his fingers with hers and led her out of the airport.

The sky was painfully bright, the kind of wintery blue that blinded you, even as it filled you with a whole new set of senses. He looked over at Talia and she was just as bright. His own personal sky.

And he was never going to stop looking up.

THE END

ACKNOWLEDGMENTS

All the usual suspects. Thank you to my darling husband who supports my dreams, rubs my shoulders, and who lies and says there's no spider and then tells me to look away, so he can get rid of the spider.

The Yes Do girls; Liz, Erin, and Meika. You're all smart and talented and funny as fuck. You're the fiercest, most loyal friends anyone could have. I love you, you crazy dumpster birds.

Sam, my favorite angst demon and fic beta. Thank you for all the laughter and support. It's so great how we both love smutty scenes and the taste of reader tears.

Everyone who has ever supported me. Victoria. Jeannie. Esperanza. Renee. Heather. Louise. And bunches of other people I didn't mention because this page would be five miles long. I love you all.

Lisa Laughman. Out of everyone, you're the person I need to thank most for this particular story. Because I wrote Talia with you in my heart. You're a light in a world that truly needs it. Every time I see you, whether it's for an office visit, or just bumping into you in the halls, you smile and give me exactly the gentle, thoughtful wisdom I didn't know

I needed. And I've held every word in my head and heart. You were the first person to ever tell me, "You were born worthy of love." Those words changed me. Because before that, I never truly considered myself worthy of anything. Thank you for talking so many of us into being brave enough to look at the sky.

ABOUT CHRISTINA

CHRISTINA MITCHELL writes contemporary romances about damaged people who need (and deserve) happy endings. When she's not writing, she drinks Moscato from novelty mugs and spends her days listening to Taylor Swift and Lewis Capaldi, obsessing over Batman, and riffing on b-movies about genetically-modified sharks. She lives in Michigan with her hilarious husband, who almost never complains about the tons of glitter makeup she leaves lying around. Find Christina at christinamitchellbooks.com.

wonderland
MEIKA USHER

For my fellow Swifties. I hope you have fun finding all the Easter eggs!

CHAPTER 1

"It kinda looks like a penis."

I tore my eyes away from the weather radar in front of me. A woman plopped into the seat beside me, iced coffee in one hand, carry-on suitcase in the other. I looked around, wondering if she was lost. There were plenty of other empty seats in the airport terminal.

"The storm," she continued as she slid her suitcase closer and balanced her iced coffee precariously on top. She tilted her head to indicate the screen on the wall before us as she wriggled out of her puffy blue coat. Once done, she reclaimed her coffee and looked my way. "It looks like a penis."

Facing forward again, I watched as a nebulous blue blob made its way across the Midwest, inch by phallus-y inch. She was not wrong. "Just the tip for now," I observed as the bulbous end of the storm eased over Michigan like the state was giving it a handy.

The woman snorted. Her eyes dragged over me, from my cropped dark hair to my well-worn Doc Martens, then back to my face. Her expression gave no hint at the results of her assessment. "Ivy," she said simply, extending a hand.

I smiled, charmed by her no-bullshit introduction. "Jane," I said, taking it. Her handshake was firm, but her skin was soft.

She held my hand for a beat longer than necessary, her lush pink lips tilting at the corner. "Come here often?"

I laughed as I pulled my hand back. "Oh, yeah. Good ole DTW is the best place to pick up ladies." I balled my hand into a fist, her warmth still sitting on my palm.

Ivy sank back in her seat and crossed her legs. I let myself briefly admire the way her jeans hugged her full thighs. "That must get expensive," she said. "All those plane tickets."

"Ahh, yes." I swiveled in my seat so that I was facing her. "But I meet the most interesting people."

She balanced her coffee on her knee and tilted her head. A lock of pale blonde hair fell over her cheek. She wore it just above her collarbone, and it did an enviable job of caressing the skin left bare by the scoop neck of her ice-blue sweater. "Do tell."

"Well, there was that one time a woman opened with a dick joke. Which was an unorthodox way to hit on a lesbian, I must say."

"Oh," Ivy said, her smirk threatening to become a full-blown smile. "You think I was hitting on you?"

I wasn't fooled. I smirked back. "Of all the empty seats in all the terminals, you chose to sit next to me."

She shook her hair away from her face and I caught a whiff of fruit. Apple? Pear? An instant burst of sunshine flashed through my mind.

"You caught me," she said, her slate gray eyes meeting mine. "I saw you heading over here while I was in line for coffee, and I spent the entire time I waited trying to come up with the perfect opening line."

I laughed, even as the warmth of flattery spread through me. "And still you went with penis."

"There's a first time for everything." Her eyes twinkled wickedly. My skin heated a couple more degrees.

"So," I said, willing the blood to drain from my face before I full-on blushed like a damn teenager. "Where you heading?"

"Chicago." She wiped a thumb over the condensation on her coffee cup. "Work trip."

"On *Christmas*?" I couldn't keep the incredulity out of my voice. "That's rude."

"Eh." She lifted a shoulder. "Christmas isn't for another couple of days, so I should be fine. Home in time for the actual holiday."

"Good." I twisted the ring around my index finger as I searched for the next thing to say. I wasn't ready for this conversation to end. Wanted to keep this sparkly, stunning creature in my orbit for just a little longer. "So—"

"How about you?" She beat me to it. "Where are you going?"

"My mom's," I said, "just outside of Naperville."

"Hmm," she murmured, her lips wrapped around her straw. "Not too far from me, then."

"If you're angling for an invite to dinner, say less." I tossed her a smile. "My mother lives for feeding people."

Ivy smiled back. "If you're there, I'm there," she said as she let her eyes linger on mine for a long, loaded moment. "I don't believe in wasted opportunities." Leaning forward, she rummaged through her gray leather tote bag. I caught a whiff of her fruity scent again. Definitely pear. Pear with something creamy, something sweet lying beneath the freshness. And I wouldn't mind a bite.

She straightened, wallet in hand and I dropped my eyes. In my peripheral, I watched as she extracted a slip of paper, then clicked open a sleek silver pen. "Here," she said as she wrote, "is my personal cell. I very much hope to hear from you." She held it out and I took it, our fingertips brushing. Something like static electricity sparked over my skin, and my gaze flew to hers. The flicker in her light eyes told me she'd felt it, too.

Our eyes held for a long, heated moment, only broken when the speaker above us crackled to life, an announcement booming through the airport.

Ivy blinked then stood, pulling her tote over her shoulder. "Safe travels, Jane." The way her lips tilted up as she said my name sent a spear of heat straight through my abdomen.

"You, too," I managed, embarrassed at the huskiness of my voice. Ivy smiled a knowing smile and turned away.

I traced my thumb over the edge of the paper she'd given me, watching as she moved further and further into the fray. Once she was out of sight, I glanced down at it. Her handwriting was sure and swoopy, the *y* curving low and long before curling back in on itself.

I didn't know if I'd call her. I probably wouldn't call her. I'd been on a lady hiatus for a while now, and, honestly, it was for the best. Dating sucked and I was burned out. But something told me that if any woman could pull me back in, it was this one.

Good thing I'd never see her again.

I dropped her number into the bottom of my messenger bag and refocused my attention on the weather radar in front of me. It totally looked like a dick. I couldn't unsee it. Fingers crossed the storm would dissipate mid-shaft, and I'd be at Mom's by dinnertime.

CHAPTER 2

The penis was an omen.

One by one, flights were canceled. I sat cross-legged in my seat and watched as flight times and terminals were replaced by *delayed* and *canceled.* The snow barely begun to fall, but the threat of a winter onslaught was enough to ground planes and delay plans. I sat back in my seat and folded one leg over the other. My flight had not been canceled yet, but at this rate, it would be. Did I want to wait around for the inevitable, or did I want to be proactive and find a solution before there were no solutions left?

My phone buzzed from its place tucked into the crook of my knee. I picked it up and looked at the screen. My sister's name glowed up at me. Swiping across the screen, I opened her text. She'd been checking in with me the entire journey, so worried I was going to miss Christmas. In the past, it would have felt like a gentle way for my big sister to check in on me, but things had changed in the last year or so. I missed the *before* us.

Tucking that thought away, I read Abby's text.

Storm's coming, it said, and I heard the words in her dry voice. *How's the flight looking?*

I swallowed around a rising lump of anxiety and glanced back to the flight screen. My plane to O'Hare was still reading on time in a sea of cancelations. My gut twisted. It wasn't going to stay that way. No way in hell was it going to stay that way.

Still on schedule, I typed back to Abby. *But seeking alternate solutions just in case.*

Shoving the phone in my jacket pocket, I stood and hefted my bag over my shoulder. What I *wasn't* gonna do was sit around and wait. Not now, not when my mother was waiting for me to come home for Christmas.

I didn't let my brain linger longer than necessary on that thought. Instead, I shifted its focus to the next step: rental car. It was about five hours by car to Mom's place. If I left now, I'd be there, if not by dinnertime, then at least at bedtime. Then, I'd have the rest of my trip to spend with my family.

The thought propelled me forward at a determined clip, weaving through the buzzing crowd until I reached the rental car counter.

"Hi," I said to the clerk. He was tall, with pale skin stretched over sharp angles and a mess of artfully tousled blond hair. I checked his name tag. "How's your day going, Gil?"

He rolled his eyes subtly, but his posture softened just barely. "We're on the cusp of a raging storm, and people are freaking out about their canceled flights and holiday plans. So...peachy."

I gave him a chagrined smile. "Sorry, dumb question," I said, to which he nodded. I laughed. "Any chance you've got a rental left for me?"

Gil did his tip-tapping thing on the keyboard in front of him, brown eyes glued to the screen. As he searched, I silently lamented not getting a jump on this sooner. Drumming my fingertips on the counter, I tried to conjure up something, anything that I could drive across state lines. Hell, I'd take a century-old jalopy at this point, as long as it'd get me where I was going.

While Gil searched, I let my eyes travel over the airport. The frantic energy that usually permeated the air was ramped up to eleven. People ran to and fro, suitcase wheels dragging behind them. A long line began to form behind me as the next round of cancelations were announced. People who'd reached the same conclusion I had.

Digging into my bag, I pulled out my wallet, preparing to hand over my license and payment. Just as I dug my credit card from its spot, Gil clucked his teeth and grimaced.

"I don't like that, Gil." I narrowed my eyes on his face. "I don't like that one bit."

"Sorry," he said, genuinely looking it. Probably due to the mob behind me more than anything. They were going to have his head on a spike. "The woman before you rented the last car on our lot."

A vein began to throb in my forehead. I leaned my elbows on the counter and bit back a groan. Pushing a deep breath slowly from my nose, I straightened. "Okay," I said with a nod. "All right. Cool. Coolcoolcoolcool."

"Sorry," Gil said again and I forced a smile. I might have to crash in the airport tonight, but Gil, he was about to spend the next few hours facing down irate customers. I did not envy him his fate.

I nodded, despite my growing dread. "Thanks anyway," I said. "And good luck."

He returned my smile and turned his attention to the next customer in line. I tucked my wallet back into my bag and grabbed the handle of my carry-on. It was fine, I told myself. Maybe the penis storm wouldn't hit after all, and all flights would resume as scheduled. Maybe it wouldn't be as bad as predicted, and we'd only be delayed. Squaring my shoulders, I marched ahead. If I was going to be sitting in the airport for who knew how long, I was going to need caffeine.

The line at the coffee shop was ungodly. Resigned to a long wait, I parked my carry-on in front of me and fished my phone from my jacket pocket. Should probably give my sister a call to update her. Swiping to unlock, I opened my contacts list. My thumb hovered over Abby's name, but before I could make the call, someone sidled up next to me.

"Fancy meeting you here," a familiar, sultry voice said.

I looked up to find Ivy smirking at me, her pale eyes dancing. "Hey," I said, mentally stomping the tiny flutter of wings in my abdomen. "You got grounded, too, huh?"

"Ugh, yes." She tossed her head back with a groan, stirring the air with her fresh scent. "But I've got an escape plan."

"Lucky you," I said, keeping my tone light. This stranger didn't need to get even a peep of my angst. "I tried renting a car, but someone else beat me to the last one on the lot."

Ivy winced ever-so-slightly, her perfect brows furrowing. "That's a bummer," she said, the sunshine back in her voice. "Any alternatives?"

"Short of this storm dissipating and all flights getting back on track…" I shook my head. "I'm not hopeful."

She studied me, eyes narrowing in on my face. I shifted under her scrutiny. "What?" I finally asked, resisting the urge to check my face for a smudge of something.

There was a loaded pause before she spoke again, her eyes never leaving my face. "Have coffee with me," she said finally.

I looked at the frenzy around us, people buzzing like bees without their queen, aimless and antsy. Ivy stood in front of me, calm and confident. It was an energy I craved. Especially right now. *One coffee,* I told myself. *One coffee, and we'll go our separate ways.*

"Okay," I said, moving ahead with the line. She smiled a satisfied smile, like a cat who'd caught its prey, and I wondered what I'd just agreed to.

CHAPTER 3

We found a seat just outside the coffee shop. Everything inside was taken, and even if there'd been a spot to sit, I'd have opted out. The tension in there was a lot. It set my teeth on edge, ticked my pulse up more than a few notches. At least outside of the shop, there was some distance from the churning chaos around us.

"So," Ivy said, giving her iced coffee a shake to mix the foamy stuff on top with the rest. "Who's Abby?"

My head shot up, peppermint latte half to my lips. "What?"

"You were about to call her when I caught up with you in the coffee line." Ivy sipped her drink. "Is she your girlfriend?"

I lowered my cup, sip untaken. "No," I replied, bewilderment my foremost emotion. "She's my sister. Why—"

"Just curious." She said it with a nonchalant shrug. "How's your coffee?"

I hadn't taken a drink yet, but I nodded anyway. This woman's aura was a tilt-a-whirl. "Good. You?"

"Oh, delicious." She twirled her straw, the silver sparkles on her ice-blue fingernails catching a glint of light. "I'm not sure how much coffee is actually in it at this point, but it makes me happy." She punctuated it with an eyes-closed, happy sip.

I watched as her pink tongue darted out and dragged over her bottom lip. "Mmm," she sighed. I gripped my cup tighter and forced myself to look away, heat crawling up my neck.

"So, what's your escape plan?" I asked, my voice tight as I found something in the distance to stare at. "Is your job sending a driver, or something?"

"No." Ivy snorted. "I'm not that fancy." She twisted the straw in her drink, eyes narrowed in thought. It seemed like she wasn't going to answer when she finally emerged from her trance. Wordlessly, she reached down into her tote bag. When she straightened, a keyring dangled from her fingertips.

I instantly recognized it as the rental company's logo. "You got the last car," I said, slapping my palm on the table. "You…you…" I trailed off. Because what was I going to say? She'd done nothing more than have better timing than me. "Dammit."

But, shit, I kinda hated her for it.

Her lips twisted in chagrin. "I did," she said, placing the key fob on the table. She pushed the fob so that it spun, then nudged it in the other direction. I watched her actions, briefly wondering if I could snatch the keys and make a run for it.

Briefly, briefly.

Realistically, I knew I'd get caught by airport security before I even made it outside. And, family or no family, spending Christmas in airport jail was not worth it.

"I have an idea," Ivy said, drawing me from my imaginary crime spree.

I looked up to find her eyes on me, stare level, but a spark of silver shining in the gray. "Yeah?" I prompted, a little uneasy. I didn't know this woman. That spark could mean a countless number of things, from *let's make out in the bathroom,* to *let's hijack a jet.*

If I was being honest with myself, I'd admit that the first one didn't sound so bad. But I'd lied to myself many times over the span of my twenty-seven years, and I'd turned out just fine. What was once more?

"What if," she started, the words slow and purposeful as they formed on her plush lips. Lips I would not mind kissing, should the opportunity arise.

Stop it, I chided myself. *Now is not the time.*

"Well, we're both heading to the same place. Generally, anyway. And you're not giving off a homicidal maniac vibe. So...what if we rode together?"

I looked from her face to the keys, still delicately between her fingers. Pulling my lip between my teeth, I rolled the proposition over in my mind, weighing it against my other options. I could wait it out and hope for the storm to clear, for flights to reschedule, for a Christmas at home instead of one spent on an airport floor. Or I could take the chance that this woman, this beautiful, poised, and confident woman, would not murder me and leave me in a snowbank, undiscovered till spring.

I refused to think of the other option. The option that involved lips and hands and...

Nope.

Giving my brain a vigorous scolding, I straightened in my seat and lifted my head to find that Ivy was watching me. The swerve of her lips told me she'd mapped every thought that crossed my mind, and she'd found the journey amusing. I clenched my molars against the flush spreading over my skin. "Why?"

My question, at least, seemed to catch her off guard. Her perfect brows drew together the teensiest bit. "Well, you need a ride," she said as if it were the simplest answer. "And I'm not an asshole. Most days."

"You don't know me," I countered. "You're a woman traveling alone, and you're offering to go on a road trip with a complete stranger. Forgive me if that doesn't make me wonder—"

I stopped abruptly. Wonder what, exactly? About her state of mind? Her motives? Her—

"You're so adorably paranoid." She was smiling. No, *laughing*. And the tiny crinkle on the bridge of her nose about did me in.

"Well, yeah." I averted my eyes. "You realize what country you're in, right?"

Her amusement dimmed a little. "You're right. Sorry." Shifting in her seat, she crossed one leg over the other, the fluorescent light glinting off her leather boot. "I wouldn't offer a ride to just anyone. You've got a good vibe."

Sitting back in my chair, I studied her. Aside from the obvious physical attraction, I hadn't picked up on any glaring red flags. Although, to be fair, usually the physical attraction *was* the red flag. I brushed that thought aside and contemplated her offer. Really contemplated it. My mom was waiting for me to come home. She'd be crushed if I didn't make it. *I'd* be crushed if I didn't make it.

"What's in it for you?" I asked before I even realized I was thinking the words.

Ivy leaned back and tapped a blue-tipped finger against her chin. "Honestly?"

"Preferably."

"I think you're hot. And I could tell when I gave you my number earlier that you had no intention of using it. And, well, I wasn't ready to give up on you yet."

She said it with not a trace of humility. Which, I had to say, was kind of hot. And flattering. And…slightly insulting?

Reaching across the table, I pretended to pick at the sleeve of her tailored jacket. "Is…is this…why, yes, I believe it is." I made like I was pulling something from her sleeve, then held the invisible object up with triumph. "It's a string! Attached to your offer!"

For the first time since we'd met, Ivy had the grace to look abashed. "Not the classiest move, I admit," she said, her fair cheeks pinkening. "But I promise you, I have no plans to ask for anything in return. I'm not a creep."

"I don't know." I arranged my face in what I hoped was a stern expression. The look on her face was so earnest that I almost caved. "That's creep behavior."

She narrowed her eyes and folded her arms over her chest. I held her stare, one corner of my mouth twitching. After a few seconds of silence, I cracked, a laugh spilling from me.

"You're an asshole," she declared, laughing. "I take back my offer. Find your own way home!" She moved as if she were getting up, ready to march off.

"Sorry, sorry." I reached across the table to place a hand on her arm. "I couldn't help myself."

She looked at my fingers curled around her forearm, then settled back into her seat. After a long moment, I moved back to my side of the table. "What do you say?" she asked, lifting the rental's keys between her thumb and forefinger. "Wanna be my road trip buddy?"

I let the question dangle in the air between us, though I already knew my answer. There was a slim chance I'd get murdered, but on the flip side, I'd get a ride home. With a beautiful woman. Who thought I was hot.

I ignored the thought that I'd let myself get talked into stupid shit before by beautiful women. Neither here, nor there.

"All right," I said, extending my hand across the table. "I'm in."

The moment Ivy's fingers closed around mine, smooth and warm, I knew I was in for a ride. Whether it ended in a Christmas miracle or a frigid disaster, only time would tell.

CHAPTER 4

"It's…kinda small."

Ivy circled the rental car, a tiny blue hatchback, an assessing look in her eyes. The burgeoning wind whipped strands of hair into her face, and she shook them away. "Now, Jane," she said, taking a step back to get the full picture. At least the rental place had brushed the snow from the car for us. "Didn't anyone ever tell you that size doesn't matter?"

"Yes, but when we're talking blizzards, I'd feel more comfortable in something…bigger." In fact, even the thought of getting into this half-pint of a car had my armpits sweating. Not great when I was about to share the small space with another human. A hot human, no less.

Ivy muttered something that sounded suspiciously like *size queen* as she clicked the unlock button on the fob and opened the hatch. My suitcase wheels struggled in the freshly fallen snow as I joined her at the rear of the car. She lugged her suitcase in, and I suppressed a grunt as I followed suit, depositing mine next to hers.

"My first car was about this size," she said as she walked

to the driver's side door. "It handled like a beast in the snow. I'm not worried."

That makes one of us, I thought as I tromped through the snow to the passenger door. I shrugged out of my leather jacket and tossed it in the backseat, along with my messenger bag. With a deep breath and a look up at the ever-darkening sky, heavy with more impending doom, I climbed in.

"You don't get car sick, do you?" Ivy asked as she settled in next to me. "Probably should have asked that before I offered you the ride."

I gave her a wry smile. "Would I be less hot if I did?"

"Well, kind of." She pulled her door shut and adjusted her seat. "Vomit is gross."

I pushed my own seat as far back as it would go, maximizing my leg room. "Well, I guess this is where our romance begins and ends," I said with a dramatic sigh. "It was fun while it lasted."

She side-eyed me. I snorted.

"Asshole," she said as she stuck the key into the ignition.

"It's best you know now," I shot back, stretching the seat-belt over my body. "Before you get attached."

Ivy shook her head, trying and failing to hide her amusement. I basked in the glow of the knowledge that she found me amusing. "This is going to be a long trip," she muttered, barely audible over the roar of the engine coming to life.

"Not if you drive fast."

She ignored me and backed out of the parking spot. As promised, the little car didn't hesitate to barrel through the snow beneath its wheels. Once we were on the road, Ivy glanced over. "Snacks?"

"Um. Yes," I replied. "One cannot have a road trip without snacks. It's the law."

"Must be some weird Michigan law I've never heard of." She flipped her blinker on and eased into the turning lane. "What are your snacks of choice?"

"Yes," I said again, earning a snort.

She pulled into the gas station parking lot and parked the car at a gas pump. "I pump you shop?"

I nodded and reached for the door handle. "Any requests?"

Ivy glanced my way before she pushed open her door. "Surprise me." And then she was out of the car.

"Okay," I said to no one as I got out, too, and headed toward the store. I held the door open for an older man with a full white beard, suppressing a shiver. Fuck, it was cold. Shouldn't have left my jacket in the car.

"Thank you, dear," the man said, giving me a kind smile and a nod. "Merry Christmas."

"Merry Christmas," I repeated, returning his smile.

Once inside, I veered for the junk food. I firmly believed that calories did not count on road trips, so it was time to load up on all the snacks. As I strolled the candy aisle, I pondered what to get Ivy. Was she a chocolate person, or a gummy person? Or maybe licorice? Tapping my chin with my pointer finger, I stared at the selection. Sweet and sour, I decided, grabbing a bag of Sour Patch Kids.

By the time I made it to the register, I had two different kinds of chips, three chocolate options, the sour gummies, and a roll of Oreos. Two water bottles were tucked under one arm, and two sodas under the other. Excessive? Maybe. But I wanted all the bases covered.

"Stocking up for the blizzard?" the cashier said as they rang me up, their dark-lined eyes taking in my stash.

"Road trip," I replied, digging my wallet from my back pocket.

Their brows dipped. They glanced toward the window, then back to me, an *are you shitting me* look on their face.

"I know," I said before they could speak. "We're trying to get ahead of it."

The cashier whistled beneath their breath. "May the odds, and all that," they said as they finished ringing up my items.

"Thanks." I handed them some cash and waited while they counted out my change and put my stuff in a bag.

Ivy was finished filling the tank by the time I made it outside. She was inside the car, drumming her fingers on the steering wheel and nodding her head in time with whatever was playing on the radio. I hunched my shoulders against the wind and crossed the parking lot. It was hard to tell how much of the slow blowing into my face was fresh and how much of it was blowing off of the gas pump covering.

"Sorry," I said to Ivy as I opened the car door. "I couldn't decide what to get."

"So you bought the whole store?" She looked pointedly at my bulging bag.

"Of course." I pulled out the waters and put them in the cup holders between us. "If you need caffeine, I've got soda. But you had, like, eight coffees before we left the airport, so…"

"Valid point." She uncapped one of the bottles and took a swig. Then, she reached for a cable I only just noticed and plugged her phone in. "You like Christmas music?"

I whipped my eyes to her. "Do *you* like Christmas music?"

The look on my face must have alerted her to my inner panic because she burst out laughing. "I'll take that as a *no*," she said once she recovered. "It's either that or murder podcasts."

"Murder podcasts," I said without hesitation. "Please, give me the murder."

"You got it." She cued up a podcast and put her phone in the center console. Then, she checked her mirrors and adjusted in her seat. "Ready?" she asked.

I secured my seatbelt and nodded. "Ready."

Minutes later, we were on the highway, moving at a steady pace toward a darkening sky.

❄

Why was she driving so slow?

It was the only thing I could think as we inched our way forward over the next hour. Traffic wasn't as horrendous as I'd expected, which eased my worry about how long the trip would take. But then Ivy never sped up, never passed anyone. She drove like a grandma fresh out of Sunday service, and I found myself hitting the imaginary gas pedal constantly.

It didn't help that I'd gotten numerous texts from Abby. Asking if my flight had been canceled, if I was still coming, what I was doing. I'd ignored her thus far, but I knew that wasn't sustainable. If I told her that I'd agreed to ride in a car with a complete stranger, in true big sister fashion, she'd kill me. Then, she'd tell Mom so Mom could kill me again.

And I rather liked being alive, thank you.

"You're fidgety."

Ivy's voice sliced through my thoughts, and I jolted. "Sorry," I said, tapping my fingers on my knees. I realized what I was doing and balled my hands into fists. "Sorry," I said again.

"Something the matter?"

I looked over. She was faced forward, eyes straight ahead, both hands on the wheel, posture perfect. The seatbelt cut across her chest and my eyes followed its line over the gentle slopes and curves of torso and across her lap. "No," I said slowly, forcing my eyes back to her face.

The gray winter light was dim inside the car but could not hide the amused tilt of her mouth. "Liar."

Shifting in my seat, I folded my hands together in my lap. "It's just," I started, urgency pushing at my ribcage. "You're driving so *slow*."

"There it is," she said softly, not taking her eyes from the road.

"I get that you're being safe," I rushed to add, "and following the rules, and all that. But we're in a hurry. Or, at least, I am. And the storm hasn't even started yet. We could be making great time right now."

Ivy didn't respond, at least not immediately. Instead, she flexed her hands around the steering wheel and appeared to straighten in her seat. I didn't know her well—or at all, really—but something told me that I'd poked the polar bear. Was this the part where she pulled off to the side of the road and offed me?

In my lap, my phone vibrated again. Yet another text from my sister, I was sure. I didn't check it, choosing instead to keep an eye on my travel companion.

"Why are you in such a hurry?" Ivy finally asked, her tone even and controlled. "I know it's almost Christmas, but it's not like we're days' worth of driving away from our destination. It's a few hours. We're going to get there in time."

"I know, it's just..." I sighed and looked down, tapping my phone screen. It lit up to reveal that I had, in fact, received another text from my sister.

Everyone is here, it read. *Just waiting on you.*

I expelled a long breath from my nostrils and looked out the passenger side window. "Christmas is a big deal in my family." I watched the snow-covered scenery pass us by. I wasn't sure how much I wanted to tell this almost-stranger, especially since everything still felt like a healing wound. Poking it hurt. "This year is especially important. I...I really need to be there."

It wasn't much. It wasn't anything. But I hoped it was enough.

Silence settled in the spaces between us, only interrupted by the faint murmur of the murder podcast on the radio. I ran my thumb over the outer ridges of my phone and breathed through the hammer-like beating of my heart. In my mind, visions of last year played on a loop. Weak smiles and teary eyes and festive head scarves. Long, tight hugs and silent prayers for another year.

My eyes burned with sudden tears, and I blinked them back.

As if she sensed the turn in my emotions, Ivy reached over and placed a hand on my knee. My head shot up and I looked her way. She flashed me a smile and squeezed my leg before returning her hand to the steering wheel. I held my breath, waiting for her to ask for more information. When she spoke, however, it wasn't what I expected.

"Please tell me you've got Sour Patch Kids in that bag."

A laugh spilled from me, dispelling the haunt of tears. "I *knew* it," I said as I reached for the bag of gas station spoils at my feet.

"Is that a yes?" She did a little shimmy in her seat, getting another laugh from me. I pulled the gummies from the bag and tore the package open. "How'd you know?" she asked as I handed the candy over.

I watched as she tipped the bag and caught a few candies in her mouth before she handed it back to me. "Intuition?" I quipped, putting the open bag in the center console for easy access.

Ivy *hmmed* as she chewed. I pulled the bag of M&Ms out for myself and stowed the rest at my feet again. We munched in silence for a while and, just as the podcast revealed the *who* in *whodunnit,* the sky opened above us, releasing fat, heavy snowflakes by the millions.

"Here we go," Ivy said, shoulders squaring. "Round two." I found myself straightening in my seat, too.

It wasn't too bad at first. The temperature was just high enough that the snowflakes melted as soon as they hit the pavement. But a quick glance at the weather app on my phone told me that the temp would drop soon. We had half an hour, forty-five minutes maybe, of decent roads before shit went south.

Ivy seemed unconcerned as I reported this to her. She shot a glance my way, lips tilted up. "I got you, babe," she assured me, and, dammit if that confidence didn't give me a tingle in my jingle. She flipped the windshield wipers onto a higher speed and eased off the gas just a touch.

My hands tightened into fists in my lap, gripping a phantom steering wheel. I wasn't accustomed to someone else driving in conditions like this, let alone someone I didn't know. For the first time, I genuinely questioned my decision to get into this car. I knew my safety wasn't at risk from Ivy herself. But I forgot to take the storm into account. The actual driving in the storm. The other drivers on the road. I didn't know Ivy's driving record. Didn't know if she'd been in any accidents, and, if yes, if they were her fault. I had not thought this through.

The snow fell faster, blurring out all but a hint of tail-lights before us. My stomach flipped. I pushed a slow breath through my nostrils, then breathed deep through my mouth.

"You good?" From the corner of my eye, I saw Ivy cast a quick look in my direction.

I pressed harder into my seat. "Yep." I kept my eyes straight ahead, counting the back and forth of the wipers silently. "Great."

"Want me to pull over?" There was concern in her voice, and it both touched me and made me feel silly.

"No, no. I'm fine," I said, tension making my own voice sound paper thin.

"I think there's a rest stop coming up soon." She glanced in the rearview, then eased the car into the next lane. "Why don't you tell me about your favorite Christmas movie."

"I—what?" I frowned in her direction. She didn't look back, keeping her eyes trained on the road instead. "Why?"

"Mine's probably *Jingle All the Way,*" she said instead of answering my question.

"*Jingle all the—*" I frowned harder. "The movie with

Arnold Schwarzenegger? Are you serious?"

"Absolutely." After a pause, she added, "Or *Gremlins*."

"*Miracle on 34th Street* is clearly the only correct answer," I said, gobsmacked. "Or *White Christmas.*"

"If you don't mind being predictable, sure." She eased the car over again. "I suppose you're also a fan of *It's a Wonderful Life*."

"Duh!" I straightened in my seat. "It's blasphemous to *not* enjoy that movie."

"Eh." She shrugged. "To each their own."

"I—it—why are we stopping?" I pulled my incredulous stare from her to find that we had pulled into the parking lot of the rest stop. I turned back to Ivy.

She shrugged. "Figured I'd give you a breather," she said simply. "Plus, I have to pee."

Before I could respond, or even think of what to say, she was out of the car.

I stared after her as she walked across the snow-covered lot with slow, methodical steps. Once she disappeared into the building, I sat back in my seat and breathed deeply, eyes closed. "Get it together," I told myself on the exhale.

My words sank into the warmth of the car's interior. When I opened my eyes, a sheet of thick snowflakes had covered the windshield. Ivy had left the car running but killed the wipers. I let my head drift to the side, squinting. No Ivy yet. Straightening, I tapped my fingers against my knees in a nonsensical rhythm. My eyes took in the neat and tidy interior of the rental. The gleam of the dash, the shine of the gear shift. The curve of the steering wheel. My hands paused their fidgeting, a thought forming. There was one for sure way to calm my anxiety about Ivy's driving.

With one more glance toward the building, I got out of the car and rounded it. Before I could second guess, I climbed behind the steering wheel. Hopefully, Ivy wouldn't mind sharing driving duties.

CHAPTER 5

"What are you doing?"

I grinned up at Ivy, who'd just pulled open the driver's side door to find me in her seat. "I, uh, thought I'd give you a break?"

"I don't need a break," she said, extending her hand as if to help me out of the car. "Thanks, though."

I looked at her hand, then back to her face, widening my smile. "I insist."

Ivy's placid expression cracked just the teensiest. She looked up at the sky, squinting against the flurries. "Look, Jane, I appreciate the offer, really," she said, snowflakes clinging to her hair and eyelashes when she met my eye again. My breathing stuttered. She looked ethereal, like a snow angel come to life. "But here's the thing—"

Her words were cut off by a loud grinding sound, followed by a chug, and then…silence. I pulled my hands away from the steering wheel and stared as every light on the dash lit up. "That can't be good."

"What was that?" she asked, leaning in to see what I was looking at.

"I…don't know." I turned the car off, then tried to restart

it. Something squealed under the hood, but the engine did not turn over. "I didn't touch anything."

"Let me try." Ivy leaned further into the car. I sank back into the seat to give her room and tried not to notice the hand she planted on my thigh for balance, or the way her scent enveloped me. With her other hand, she tried the key in the ignition once, twice, three times, getting the same result. "Shit," she whispered, easing back out of the car.

To distract myself from the sudden rush of cold that followed her distance, I climbed out of the car to join her. Side-by-side, we stood, staring at the traitorous car. Above us, the snow fell harder, as if the sky itself was taunting us.

Wrapping my arms around myself, I suppressed a shiver. "What do we do?"

Ivy pulled the sleeves of her sweater over her hands. "Roadside assistance," she said with a resolute nod. Then, she yanked the car door open again and leaned inside to open the glove box. Her sweater rode up enough to reveal an excellent view of her backside in those snug jeans. I tried—I swear I tried—to not stare. I lost the battle, however, because the way her jeans molded over the full curve of her ass was simply illegal.

When she straightened, I took a step back, as if I'd been caught committing a crime. "You find it?" I asked stupidly. The paperwork was in her hand.

She didn't seem to notice as she thumbed through the papers, locating what she was looking for. Then, she pulled her phone from her back pocket and tapped at the screen. As she put the phone to her ear, she began to pace, her boots crunching in the snow and ice.

I grabbed our coats from the backseat and held Ivy's open so she could shrug into it. She mouthed a thank you, just as she reached a real person on the phone. "Hi, yes," she said, cradling the phone between her shoulder and cheek while she zipped her coat. "I rented a car from you guys a while ago, and—"

I tuned out as I pulled my own coat on. Jamming my hands into my pockets, I wandered a few steps away. The sound of the highway hummed behind us, the glow of the rest stop ahead. Ivy's voice was a steady murmur as she spoke to the rental company, and I tried to let her calm cadence convince me that everything was fine.

Everything was not fine.

Leaning against a tree, I looked upward. The sky was purple-gray with the promise of more snow, snuffing out any traces of daylight. Of hope. The white flakes danced on a quickening wind, coating the trees, my face, the ground. There were no signs of reprieve.

Exhaling, my breath puffed white in front of my face. I'd have to call my family. Tell my mom I wasn't going to make it. Hear the disappointment in her voice. The hurt. It was going to suck.

"Shit," I whispered, pushing away from the tree.

Ivy was just finishing up the call when I made it back to her. "Tow truck is on the way," she said. "There's a town not far from here with a shop."

I nodded. Okay, I thought but didn't say.

"Let's wait inside," she continued, jabbing her thumb toward the building. "I'll buy you a coffee." Without waiting for me to agree, she looped her arm through mine and led us into the building. "Shouldn't be too long," she said as she fished her wallet out of her coat pocket. "We'll get on the road in no time."

I knew she was underplaying things, and I let her. She punched some buttons on the machine, and, about a minute later, I had a steaming paper cup in my hand.

"Thanks," I said, cradling it between both hands. I blew on the hot liquid as she ordered her own. My thoughts whirred along with the coffee machine. Christmas was hours away.

My family was hours away. It was a race. Snow versus car. Nature versus human. Hope versus reality.

I felt hopeless.

"Chin up, buttercup." Ivy bumped her cup against mine. I looked up. Her gray eyes shimmered in the fluorescent light. "It's not over yet."

Her words were warm and thawed my fragile reserve. My eyes stung with the tears that had been hovering for hours now. I blinked and looked away. "Sorry," I said, staring hard into my coffee cup. "I'm not usually so…all over the place." I winced as I replayed the array of emotions I'd exhibited today. Stable, I was not.

"It's the holidays," Ivy replied. "Even the most put-together person loses it a little bit this time of year."

I laughed. "Well, I'm not exactly *put together* under the best of circumstances. In fact, I'm usually a walking disaster. I—" I looked up to find her eyes steady on my face. She smiled, a soft tilt of her lips, and reached across the distance to brush my bangs out of my eyes. My next breath caught in my throat.

"I happen to like walking disasters," she said. "Especially when they've got legs like yours."

Another laugh fell from my lips. "That was bad."

She laughed, too, a throaty sound that raked across my nerve endings and lit them like a strand of twinkling lights. "Yeah," she agreed. "It was real bad. But, hey." She shook her hair away from her face and smiled wider. "I got you to laugh, so it was worth it."

"You are a giant cheese ball, aren't you?" I hadn't meant to, but I stepped forward. I looked down. The toes of our shoes touched, my black Doc Martens kissing the pointed tips of her fancy cream boots.

Ivy looked down, too, then back to my face. "I kinda want to kiss you."

"Kinda?" I repeated, lifting a brow.

She flushed, a pretty, pretty pink. "Yeah, okay. I wanted to kiss you the moment I saw you in the airport, staring down at your phone with this…laser-focus concentration on your face. I wanted to be the one to break it."

I inched closer, reaching behind her to set my coffee down on the sliver of a counter beside the coffee machine. "Well, you definitely did that."

Ivy smirked, a sexy twist of her lips. "I did, didn't I?"

"Mmhmm." I took another step forward. "And you haven't stopped since."

The smirk transformed into a full-on smile, and, in a blink, she took control back. Placing her coffee cup next to mine, she looped her fingers in the pockets of my coat and pulled me to her. I could feel her warmth, even through the layers between us, and I wanted more.

I didn't have to lean down or stand on tiptoe to kiss her—a revelation I came to as she closed the remaining distance, pressing her lips to mine. They were as soft as I thought they'd be. Softer, maybe. And I sighed as I let myself sink into them, kissing her back, slow and savoring. She slipped her hands into my open coat, winding them around my back, and I arched into her, threading my fingers through her hair. *Silk,* I thought as I deepened the kiss. Her hair was like silk.

Her tongue slid over my bottom lip; I hummed my appreciation. She smiled against my lips, and I couldn't help it. I smiled back.

We parted, both laughing as we rested our foreheads together. "How's that concentration doing now?" she asked, her breath coming out in quick little huffs.

I slid my hand to the base of her neck, my thumb stroking her jaw. "Mmm," I murmured, my own breathing ragged, "I think I've found a new fixation." And then I tilted my head to kiss her again.

This kiss caught fire quickly, her lips opening beneath mine in an invitation I gladly took. Her fingers found the hem of my sweater and lifted, stroking the bare skin at my waist. I shivered, my own fingers tightening in the hair at the nape of her neck. Taking one final step forward, I backed her into the vending machine. She moaned and arched away from it, pulling me tighter against her.

Ivy's hands slid further up my sweater, over my stomach and across my ribcage, and I gasped against her lips. She took the opportunity to slip her tongue into my mouth, caressing my own in soft, sure strokes. My thighs clenched as I imagined her mirroring that motion somewhere else. "Fuck," I said, and I wasn't sure if it was an invitation or a curse.

She chuckled, dragging her mouth from mine to nip at my jaw. "Maybe later," she whispered into my ear, the promise in her words sending a flood of liquid heat straight to the core of me. It was in that moment that I knew she would be so much more than I imagined.

I leaned in for another kiss but froze halfway as the crunch of tires on snow and the roar of an engine broke the silence. We turned in unison to find a tow truck pulling into the parking lot.

"Our chariot has arrived," Ivy said, leaning her head against the glass of the vending machine. A smile played at the corners of her mouth, swollen and shining from my kisses, and there was no missing the promise there.

CHAPTER 6

We ended up about thirty minutes away, in a small, blip-on-the-map town, complete with a lone stop light. The mom-and-pop motel was within walking distance from the car shop.

And there was only one room available.

Of course there was only one room available.

Ivy was outside on the phone with her boss. She paced back and forth in front of the door, phone clamped to her ear. I wasn't the only one getting detoured, a fact that I'd managed to forget in my selfish haze. I hadn't even asked her what her job was. I had, however, spent the entirety of the ride here thinking about what would have happened if the tow truck hadn't interrupted. Nothing. Nothing would have happened. It wasn't like we were going to bang it out in the grungy bathroom of a highway rest stop.

The sole room left at a small-town motel, though...

I shoved that thought away and forced my attention back to the motel clerk. She'd just finished putting my information into her computer, and slid my driver's license across the counter, along with two key cards. "Thanks," I said, hoping my inappropriate thoughts weren't written all over my face.

She nodded, seemingly clueless. Phew. "Merry Christmas."

"You, too," I said with a smile as I pushed the door open.

Ivy was still on the phone when I got outside. I caught her eye and held up the cards. She nodded and followed my lead.

"What do you want me to do, Steve?" she said as I led us along the front of the building, eyeing the door numbers as we passed. "Unless you've got an in with Santa, and you can get his goddamn sleigh of reindeer here to pick me up, I'm staying put."

I bit back a smile as I located our room and unlocked the door. I motioned for her to go in and closed the door behind us. Ivy dropped her bag on the foot of the bed closest to the door—at least there were two beds—and shrugged out of her coat.

"Look," she said into the phone. "It's been a long day, and there's nothing to be done with the rest of it. So, I'm going to let you go, take a hot shower, and get some damn sleep." She paused so the person on the other end could speak. "That's what I thought," she said after a moment. "Talk tomorrow."

She hung up the phone and tossed it onto the bed beside her bag. Then, she turned to face me. The look on her face said she'd expected me to drop her off and leave. Probably to head to my own room.

"So, they only had one room," I said with a *ta-da-like* gesture. "And here we are."

"Oh," was all she said, her gray eyes fixed on my face. Instantly, my body recalled the taste of her lips and the feel of her hands on my skin. She looked from me to the bed, then back again. I was positive my face could guide Santa home. I looked away first.

"On the upside," I said as I leaned down to untie my boots. "I don't snore."

She leaned forward to unzip hers. "Is that the only upside?" she asked innocently.

I wasn't fooled.

Boots off, I stood and sat them near the door, then shrugged out of my coat. "I mean, we might have cable," I said, tilting my head toward the TV. "That doesn't suck."

Ivy let out a snort. I glanced over to find her reclining on the bed, elbows propping her up, socked feet hanging off the edge. I waited for her to speak. She stayed silent and just… looked at me.

I turned away. What was it about this woman that turned me into an awkward teenager all over again? "So," I said as I stretched my arms far above my head. "Is it just me, or has it been the longest day of all time?"

"I don't know." Ivy stood and peeled the outer layers of her clothing off as well. "I think the longest day of all time was probably when my ex took me to see *Les Mis* at her little sister's high school."

I let out a low whistle of sympathy and tried not to notice the way her blue sweater stretched across her breasts as she arched her back. Tried not to think about how they'd felt pressed against me. "Did your ex hate you?"

"By that point in our relationship? Maybe a little." She leaned forward, letting her arms dangle loosely. "You can shower first. I'm gonna work on this knot in my back."

"Do you," I started, but I snapped my mouth shut before I could finish the sentence. No way was I going to ask her if she wanted me to rub her back. Had I been commended on my most excellent back rub skills by many a partner? Sure. Did that mean I should offer them up to an almost-stranger I'd be sharing a motel room with for the night? Probably not.

Then again…

"Do I what?" Ivy asked, not looking up from her bent over position.

"Do you, uh, think a hot shower would help?" I jabbed my

thumb over my shoulder in the direction of the bathroom, as if she could see me, then winced at yet another display of awkwardness.

"Maybe." She straightened, her cheeks flushed, her hair mussed. My mouth went dry. "But I don't want to use up all the hot water before you get in there." She pushed both hands through her cornsilk hair, and I could almost feel it, cool and soft against my fingers.

I ripped my gaze away and yanked the zipper on my suitcase. "Okay," I said, deliberately not looking at her as I fished my toiletry kit and a change of clothes out. "I'll save you some."

Shouldn't be too hard, I thought to myself as I walked into the bathroom, since my shower was going to be ice cold.

❄

Fast forward to forty-five minutes later. I sat on my bed, freshly showered and in my old college t-shirt and joggers, trying not to think about Ivy on the other side of the bathroom door. The shower had been running for a while now, and my imagination had been running wild just as long.

Rubbing the heels of my hands into my eyes, I tried to erase made-up images of slick, pale skin, plump lips begging to be kissed, rivulets of water running over full curves, my lips chasing each drop, pursuing what we started earlier—

"I feel a thousand times better."

I jolted, my heart leaping from my ribcage. "Shit," I hissed, putting a hand to my chest. "You scared me."

"Sorry," Ivy said. I opened my eyes to find her tilting her head to dry her hair with a towel, and, fuck me, she wasn't wearing any clothes.

She had a towel wrapped around her, but it was a motel-provided towel, which didn't cover…well, a whole lot of anything. It fell mid-thigh, and was pulled so tight at her chest that her ample breasts nearly spilled over the top. And…and I was staring.

I dropped my eyes to my lap, watching my fingers tangle and twist together. "How was your shower?" I asked, my voice tight.

"Not bad." There was amusement in her tone. Confidence. Knowledge. Like she knew I'd been looking and had enjoyed the view.

She wasn't wrong.

"Would've been better with some company."

Instant heat flooded my body. I looked up to find her smiling, a wicked gleam in her eyes. That gleam was the push I needed, the concrete confirmation that she wanted this as much as I did. Unfolding my legs, I pushed up onto my knees and moved to the foot of the bed. If I reached out, I could touch her. I didn't. "What would you have done," I started as I sat back, swinging my legs over the edge of the bed, "if I'd joined you?"

Her smile widened. She turned so that she faced me. I could feel the heat radiating off her shower-warmed skin. My mouth watered.

"Because I think you're all talk," I continued as I reached out, planting my hands on her hips and tugging until she stumbled forward to stand between my knees. "I think if I had pulled back that shower curtain to find you there, naked and wet, you would have covered yourself and kicked me out."

"No," she said softly, her fingers hovering at the top of the towel.

"No?" I let my fingers tease at the hem of the towel, at her damp skin, watching her face. Her eyelashes fluttered the teensiest bit. Satisfaction bloomed hot inside me. If it felt this good wring such a tiny reaction from her, what would it feel like to make her come? To watch her fall apart?

I needed to know.

"Ivy," I said, my voice tight with want. "I need to know what you want from me."

Her breathing was coming faster now, her breasts lifting and falling beneath the towel. It would take so little to loosen it, to let it fall to the floor, to—

As if she heard my thoughts, Ivy's hands dropped to her sides, letting the towel fall to the floor.

"Fuck," I hissed, taking in the vision before me. The lush curve of her hips, the soft swell of her stomach, the full, perfect thighs. "You're stunning."

"Yeah?" she asked, and the tone of her voice drew my eyes to hers. She knew. Oh, she knew. There was not a single uncertainty in her face. She goddamn knew she was a goddess.

"Oh, yeah." I reached out, pausing with my hands hovering just above her waist. "Can I touch you?"

"You fucking better." And then she covered my hands with hers and put them on her body. Slid them down her hips and over her stomach. Back up to cover her breasts. Her nipples hardened beneath my palms, and I couldn't suppress the growl that left my lips.

Watching her face, I ran my thumbs over the hardened peaks. She pulled her plump lower lip into her mouth, a sound catching itself in the back of her throat. I wanted to free it. Sliding one hand down, I settled it at her ribcage, fingers lightly trailing the underside of her heavy breast. Then, I leaned forward, taking her nipple lightly in my teeth.

She hissed.

I smiled.

Without slowing the teasing pace of my thumb on her other breast, I pulled her nipple into my mouth, flicking my tongue over it. She arched her back, sighing, and I took that as a sign of encouragement. I gave one nipple a light pinch while I nipped the other with my teeth, and...there it was. A moan, low and throaty, as she pushed her fingers into my hair. I smiled against her skin, feeling a hot twist of need between my own legs.

"Jane," Ivy whispered, holding my head in place while I sucked and nipped at her soft, sweet skin. "Touch me."

I lifted my head just enough to look her in the eye. "I thought I *was* touching you," I murmured back, giving her breast a soft knead.

"No." Her fingers tightened in my hair. "*Lower.*"

I wasn't sure what was hotter—the desperate ache in her voice or the directness in her command. Whatever it was, I was helpless to obey. Gripping her hips in my hand, I eased backward onto the bed and pulled her with me, so that she straddled me, naked and glorious. And surprised. From soft *oh* of her mouth to the deep flush in her cheeks, it looked good on her.

Reaching behind me, I adjusted the pillows beneath my head. Confusion flitted across her face, and I smiled.

"What—" she started, her question stalling on her perfect lips as I pressed my fingertips into her hips and urged her closer.

"Come here," I said.

I didn't have to tell her twice.

Almost before I got the words out, Ivy had her knees settled on either side of my head, her pussy presented to me like the prettiest of Christmas gifts. Above me, she braced her hands on the headboard. I smiled to myself as I ran my thumbs along her inner thighs. Her hips bucked, urging me on.

"How wet are you?" I asked as I traced a finger along the seam of her golden curls.

Her breathing hitched. "Fuck me and find out," she said, and her words cut right through the last of my resolve. She barely finished her sentence before I wrapped my arms around her thighs and pulled her down, my mouth melting into her. Both our groans filled the room. I drank her in, her slick softness heaven against my tongue. Holding her legs steady, I found her clit and teased, flicking my tongue over it, slowly, slowly, so slow, until she was straining against my hold, trying to get closer, to feel more.

I let go, reaching back to cup her ass instead. She pressed herself closer, moving her hips, grinding her clit against my tongue. Above me, I could hear her breathing halt, replaced by whimpers and murmurs, nonsensical words of begging, of prayer, as she drew closer and closer. I dug my fingernails into the smooth skin of her ass and moaned, urging her on, needing her to come.

I squeezed my own thighs together, trying to assuage the ache, the pulsating demand to be touched. Ivy took notice and reached back, taking my hand from her body. "Touch yourself," she commanded, placing my hand between my legs.

I obeyed. Of course I obeyed. Slipping my fingers beneath the waistband of my pants, I ran them over my smooth skin. Parting my lips, I ran the pad of my middle finger over my throbbing clit, moaning with relief against Ivy's soaking slit.

"Yes," she hissed, her fingers pushing through my hair. She ground herself into me, and I flicked my tongue over her sensitive bud, matching the pace of my finger's stroke. I dug my heels into the mattress, raising my hips to meet my hand as Ivy's body held my torso down. "Come for me, Jane," she said, and her voice was husky and bossy and so. Fucking. Hot. "Come for me, and I'll come for you."

I whimpered into her pussy, fingering my own, drawing nearer and nearer to the edge, wanting to hold off, desperate to jump.

"Yes," Ivy hissed, fucking my face. "That's it, just like that, don't fucking move." And then her thighs tightened on either side of my head and her long, throaty groan bounced off the walls, vibrating through my entire body, sending an electric pulse directly to my pussy. I shattered, a hard, pulsing orgasm that wracked my entire body. I grasped for something, anything to hold with my free hand, and found Ivy's. She held tight as we rode the wave together, as we floated into the aftershock, as we came down from the unfathomable highs we'd just reached.

Even the well-worn, creaky mattress couldn't ward off the deep slumber we sank into as we curled up in each other's arms.

CHAPTER 7

We awoke sometime during the night, a mess of tangled limbs and blankets. After we took turns with the bathroom, Ivy laid on her back and beckoned me over. I laid my head on her chest and let my still-heavy eyelids drift closed.

Her fingers pushed my bangs off my forehead, and her warm lips pressed against the newly exposed skin. The silence cradled us, our breaths synchronizing, until Ivy finally spoke.

"Tell me about your family."

I lifted my head to look at her. "This your idea of pillow talk?"

She chuckled, the sound vibrating into every inch of my body still touching hers. "It was either that or asking you to do that thing with your tongue again, but I'm still recovering from the first time you did it. So…"

I put my head back on her chest. "You think you can flatter me into telling you my life story?"

"I mean, yeah." Her fingers trailed over the nape of my neck and down my spine. I shivered. "Is it working?"

"Hmm." I nestled closer, focusing my eyes on the tiny red

light on the TV across the room. My brain rolled over the details of my life, sifting through them like a gold digger. There were nuggets of gold, for sure, but I knew that wasn't what she was looking for.

It wasn't what anyone was looking for. Not really. Most everyone wanted the juicy details. The trauma, the drama. And I had those, too.

I sighed. "My mom had cancer last year." The words spoken aloud were like rusty barbs in my skin. My fingers tightened around the sheet at Ivy's side. "Breast cancer. Bad." I let out a short laugh. "It's all bad, I guess. But it was my mom, you know?" My chest tightened and I forced myself to take a deep breath. "Anyway, she's in remission now. It was a long, hard year of hospitals and surgeries and chemo infusions and—" I squeezed my eyes shut and shook my head once, briskly, to clear the images that had haunted me most every night. "It was hard for me to not be there the whole time, but she insisted."

Ivy didn't speak. She didn't stop touching me, either. Her touch had gone from soft fingertips to a solid palm journeying across my back. I kept my eyes closed as I continued. "This Christmas is…important. Before, we were all over the place. My sister in Colorado, my mom in Illinois. Me in Michigan. We didn't make it a priority to spend the holidays together. But now…"

"Now you know how valuable your time together is," Ivy concluded. "And you're making it a priority."

I nodded. "I wasn't able to get home sooner, and now… who knows if I'll make it at all. And Abby is already there. She moved home after—" I turned my face into Ivy's chest and let the scent of her fill my senses. She smelled like summer in the dead of winter. Sunshine glinting on snow. Her hand kept its steady pace across my back. I focused on matching my breathing to each back-and-forth movement.

In and out. In and out. When I spoke again, my voice was a whisper. "I have to be there."

"Hey." Ivy's other hand found my face, tilting my chin up so that I was looking at her. "We're gonna get you there."

"But what if—"

"We are going to. Get. You. There." The moonlight coming through a crack in the curtains caught a steely glint in her eyes and, for some reason, I believed her.

I needed to believe her.

I nodded and her thumb traced along my jawbone. Leaning her head down, she pressed her lips to mine.

It was a soft kiss. Sweet. Utterly different from any other touch we'd shared. I let myself melt into it, kissing her back, showing her with my lips how much I appreciated her words, her confidence, her…well, *her*.

The flicker caught flame, and soon we were a flurry of hands and tongues and teeth, skin on skin, quickened breaths. Ivy eased me onto my back, not taking her lips from mine, and her soft palm slid over my torso, up my shirt, skimming my breasts, ghosting over my waist. A whimper caught in my throat as I felt the heat of her hand hovering over my center, and my hips lifted of their own accord. I'd have been embarrassed at my obvious neediness, but the desperation in Ivy's kiss assured me I was not alone.

"I need to touch you," she whispered, her lips moving over my jaw to pause at my ear. I shivered as her words skittered over me. "I need to feel you come."

I nodded. "Yes," I hissed, every nerve ending in my body sparking to life. "Please."

She smiled then, and it was a flash of brilliance in the darkened room. I'd have marveled at her beauty if I weren't so on fire for her touch. "*Please,*" I repeated, unashamed to be begging.

She obeyed. In one smooth movement, her lips were on my skin, hot kisses down my neck and over my collarbone, along the tops of my breasts. My nipples tightened in anticipation, but she circumvented them, creating an all-new ache. Lower, her fingers pressed trails into my hips, my stomach, my thighs. Everywhere except where I needed her touch most.

"I thought you wanted to touch me," I gasped, digging my nails into the smooth skin of her back.

She huffed out a little laugh, the sound a vibration against the side of my breast. "What do you think I'm doing?"

"Torture." The word caught on a moan as she pulled my nipple into her mouth, flicking her tongue over the hardened peak. I arched my back, shoving my fingers through her hair to hold her head in place. She growled. I shivered.

Lower, I was throbbing, wet, ready for her touch. Still, she held back. I squeezed my thighs together, trying to alleviate the ache. She reached down and pulled my legs apart. I whimpered. "Ivy. Please. *Please.*"

She lifted her head from my breast. I blinked open my eyes to find her watching me, her lips glistening, her eyes sparkling. Holding my gaze, she slid her hand down my belly. Lower, lower, until her middle finger slid between my folds, just grazing my clit.

I hissed, my hips bucking, asking—begging—for more. She smiled as she slowly…so fucking slowly…teased my aching bud. "Like that?" she asked, barely-restrained desire in her voice.

I nodded frantically, bringing my hand to my own breast. I teased my nipple and lifted my hips to meet her touch, heels digging into the mattress. "I…I need…" I panted, frantically clawing at her back with my other hand.

"What do you need?" she asked. "Tell me, Jane."

The sound of my name on her lips, in her husky voice, sent a fresh wave of need through me. I ground my pussy against her hand, reaching down to guide her. "Inside," I gasped. "Please."

I'd barely gotten the words out when she slid two fingers deep inside me. Throwing my head back, I moaned, parting my thighs to grant her better access.

"Like that?" she asked, slowly pulling her fingers out and thrusting them in again.

"Yes," I whimpered. "More."

She obeyed, slipping a third finger into my soaking pussy. As she did, she ground the heel of her hand against my clit. A wave of sharp pleasure pierced through me, rushing to the very place she touched me. I was close. God, I was close.

"Don't stop," I gasped, my hand tightening on my breast.

Ivy took my other nipple between her teeth, creating a new layer of sensation that pushed me closer to the edge. "I'm gonna come," I somehow managed. I threw my head back into the pillows, eyes closed, mouth open, desperate gasps and moans filling the space around me. Were those sounds coming from me? I didn't know. All I knew was Ivy. Her hands. Her mouth. The sweet, torturous pressure of her fingers inside me. I ground myself into her hand. She sucked my nipple hard just as her fingers found that secret place. I moaned, loud and long, explosions of light behind my eyes mirroring the pulse and throb and sweet, sweet release of my orgasm.

She held me through it, gradually gentling her touch, and once the waves subsided, she pulled her fingers from me and lifted her head from my breast. I gasped for air, my entire body feeling like static electricity. She dropped sweet kisses over my forehead and shoulders. "You okay?"

I nodded. "Give me a second to recover," I managed, my voice shaky, "and I'll show you just how *okay* I am."

Her answering chuckle told me there wouldn't be much sleeping tonight.

CHAPTER 8

Morning came in the sound of a snowplow scraping its way across the parking lot just outside our window. I opened my eyes to find Ivy already sitting up, her bare back to me. I reached out to run a finger down her spine. She shivered and looked over her shoulder, a smile on her mouth.

"Morning," she said, her sleepy voice a sexy kind of husky.

"Morning," I said back, knowing my own voice was not. "How'd you sleep?"

Instead of answering, she leaned on her elbow and brought her face to mine. I lifted my chin so that our lips could meet and say their own good mornings, slow and languorous. When we parted, Ivy straightened and tilted her head toward the window. "It stopped snowing."

Relief was warm and quick as it melted through me. "Oh, good." I sat up and stretched my arms high above my head, letting out an uproarious yawn. Then I remembered the car. Dropping my arms, I sighed. "Which does us exactly no good if the car is still out of commission."

"Hey." Ivy's tone was stern. I looked up to find her face matched. "I said we'd get you home."

I held her eyes for a long couple of seconds, doubt warring with the certainty on her face, and the deep down need to believe her. Finally, I looked away. "Okay," I said, though hope felt like tinsel slipping through my fingers.

Ivy stood, naked and beautiful, and held her hand out. "Come on. Let's get moving. We have a mechanic to talk to."

❄

The car shop was closed.

We stood in front of the building, the cheerful sign a mockery from its place in the window. Exclamation points were a downright disrespectful way to inform someone that they would not be able to get their car repaired in time to make it home for Christmas.

"What now?" I asked, hating that I sounded like a lost kid.

Ivy squeezed my hand through our layers of mittens (her) and gloves (me). "Give me a minute." She pulled her full bottom lip into her mouth, a thoughtful look overtaking her face.

I exhaled, my breath coming out in a white puff. Turning away from the offensive sign, I surveyed our surroundings. We'd landed in a quiet in-between town, its sole traffic light blinking red just up the block. A post office on one corner, a small grocery store on the next. Across the street, there was a diner, miraculously open on Christmas Eve.

As if on cue, my stomach rumbled loudly, breaking the peace of the quiet winter morning.

Ivy took notice, then followed my gaze. "Breakfast," she said with a firm nod. "Good idea." Then, we were marching across the empty street, our boots crunching in the snow and ice.

There was a surprising amount of business in the diner. We stopped just inside the door, taken aback by the near-full state of it.

"Morning!" a waitress in a green sweater showcasing two reindeer, one on each boob, complete with red noses in the nippular region, greeted us with a bright smile. "Go on and seat yourselves and I'll be right with you!"

Again with the exclamation points, I thought as I followed Ivy to the nearest empty table. Somehow, the audible ones were almost worse.

"Wow," Ivy said as she settled into her seat across from me and wriggled out of her coat. "It's like Christmas barfed in here."

"Please don't talk about barf when we're about to eat breakfast," I said, though a cursory glance at the restaurant proved her right. Garland in red and green framed every window along the front of the building, punctuated by stockings in between each, glittery names along the tops. On the men's room door hung a life-sized Santa, and on the women's, Mrs. Claus. Every other table sported a tiny Christmas tree, and the ones without—like ours—held teensy gingerbread houses.

"Sorry." Ivy pushed a piece of silken hair behind her ear, and my eyes fell to the spot just below it. I could almost hear the sound she made last night when I'd kissed her there. Instantly, my face heated. Among other places.

Clearing my throat, I looked away. "What's your go-to for breakfast?" I asked as I scooped up one of the menus. "Savory or sweet?"

"Hmm." She picked up the other menu and opened it. "My sweet tooth is usually insatiable." She paused until I looked up. "But I think I had my fill of sweets last night." The smirk she tossed across the table said she meant more than just her breakfast food preferences.

I rested my chin in my hand, ignoring the burn in my cheeks, and held her gaze. "Oh?" I asked, blinking innocently. "Did you make a trip to the vending machine for a midnight snack and not share?"

She didn't answer, but her eyes took a slow journey over my face, lingering on my mouth. Then, she lifted her menu and perused.

Smiling to myself, I followed suit. A couple minutes later, the waitress—Candy, her name badge read—came to take our orders. A short stack of pancakes with a side of bacon for me, a western omelet for Ivy. Coffee for both of us.

"So," Ivy said after Candy went to put our orders in. "We need a plan." She grabbed three sugar packets from the cup in the center of the table and shook them. "I vote we hotwire the FedEx truck across the street and make a run for it."

I snorted and poured a hefty amount of milk into my mug. "Is that your job? Car thief?"

"Cars, motor homes, battle tanks." She shrugged as she emptied the sugar packets into her coffee. "All in a day's work."

The clink of our spoons against ceramic as we stirred our coffee filled the space between us. After our first fortifying sips, I spoke again. "What *do* you do?"

She lifted a sharp brow. "You don't believe I hijack battle tanks?"

"I believe you *could*. I don't believe you *do*." I cradled my mug between my hands and rested my arms atop the table. "I can't believe I slept with a woman whose job I don't even know."

"Is that unusual for you?" She sat back in her chair, her fingertips against her own mug. Her gray eyes were steady on my face.

"Yes." I saw no point in being coy or denying it. I wasn't a casual person.

Ivy didn't answer immediately. She didn't look away, either.

Candy chose that moment to bring us our food. "Here you go," she sang, placing our plates in front of us with a flourish. I looked down at my pancakes and a short bark of laughter escaped me. The cook had drawn a Santa face in whipped cream, complete with beard and a maraschino cherry for his nose. Candy grinned. "Merry Christmas!" she sang as she walked away.

Ivy leaned over to see what I was laughing at, and she smiled in return. "Cute." Her own plate had a sprig of herbs on top of the omelet with a little red bow on them to resemble mistletoe. She picked it up and wriggled her brows at me. "Saving this for later."

"You think I'm gonna give it up for a knock-off sprig of mistletoe?" I asked primly as I unfolded my napkin and spread it over my lap. "What do you think I am, a mistle-*hoe*?"

This earned a straight-up cackle from my breakfast date. She dropped the sprig and threw her head back, the sound both husky and joyful, and I found I couldn't look away. My heart did a little skip and jump, and I forced myself to breathe through it.

Too soon, I thought. *It's too soon for the heart to get involved.*

Once Ivy recovered, she looked over at me, her cheeks pink, her eyes sparkling, and I clenched my teeth against the resounding swell of warmth in my chest. God, she was beautiful. I had the visceral need to touch her, to trace my fingers along the soft skin of her cheeks and over her jawline. To press a fingertip into the soft pillow of her lips. To follow it with a kiss. To—

She reached for her own napkin and unfolded it, the motion breaking the spell. I cleared my throat and looked away. *Get it together,* I told myself.

I forced myself to focus on the simple act of eating. I picked up my fork and cut into my pancakes, ruining Santa's beard. Ivy followed suit, digging into her omelet. We ate in silence for a couple minutes, the sounds of silverware clinking, jovial chatter, and Mariah Carey filling the air around us. I hadn't realized how hungry I was until I started eating, and then it was all I could do to not shove my whole face into the plate.

Barely restraining myself, I reached for my coffee cup. Ivy was watching me. I froze, cup halfway to my lips.

"Me, too, by the way," she said, her voice soft in the din of the restaurant.

"I'm sorry?" I frowned. Had she read my mind, and was also keeping herself from face-planting into her breakfast?

"It's unusual for me, too." She traced the tines of her fork over the plush yellow of her omelet. "The *sleeping with someone whose job I don't know* thing."

"Oh." I sat my fork down and sank back in my seat.

"You look surprised," she said with a smile.

"I am. I mean…" I shook my head. "When you approached me at the airport—"

"I laid it on a little thick." She exhaled a tiny laugh. "I know." Squaring her shoulders, she shook her hair away from her face. "I was all false bravado. I saw you there, and I thought, *my god, she's gorgeous.* And then I thought, *too bad I'll never see her again.*" She met my eyes, a new shimmer in hers, something like uncertainty. "And the thought of not seeing you again…well, it really bummed me out. So, I made a deal with myself: I'd shoot my shot, and if it didn't land, well, I tried. If it did…"

I leaned in, resting my chin on my fist. I didn't know why, but her next words felt vital. Like they would pivot my entire existence.

"If it did?" I prompted, desperate to hear the rest of the sentence.

She laughed, a tiny self-deprecating sound. "I figured we'd fool around and go our separate ways. But then…"

Without thinking, I reached across the table and took her hand in mine, lacing our fingers. "But then," I echoed, knowing exactly what she meant.

We let the words hang there, in the warm space between

us, not pushing, not asking, not analyzing. There would be plenty of time for that later.

For now. It was enough.

"Accountant, by the way," Ivy said as she pulled her hand back.

I caught her eye. "Accountant," I repeated, "or *accountant?*"

She snorted and picked up her fork. "The boring kind, definitely."

Smiling, I reclaimed my own fork. "Waitress slash photographer," I replied with a smile. Then, we went back to our breakfast, the diner sparkling a little brighter around us.

CHAPTER 9

"Any idea when the car shop will be open?" Ivy asked Candy as she brought us our check a little later.

"It's Christmas Eve, dear," she said with a regretful shake of her head. "Nick's shop is closed up till after the holidays."

A sound that fell somewhere between a howl and a whimper escaped me and I slapped a hand over my mouth. "Sorry," I mumbled behind my hand. Ivy shot me a sympathetic look then turned back to Candy.

"We had a car towed to his shop last night," she explained, "and we were really hoping to find out if there's any chance we'll get on the road in time to make it home for Christmas."

Candy's eyes softened and she clasped her hands to her chest, between the two reindeer. "Oh, no," she said. "That's just awful."

The pancakes I'd just eaten turned to stone in my stomach. I sank back in my seat, defeated. I could already see the disappointment on Mom's face. I really should have left days ago, like my sister suggested, instead of staying home a bit longer for work. My eyes burned. I blinked, but a tear fell anyway.

"We'll figure it out," Ivy said, her voice soothing as she

hopped up from her seat to stoop next to me. She wiped the tear away with her thumb and squeezed my wringing hands. Looking up at Candy, she asked, "Is there anywhere around here we could maybe rent another car? Or something?"

Candy looked down at us, her own eyes welling. "Let me see what I can do," she said, spinning on her heels. "I'll be right back."

Ivy stayed put, her hand still on mine. "I will absolutely hijack some shit if I have to, to get you home in time."

I laughed, the sound more watery than I would have liked. "I appreciate the sentiment," I said, turning my hand so we were palm-to-palm. "But I could never let you risk jail time for me."

She grinned, eyes flashing devilishly. "They'd have to catch me first."

"With the way you drive? Shouldn't be too hard," I shot back, returning her grin.

She threw a dirty look my way, but quickly replaced it with a laugh.

I reached over and threaded our fingers together. "Thank you," I said, overwhelmed by her kindness, her fierceness. Overcome with the need to kiss her, diners be damned. I leaned in, my eyes dropping to her mouth. They tilted up at the corner, accentuating the fullness of her bottom lip, and I wanted nothing more in that moment than to revel in that fullness.

"There are people everywhere," she whispered.

"I don't care," I whispered back. And then her smile took over her entire mouth. Bracing her hand on my thigh, she leaned closer, close enough that I could feel her breath against my lips. My heartbeat thrummed faster as we drew closer and closer, until—

"I've got good news," Candy said, her chipper voice like an icy gust of wind.

We flew apart, and Ivy stood, smoothing her hands over

her pants. I swallowed and looked down, forcing my breathing to regulate.

"Turns out, Nick's got a loaner just collecting snow on his lot, and it's all yours."

"Wait, really?" I said, hope flaring bright.

"Really." She gestured toward a man sitting at the end of the counter, a red Christmas sweater and fluffy white beard making him look more like *Santa* than *Nick*. "He'll get the rental fixed up after the holiday, and you girls can swap cars on your way back through."

I glanced at Ivy. I didn't know her plans. Was she staying in Chicago after Christmas, or did she have a flight back to… fuck, where was she even flying in from?

The thought that I'd started something with a person I knew next to nothing about reared up again. My mouth went dry. "I—"

"That's perfect," Ivy interjected. "I've got a flight out of Detroit next week."

"Great," Candy said. "If you two are all set, Nick'll walk you on over and get you set up."

I nodded, shrugging into my coat. Ivy pulled her own off the back of her chair and put it on. After putting a handful of bills on the table, she nodded. "We're ready."

❄

"From one extreme to the other, huh?" Ivy said as we got settled into the giant cherry red pick-up. "Tiny car to big ole truck."

I snorted and pulled my seatbelt on. The truck had to be a couple decades old, at least. It had one of those endless bench seats like a giant couch, and it made me want to pull my feet up and take a nap. "Hey, as long as it gets us where we need to go." I glanced over. "You comfortable driving something this size?"

Ivy waved me off. "Don't you worry. Just sit back and enjoy the ride."

"You should know by now that I much prefer to be an active participant," I shot back before I could think better of it.

Her head swiveled my way, a devilish curve on her lips. "Oh, I know."

I blushed and faced forward. She chuckled and started the truck.

The first part of the drive was quiet. The snow had stopped a while ago, so the roads were surprisingly clear. Or, at least, manageable. I was beginning to feel downright optimistic about making it home in time for Christmas when we pulled onto the highway.

A standstill.

Of course.

"Fuck," I muttered, taking in the long, slow-moving line of cars ahead of us.

Ivy eased the truck to a stop behind a long line of cars and reached over to take my hand. "Plenty of time," she said. "We're gonna make it."

I squeezed her hand to show her I appreciated her assurance, though I wasn't sure I believed her. Then, I angled my body toward her. An opportunity had presented itself in the form of a traffic jam. Narrowing my eyes, I studied her profile.

She glanced at me out of the corner of her eye. "What?"

"Nothing." I tapped a finger against my chin. "Where'd you grow up?"

A laugh tumbled out of her. "Oh, I see what you're doing," she said, easing on the gas to inch forward. "Get-to-know-you time, huh?"

I shrugged. "What else are we gonna do?" Reaching over, I tucked a lock of silken hair behind her ear. "I mean, I'd very like to know the person I had mind-blowing sex with all night."

Her cheeks pinkened. "Mind-blowing, huh?"

"Mind-blowing," I confirmed, my body heating at the memory.

She smiled my way, and it was a sweet, heart-tripping type smile. The kind of smile people went to war over.

I clenched my teeth and told my brain to STFU with the romantic shit. Odds were, we'd part ways once we hit Illinois, and I'd never see her again. No point in getting all infatuated.

Too late.

"New Jersey," she said, bringing my focus back to our conversation. "One brother, one sister. Both married. They spend Christmas with their in-laws. My parents are in Florida, avoiding winter like the plague." She glanced over. "Normally, I'd head down there to spend the holiday with them, but my plans were cock-blocked by work. One of my firm's clients has a branch in Chicago, and they need someone to un-fuck some things before the new year. Easier to do in-person."

"Hopefully, there's a big, fat bonus involved."

She released a silent laugh through her nose. "Oh, yeah."

I smiled as I rested my head against my seat and let it drift to the side. The cab of the truck was warm and smelled like summertime. I could almost pretend that the winter wonderland outside our windows didn't exist.

And, I decided, I was going to let myself do just that.

CHAPTER 10

We hit a steady pace about forty-five minutes later. Not fast by any means, but not standing still anymore. About twenty miles of a slow crawl and Ivy decided to get off the highway. "Need anything to eat?" she asked as a gas station rolled into view.

I eyed the clock on the dash. It was nearing noon. My stomach rumbled at the thought of sustenance, but I didn't want to stop, didn't want to slow our journey home. My travel companion, on the other hand, chose logic.

"I don't know what happens when you get hungry," she said, turning into the gas station parking lot. "And I'd prefer not to find out while confined to a small space with you."

I snorted. "Valid."

She parked the car and we went inside, gathering protein bars and beef jerky to tide us over until, hopefully, Christmas Eve dinner. As we walked back to the truck, Ivy linked her fingers with mine. I glanced between us, my heart faltering, then thumping double time. I looked up, catching Ivy's eye. We smiled like two high schoolers.

I didn't let myself think too hard about what we were doing. How much time we had left. What would happen when we pulled up outside of my mom's house. Instead, I made the conscious choice to live in this moment. And this moment? It was pretty good.

When we reached the truck, she pulled my hand to her lips and dropped a kiss against my knuckles before opening my door for me. I climbed inside, and she handed me the bag of snacks before shutting me safely inside the warmth. I watched as she rounded the truck, the winter wind lifting her hair like a golden halo around her head, and I held my breath, a rush of affection, of…something more, rushing through me.

I always fell too fast. I knew I did. But all the knowledge in the world could not stop it from happening. And so instead of shoving it down, pretending away the glow in my chest, I let it warm me.

Heartache would come soon enough. What was the harm in letting myself feel happy for a while?

"Brr," Ivy said as she got in next to me, bringing a rush of cold air in with her. "I think it's getting colder."

I leaned forward to look out the windshield at the sky. It was gray and growing grayer by the minute. "Our reprieve may be over soon."

"In that case, we better get moving." She started the truck and pulled out of the parking lot.

While she drove, I opened the package of Oreos she'd bought and held it out to her. She helped herself to a few, and I sat the rest on the seat between us. Leaning forward, I flipped the radio on, filling the cab with the jolly sound of Christmas music.

And we drove on.

❄

"This storm is not fucking around."

Ivy flipped the windshield wipers to the next highest speed and shifted in her seat. Glancing over at me, she asked, "You doing okay?"

I had a white-knuckle grip on the door handle, but I gave her a strained smile and a thumbs up with my free hand. She looked like she wanted to reach over, maybe take my hand or squeeze my leg, but didn't want to take a hand from the wheel, lest I freak out more.

I appreciated that.

I unwrapped my fingers from the handle and pulled my phone from its spot beneath my butt. I'd been keeping track of our journey on a navigation app. Ivy seemed to know where she was going without it, which was both impressive and hot.

We were about two hours from home. Two hours in good weather. Who knew how long in the storm that wouldn't end.

"Tell me more about you," I said, tossing my phone onto my lap. "Distract me."

Ivy *hmm'd*, tapping her fingers against the steering wheel. "What would you like to know?"

Everything, I thought.

"Everything," I said.

She chuckled, the sound soft and warm. "Everything, huh?" she said, her voice like balm over my rankled nerves.

I lay my head against the headrest and closed my eyes. "Mm hmm."

"Well." I felt her shift and then the Christmas music grew quieter. "There's not enough driving left for me to get through *that* story. How about I tell you about the time I hooked up with the head cheerleader during our senior homecoming game?"

The gentle murmur of her voice, combined with the

strains of "Have Yourself a Merry Little Christmas," and the rumble of the engine created the most magical lullaby. And I was helpless to resist. My limbs grew heavy, eyelids drooping.

The next thing I knew, Ivy was gently shaking my shoulder.

"Hey," she said. "Jane, wake up."

"Mmm," I mumbled, frowning. "Why?"

She laughed. "Because we're here."

Her words sank in, then registered like a shock to the system. I sat up so fast, the seatbelt locked and pulled me back. "Here?" I repeated, looking around. It was dark, which was all I could really register. "Home?"

"Well, no." She straightened away from me. "At my hotel." At my questioning look, she added, "I figured I'd stay here and you could take the truck."

I rubbed the heels of my hands into my eyes, rubbing the sleepiness away. Then, I looked at Ivy. She looked tired from the long drive, but the way the streetlight caught her face, the snow glittering in the light behind her…it was like I was in a snow globe, with my very own Christmas angel.

Reaching out, I pushed a lock of hair away from her face. "No."

Her brow furrowed. "No?"

I shook my head. "No. You're coming with me."

"Jane…" She twined our fingers together and held them in her lap. "I don't want to interfere with your family time. I know how important it is to you. I—"

"If it weren't for you, I'd still be in Detroit, sleeping on an airport floor." I squeezed her fingers. "You're a goddamn Christmas miracle, and I guarantee my family will be more than happy to have you."

An uncertain look flashed over her pretty face. I thought she was going to refuse, insist I leave her here, in this cold, impersonal hotel—granted, it was nicer than the place we'd crashed last night, but still. It wasn't good enough. Not for her.

Finally, she sighed, the sound soft and sweet with the sound of acceptance. "Fine. Okay."

My heart leapt. "Great. Let's get—"

"But—" She held up her other hand. "I refuse to meet your family in my wrinkled and smelly travel clothes. Let's at least go freshen up."

"Okay." I smiled. "But I think you look great. I mean. I'd do you."

Ivy laughed. "You *did* do me," she shot back as she killed the engine.

I smirked back, pushing my door open. She did the same, rounding the truck to join me. "Damn right I did," I said as she reached me, looping my arms over her shoulders.

We locked eyes, heat flaring between us, even as the frigid wind spun snowflakes around us. Leaning in, she kissed me, and it was softer than it had any right to be.

"Come on," she said when we parted. "Let's go get cleaned up."

CHAPTER 11

It was nearing six o'clock by the time we got checked into Ivy's room. My family had probably already eaten dinner. I'd missed out on so much family time already. I needed to get home.

I had second thoughts about my level of urgency to get home when Ivy walked out of the bathroom in a matching green lace bra and panty set, looking like a Christmas gift I couldn't wait to unwrap.

"Unfair," I growled, drinking her in with my eyes. "How am I supposed to focus on my family when I know you're wearing *that* under your dress?"

She smiled as she pulled her red sheath dress off its hanger. She'd steamed it in the bathroom while she showered, so now it was wrinkle-free and nearly as perfect as her ass in those panties.

I sighed with disappointment as she stepped into it. She laughed and looked over her shoulder. "Zip me up?"

Dragging my feet, I crossed the room to her. As I grabbed the zipper, I leaned in, dropping an open-mouthed kiss at the space where her neck and shoulder met, scraping her smooth skin with my teeth. She hissed. I straightened and zipped her up. "All set."

"Evil," she shot back, turning around. Her blue gaze skimmed slowly over me, from my black satin cigar pants to the lace-trimmed camisole, lingering on my cleavage. "You know it's still snowing, right?"

I snorted. "Kinda hard to forget," I replied as I crossed the room to where my suitcase lay open on the foot of the bed. I pulled out a sweater and held it up so that Ivy could inspect it. Her eyes widened as they took in the glory I presented her with.

It was a green sweater, with strands of red and gold garland draped over it, winding all the way around the torso and down both arms.

"What," she started, bringing her eyes back to my face, "the hell is that?"

"Tradition." I pulled it over my head, then reached back into the suitcase. "And I'm not even done yet." Turning around, I made a few adjustments, then faced her again. With the flip of a switch, the little lights turned on and blinked. Ivy started to laugh, but I held up a finger, turned back to the suitcase, and opened a Ziplock bag, pulling tiny ornaments out. One-by-one, I hung them from the garland.

"Oh, my god." Ivy leaned forward, laughter tumbling from her like the notes to my favorite Christmas carol. "I am *so* underdressed."

I grinned, putting my hands on my hips. "It's okay, I'm sure they'll still let you in." Then, I reached for her coat and held it open. "Shall we?"

❄

The snow had slowed to a light sprinkle by the time we pulled up outside of my family home. Colorful strands of lights outlined the two-story Craftsman, and a blow-up

Santa waved at us from the front lawn, complete with sleigh and reindeer.

"Mom must have gotten Uncle Benjamin to decorate," I said as Ivy put the truck into park at the curb.

She leaned forward to peer around me. "Looks good," she said. "Festive."

"Would you expect any less from a family that mandates ugly Christmas sweaters for dinner?"

"I think I expected more."

"Fair." I laughed and unbuckled. "Ready?"

Ivy sat back and exhaled one quick puff, nodding. "Yes."

Narrowing my eyes, I looked her over. "You nervous?"

She cast a sidelong glance my way. "No."

"Liar."

The truck cab filled with the sound of her sighing as she leaned her head back against the seat. "Fine," she said, not looking at me. "I'm a little nervous."

I slid across the seat and nestled tight against her side, resting my head on her shoulder. "I promise you're not walking into some tragic Christmas murder story. They're harmless. Weird, but harmless."

"Oh, my god," she laughed, lifting her head just enough to look down at me. "I wasn't even thinking about the possibility of murder!"

"Good!" I linked my fingers with hers and brought them to my lips for a kiss. "Don't!"

"Well, now I'm gonna." The lights from my mom's decorations flashed pinks and greens and yellows across Ivy's face as she looked at me. "All I'm going to think about is getting murdered, like some real-life Krampus shit."

I snorted and straightened away from her. "Well, then there's no way you'll be disappointed, as long as the night doesn't end in murder."

She narrowed her eyes. I widened mine. "You did that on purpose."

Grinning, I leaned in to smack a kiss against her cheek. "You're welcome!" Then, I slid back to my side of the cab and pushed open my door. "Come on. Let's go not get murdered."

Ivy turned the truck off and climbed out, joining me on the other side. Excitement flickered inside me as I looped my arm through hers and marched us forward. I couldn't wait to see Mom, to hug my uncle, who always smelled like black licorice and Old Spice, and, yeah, I even couldn't wait to see Abby. It'd been a while, after all.

We headed up the walk, rock salt crunching under our boots. When we reached the porch, the front door swung open.

"There you are!" Mom said from the doorway, a silhouette against the warm light of the interior. "You're just in time for din—."

She didn't get to finish. I rushed forward, taking the stairs two at a time, and enveloped her in a hug. Her arms wrapped around me, and she held me just as tight. She smelled like cinnamon and laundry and home, and I breathed deep, something broken in me healing. "I didn't think I was gonna make it," I said against her hair, still short from the chemo.

She squeezed tighter. "But you did, and I'm so happy to see you." She stepped back and placed a soft hand against my cheek. Her chocolate brown eyes were warm on my face as she smiled up at me. Then, she glanced over my shoulder. "Who do we have here?"

I turned to find Ivy still at the bottom of the stairs, hands stuffed into her coat pockets, polite smile on her face.

"Oh!" I said, the spark of joy at seeing my mom growing brighter as my eyes met Ivy's. "Mom, this is Ivy." I held a hand out to her. She stepped forward and took it. "She's the reason I'm here."

Ivy stood next to me and held out a hand for Mom to shake. "Nice to meet you, Mrs.—" She frowned and looked from me to Mom, realizing that she'd never learned my last name. "Er...Jane's mom."

Mom and I both laughed, though probably for different reasons. "Archer," Mom said as she pulled Ivy in for a hug. "Call me Betty."

Ivy looked over my shoulder, eyes wide, as she hugged my mom back. "Thank you for getting my baby here," Mom said as they parted. "Now let's get inside. It's *freezing!*"

We followed her into the house, instantly enveloped by warmth and sound. "My last name's Stephens, by the way," Ivy whispered as I closed the door behind us. We shared a smile before facing forward.

Further in, I could hear chatter and laughter, with an undercurrent of jolly music, and I turned to smile at Ivy. "Give me your coat," I said as I shrugged out of my own. She obliged, and I tucked them both into the hall closet. Then, I took her hand, giving it a squeeze. "Remember. It's gonna be a hell of a night, as long as you don't get murdered."

She made a face but let me link our arms. "My family doesn't do the whole holiday thing," she murmured as we headed toward the wall of sound that was my family. "At least not like this."

"Well, you're in for a treat." I grinned over at her, squeezing her arm reassuringly. Then, we walked into the room.

"Janey!" went the immediate chorus as we entered. There was a large sectional couch lined with uncles and aunts and cousins, all decked out in their Christmas uglies. The floor was a mess of kids, all playing with their new Christmas Eve toys. They barely looked up.

I patted Ivy's arm, then picked my way through the maze of little limbs and bodies, making sure not to step on any kids, then I went down the line, leaning in for hugs and kisses and *how are you's*. When I reached Abby, she gave me a squeeze and murmured, "Glad you made it." I pressed my lips together in a half-smile and moved on to her husband, Anthony. Once I reached the end of the couch, I stood beside my mom and motioned across the room. "Everyone," I said, "this is Ivy. Ivy…everyone."

She lifted a hand and wiggled her fingers. "Hi, everyone."

"What the hell are you wearing?" Uncle Benjamin demanded, earning a roar of laughter from the room.

Ivy looked down at her simple dress—a dress that hugged every curve and dip of her body so lovingly that I was envious—then back up to my uncle. "I told Jane when I saw her sweater that I'd be underdressed," she said, laughing.

"Janey," Uncle Benjamin said. "Get this girl something more appropriate."

"Yes sir," I laughed, shaking my head. "Come on." I brushed past Ivy and motioned for her to follow. "Let's see what I've got upstairs."

I led Ivy to the guest bedroom, with its hidden stash of Christmas garb, and flung open the closet. "Pick your poison," I said with a dramatic wave.

Ivy took in the glorious assortment of reds and greens and golds, sparkly and spangly and otherwise adorned, blue eyes wide. "Your family does not fuck around." As she said it, she approached the closet and began flipping through sweaters.

I sat on the edge of the bed and watched her. My brain strived to reconcile her in this space, in my home. This person I'd only known for a couple days. This woman I'd held and touched and tasted.

This woman that would be leaving at the end of the night, maybe out of my life for good.

The thought brought a thread of icy dread through my blood, and suddenly, I wanted to slow time.

"What about this?" Ivy spun around, holding a sweater to her chest.

I swallowed down the burgeoning anxiety and took her

in. She'd picked a Rudolph red cardigan covered in velvety gingerbread people. It was awful.

It was perfect.

Grinning, I hopped up from the bed and reached for the sweater. I took it off the hanger and held it out. "It's so you," I said as she threaded her arms through the sleeves.

She laughed as she faced me, a rush of summer pear filling my senses. I reached out and straightened the sweater, buttoning it up. Once I reached the last one, she covered my hands with hers. I looked up to find her watching me, something unreadable on her face.

"What?" I asked, my voice barely above a whisper.

She held my gaze for a long moment before looking away, an imperceptible shake of her head. "Nothing." She smiled, too bright, too cheery, and stepped back. "How do I look?"

My heart thudded heavily against my breastbone. I forced myself to exhale and returned her smile. "Stunning," I said, even as my mind spun with possibilities of what she'd been about to say. "I've never seen anyone look so sexy in an ugly Christmas sweater."

"Lies." She moved past me, catching my hand in hers on the way. "But thank you."

When we returned to the living room, all eyes were on us. A cacophony of whistles and approvals filled the room.

"Much better," Uncle Benjamin decreed, louder than all the rest. "Now, let's eat!"

CHAPTER 12

Dinner was…well, it was an ordeal. Not that that was unusual in the Archer household. There was always some drama or another, usually involving my mom's younger sisters, who'd been competitive from birth. This year, it resulted in three different sweet potato casseroles, three different types of potatoes, and three different pumpkin pies. Mom, in her consummate wisdom, knew that neither of her sisters were adept at cooking, so her dishes were there simply to ensure we'd have an edible meal.

The real fun, however, came after dinner, when a game of White Elephant tipped things over the edge. Aunt Meredith opened her chosen present to reveal a gag gift—a bedpan with fudge resembling poops—and declared that this wasn't the gift she'd meant to choose. She wanted a do-over. Her sister, Aunt Olivia, informed her that there were no do-overs in White Elephant, and to sit down and *deal with your shit*.

I settled into my seat next to Ivy, popping a piece of sugar cookie into my mouth, wishing it was popcorn. Ivy looked my way, brows lifted in alarm. "Don't worry," I said, offering her a cookie shaped like a snowflake. "This is normal."

"Totally normal," Mom agreed from Ivy's other side. "If it gets physical, we'll hose them down."

I huffed out a silent laugh and rested my head against Ivy's shoulder. Dinner was delicious, and I'd definitely eaten too much. The food coma was fast approaching.

"So," Mom said as the Annual Aunt Rumble continued around us, "did you two really *just* meet?"

I felt Ivy tense against me. Glancing toward Mom, she answered, her voice calm and steady. "Yes, yesterday, actually."

How did she do that? Always calm. Always steady.

Not always, a voice whispered, drawing forth explicit images of Ivy coming undone. A twist of heat radiated low in my abdomen, and I shifted in my seat. "Was it really just yesterday?" I asked, straining to keep the tension out of my voice.

Ivy's lips curved in that soft way that meant she was about to tease me, and I found I couldn't wait. "I hope you asked Santa for a calendar."

I made a face at her, and she laughed. Her laugh really was quickly becoming my favorite sound.

"Huh," Mom said, her brown eyes twinkling as she took us in. "Interesting." She stood before I could question just what she thought was so *interesting*. "I'm gonna break this up."

We watched as my mother crossed the room, the air of authority surrounding her much stronger than one would expect from a person that still looked so frail. Without hesitation, she stepped between the sisters just before Aunt Meredith whacked Aunt Olivia with the bedpan. We couldn't hear what Mom said, but it seemed to put some sense into the other two. They stood down, returning to their seats while Mom took the bedpan from Aunt Meredith. Without missing a beat, she extracted a piece of the fudge and bit into it, causing an uproar of laughter and groans from the room.

"Your mom is great," Ivy said, laughing as she stole the last cookie from the plate I held.

I smiled, warmth like a radiator inside me. "I know."

"Your whole family is pretty great." She settled deeper into the couch, looking so cozy that I wanted to snuggle up against her and stay there all winter through, like a hibernating bear.

I resisted, aware that, after tonight, I'd be fielding questions about Ivy for the rest of my stay. Probably beyond. Especially from Mom. I didn't want to fuel them any further. "Yeah, I'm a fan." I sat my now-empty plate on the arm of the couch and dusted cookie crumbs from my garland-covered chest.

"Thank you." Ivy's head drifted sideways against the back of the couch so she was looking at me. "For bringing me. This sure as hell beats Christmas Eve alone in a hotel room with takeout and cable." She turned her wrist to glance at her watch. "I should probably get going soon."

The image her words brought to mind hit me like an icicle to the gut. It was lonely. Cold. I didn't want that for her. Not tonight. Not ever.

"Stay," I said before I thought it through. "Stay tonight."

"Oh, no." She frowned. "I couldn't intrude like that."

"You wouldn't be." I faced her, laying my head on the back of the couch, too. "In fact, I'm pretty sure that if my mother knew that you planned to spend Christmas alone and I let you leave, she'd kill me. Krampus-style."

That earned a laugh, tinkling and light. "Are you sure?" she asked once she sobered.

"Yes." I reached over and reclaimed the last cookie, taking a big bite. "Deadly."

Rolling her eyes, she took the rest of the cookie from my hand and popped it into her mouth. "Fine. But don't expect me to join into any Christmas sing-alongs."

"I make no guarantees," I shot back. "I've always needed a duet partner for Christmas Karaoke."

❄

As expected, Mom was more than happy to have Ivy stay the night. The moment it was brought up, everyone kicked into high gear. The aunts made it a mission to find something for Ivy to sleep in while my mom grabbed extra bedding from the linen closet for the pull-out. She handed the stack of bedding to me, and the look she gave me indicated that she knew it was all for show. Ivy would be sleeping in my room.

After a constant rotation of family members doing their nightly bathroom routines, Ivy and I got our turns. I let Ivy go first, then did my thing, reconvening in my childhood bedroom. She stood on the far side of the room in a red and black flannel PJ set, courtesy of Aunt Meredith, her hair pulled into a messy top-knot, her face naked of makeup. My heart stuttered at the sight of this perfect specimen in the very room I'd spent my most awkward and confusing years in. Past me would have never believed it.

Ivy reached for one of the black throw pillows on the bed, the tilt of her perfect brow saying everything she didn't vocalize. The full-size bed was still dressed in the zebra-print duvet and hot pink sheets I swore were cool back when I was sixteen.

"I know." Reaching for the other throw pillow, I tossed it at her. "Shut up."

She laughed as she caught it, then set both aside. "I'm pretty sure my room didn't look any better," she said as she peeled the blankets back. "Probably worse, actually."

"Don't lie to make me feel better." I toed off my slippers and fluffed up my pillows before climbing into the bed.

"Okay." Ivy joined me, laying on her back. She lifted her

arm so I could snuggle against her side, my face nestled onto her chest. "I won't." She kissed the top of my head, her fingers playing with the hair at the nape of my neck. I sighed and snuggled closer, draping my arm over her soft belly.

Beneath the blankets, our legs tangled together. I sighed, contentment flowing through me. "I like you," I murmured against her neck as warm strands of sleep pulled at my limbs.

She laced the fingers of her other hand with mine, giving them a light squeeze. "I like you, too," she whispered.

I smiled to myself, eyes closed, and let our breaths sync as we settled into the silence. The thrum of her heart beneath my ear eventually slowed to a steady pace, her even breaths rustling my hair. A train of thoughts niggled at my subconscious, the *what if* kind of thoughts. I brushed them aside and let myself drift off, too. Sorting out what came next would be a problem for Tomorrow Jane.

CHAPTER 13

Morning came in the form of breakfast smells wafting upstairs, the sweet and savory aromas woven through with joyful chatter and laughter. The sounds of every Christmas of years passed. Smiling to myself, I snuggled deeper into my pillow, the feeling of home a glow inside my chest. The bed shifted beside me, and it took a moment to remember that I was not alone.

I opened my eyes to find Ivy already awake, the gray winter light caressing her face, rendering her almost ethereal. "God, you're beautiful," I whispered, reaching over to brush a lock of hair away from her face.

"You're Christmas drunk," she replied, turning her face into the pillow to hide her smile.

"There's no such thing." I scootched closer, until our bodies were pressed together, then wound my arms and legs around her, smacking loud kisses against her cheek until she emerged, laughing.

She folded her hands beneath her cheek and met my eye, her lips still curved in a smile. "Morning."

"Morning," I said back, unable to quell the grin overtaking my face. "How'd you sleep?"

Ivy opened her mouth to answer, but a knock on the door cut her off. "Rise and shine," my mom's voice sang from the hall. "Breakfast is ready!"

"Be right there," I called back, not taking my eyes from Ivy. When I heard Mom's footsteps fade down the hall, I slid my hand over Ivy's waist and pulled her closer. She was warm and soft, and I wasn't ready to let her go.

You're going to have to, my brain whispered, *soon.*

I shoved the niggling thought to the back of my mind, but it must have shown on my face, anyway. "What's wrong?" Ivy asked, twining her fingers with mine at her waist.

"Nothing." I turned my face into my pillow and exhaled, urging all thoughts beyond this moment out of my brain. "I'm good."

She shifted beside me and her soft fingertips pushed through the hair at the nape of my neck. My pillow dipped as she lay her head next to mine. "Jane."

"Uh-uh," I mumbled into the pillow, shaking my head. If I looked at her, I'd spill my guts. And my guts were filled with confessions. Of feelings and fears and heart-tripping wishes. Unrealistic wishes. Best to keep it all to myself.

Ivy moved closer, till her forehead was pressed to the side of my face. "Jane," she said again.

I squeezed my eyes shut, as if I could will myself out of this moment and into the next. Apple pancakes and bacon and Uncle Benjamin's eggnog for breakfast. My stomach rumbled, loud and obscene, at the thought.

Ivy huffed out a silent laugh at the sound. "You can't hide forever," she murmured, her voice a melody in my ear. "You'll starve."

Growling, I rolled onto my back. "What happens next?" I stared at the ceiling as I spoke, afraid of what I'd see if I looked at her. Squinting, I traced the outline of a long-ago-fallen glow in the dark star. Not the wishing kind, unfortunately. If it were, what would I wish for?

More time.

The answer was as immediate as it was impossible. Time stopped for no one, slowed for no one. No matter how much you wanted it to.

I closed my eyes, the star's outline dancing behind my lids. Ivy still hadn't spoken.

Maybe that was my answer.

"We should get downstairs," I said, sitting up. "Breakfast is getting co—"

Ivy cut me off by pulling me back down onto the bed. "Not yet," she said, nestling her face into the crook of my neck. Her arm snaked around my middle and squeezed tight. "A few more minutes."

I leaned my cheek against her forehead, my insides going gooey like a melted marshmallow, despite the creeping knowledge that this could not last. Outside of this room, this house, this city and state, we each had lives to return to. The wonderland we'd let ourselves get lost in didn't exist in the real world.

But maybe it could, a voice whispered from the hopelessly romantic part of my brain. The thought had me pressing my lips to Ivy's forehead, a tender gesture that, I hoped, signaled more than just a casual fling.

"I don't know what happens next," she murmured into my skin. "Do we have to decide now?"

My heart lurched. I breathed through it. "No," I said, keeping my tone light. "We don't have to figure anything out right now."

Ivy rolled away and squinted at my face. She was the single most adorable sight I'd ever seen, with her scrunched up face and bedhead halo. "Except for breakfast," she declared with a resolute nod.

I laughed, despite the wonky beating of my heart. "Except for breakfast," I agreed, pushing myself upright. I climbed out of bed and held out my hand. "Come on. The pancakes tend to go first, and you don't want to miss my mom's world-famous apple pancakes."

Her eyes widened. She took my hand and let me pull her out of our little haven. Together, we headed downstairs for breakfast.

❄

The next few hours were a blur of Christmas chaos. Breakfast was devoured in record time, with the aunts fighting over the last slice of bacon like two vultures battling for one carcass. They were thwarted by Mom swooping in to claim the prize for herself. After, we gathered in the living room, where Uncle Benjamin played Santa and doled out gifts, one by one, to adults and children alike. Somehow, whether it be by Christmas miracle or my mother's quick thinking, there were even gifts for Ivy. I tried not to melt at the earnest way she thanked Mom, her blue eyes wide with surprise and emotion.

"Oh, sweetheart," Mom said, hugging Ivy tight. "It's just a sweater."

I hid my smile behind my glass of eggnog and wondered for the hundredth time just how I was supposed to let Ivy leave.

"What's going on there?"

I looked over to find Abby settling into the seat beside me, her dark eyes shrewd on our mom and Ivy.

"Oh, you know," I said, keeping my tone light, "figured I'd bring a hitchhiker home for the holidays. She might go on a killing spree later. We'll see."

"Hmm." Abby clinked her red-and-gold manicure against her own glass of nog. "If you could convince her to off me first, that'd be great. I'd rather get it over and done with."

"I'll see what I can do." I gave my sister a sidelong look.

She'd cut her hair since the last time I saw her, a sleek bob now. It suited her. "I like your hair."

Abby lifted a hand and smoothed it over her dark locks. "Thanks." Dropping her hand to her lap, she wrapped it around her glass. "I like *her*."

I looked back to Ivy, who was talking with our mom, heads low, conspiratorial. A soft smile hijacked my lips. "Yeah, me, too." Heaving a sigh, I added, "It's gonna suck when she kills us all."

"So much," Abby agreed. We sipped our nog in silence for a few seconds before Abby spoke again. "I'm sorry if I've been hard on you, Janie."

My head shot up so fast the room spun. "What?"

Abby sighed and leaned forward, putting her glass on the coffee table. Then, she turned to face me, pulling one leg onto the couch. "I've been a shitty big sister. I think I just got so lost in my own fear and sadness, and you weren't here, you know? And I know that's because Mom didn't want you putting your life on hold for her, but emotions aren't rational." She pulled her knee to her chest, her candy-cane-covered sock peeking out from her pant leg. "And I couldn't get mad at Mom, so—" She cut herself off with a helpless shrug.

Realization buzzed in the back of my brain, spreading through me like a shot of whiskey. "Abs…"

"Nope." She stretched her leg out and shoved me lightly with her foot. "That's it. That's all I had to say."

I laughed and grabbed her foot. She shrieked and tried to pull back. We devolved into a childhood wrestling match, a tornado of flailing limbs and screeching, until, inevitably, our mother broke it up.

"You'd think they would have outgrown it," she said to Ivy as she parked herself between us on the couch. "Alas."

"Alas," Ivy agreed, an amused glint in her eye as she looked at me.

I didn't have it in me to be embarrassed, so I simply shrugged. "She started it."

Abby snorted. "Did not."

Leaning forward, I peered past our mother, ready to bicker, but Ivy spoke up before I could say anything. "Your mom was telling me about the Christmas lights in the town square."

I looked back to Ivy, my sister forgotten. "Oh," I said, dropping my feet to the floor. "I haven't seen the town square lit up in forever."

"You two should go." She grabbed the blue wool scarf she'd gifted Ivy, draping it over Ivy's shoulders. "I bet it's extra beautiful with all this fresh snow."

Ivy looked over at me, her hand lifting to touch the scarf. A smile played on her lips, hope glinting in her eyes.

I was such a sucker.

❄

Mom's house was only a few blocks from the center of town. The walk was brisk and quiet, beautifully bathed in the periwinkle light of winter. The streets were lined with homes glowing bright and colorful against the sparkling white backdrop of fresh snow.

"It's so quiet," Ivy said, her voice reverent, as if she was afraid to disturb the peace.

"Everyone's inside, all warm and cozy," I whispered back, shoving my hands deeper into my coat pockets. "Why did I let you talk me into this?"

She smiled over at me, and the swoop of my stomach answered my question before she could utter a sound.

"Shut up," I grumbled, bumping my shoulder against hers.

She laughed, the sound a joyful tinkle in the peaceful quiet. "How much farther?"

Instead of answering, I pointed straight ahead. A golden

glow radiated at the end of the street, as if it were the gates of Olympus.

"Oh," Ivy breathed. I threaded my arm through hers and marched us forward faster.

The side street spilled out onto town square like we'd emerged from a thick, dark forest to find a sunny, spacious meadow. Only the meadow was covered in snow and lined with brick buildings trimmed in twinkle lights. In the center of the square, a beautiful gazebo, glowing like a beacon of hope on a long, dark night.

"Wow." Ivy stepped forward, eyes wide as she took it all in. I hung back, taking *her* in as she spun full-circle, eyes wide with awe. Snow shimmered in the glow of countless strands of lights, like a million diamonds on the ground. Slow, lackadaisical snowflakes fell from above, and it felt like we were in a snow globe flipped upright.

Ivy spun to face me, the smile on her face luminous. My heart beat harder in my chest. "Wow," I repeated, taking the hand she held out to me.

She pulled me against her, arms draped over my shoulders. I wrapped mine around her middle. And then we swayed to music that didn't exist, but for the beat of our hearts. Eyes locked on one another, we sank into the magic of the moment.

I didn't want it to end.

"I have to go soon," Ivy murmured against my hair, as if she'd read my mind. "I've got work tomorrow."

My arms tightened around her. "How long will you be in town?"

"A couple days." She dipped her fingers beneath my scarf, the frozen tips against my neck making me shiver. "My flight home is on the twenty-ninth."

"Where's home?" I couldn't believe I hadn't asked this earlier, but now it seemed like the most important question I'd ever asked.

"Windsor, for now." She rested her cheek against my temple. I leaned into the touch. "You?"

"Detroit," I answered, a glimmer of hope in my veins. Windsor was both an entire country away and a mere river's width from Detroit. We could make that work. The hope was immediately tamped down by the thought that maybe Ivy had no desire to continue this. Whatever this was. I kept my tone light when I added, "You're not too far away."

Ivy eased away from me, and I squared my shoulders, preparing for the *this was fun, but* speech. It'd be totally valid. It'd only been a couple days. Forced proximity plus holidays definitely had contributed to…whatever was going on here. But it felt like more. To me, at least, it felt like more.

I hoped I wasn't the only one feeling it.

"Jane," she started, her thumbs tracing the curve of my jaw.

I thought I was brave enough to hold her eye while she did this. I was not.

"I know," I said, stepping out of her embrace. "Sorry, I—"

"What are you sorry for?" Ivy grabbed my hand, pulling me back to her.

"I always do this." I tried to pull away, but she held tight. "I always fall too fast, and then I freak the other person out. Or I fall too fast, and they think they have, too, but then they—"

"You fell for me?"

My mouth snapped shut. I looked at Ivy, so beautiful in the glimmering light, and my heart twisted. "Yes," I said, soft and low, like I didn't want her to hear me.

Her face softened, blue eyes warm. She pulled my hand until I stumbled forward, crashing into her softness. "Me, too," she whispered, cupping my face in her palm. "Isn't that crazy?"

I laughed, my eyes going blurry. "So crazy."

"What are we gonna do about it?"

“Well, obviously we have to go to the courthouse first thing tomorrow morning and get married,” I said as if it were the most logical thing in the world. “And then we have to get a cat.”

“Good news,” Ivy said, laughing. “I already have a cat.”

“Great, we’ve got a head start, then.” I stepped closer, leaning my body into hers. “What’s my newly acquired fur child’s name?”

“Sir William Catner.” She brushed her nose against mine. I lifted my face to hers and looked into her blizzard blue eyes. “You’re going to love him,” she murmured just before pressing her lips to mine.

“Merry Christmas,” I whispered, and then we kissed as the snow swirled around us and the stars sparkled above.

Tomorrow would be an ordinary day. No more Christmas magic glittering in the air. The gifts would all be opened, the carols all sung. But I knew, down to the marrow of my bones, that Ivy was the one I wanted beside me as we cleaned up the wrapping paper and bows.

And I couldn’t wait.

THE END

ACKNOWLEDGMENTS

My Yes Do girls, Christina, Erin, & Liz. Your support and love are absolutely invaluable. As are the endless laughs. I love you all.

The Grumpy to my Sunshine, James. Thank you for being a hard ass, but not doubting for a second that I would get this book (and every book) done. I will never not be surprised that you believe in me so much.

Bri & Jessica for being SO EXCITED to read everything I write, for sharing my posts, and for shouting from the rooftops that everyone should read my books. I love, love, love you both.

Louise, Alyssa, Kelly, & Victoria. When I need a pep talk or to brainstorm a plot hole or to vent about this crazy publishing world, you're always there. Your insight and advice are invaluable, but your friendships mean even more.

Brian, for keeping me fed and entertained, and for taking care of the fur girls when I'm on deadline. I'd wither away without you.

Taylor Swift, for writing the soundtrack to countless stories I've written and will write someday.

Mom for reading every word I write, and for pimping me

out at every chance you get. Dad and Jason for always being supportive but never reading my books.

And last but definitely not least, the people who DO read my books! I will never stop being surprised that you exist, and forever grateful that you do. Thank you, thank you, THANK YOU!

ABOUT MEIKA

MEIKA USHER is a sucker for an HEA. She writes love stories laced with snark, sex, and swears. When she's not writing, she loves to travel (Amsterdam is her favorite city), scream-sing Taylor Swift in her car (All Too Well, anyone?), and get tattoos (a dozen and counting). She lives in Michigan with her two snooty cats and one scrappy little dog. Oh, and a never-ending pile of romance novels she swears she's going to read. Find her at meikausher.com.

a merry little
christmas
LIZ ZERKEL

TO MY HUSBAND, JEREMY—

You are better than any book boyfriend could ever dream of being!

CHAPTER 1

Mae Thompson
December 23, 9:30am
55.5 hours until Christmas Dinner

"Good morning, this is your pilot speaking with an important announcement. Unfortunately, the snowstorm arrived earlier than expected in St. Louis, and the airport has shut down. We will divert to Detroit for everyone's safety. We apologize for the inconvenience and will do all we can to get you to your holiday destinations. We will arrive in approximately an hour and fifteen minutes."

I groaned as my head fell back while the pilot spoke. This was terrible news, but it wasn't even the worst I'd received in the last 24 hours. I could practically recite the email by heart, I'd read it so many times.

. . .

"*Hello, Mae Thompson,*

With our greatest regret, we must inform you MidWest Love Publishing will close its doors permanently the first of January. Since you're currently on vacation, there is no need to return to the office other than to gather your belongings by December 30. We will send all our employees a $1,000.00 bonus as a thank you for all you've done. Best of luck with your search for your next journey. Please reach out if you need a reference.

Best, Juliet and Adam Wright"

I'd spent the last four years working every position asked of me, from assistant to fact checking to proofreading until my eyes blurred.Three months ago, I finally became the acquisitions editor for the sci-fi and fantasy romance department. It was my job to figure out which submissions had the special something we looked for and I helped make those authors' dreams come true.

And now all those dreams are crushed, including my own.

Fuck.

"You've *got* to be shitting me." The white man sitting next to me was unfortunately good looking but had the manners of an angry bear. As he crossed his leg, his expensive-looking shoe jostled my seat-back tray, sloshing my wine and nearly getting it on my book.

Not only had I unexpectedly lost my dream job after taking my first vacation in years, now I was stuck on the plane next to an arrogant man in a suit who'd been rude from the moment we sat down. Earlier he'd refused to move when I needed to use the bathroom and I tripped over his legs. And he had the nerve to glare at me as if I wanted to be sprawled across the aisle.

"Could you maybe move your foot?" I asked, frustration

coloring my voice as I grabbed my napkin to clean up the mess.

He cracked open a dark brown eye. "What?"

I pointed at the red stained napkin on my tray. "You spilled my wine. Could you try to be mindful of your space? I paid for that!"

"If I bought you another one, would you stop talking for the rest of this miserable flight?"

My mouth dropped open at his audacity. "Wow, that's some fan-fucking-tastic Christmas cheer you got there, buddy. I'm trying to make the best of this crap situation, alright?"

He jerked his foot away without an apology. I glared at him but his eyes were already closed. I opened my book, hoping it would help me ignore that I'd lost the job I'd worked so hard for and hadn't had long enough to gain the experience needed for similar roles elsewhere. Add in my dwindling bank account and not getting home tonight?

Merry Christmas to me.

❄

If I looked up Hell in the dictionary, it would show Detroit Airport right before Christmas while snow and sleet pelted outside as flights were grounded and canceled one by one.

The terminal was in utter chaos as people scrambled to find any possible flights. I glanced towards the swarmed baggage claim and cursed my past self for bringing a checked suitcase instead of a carry-on. Damn my inability to pack light.

I pulled out my phone and decided to bite the bullet and tell my family I didn't know when I'd make it home.

Within a few rings, my mom's worried voice and soft

Christmas music reached my ears. "Sweetie, shouldn't you be in the air?"

I explained my predicament about the blizzard but decided to wait until I saw her to tell her about my job. I didn't have the mental bandwidth to handle her reaction to both tidbits.

"Blizzard? I thought it wasn't hitting until much later."

I closed my eyes and tried to keep my voice calm. "When was the last time you looked outside?"

"Oh, hold on real quick, sweetie," she said to me before a muffled, "Viola, can you check the cookies? I'm on the phone with your sister."

"Got it," my younger sister called back.

"Xander, Jake, and the kids will be here later tonight for dinner. You're going to miss the gingerbread decorating," Mom said, her attention back at me.

The carousel began moving, and the first pieces of luggage made their way slowly around. I kept my eyes peeled for my light green suitcase, but so far it was a sea of black, navy, and gray bags. "I want to be there, but there's no way I'm getting to St. Louis tonight."

"I know. I'm sorry about how stressful this must be. Have you found a hotel?"

Crap. I forgot about the whole sleeping thing. I glanced around and noticed people already hunkering down in the airport. I briefly considered doing the same to save money, but I was certain my parents would kill me if they found out. Sometimes I think they forgot I was an adult who lived on her own.

"—and I swear to God, if you think you're sleeping alone in the airport, you've got another thing coming. You have no idea what sort of gross perverts might be around."

At least my mother was predictable.

"I'll find a safe place to stay, don't worry." I saw my flashy suitcase drop down, a bright dot amongst so many bland bags. "I see my bag, so I gotta run. I'll touch base with you soon." After a rushed goodbye, I lunged for my bag before it could get past me.

I was semi-comforted that no one else knew how to handle the blizzard situation. I briefly considered getting a rental car, but despite growing up in the Midwest, I wasn't comfortable driving in storms. As I walked toward a less crowded area to consider my options, I noticed my suitcase felt different. Lighter and the wheel wasn't pulling. I stepped out of the foot traffic and squatted to examine it. I had packed it to capacity, and this felt like stuff was missing. I did *not* have the spoons to deal with possible theft, especially since hotels were probably filling up by the minute.

I reached to unzip it and saw a sleek luggage tag I didn't recognize. Oh no, oh shit, no, no, no! What had I done? I slowly turned it around to read the name on it: Alonzo Davis.

Apparently, the only thief around was me.

CHAPTER 2

Alonzo Davis
December 23, 12:30 PM
52.5 Hours Until Christmas Dinner

"No, you don't understand," I said, trying to keep my cool. "*This* bag isn't mine. It belongs to someone named Mae. She grabbed *my* bag instead of hers. Is it possible to page her so we could swap? I tried calling the number listed on the tag, but it went straight to voicemail." Not that I was hopeful she was still in the airport since I'd waited for almost an hour to be assisted.

"Oh, what a mess. Give me a moment, and let's see if we can find her." The older woman pressed a few buttons on the phone before saying, "Paging Mae Thompson from flight number 356. Please report to the baggage desk."

"Actually, hi! I'm already here." an out-of-breath voice called. I turned to see a frantic woman with her hair in a messy bun and sweater slipping from her shoulder rush into the room. I frowned, realizing she was the woman I sat next to on the plane.

Her entire face dropped as she recognized me. "You're Alonzo? Of course you are."

I crossed my arms and stood a little taller. "You're the one who grabbed the wrong bag, *Mae,* not me." I pushed her suitcase towards her. She rolled her eyes and grabbed it before shoving mine toward me.

"I know, and I'm sorry. Things are a bit hectic here if you haven't noticed. Now, if you'd excuse me, I need to find a taxi so I can get to a hotel." Mae turned toward the counter and her entire body language shifted. She smiled kindly at the woman helping me and said, "I'm sorry for this mix-up. Thank you for your help. Is there anything else you need from me?"

"No, dear, easy mistake. Just be more mindful next time you fly. Have a Merry Christmas."

She beamed at the woman before practically sprinting away, her long legs practically a blur.

I thanked the woman and hurried after my suitcase bandit. Mae walked with purpose, making me think she had a plan. Since I wasted the last hour of my life dealing with the luggage disaster thanks to her, I figured she owed me. It only seemed fair.

But I didn't expect her to be so damn fast as she navigated the airport. Luckily I could spot her giant bun bobbing up and down amongst the bustling crowd as she dodged around people. Finally, she pushed through the exit into the crowd waiting for rides.

Unsurprisingly, yet absolutely frustratingly, there were no cabs. Mae leaned into the street, desperately searching for one to wave down. I quickly contemplated my options: I could be an ass and take the first available taxi, leaving her behind, or I could convince her we ought to share since rides were limited and we'd already wasted enough time.

I hovered behind her, still debating what I wanted to do, as an available cab pulled up and half a dozen people stared it down. I had to act fast before anyone else could snatch it away. I rushed forward and grabbed for the door before it completely stopped. I needed everyone to know this one was mine.

A building roar of angry voices from the waiting crowd increased as I yanked the door open, but one voice rose above them all.

"Oh *hell no,* not today, Satan!" Mae shrieked, her pale face reddening, either from the cold or her anger. I ducked my head into the cab to greet the driver. He must've heard her indignation because he frowned at me, and for a moment, I thought he might refuse me service.

I threw my suitcase in and turned, plastering the best grin I could manage, and said through gritted teeth, "*Sweetheart,* I got this cab for us, so how about you load your stuff so we can head to a hotel, alright?"

Her brow furrowed, and she stared at me in confusion for a beat before turning her focus back on the driver. He leaned across the passenger seat. "Miss, is this guy bothering you?"

The look she shot at me screamed, "Yes, he's bothering me." So I silently begged her to play along so we both could get out of here before shit got worse and the crowd turned on me. Snow was steadily falling, and I refused to spend the night at the airport. She sighed in defeat and said, "No sir, I'm fine. My boyfriend was being an annoying prick on the plane, and I'm grumpy about it. Sorry. Can I throw my bag in the trunk?"

My lips twitched at her calling me her boyfriend. At least she was willing to play along.

The driver studied us, determining if we were liars—which we *were*—or not. Finally, he nodded curtly, and the trunk popped open. Without thinking, I grabbed her suitcase to load it.

“Oh. Um. Thanks…Alonzo?” She said my name like a question, and I couldn’t fight the grin at the absurdity of the whole situation.

I lowered my voice so the driver couldn’t hear. “You can call me Lon. Or Alonzo. Whichever.”

“Alright, Lon. Since when are you so selfless?”

“I’m not. I figured you owed me after stealing my suitcase,” I said with a wink before gesturing for her to get into the cab. She hesitated so I gritted though a smile, “Look, do you honestly think the cab would’ve stopped for you if I hadn’t jumped forward?”

Her green eyes narrowed, but I could tell she knew we were in it together.

The driver looked at us through the rearview mirror. “Where to, folks?”

I turned to Mae. She stared back at me with wide, expectant eyes. “Wait, you didn’t have a plan? I assumed you found a hotel while I was in the office dealing with the luggage.”

She blushed in a way that emphasized her ivory skin, like berries in cream meant to be savored. But now wasn’t the time to think about how attractive she was. I needed to focus on the issue at hand. And her silence made it abundantly clear I’d forced my way into a cab with someone with zero plan.

Shit.

CHAPTER 3

Mae Thompson
December 23, 1:30 PM
51.5 Hours Until Christmas Dinner

I totally didn't have a plan. And now I had an unwanted travel companion. Suited-Up Asshole—Lon, I mentally corrected myself since he was now my fake boyfriend—might not be the dick I initially thought, but that didn't mean I wanted to work with him.

I cleared my throat and leaned toward the driver. "Sir, do you know of any hotels with openings? We were supposed to fly to St. Louis and now are stuck."

Next to me, Lon muttered, "We're screwed," and it took everything in me to not question his use of "we." Outside of this car, there was no "we."

The driver scratched at his white beard and thought for a moment. "Anywhere you go will probably be pretty busy, but if I take you to one not *right* next to the airport, you might have better luck. Does the star rating matter?"

"Doesn't matter as long as the bed's clean," I said. I'd certainly stayed in some questionable motels in my day, so I could handle most anything.

"And money's not an issue," Lon added.

I furrowed my brow wanting to say, "Uhhh, yes, it's *extremely* an issue," but I kept my mouth shut. Right now we needed to find somewhere with space.

"Alright, I have a place to try. It's not the Ritz, but it's nice. Let's go before the roads ice over."

I nodded in agreement and leaned back in my seat and wished away the tension in my muscles. I knew I wouldn't relax until I was home with a new job lined up. My bank account was dwindling by the second with this unforeseen detour along with my feelings of self-worth. I worked my ass off at MidWest Love and for what? A pile of student debt and the fear I wouldn't be able to stay in the city I loved with a fulfilling job.

I closed my eyes, trying to ignore my swirling thoughts. I must've dozed off because suddenly I was shaken awake. "Mae, we're here. Hurry up and get your stuff."

I blinked rapidly, trying to place where I was and who was talking. "Oh, Lon, right. Sorry." Just then, the driver came to my side of the cab and opened my door. "Thank you, sir." I studied him while I undid my seatbelt. "Has anyone ever told you that you look like Santa?"

He chuckled, his breath causing little white puffs in the cold. "All the time, miss. All the time."

I pulled out my wallet, and he shook his head. "Seems like you two are having a rough day. The ride's on me."

I sputtered, unsure I heard him correctly, "That's not necessary—"

"Consider it a Christmas present." He winked as he handed me my suitcase. "It's adorable you two have matching bags. You make such a nice young couple. I hope you get home in time for the holidays."

I avoided his gaze as I thanked him, fighting back tears at his sweet gesture I didn't deserve. My stomach knotted with the guilt of lying to such a kind man. Moving faster than he had exited the car, Taxi Santa climbed in, waved, and drove off.

"Shit, I wanted to at least tip him," I muttered.

"I left some money on my seat when he wasn't looking." Lon grabbed the handle on his bag and nodded toward the hotel. "It's freezing out here. Come on."

I stood there stunned and studied Lon as he hurried to the entrance. The more I was around the man, the more confused I became. Him leaving a tip didn't compute with the man who was rude as hell on the plane. And damn, he looked good in those suit pants. He looked like a businessman, but apparently wasn't the kind who spent all day at a desk. I didn't want to keep staring but my eyes seemed to have a mind of their own.

I blamed the stress.

A handful of other travelers milled around the lobby, but no one else had luggage. I crossed my fingers for things to work in my favor. Lon made it to the desk first, so I awkwardly lingered behind him, daydreaming about a warm, cozy fire where I could wrap up in a blanket with a book. Or at the very least a bed I could curl in for the night. I was exhausted and peopled out after all the time spent at the airport.

"Good afternoon, and welcome to Capri Hotel. How can I help you?" the young woman behind the desk asked Lon.

Lon leaned casually on the desk. "I don't have a reservation but hoped you had an available room?"

She smiled and started typing. Her eyes flicked to me and asked, "I noticed the two of you walked in together—are you needing only one room?"

"Oh, we're not together. We happened to share a cab from

the airport," I chimed in before Lon could speak. "We're stuck because of the weather."

She made a tsking sound and nodded. "I'd heard the airport was shutting down. Horrible time of year for that to happen." She finally looked up and smiled at Lon. "So, the good news is I do have a room. However," she gave me a sympathetic glance. "It *is* the only room available, and since this gentleman was first in line, I have to offer it to him first. I'm sorry, ma'am."

My head buzzed with anxiety as I closed my eyes, trying not to unfairly lose my cool at the woman. This was Lon's fault for hijacking my cab and having longer legs so he could get to the desk first. I opened my eyes to see them both staring at me, and at least Lon had the decency to look sheepish. I nodded and said, "No, I totally get it. I'll just google to see if there's any other place around here with availability. And then find a cab willing to drive in this storm."

Lon ran a hand through his dark but no longer perfect hair and let out an exhausted sigh. "I can't believe I'm about to do this, but you should take the room, Mae. I did technically steal it from you."

My eyes widened, yet again shocked at the decency he showed. I took a few steps closer to the desk, unsure what to do. "That would be amazing if you wouldn't mind." He simply shrugged and pulled out his phone. I looked at the woman and asked, "What type of room is it?"

"It's our presidential suite, one of the nicest rooms in the hotel. I'm a little surprised it's even available because it's normally booked for Christmas," she chirped. All I heard was my bank account flushing down the toilet.

"How much is it per night?" I asked softly, wishing and praying it would be reasonable.

"Let me check." She pressed a few more buttons and said,

"Currently, the nightly rate for the suite is $735.00 plus tax. The airport will probably still be closed tomorrow, so you might be here for two nights."

I choked on spit at her words. Game over for me.

CHAPTER 4

CHAPTER 4

Alonzo Davis
December 23, 3:00 PM
50 Hours Until Christmas Dinner

I looked up from searching on my phone for an available hotel when Mae started sputtering and coughing. I smacked her back in case she was choking, but she glared at me as she caught her breath. “You okay?”

Her cheeks flushed bright red, and she chewed nervously on her lip. “There’s no way I can afford it without maxing my credit card, and that’s not a good idea at the moment.” She looked up at me, embarrassment painting her face as she shrugged helplessly. “Turns out the room’s all yours.”

I frowned and turned to look at the receptionist, whose name tag read Sierra. “I’m so sorry, Sierra. I wasn’t listening. How much is the suite?”

She repeated the number, and I let out a low whistle because it seemed excessive for one person, but I had the money and needed a place to stay. I pulled out my wallet and slid my card over to her.

Mae straightened her purse on her slumped shoulders and took a few steps away from me. "I guess this is our goodbye. Good luck making it to St. Louis." She gave Sierra a little wave and pulled her suitcase toward the front door.

I tapped my fingers, debating what to do. Past the protective shield of the windows, the storm was swirling and the roads were more white than not. I couldn't let her go out there and rest comfortably in my massive bed tonight without feeling like the biggest dick in the world. I turned and called, "What, so that's it? I think a fake boyfriend deserves a better goodbye."

She glanced over her shoulder, barely contained tears glittering in her eyes, and that sealed it for me. She wasn't going anywhere. "I'm not in the mood for this, okay? I'd say it was nice to meet you, but today's been absolutely hell."

I closed the space between us. "Hey," I said softly, "I'm happy to share the suite with you if you want. I know we just met, so this whole thing is weird, but I'm not okay letting you go out in the blizzard. I mean, it's the presidential suite, right? It probably has plenty of room. Certainly, way more than I need by myself." I turned toward the desk and asked, "Hey, Sierra, how many beds are in the suite?"

"Two king beds, each in their own rooms, and a pull-out couch in the living room area."

"See, tons of space. What do you say?"

She looked down at her shoes, refusing to look me in the eye as her cheeks flushed a deep pink. "Look, I'm not comfortable admitting this but I don't have the money for it. Even splitting the room is too expensive for me, especially if we're stuck here for two nights."

I shrugged. "I'm perfectly fine with footing the bill."

Mae's eyes shot up. "No, absolutely not."

"The taxi driver gave us the ride for free, this is the same thing," I said, holding my arms out wide. "Merry Christmas and all that shit."

"A thirty dollar ride isn't the same thing as you paying for this!"

"Say yes so we can get settled and get drunk in the lobby bar. I want to get this damn suit off."

She finally cracked a smile. "Yeah, I don't know how the hell you stand traveling in a suit." She glanced out the front door and sighed heavily. "Okay, you know what? Fine. Let's do this." Mae sternly pointed at me and said, "No funny business, okay? This isn't an 'I thank you for your generosity by getting in bed with you' sort of deal."

I held my hands up in surrender. "I would *never* assume anything like that." I paused for a moment and then grinned, "However, I wouldn't say no to consensual just-because fucking if you change your mind later." I winked and turned back to Sierra to finish checking in.

"You're such an asshole," she muttered, but her eyes flashed with amusement.

As we rode the elevator to our floor, I studied her. Mae seemed to be radiating tension with her shoulders practically up to her ears, and I couldn't tell if it was because of the blizzard situation or my ill-timed jokes about sex. I cleared my throat. "I shouldn't have made the comment about sleeping together. You don't actually know me and I understand this isn't exactly an ideal situation for a single woman to be in." Wait, is she single? I flushed, embarrassed for potentially making it all worse. "Assuming you're single. Or that you like men. Which is a shitty thing to assume."

Mae's shoulders relaxed as she smiled in amusement. "I am single. And unfortunately, I do like men."

"We're the worst, so my condolences."

She finally smiled as the elevator door opened at the top

floor. I'd stayed in many hotels around the country and was glad to see this seemed perfectly clean and comfortable. I pressed the card key against the door and pushed it open. Once I clicked on the light, we saw the massive living room with a kitchenette to the left and a sizable bathroom to the right, and two doors I assumed led to the bedrooms.

"Not too shabby," I said, dropping my messenger bag on the coffee table until we figured out who'd get what room. "Nice size TV."

Mae snorted and walked around the room, examining it. "This place better be damn nice with how much it costs." She turned and looked at me, tucking a strand of loose hair behind her ear. "Thanks again for letting me stay with you. I didn't want to spend all my time searching for a room only to end up on the floor in the airport."

"There's no way I would've let you do that, so no worries." As soon as the words left my mouth, I realized they sounded weird and possessive, especially having just met the woman. "Not that I could've stopped you, of course. But, I would've worried all night."

Yeah, I wasn't making it any less weird. I cleared my throat and awkwardly gestured toward the bedrooms. "So, uh, want to pick which room is yours?"

Mae smirked and peeked inside the closest room. Well, at least my foot-in-mouth situation hadn't made her grab her bag and run for the nearest exit.

CHAPTER 5

Mae Thompson
December 23, 4:30 PM
48.5 Hours Until Christmas Dinner

I couldn't remember the last time a shower felt so good. It had a rain shower head which felt amazing against my overstressed body, and I wished I could stand there for the rest of the night, but I knew Lon was waiting for me to finish so we could venture downstairs to the bar. I'd told him he could go down without me, and I'd meet him there, but he shrugged the idea away and said he'd relax until I was ready.

The scent of his body wash lingered in the air, and I breathed it in, enjoying it like the total creep I was. Damn, it had apparently been far too long since a man had been in my life if the hint of him made my stomach tingle with desire. But, it wasn't simply his clean-cut handsome looks that appealed to me. He kept me on my toes and kept surprising me with his kindness and generosity. I wanted to peel back his layers and find out exactly how wrong my initial impression of him was.

I quickly finished rinsing the conditioner out of my hair and considered shaving my legs– among other areas– with the thought of Lon discovering my freshly smooth skin. I forced my brain to stop. Hadn't I *just* told him I wouldn't get in bed with him?

I scrubbed harder at my hair and decided to skip shaving. I never felt the need to be totally smooth to sleep with someone, but this felt like putting a physical reminder to keep things strictly friendly with Lon.

I tried my best to not focus on the memory of Lon walking from the bathroom, white towel wrapped low on his hips, defined muscles on display as he grinned at me with a shrug. "I don't like getting changed in the bathroom after I shower because I never feel like I can get dry enough. Sorry about that," he said as my eyes tried to look anywhere but his mostly-naked self.

"I get it," I squeaked out, staring intensely at my phone so I wouldn't count the number of water droplets going down his abs. "I totally hate an unwanted wet feeling."

He snickered, and right before he closed his bedroom door, he poked his head back. "I want you to know how much restraint it took to not make a 'wet' comment back at you, so you're welcome."

I shoved those dangerous thoughts away and focused on the phone call I had with my mom while waiting for my turn in the bathroom. She wasn't thrilled the storm ruined my travel plans, but she was thankful I'd made it safely to a hotel.

She seemed *incredibly* interested when I mentioned I planned to hang out with a man from my flight since we were staying in the same hotel. I decided she didn't need to know I was sharing a hotel *room* with said man. I was in my mid-twenties, I deserved a few guilt-free secrets of my own.

Talking to her had brought back my guilt about having

not told her about my lack of job situation in full force. St. Louis wasn't a small city per se, but it wasn't full of publishers needing editors like Chicago or New York was. And since all of us suddenly needed jobs, I would be fighting some tough competition to find a new one.

No. There was no reason to focus on that right now. Not when I had a hot as sin man sitting out there waiting to get drunk with me. There was absolutely nothing I could do about being unemployed or being stuck in Detroit, so I might as well let myself have a good time. I quickly finished getting the last of the soap off me and turned off the water.

After drying off, I slipped into clean underwear and a bra. I'd debated what outfit to wear since a big part of me wanted to slip on a pair of sweatpants and slippers, but the bar seemed nicer than that. Granted, I personally thought all fashion rules ought to be tossed out the window when dealing with a blizzard. Since I thought I'd be home doing laundry by now, my options were limited, but I decided on a pair of relaxed jeans, a simple black tank top, and for the hell of it, a festive Christmas sweater my Grandma gave me. It might've been over the top and cheesy, but I figured everyone could use some extra Christmas spirit.

I left the bathroom to drop off my dirty clothes in my room and found Lon sprawled out on the couch in the living room with his laptop on his chest. "Are you working on Christmas Eve Eve during a blizzard? It's time to relax and make this shitty day better." At least he ditched the suit for a pair of jeans and a cozy gray henley.

He looked up at me, and I nearly tripped over my feet when I noticed the pair of dark-rimmed glasses that emphasized his deep brown eyes even more. "Nice sweater. Did an elf knit it for you?" He sat up and closed his laptop. "For the record, I wasn't working. I was checking the weather radar, and it's looking pretty nasty."

I fingered the edge of my colorful festive cardigan. "Hey

man, this thing is older than you and handmade by my Grandma. It's a classic."

He smirked and stood up with a stretch, exposing a sliver of his toned stomach. "Whatever you say, Mrs. Claus."

I rolled my eyes and continued to my room to put away my clothing. "Better Mrs. Claus then a grinch like you."

“A grinch? I’m a regular ol’ Buddy the Elf. Just you wait.” His lips twitched like he was trying his best to not start laughing. “I might need a drink or two to get there.”

I grinned, already feeling more at ease with Lon. I grabbed my purse and turned to face him. “Well, then. Let’s get your inner elf ready to party. Ready to go to the bar?"

"You have no idea." He shocked me by holding the door open for me like a gentleman. "After you."

CHAPTER 6

Alonzo Davis
December 23, 6:00 PM
47 Hours Until Christmas Dinner

We managed to snag two spots at the bar despite many other hotel patrons taking their travel grief out on a few drinks. The bartender stopped in front of us when he noticed my empty glass. "Need a refill?"

I glanced at Mae as she downed the rest of her drink, and I nodded. "Yeah, I'll have another negroni. Mae, what do you want?"

She wiped her mouth with a napkin and leaned forward so she could better look at the bottles lining the back of the bar. "Can I have a rye Manhattan, please? Oh, and two glasses of water?" Mae turned my way. "We should probably also order food. I totally forgot to eat lunch with all the blizzard shit going on."

I chuckled and studied my unexpected companion. Her hideous sweater was starting to grow on me because she looked so damn cheerful in it despite our current circumstances. "Don't tell me two drinks gets you drunk."

She'd been spinning side to side on the stool and stopped to raise a dark brow at me. "I'm not drunk. But I plan to drink more, hence the need for food." The bartender placed the waters in front of us, and Mae immediately grabbed one and took a long swallow. She let out a throaty hum and smiled. "Don't you love how refreshing ice water is?"

Jesus, she needed to stop making those appreciative sounds every time she tasted something she liked. I cleared my throat and chugged half of my water. "We definitely need food. Order whatever you want."

She eyed me, her straw resting against her lips for a moment before saying, "You do know you're not paying for me. You're already taking care of the room, so I'm not going to let you pay for this."

I figured there was zero point in arguing with her at the moment, so I waved her words away and said, "Whatever you say." Our cocktails appeared and I swapped mine out for the water I'd been holding. "So, do you live in St. Louis, or are you only there for Christmas?"

"Born and raised and still living there," she said before taking a sip of her drink. "I went to grad school in Chicago but decided to move back home when I finished." She paused, tapping her fingers on the bar along to the soft Christmas music. "If I can't find a new job soon, I might have to look into moving back there. Chicago has way more publishing opportunities than St. Louis. Which sucks. I'd rather not leave my friends and family."

"If St. Louis doesn't have the opportunities you need, why not make them yourself? Start your own publishing company."

She snorted and dipped her face, allowing her hair to cover it from view. "I wish. But that takes start-up money and knowledge of how to run a business. I might be a damn good editor, but I don't know shit about the business side of it all."

"Well, how about—" My words trailed off as I realized she was shrinking on her stool in front of me, her shoulders slumped in a protective stance. Note to self, lay off on the job ideas for now. I cleared my throat and changed the subject with absolutely no finesse at all. "So were you in New York for business or for fun?"

She seemed immediately relieved. "I was visiting friends who moved out there several years ago. It was my first time seeing all the holiday lights and decorations." She sipped her cocktail before leaning her elbow on the bar and resting her chin on her hand. "What about you? Why're you headed to St. Louis?"

I forced myself not to down the rest of my drink to avoid speaking and instead sighed deeply. "I also grew up in St. Louis but moved away for college and only come back when necessary."

"You don't like it there? What a shame, I love the city."

I didn't truly dislike St. Louis. I hadn't spent enough time there as an adult to form a genuine opinion of it as a city. I just absolutely did *not* like my father, so I chose to avoid him as much as possible, but I didn't want to blurt out to a stranger.

Weirdly enough, Mae didn't actually feel like a stranger anymore.

"Uh, I have a rather…volatile relationship with my dad. We're better off not being around each other."

"Oh," she said quietly, and slowly reached out her hand to gently rest it over mine. I hadn't noticed it was in a tight fist until her touch calmed my nerves and allowed me to relax my grip. "You don't have to talk about it if you don't want to, but if you dislike him so much, why go at all?"

"Because, believe it or not, I'm a big ol' mama's boy," I said with a wry chuckle. "And when she asks me to fly home for Christmas, I can't say no."

"That's pretty adorable, and I would've never guessed that based on how atrocious you were during the flight."

My mouth fell open. *Atrocious*? I'd been in a sour mood, but surely I wasn't *that* bad. I should've had a first-class seat, but there was a glitch, and I wound up in coach. I'd been irritated, plus the airport was a shitshow with holiday traffic. I pinched the bridge of my nose and sagged my shoulders. "Yeah, alright, I was a dick, and I'm sorry."

She shrugged. "We all have our own shit. You can fix it by ordering pesto chicken flatbread, though."

"I see your flatbread and raise you a plate of chicken wings, too."

"You got yourself a deal."

CHAPTER 7

Mae Thompson
December 23, 9:30 PM
43.5 Hours Until Christmas Dinner

"So, what did your mom say about the whole being stuck in Detroit thing, because lemme tell you, my mom seemed totally anxious," I said before shoving a mozzarella stick in my mouth. We were starving after a long ass day of travel and ordered a few other snacks as we kept drinking. I chewed and then added, "Well, once she even knew a massive storm was happening. I love my mom, but when she's focused on something like making enough Christmas cookies to feed the entire city, she's oblivious to the world around her."

"Oh, shit," Lon breathed out, suddenly sitting so his spine was perfectly straight. "I forgot to tell my mom about being stuck here. Oh my God."

"I mean, surely she's well aware of the situation if she

watches the news or, you know, looks outside. Though, maybe she doesn't if she's anything like my mom."

"I'm going to call her real fast. Do we want another round down here or get a bottle of wine to bring up to our room?"

Our room. For some reason, the sound of that made me shiver in pleasure. "I'm fine either way," I said as a giant yawn took over. "Jeeze, sorry. Guess I'm more tired than I expected."

"It's been an overwhelming day, so it makes sense." He hopped off the stool and let his hand linger on my shoulder slightly longer than necessary before he headed to the lobby to make the phone call. As I finished the last little bit of my drink, I thought about how weird this day ended up being. How had this man gone from the obnoxious asshole on the plane to some sort of friend who totally saved my ass by letting me share the suite with him?

An incredibly sexy friend with abs I wouldn't mind licking.

The longer we sat next to each other, talking and laughing over the most random things, the more I liked him. Obviously, he was attractive with his inky black hair, dark eyes, and toned body, but that was easy to ignore when I thought he was a jerk.

Now I felt compelled to find reasons to touch him as much as possible. I'd never been a casual hook-up sort of person, but the idea was beyond appealing right now. I was newly jobless, he was stressed out about having to see his dad, and we were stuck in this hotel together. Why shouldn't we help each other relax and forget about the shit surrounding us? I bet if I suggested a no-strings-attached boning, he'd be down. Not to toot my own horn, but I was a total babe, and he seemed to enjoy spending time with me.

Those thoughts still danced in my mind as Lon returned to the bar and sat down. "Everything good with your mom?"

"Yeah, she said she understood there wasn't anything I

could do about the weather, and was happy I found somewhere safe and warm to wait it out."

I nodded, suddenly feeling shy around him. What if he wasn't into my new plan to bang out our stress? Would it make sharing the suite with him painfully awkward? We were both adults, and it wasn't like I wanted to propose marriage or anything. I simply wanted someone to make me feel good.

I cleared my throat and lowered my voice to say, "So, I've been thinking. And I'm sure I'm going about this all wrong because I've seriously never done this before, but I feel like we're getting along well, right?" I glanced up at him, reminding myself I should probably make eye contact with the person I was propositioning sex from. He nodded, clearly curious where I was going with my rambling. "Cool, me too. I think you're a handsome guy, and I think you think I'm at least fairly attractive—"

"I think you're more than *fairly* attractive, but go on."

"Ah, right. Good to know. But alright. As I was saying, we both think the other's attractive, and like, we're stuck here, which sucks and, I don't know, I thought we could try to make things a bit better?"

I could tell he was trying his best not to laugh, which wasn't exactly doing my ego any favors, so maybe I'd read the entire situation wrong. Fuck. How would I backtrack out of this and save face? "Ahhh, yeah. How about that next drink?"

He frowned, leaning back on his stool to examine me. "Wait, what? I mean, yeah, I'll happily get us another, but I think you should finish the train of thought we were riding."

Oh my God, he was going to make me say it and then reject me, wasn't he? My face flushed warm yet again, and I suddenly wanted to be back in my room with the door locked and safely under the covers. I grabbed my purse and started to stand, muttering, "Actually, I don't think I want another drink." I gestured toward the exit and started to stand.

He reached out and grabbed my arm lightly to halt my movements. I paused but didn't look at him. He let go, sliding his hand up my arm, trailing it slowly to my shoulder until reaching my chin so he could tilt my head to look me in the eye.

"If you want to go back upstairs and call it a night, obviously that's fine, and I won't stop you. But..." he paused, and my heart stuttered as his dark gaze bored into me. "I think you should ask me the question because if it's what I think it is, the answer is yes."

I swallowed hard, replaying his words to make sure I heard him correctly. I could do this. I was an independent grown woman with decent sexual experience. I could tell a man I wanted him to sex me up. I could.

I simply had to open my mouth and do it.

"You're not going to make this easy on me, are you?" I asked softly.

His cocky grin turned into a serious smolder as he gently tucked a loose strand of hair behind my ear. "If anything happens between us, I want it to be because *you* initiated it and went into it with a clear mind. You're tired—"

"I'm not that tired," I interrupted, realizing how electric I felt.

"You're stressed—"

"So are you."

"And I'm not entirely sure what level of sober you are."

I paused and considered. I felt a little tipsy, but just enough for my shoulders to relax and make me brave enough to ask for what I wanted from him. Or at least nearly brave enough.

"I have a nice little buzz going, so I wouldn't operate any heavy machinery, you know, in case any is lying around this hotel. But, I'm making clear and sound choices right now."

A slow grin spread across his face, and he turned toward the bar to motion for the bartender to come over when he had a chance. "I'd like our check, please," he said once the bartender stood in front of us. Lon glanced at me for a moment and then added, "And is it possible for a chilled bottle of champagne we could bring up to our room?"

I opened my mouth to fight him about paying the bill I said I wanted to split, but he handed his card to the bartender before I could. I shut my mouth and sank back into my chair. If he wanted to pay, who was I to stop him?

"Of course. Let me get that for you and two glasses, and I'll be right back with your check."

"Champagne? How fancy," I said, excitement bubbling inside me.

"Well, it *is* Christmastime, after all. We might as well celebrate."

CHAPTER 8

Alonzo Davis
December 23, 10:00 PM
43 Hours Until Christmas Dinner

I held the door open for her and then walked to the couch to place the bottle and glasses on the coffee table. If she was uncomfortable, I wasn't interested in anything physical going down between us tonight, so I turned toward her and crossed my arms. "I want to clarify nothing will happen here unless you want it to."

"I want it to," she said quickly, taking a few steps toward me. "I've never had a one-night stand before," she said softly. "I'm kind of out of my depth here."

"Never? Not even during wild college years?"

"I had the same boyfriend for a chunk of college, so not so much. We broke up a few months after I went to grad school in Chicago. What about you? Is this your usual sort of thing? Not that you need to give me your entire sexual history or anything, but some basic information might be nice."

"Would you believe I've never actually slept with someone who hadn't at least been a planned date?" I stretched my legs, toeing off one shoe and then the other. I hated wearing shoes unnecessarily. "Before we fully explore my dating and sex history, would you like a glass of champagne?"

"Yeah, that sounds great." She bit her lip and untwined her feet to stand. "Actually, I'm going to change into lounge clothes. I don't normally chill in jeans and whatnot."

"Good idea. I'll change too, and we'll meet back for a drink." I pushed off the couch and held my hand out to her to help her to her feet. I must've misjudged my strength and how quickly she planned to jump because I pulled her hard enough that she stumbled into me. Her forehead nearly smacked my chin, and her hand landed heavily on my chest. I let out a small grunt upon impact and immediately started laughing. "I'm *so* sorry. This didn't go according to plan at all."

Her fingers gripped my shirt as if she was still worried about losing her balance and blinked up at me. "What the hell just happened?"

"Uh, I attempted to be suave and failed," I said, taking a small step back before I was tempted to wrap my arms around her waist and pull her tighter against me.

"I hope your moves in the bedroom are better than that little show, or else I might change my mind about sleeping with you later," she said, letting go of me and turning to walk towards her room. Before going through the doorway, she shot me a cheeky grin and winked, and immediately my jeans felt uncomfortably tight. Dear God, I wanted to follow behind her and help her strip down until she had nothing on, but I knew taking it slow and spending more time together was the best option here.

Patience. I quickly adjusted myself in my jeans before heading to my room to change into a pair of navy flannel pajama pants and a white undershirt. I glanced in the mirror to make sure I wasn't a total mess and returned to the living room, where Mae was already lounging on the couch. Her long, wavy hair was back to being piled up on top of her head, and my fingers itched to reach forward, and let her hair flow like it had been down at the bar. She wore oversized sweatpants and a tank top that emphasized her trim waist. I raised my eyebrows and asked, "Won't you get chilly in a tank top?"

She smiled and reached down to grab a throw blanket she must've brought from her room. "I like being able to wrap up in a fluffy blanket while watching TV, so I wear a lot of tanks even in the winter." She shrugged and said, "Also my clean clothing leftover from vacation is sort of lacking, to be totally honest."

Ah, right. She was ending a trip, whereas I was starting one. "Well, if you need a clean t-shirt to wear or something, let me know. I have a whole suitcase of clean clothes and can do laundry at my parents' house."

She watched me as I moved to the table to open the bottle and pour each of us a glass. "It's so weird seeing you in PJ pants when you wore a suit on a plane this morning. Who does that unless you're headed straight to a business meeting and don't have time to change?"

I chuckled, handing her the drink before sitting back on the couch. "Normally, I'm flying to or from a meeting, so I guess I'm used to it? Back in the day, people did dress up to travel."

"Yeah, well, those people didn't have to take their shoes off and remove outer layers to go through security. I like the ease of yoga pants and a comfy top compared to looking stylish on a plane."

"Fair point. It's also easier for me to wear the suit instead of trying to pack it in a way that won't wrinkle it. I didn't feel like bringing my garment bag and needed a suit for

Christmas Mass." My mom always wanted us to go to church as a family over the holidays, and I didn't have it in me to tell her no.

She took a long sip of her champagne and closed her eyes as the bubbles hit her tongue. "This is tasty. Thank you for getting it."

"Of course." With each minute ticking by, I was more than happy to do whatever I could to see Mae relax and smile. Initially, I offered to let her stay with me out of guilt, but now I couldn't imagine spending this time with anyone else. Or worse, alone. "Like I said before, money isn't an issue for me, and I hope that doesn't come across as like a rich asshole thing to say, but it's one aspect of my life I have figured out. I don't want you to not enjoy yourself because money's tight at the moment."

"Even though letting someone help me out makes me incredibly uncomfortable… I appreciate it." She let out a sigh. "I am *not* looking forward to admitting to my family the press shut down. I know I'll find another job, but I might not be able to be picky." Mae rolled her eyes before adding, "Cue yet another conversation from my parents about how I should've picked a more lucrative major and blah blah blah."

I made a face because I was familiar with that type of conversation through the years. "I was a math major with an actuary minor, so my parents were fine with my career plans. It was all my extracurricular activities in high school my dad gave me shit about." I deepened my voice to imitate my dad and said, "Son, why aren't you trying out for the football team? No one cares about you being on the chess team. Stop dicking around with the other robot dorks and hit the gym."

"He made fun of you for being smart and enjoying groups that could lead to things like engineering or computer science? Why? My dad would've been ecstatic if I'd been more into the STEM classes."

I ran my fingers through my hair, trying to decide how

much I wanted to get into my relationship with my dad when we should be having fun. "My dad was the star quarterback, homecoming king type, and he never understood how his only son, regardless of all his pushing, had zero interest in being an athlete and wanted to play D&D with his friends." I shrugged my shoulders and took a gulp of my drink before leaning forward and grabbing the bottle to top us both off.

She held her glass out to me to make filling it easier and gave a little snort of disbelief. "I'm sorry, but has your father *seen* your body? You're obviously working those muscles somehow." She scrunched her face up in an adorable way and added, "Sorry that was such a weird thing to say. I totally didn't mean to suggest your dad should check out your abs or anything. I keep making this worse."

I grinned and turned on the couch to face her. "Ah, so you *were* checking me out earlier."

"Uh, dude, you were walking around in only a towel. Of course I was."

"And I take it you liked what you saw?"

Mae's cheeks flushed an adorable shade of pink I was already addicted to causing. She shifted on the couch and took a small sip of her glass. Her movements made my eyes focus on her chest, bringing attention to her tight, hard nipples under her thin tank top. God, I itched to lean over and lick them.

I crossed my legs to conceal my growing hard-on since these pants weren't going to hide anything, but I wanted to kiss her and let my hands roam all over her body as she squirmed under me. I glanced at her and noticed her eyes staring at my crotch. I guess I wasn't doing a great job of hiding my situation.

CHAPTER 9

Mae Thompson
December 23, 11:00 PM
42 Hours until Christmas Dinner

Oh my God, he had an erection. He was sitting there, less than a foot away, and his dick was hard. He was trying to be discreet, but nothing could hide what was going on below those well-worn flannel pants. Who needed gray sweatpants when this seemingly well-endowed man had navy plaid PJs?

Or maybe I was tipsy and horny. That was probably it.

I leaned forward to place my glass on the table and scooted closer to Lon. I cleared my throat to finally answer his question from before. "Yes. I definitely liked what I saw. And I like what I see now." I let my fingers trail up from his knee to about mid-thigh. "Is it okay for me to touch you like this?"

He nodded and leaned deeper into the couch, sliding his hips forward to give me more room to explore. "I'd never stop you from touching me," he hissed out. "Do what you want to me. You're in control."

The power of his words tingled through me, making me all the more excited. His white undershirt barely hid any of his muscle definition, waiting for me to touch skin to skin. I bit my lower lip, not entirely sure what to do next.

"Would you be okay removing your shirt?" I asked, my voice not sounding as confident as I'd hoped.

Without responding, he grabbed the hem of his shirt and ripped it over his head, tossing it to the ground. He then looked at me as if waiting for my next request. I didn't want to disappoint him, so I moved toward him as much as possible until our legs touched. But it wasn't close enough. I grabbed his shoulders to anchor myself and swung my right leg over his, making sure to not accidentally knee him or topple over him.

Lon's hands immediately went to my waist and gripped me tightly. "Well, hello," He breathed out, his eyes shining with anticipation. His fingers gently slid up and down my back as if wanting to touch me everywhere but was waiting for my consent. Like he said before, I was the one with the power here. I was in control of this situation.

And I loved it.

I took in every firm muscle from his abs to his pecs to his impressively broad shoulders. "How the hell does an actuary look like this?"

He chuckled and shrugged. "I ride my bicycle to the office most days, and one of my buddies got me into weight lifting with him a few years back. Also, I like using my time efficiently, so I meal-prep for the week on Sundays. Which meant lots of lean proteins and veggies since they keep well."

"Ah, so the key to being fit and thin is liking boring food, got it," I said, amusement coloring my voice.

His grin only grew. "Seems like it. But I'll have you know,

I'm pretty solid at cooking. I use a ton of seasoning. No bland tasting food in my home."

"Oh, thank God, because that would be a shame." I settled my ass more firmly on his legs, purposefully leaving space between his dick and me for now. We hadn't even kissed, so grinding up on him seemed a bit much.

"So, are we going to just chat about food with you on my lap, or did you want to, I don't know, kiss me?"

"I'm rather enjoying this view at the moment." In actuality I was trying to gather my courage to make the next move, which was ridiculous since he obviously wanted me. I slid my hands down his shoulders to his hard chest, and I loved how the muscles moved under my touch. He let out a low puff of air as if even that simple touch pleased him.

"What do you think about me losing my shirt, too?"

"I'd say about damn time."

I smiled and quickly removed my tank top. I only had on a light pink lace bralette under it. I wasn't blessed with large breasts like some women, and when I was younger, I felt self-conscious. He stared at my chest with such apparent hunger that I forgot why I'd ever felt less than.

"Dear Lord, I want to taste these," he said, his hand moving up my side to cup my right breast. His thumb gently grazed my nipple, and I hummed as the pleasure seemed to shoot through me. A wolfish grin appeared as he studied me for a moment before adding more pressure to my nipple. I wiggled on his lap, wishing his thumb was moving against my clit in the same way. "Do you know how sexy it is watching you like this?" he asked, his deep voice thick with want.

I couldn't even answer. The sensation of him playing with my breasts was only making me needier. I wanted *more*. So, instead, I grabbed his face and desperately pressed my mouth to his. Immediately his other hand went to the back of my neck to hold me to him as he bit my lower lip for me to open to him. It was as if I couldn't kiss him fast enough or deep enough. I didn't care I was so out of my mind with want, that this was probably not my best work, and the way Lon was reacting, I didn't think he cared, either.

My tongue ran against his lips, hoping he'd open his mouth for me. He did, and his tongue immediately sought my own as they moved against each other in a push and pull of dominance. He let out a low moan as my fingers slid into his now utterly unruly thick hair. I tugged gently, and his moan turned into a growl. Oh, I liked that reaction a lot.

He pulled back and rested his forehead against mine, both of us panting for breath. "You're killing me," he muttered, his eyes still closed as if trying to calm himself. But I didn't want him calm, I wanted him wild with lust.

"I think it's time for your pants to come off," I said, letting my fingers trail down his stomach to the drawstring at his waist. "What do you think?"

Suddenly, he surged to his feet, picking me up effortlessly so my legs wrapped around him. I gasped, shocked at his movements, and threw my arms around his neck to hold on tight. "What are you doing?" I squeaked out.

"Well, I can't take my pants off sitting down when you're on my lap, can I?" He then turned and stalked to his bedroom, kicking the door open like a man on a mission.

Before I knew it, my back was pressed against his bed, and he let go of me to straighten once more to roughly tug at his drawstring.

"You're sure you want me to take these off, Mae?" he asked, his thumbs tucked into the waistband, preparing to yank them down.

I nodded and said, "Yes. Yes, I do."

"I'm not wearing boxers, so once these are off, that's it. I'll be buck ass naked." He raised his brows, waiting for me to respond.

My mouth suddenly felt dry at the thought of seeing this

beautiful man in all his glory. The idea was a little scary but more exciting than anything. "Do it."

As soon as the words left my mouth, his pants were down around his ankles, and he kicked them away. I thought he'd quickly hop onto the bed to join me, but instead, he stood there and ran a hand over his mouth. "And you're sure you want to do this?"

I propped myself up with my elbows and took all of him in from his amazing arms, toned stomach, strong legs, and his proud, thick erection. It was ready and waiting, and looking at it sent a shiver down my spine all the way to my pussy.

"Yes. Very much so. But I don't like how many clothes I still have on."

He stepped forward until he stood at the end of the bed. "I'm more than happy to help fix that."

CHAPTER 10

Alonzo Davis
December 23, 11:30 PM
41.5 Hours Until Christmas Dinner

The way Mae stared at me only made me even more turned on which I hadn't known was possible. Her cheeks were flushed, and her chest rose and fell quickly as she bit her lip and watched me get on the bed and move over towards her.

"Well?" I asked since she hadn't said yes or no to me helping her undress. "Can we take these sweats off?" My hands slid up her legs, gently caressing her thighs until I reached her waistband. She asked permission to remove my pants, and I had to do the same for her. Just because I was completely naked didn't mean she was ready to be.

But, dear lord, I hoped she was.

"Yes," she breathed out, lifting her hips and giving me the permission I desperately wanted. I leaned down, letting my lips graze against her soft stomach, peppering kisses across her skin. I studied her face to see how she'd react, but her eyes were squeezed shut as if concentrating hard.

My teeth gently nipped slightly above her hip, and her entire body seemed to shake. "Was that a good reaction or bad?"

"Good. Very good."

I grinned against her pale, warm skin and slipped my fingers under the band of her sweatpants. I tugged the baggy pants down, letting inch after inch of skin become exposed, as I drank in the sight of her. Finally, slowly, her pants were to her ankles, and I tossed them aside. I sat back and studied her for a moment. She wore a pair of black boy short style underwear with a lace edge, and I couldn't wait to see how good her ass looked in them.

"Wow."

"Wow…what?" She asked, squirming under the intensity of my stare.

"You're amazing. I obviously already knew you're hot, but wow." Before I could think, I leaned back down and kissed her inner leg, making my way up to the apex of her thighs. Like the jerk I am, I moved to the top of her panties and pressed a kiss there, avoiding where I knew she wanted me. I'd happily go down on her and planned to if she wanted it, but all in good time.

"Alonzo," she hissed out, startling me with my full name for the first time since we swapped suitcases.

I lifted my lips from her skin to peer at her. "Am I in trouble?"

"You will be if you keep being such a damn tease!"

I chuckled against her skin before moving up her body so I could run my tongue over a lace-covered nipple, enjoying the sound of her breath catching in her throat. She was so responsive to my touch, which made me want to explore her all the more.

“I think it’s time to remove this,” I said between licking and sucking, toying with the strap of her bra.

“Yes,” she said, nodding enthusiastically in agreement. I started to reach behind her to unhook it, but she pushed my hand away to sit up. “There aren’t any hooks, so I have to—” She paused and began pulling it off over her head. With a sigh of relief, she tossed it toward the other clothes. “That’s better.”

Mae’s small but perky tits looked so damn inviting that I couldn’t stop myself from dipping my head back to them, focusing on her left nipple while my hand gently squeezed and kneaded at her right breast. She arched her back and grabbed my hair, holding me to her, silently begging me to keep grazing her sensitive skin with my teeth.

As my mouth worked her, my hand stroked down her stomach, making its way back to her underwear. I lifted my head long enough to ask, “What about these? Do these stay on?”

She opened her eyes to look where my hand sat and bit her lower lip for a moment. I moved my hand up some to not pressure her. A sly smile spread across her face, and she let her hands drift down her torso until they reached mine, guiding it to the last remaining bit of material between us. She hooked her fingers under the underwear band and tugged them down, giving me her answer. I groaned as she became fully exposed to me, and I was struck by the undeniable need to taste her immediately.

I kissed my way back down her stomach until I reached her pelvis again. She let out a huff of frustration and covered her face with her hand. “I swear to God, if you’re only going to tease me, I’m getting out of this bed and putting my clothes back on.”

I bit her inner thigh gently before grabbing her legs, spreading them open so I could better fit my torso between them. "Not teasing. I'm actually quite serious about going down on you right now."

She adjusted her legs, opening herself to me even more, giving me better access. "Oh my God, yes."

I hooked her legs over my shoulder and simply took her in for a few moments until she started squirming under my gaze. "You don't need to memorize every single detail down there," she muttered uncomfortably. She was wrong, though, because I needed to put this to memory in case this was the only time I was lucky enough to have her.

Instead of answering, I licked and nibbled my way up her thigh until her pussy was right there, ready for me to feast. I tightened my hold on her hips and tilted her towards me to better the angle. My tongue explored her folds as I took in the earthy smell of her arousal. If it were possible, I felt myself become harder and ached for her to touch me. But her coming first was far more important than my own needs. My tongue moved to her clit and circled around the sensitive nub to see what sort of movement she enjoyed the best.

"Don't be scared to tell me what you like. I want you to feel good," I growled, barely lifting my head from her before sucking on her clit, adding more pressure.

"Holy shit, *that* felt amazing," she breathed out, her hand yet again weaving its way into my hair to hold onto me.

I continued sucking and licking for a few moments before moving my pointer finger to her core. Oh, dear lord, she was so wet that my cock twitched, wanting its turn. Instead, I pressed my finger in, moving it slowly in and out to see how her body reacted to it. She let out a low moan as I fucked her with my finger, increasing the speed of my thrusts. "How's that," I asked, lifting my head enough to see her face. Her eyes were clenched shut, her mouth wide open. "You're so damn wet for me, Mae. I can't fucking stand it."

Her hips moved with each in and out motion of my finger, so as I bent my head back to lick her, I added another finger and sped up my movements. "Oh my God," she squeaked out. "I'm so close…"

Thank God, because I was wound so tight from watching her that I felt I might embarrass myself by losing control. And I couldn't have that. Not yet, at least. I needed to make her come, and quickly.

As I pressed my fingers back in, I bent them and began tapping against her G-spot while increasing my tongue on her clit. A sound like a muted scream seemed to catch in Mae's throat, and her inner walls suddenly gripped my fingers even harder. A few moments later, her entire body went limp as I gave her a few slow licks before gently removing my fingers.

"I think I'm dead," she panted, pushing her now loose hair from her face.

"Was it at least a good death?" I pressed a few kisses on her hip bone before sliding my way back up to be next to her on the bed.

"The best."

CHAPTER 11

Mae Thompson
December 24 12:00 AM
41 Hours Until Christmas Dinner

I was still trying to catch my breath when Lon laid down beside me and wrapped his arms around my waist, pulling me to him. His erection pressed against my hip, but he seemed more focused on me than on his needs. I turned to face him better and wrapped my arms around his neck, pulling him to me to give him a deep kiss.

I sighed happily, feeling more relaxed than I had in days, and said, "You're damn good at that."

He chuckled, then leaned over to kiss my neck. "You deserve to feel good."

I skated my hand down his back until I could grab his muscular butt. "So do you, you know."

He cocked a brow at me and smiled. "Oh? Do I?"

"I think you've proved you do."

I moved my hand to tease his cock, gently trailing my

fingers from the head down to his base and back up again. Two could play the game he so enjoyed earlier.

"You're an evil woman," he groaned before wrapping his hand around my fingers and his cock, making me squeeze him. We stroked him a few times together until I decided I'd had enough of that.

I rolled over so I could straddle him. "Do you have any condoms?" I hadn't thought to bring any with me on vacation because hooking up with a hot stranger hadn't been on my to-do list.

"I have no idea, actually. When I packed to see my parents I wasn't exactly thinking about sex."

I accidentally snorted at that. "I'm… flattered? That was nearly romantic." He gently smacked my hip to signal me to get off him so he could check.

His muscles flexed in the most delicious way when he hurried over to his desk. "Come on…" he muttered as he dug through the bag.

"Even if you do find a lonely little condom—"

"Perfectly average-sized condom, thank you very much," he interrupted, briefly pausing his search.

"Sorry, I didn't mean to offend your…*condoms*…but if it isn't one you purposefully packed in there recently, I'm not comfortable using it anyway. Who knows how long it's been in there or if your nail clippers got a little too close to it."

He looked up and pushed his hair away from his face. "Good point." He put the bag down and turned to me, looking apologetic. "I don't have anything. What about in your room?"

I bit my lip and shook my head. "Negative. Like I said before, I don't do the random hookup thing, so it didn't occur to me to pack some *just in case*."

"Damnit, clearly neither one of us has enough sex, or else packing condoms wouldn't have even been a question."

I chuckled at that because he wasn't wrong, and it was my

damn luck that the one time in far too long that sex was even on the table, I wasn't prepared for it. My chuckles quickly turned into full-body belly laughter until Lon collapsed on the bed with me.

I wiped a little tear of laughter away with the back of my hand and tried my best to catch my breath. Laughing that hard after how incredibly crappy the last few days had been felt nearly as good and cathartic as the orgasm he gave me earlier. Nearly.

"We're a little pathetic," I said, crawling over to where he sat on the bed, wrapping my arms around him, so my chest was pressed to his back.

"A bit, but hey, it's not over yet. This is a nice hotel. Surely they have things at the front desk, right?"

Hope blossomed in me. "Oh my God, you're right. You're a genius!" I leaned around and pressed a kiss to his cheek.

"Well, not to brag, but I was in Gifted and Talented back in the day so basically that's true." He winked at me and then reached for the phone on the bedside table. He pressed the number for the front desk and waited a few seconds for them to pick up.

"Yes, hello, this is Alonzo Davis in room 1532. I'm sorry to bother you so late, but I wanted to see if the front desk had personal items we might have failed to pack? Like condoms?"

I grabbed one of his pillows to shove my face in because this situation had me far out of my comfort zone, and there was a significant chance of awkward giggling.

He was quiet for a moment but nodded at whatever was being said on the other side. "Got it. Yes. The multi-pack would be great. Uh-huh..." He glanced at me and shot me a cocky grin, and all I could do was roll my eyes at him. "Oh, anything else? Let me ask."

He covered the mouthpiece with his hand and asked, "Is

there anything else we need? I was thinking about a bottle of red wine, if they have any?"

"I could totally go for some snacks, actually. Like chips or something?"

He gave me a thumbs up and returned to the person on the phone. "Can we order a bottle of red wine and several bags of assorted chips? Anything you have is fine."

"And I want something sweet. Chocolate preferably."

He nodded, all business and added, "And a few types of chocolate?" He looked at me with a brow raised as if to ask if there was anything else. I shook my head, pleased he was going along with all of this. "Yeah, that's all. Charge it to the room, yeah. I'm happy to come down there to get it if you all are too busy. Oh, well, that sounds great then. See you soon." He hung up the phone and turned to me. Before I even knew what was happening, I was flat on my back with his large, still incredibly naked form on top of me.

"You looked so sexy sitting here while I was on the phone." He peppered kisses all over my skin as he talked until I grabbed his face and made him look at me.

"Thank you for ordering all of that. I'm having a fantastic time with you tonight."

His grin returned, and he leaned down to finally kiss my lips, lingering for a few moments. "You've made this bad day so much better. And it's not even over yet."

CHAPTER 12

Alonzo Davis
December 24, 12:30 AM
40.5 Hours Until Christmas Dinner

I got off the bed and stretched my back before grabbing my boxer briefs to put on. On the plus side, trying to find a condom and needing to call the front desk calmed my dick down. I glanced at Mae, currently sprawled across the bed, looking comfortable, and I couldn't help my smile at the sight. I liked her being there, in my bed, naked. That felt right, even if just for now.

But, God, part of me didn't want it to be only now, and that realization hit me like a ton of bricks as I watched her lean over and grab the remote to turn on the TV.

I hadn't wanted more with someone in a long time, but this was only supposed to be a no strings attached thing. We lived in two vastly different places and hadn't even known each other for twenty-four hours. Who the hell started falling for someone the day they met? But she made me constantly laugh and I found myself so utterly relaxed in her presence. I was *happy* and truthfully? I wasn't sure the last time I'd felt that way.

I calculated risk levels for my job. Yet here I was, beginning to want something with a woman, where all the facts of our situation pointed towards, at best, an amicable parting or, at worst, utter heartbreak.

I hadn't even had sex with Mae, and my brain was already trying to find a way to make us make sense together. This was bad.

"Oh," she gasped, drawing my focus back to her. She'd pulled the blankets up so I could only see the tops of her breasts as she leaned against a mountain of pillows. "I found *It's a Wonderful Life* on. I love this movie. I grew up watching this with my parents and siblings, all of us piled on the couches in the living room with bowls of popcorn and far more cookies than we'd ever need. Hot chocolate for all of us—my parents would spike theirs with Baileys or peppermint schnapps." She let out a sigh that, while content, seemed tinged with sadness.

I walked around the bed to sit next to her for a moment. "Are you alright?" I grabbed her hand, bringing it to my lips to press a kiss on her knuckles.

She smiled softly at me. "I am. But I've never missed Christmas with my family before. Assuming the weather permitted it, they all gathered for dinner and gingerbread house decorating tonight. I'm sure they watched *The Muppets Christmas Carol*. That's one of our favorites."

I stayed silent for a moment, unsure of what to say. I was an only child and didn't have the same sort of holiday memories she held. I typically went home for Christmas, but there were still plenty of years when I'd find reasons and excuses to stay away. The older my parents became, the more I did my best to make it home because I knew it was important to my mom. But it was obvious Mae and I had utterly different family experiences, but just because I didn't fully understand what she felt didn't mean I couldn't try to help.

"My mom loves *White Christmas*, so she always makes us watch it together when I'm home," I offered. "I went through a phase where I absolutely hated it because of the love story within it, but last time I watched it with her, I totally cried."

Mae turned her full attention to me with wide eyes. "For real? I mean, I don't blame you, I love that movie, but that's absolutely adorable."

"Sure, we'll go with adorable."

A knock at the door made us both startle. I jumped off the bed and hurried to the closet to throw on the hotel robe. "I'll go get our stuff and be right back."

A few moments later, I re-entered my room with several bags full of the items we ordered. "I hope you're actually hungry because they gave us *a lot* of snacks. They even included brownies made in-house."

Mae was burrowed so deeply into the blankets looking content and happy, that I immediately realized that we would not be having sex that night. And honestly? I was totally fine with that. If the weather forecast was any indication, we'd still be stuck here tomorrow.

And I was sort of looking forward to that.

Mae turned and sat up, nearly showing me more than she probably meant to. "Did you say brownies?"

I pulled the container out and handed it to her. "They'll go great with the bottle of Cabernet they picked out," I said, holding out the bottle. "Want to have wine and eat snacks while we watch this?" I nodded to the television where the classic movie still played.

She bit her lip as if unsure I was actually okay with this plan since we initially placed the order so we could have sex. "I mean, that sounds absolutely amazing to me, but…"

"Mae. Seriously. We've had a long day and deserve to be lazy and enjoy ourselves, right? And if that means eating snacks in bed while watching a Christmas movie, that's what we're going to do. We have all of tomorrow for the other stuff." I winked at her before turning to my suitcase to find a shirt for her to throw on. I turned and held out a flannel shirt. "Want to wear this? Or I can grab you a robe or something instead?"

"Oh, you don't want me to stay naked?" she asked, giving me a joking glance.

"Don't get me wrong, if you want to stay naked, do it. But if you want to cover up, I can grab your PJs, or you can slip on something of mine."

"I'd love the flannel, actually. My arms are a bit chilly."

I tossed it to her and watched as she slid her arms into it and buttoned it. The shirt was oversized on her, but I loved how it looked. "That looks better on you than me," I admitted, the view of her in my clothing warming my chest.

Yeah, I was definitely in trouble.

CHAPTER 13

Mae Thompson
December 24, 6:30 AM
34.5 Hours Until Christmas Dinner

Oh my God, I needed to pee so badly that it hurt. I blinked into the still dim room and realized a few things: this wasn't my room, a crumpled bag of chips was next to me, and a strong pair of arms had me trapped against a firm body.

I shoved the bag of chips to the ground, figuring we'd clean up the room later, and momentarily basked in how amazing it felt to be held. I hadn't been wrapped up in someone for far too long, and it felt so *nice*.

Other than the desperate need to pee.

I waited as long as I could until there was no denying the need to run to the bathroom. I slowly pried Lon's hand off so I could slide out of bed unnoticed and luckily managed it without waking him up. I walked toward the bathroom and took care of business while thinking about the night before.

We chatted while watching *It's A Wonderful Life*, ate too much junk food, and enjoyed a glass of wine. I had no idea when we fell asleep, but I'm pretty sure I never brushed my teeth before passing out. I actually felt bad about crashing in his room and not my own. Was that rude of me? At least he hadn't seemed mad that I was there, if him being wrapped around me like a blanket was any indication.

I quickly chugged a much needed cup of water and left the bathroom. I stopped in the middle of the living room, unsure if I was supposed to go back to Lon's bed or my own. We hadn't decided to share the bed; it had happened naturally, so would it be presumptuous of me to return to his space instead of my own?

I figured I should take the safe route and go to my own room until it was time for us to get up for the day. I started walking in that direction and heard a gravely, mostly-asleep voice say, "What are you doing?"

"Oh!" I nearly jumped out of my skin at his voice. Lon leaned against the doorframe of his room, wearing only his boxer briefs, and I couldn't stop my eyes from taking in how amazing he looked, even sleep-rumpled. "Shit, I'm so sorry. I didn't mean to wake you. I had to go to the bathroom and didn't want to bother you, so I figured I'd finish sleeping in my own bed?"

He pushed some of his disheveled hair out of his eyes and blinked slowly at me. "That's ridiculous. Come back to bed. In here, I mean."

Lon turned on his heel and walked back to his bed, getting under the sheets without another word. Well. Alright then, I guess that answered my question of where to go. "Sorry I fell asleep in here last night." I crawled back into bed, happy he wanted me to stay. "Did we even finish the movie?"

"I did, but you were asleep before it ended."

Which meant he purposefully let me stay in his room with him. My chest fluttered with the excitement of what that might mean. Every passing minute with Lon, I seemed to like him more and more. I knew that was silly and probably dangerous to my emotions, but I couldn't help it. He made me laugh, he was unexpectedly sweet, and he made me happy. And dammit, feeling happy felt *good*.

I snuggled under the blankets and turned to face Lon. "I didn't mean to sleep here." I said with a shy smile.

He reached forward and tucked a loose strand of hair behind my ear. "Trust me, I didn't mind at all." He paused, and his lips lifted in a half smile. "You *are* a bed hog at times, though. You kept rolling over to try and steal my pillows."

"Well, you're a major sleep snuggler. When I woke up to use the bathroom, you were wrapped around me like a koala bear on a tree."

"I can't help if Asleep Me wants to touch you all night long." His dark eyes darkened with heat as he studied my face, and all I wanted to do was lean forward and kiss him.

So I did.

This somehow felt even more intimate than the night before, even though his mouth had made me come. We weren't using each other to work out stress and pent-up sexual energy. This was simply because we couldn't help ourselves.

Lon deepened the kiss, his tongue moving across my lips, seeking entrance. I opened to him and couldn't help the moan that escaped me as he moved his body over mine. His hard cock pressed against my thigh, and I realized I didn't want to wait any longer. I needed him right now.

"Are the condoms close by," I asked, my voice sounding breathless and needy.

His teeth grazed the shell of my ear, sending a shiver down me. "Yes, should I grab one?"

I nodded enthusiastically, and he immediately rolled off me to grab the box and pulled out a foil. My fingers went to the buttons of the flannel shirt I wore and began quickly undoing them. I kept tripping up since I wasn't used to the way men's shirts buttoned, so finally, I yanked it up and over my head while kicking the blankets off me.

He chuckled, but the look on his face was anything but humorous as his eyes drank me in. Despite my hair being a mop on top of my head, my makeup from the night before sleep-smudged, and not having the biggest or perkiest breasts in the world, I'd never felt more beautiful than in that moment. He bit his lip as his eyes finally made it to my underwear.

"Well, those are going to have to go too, you know," he said, his already rich voice sounding even deeper.

I scooted down on the bed and lifted my hips a little. "Will you help me with that?"

"Gladly." His mouth was on me in a flash, kissing my breasts in the way he already knew I liked. The slight scruff that grew overnight on his cheeks scraped against my skin in the most delicious way. His fingers made their way down to my underwear as his lips kept kissing and nibbling one breast and then the other. The sensations of his lips and teeth and facial hair had me squirming under him, wanting even more.

"Lon, please," I hissed as his teeth gently grazed my nipple again. It felt beyond amazing, but my body was buzzing with desire. "Touch me."

He looked up with a glint in his eyes. "Isn't that what I'm doing? I'm touching you all over." And he was, but not in the way I wanted, and he knew it. His fingers gripped my underwear and tugged them down painfully slowly. His mouth followed the movement of the material until I was fully exposed to him once more.

"Jesus Christ, you're already so wet, aren't you? I love how you react to me." His fingers spread me open, and he groaned at the sight of me. "I want to taste you again," he said before ducking his head to lick me through my folds from my opening up to my clit. My hips bucked at the feeling, desperate for him to increase the pressure and speed as he slowly, teasingly sucked.

"Do you get a sick pleasure from torturing me like this?" I whined, not caring if I sounded ridiculous. His mouth and hands felt terrific, but it wasn't what I wanted right now.

The bastard lifted his gaze and winked before giving me another long lick. I grabbed his hair and tugged him up and away. He immediately moved next to me, his expression suddenly serious. "Was that not what you wanted?"

"No, that's not the problem," I said, rubbing my hand up and down his arm to calm him. Without warning, I shoved him by the shoulder, forcing him onto his back, and he blinked up at me, unsure of what to do. "You were doing a great job. I just wanted attention from a different part of you." I straddled his legs and let my palm rub against his thick erection, still covered by his boxers.

He closed his eyes at the sensation and pressed himself against my hand, his hips gently rolling.

"I didn't get to properly investigate this part of you last night," I said, fully gripping him through the material. The tip of his length was peeking out from the waistband, so I bent down and gently licked it.

"Holy shit," Lon hissed out, gripping the sheets tightly as he watched my tongue circle him a few times. "Now who's the tease here."

I shrugged and gave him a sly smile. "I learned from the best, I guess."

"Fuck this," he huffed and tugged off his boxers, freeing his cock from the tight material. I giggled and lifted my hips so together we could get him undressed.

We were both totally naked, and I was suddenly incredibly aware of how close he was to my entrance. I only had to adjust my position slightly and I'd be able to sink down on him. "Condom. Now," I practically panted, unable to think about anything other than wanting to ride him.

"Yes, ma'am," he simply said, and ripped open the wrapper. Within a few seconds, he was fully covered. "I want you to know that my last physical was recently, and I'm totally healthy. And I haven't slept with anyone since then. In case you were wondering."

"We probably should've finished this conversation last night, but now is better than never. I am on birth control, and I'm healthy and clear of anything, too."

His hands roamed from mid-thigh, up to my hips, and around my ass. Goosebumps popped up as he gripped my ass, it felt so good. "Well then. I think that covers it all."

I propped myself up to a kneeling position and grabbed his cock so I could guide him to me. "Yes," I said, loving how he felt pressed against me. I sank down, letting his cock push into me inch by inch. "Yes," I breathed out again. "Oh my God, you feel amazing already."

I closed my eyes, my head falling back for a moment to bask in the sensation of being filled by Lon. His hands went back to gripping my hips tightly, holding me to him. "Mae, I can't—oh my God. Please. I need us to move. Let me thrust into you." His left hand reached down between us, and his thumb circled my clit, sending a shock through me, and I felt like I would come right then and there.

I lifted my hips before pressing down on him repeatedly, swiveling them in a way that made me lose my mind a little each time his cock hit right where I wanted it.

Lon thrusted up with every down movement of my own, and soon I felt an orgasm build until it suddenly overwhelmed me. I tried to shut my eyes, but Lon growled, "No. Look at me while you come."

And God, that command made me explode even harder, the orgasm seemingly never-ending as I clenched around him again and again. As I finally felt myself coming down from the high, Lon's hips moved harder, losing any sense of rhythm until his mouth dropped open in ecstasy. "Mae," he groaned as he thrust into me one more time, keeping his eyes locked on me as he finally let himself come.

He let out a long sigh and pulled me to him. I carefully got off him and curled against his chest, letting his strong arms wrap around me, not caring that we both were a little sweaty.

"Shit," he breathed out. "This might've become my all-time best morning ever." He pressed a kiss to my temple, and I felt the same tingles of excitement flutter in my stomach again. I had to be honest with myself. After that, I was, without a doubt, a total goner for his man.

CHAPTER 14

Alonzo Davis
December 24, 12:30 PM
28.5 Hours Until Christmas Dinner

After we cleaned ourselves up and gulped down some water, we climbed back into bed and slept until after breakfast. Once we were finally willing to wake up and get out of bed, I convinced Mae to shower with me. We *might* have stayed there until the water ran cold, and seeing her still-damp hair made me think of her pressed against the tiled wall with her legs propped up by my shoulders.

We lounged in the living room wearing only the hotel's white robes while enjoying some leftover snacks and wine from the night before as we figured out how we wanted to spend the day.

"By the way, I checked the weather forecast and the airport's status," I said, taking another bite of brownie. I'd have to ask the front desk who made them because they were fantastic, with chunks of dark chocolate mixed in. "They're hoping the airport will be up and running tomorrow, but this storm is lingering way longer than anticipated." We opened the living room's floor-to-ceiling windows to watch the snow. It looked magical from the top floor of the hotel.

Mae curled her legs up and took a small sip of wine. "Is it bad that I'm actually thrilled we're here for another day? Obviously, I don't want to miss Christmas, but..."

I leaned over to kiss her softly. "Is it bad that I hope the storm lasts even longer and I can stay here with you instead of seeing my parents?" I glanced up and noticed she was staring at me, an adorable look on her face that I couldn't quite read. "What? Am I horrible for that?"

She seemed to be fighting a grin and turned her attention toward the TV, which was showing a Christmas-themed cooking competition. "I mean, I think it's pretty sweet you want to spend more time with me, but your mother might not be okay with it."

I shrugged, not knowing what to say. My mom would be disappointed, but she knew the weather was out of our hands. Mom would probably be ecstatic to know I met someone who made me feel this happy and at ease.

Not that I planned to tell Mom about Mae because that would be utterly ridiculous since tomorrow we would be going our separate ways.

Wouldn't we?

I mean, we were going to the same place, right? Why couldn't I see her again while in town? Then again, I didn't see the point in prolonging our goodbyes. I'd make the absolute most out of today, and tomorrow we'd part ways, and that would be that.

❄

"Hey there, what can I get you two?" A young woman with short, tight curls smiled at the two of us from behind the bar. We decided we needed some actual sustenance and not only junk food.

"I'm absolutely *starving*," Mae said, scanning the menu. "Can I have a glass of the house white wine, and I think I'll do the double bacon cheeseburger with fries."

I mentally debated between a french dip sandwich and a salad with grilled chicken since I was starting to feel the need for more vegetables after all the fried bar food and snacks I'd consumed in the last day. "I'm going to get the french dip sandwich." I paused before saying, "And I'd like to sub the fries for a side house salad, please." There. Best of both worlds.

Mae bumped me with her shoulder and said, "If you share your salad with me, I'll share my fries with you."

"God, you're amazing," I said quickly because, honestly, I did want those fries.

I ordered a beer and then turned to look at Mae. She wore leggings again with an oversized light gray sweatshirt. I couldn't understand how she managed to take something so simple and make it feel cozy and alluring simultaneously.

"Why are you staring at me like that?" she asked, fidgeting with the coaster in front of her.

I leaned forward to cup her cheek gently and kissed her. It took every ounce of strength to pull back since we weren't alone, and I wasn't usually keen on public displays of affection.

"I just wanted to do that," I said, turning back toward the bar and taking a sip of my water.

For a moment, I worried I'd crossed a line since we weren't actually together, and we hadn't discussed what this was between us. Because there *was* something between us even if we hadn't planned for there to be. I glanced back at her, and when I saw a startled but happy look on her face, I let out the breath I'd been holding.

"Well. Alright then." At that moment, the bartender placed our drinks in front of us, and Mae smiled kindly at her. "Oh, thank you. Hey, by the way, thanks for being here working. Between the blizzard and it being Christmastime, I'm sure work isn't exactly ideal right now."

The bartender gave her a genuine smile instead of a practiced customer service expression. "It's not a problem at all. Most of us stayed here last night since the roads are practically shut down. I'd never had a work sleepover, but it was shockingly fun. We brainstormed some events to host throughout today to keep things festive."

I'd already planned on tipping her well for working over the holidays, but now I'd be sure to tip her double for having to stay at work so long. "Wow, that's above and beyond for you guys. What sort of stuff?"

She shrugged off my words and said, "It's as much for the guests as it is for us, too. There's a cookie decorating event starting soon with hot chocolate and coffee." She leaned forward and put her hand to her mouth as if telling us a big secret. "And yes, you can make them adult beverages if you want. And later, we're setting up a big projector in the lounge to show some Christmas classics."

Another worker approached with our food and added, "Oh, and don't forget the snowpeople competition outside. Guests have until six o'clock tonight, and then we'll pick a winner."

Mae gasped in excitement at that. "Oh my God, really? Lon, can we make a snowman? It always makes me think of the scene in *Meet Me In St. Louis* where they make the snow family, and then Tootie destroys them all while 'Have Yourself A Merry Little Christmas' plays in the background. I love that movie."

"So does my mother. Why do you think my name is Alonzo?" I asked, grinning over my beer.

Her eyes widened at this. "What! No way. That's amazing. If she had a daughter, would she name them Esther or Rose?"

"Oh, Esther, for sure. But, yes, we'll definitely build a snowman. I'm fairly certain I have gloves packed…" And if I didn't, I'd suffer through the cold for her.

CHAPTER 15

Mae Thompson
December 24, 2:00 PM
27 Hours Until Christmas Dinner

"I swear to God, Mae, if you throw one more snowball at me, I'll..." Lon paused to think up a proper threat as he removed his hat to shake the snow off. I hadn't meant to hit him in the back of the head, but it turned out my aim wasn't that great. "I'll kick over our snowman!"

"You leave poor George out of this," I scolded, covering the sides of the snowman's head to shield him from Lon's horrible words. "He's innocent."

"Then you'll have his death on *your* conscience knowing you could've prevented it." His hair was adorably rumpled from wearing his knit hat the last hour or so, and it hit me yet again how much I enjoyed the relaxed version of this man.

"Ignore him, George! He doesn't mean it," I said, patting our snowman on the back as if comforting a small child.

"Daddy's grumpy that his snowperson idea wasn't as good as mine."

"Did you seriously just refer to me as 'Daddy', and not even in a sexy way? I don't think I'm okay with this."

I snorted and turned to look at him with a raised brow. "If you're expecting me to call you Daddy for any other reason besides our beloved George, you'll be waiting a long ass time, my dude."

He flashed me a wicked grin and said in a low voice, "We'll see about that." I felt my cheeks flush despite the cold air, and my skin buzzed with the promise of his words.

I glanced around to see if any other hotel guests working on their snow creations could hear what we were talking about. Much to my relief, no one else seemed to be paying attention.

Suddenly, warm lips brushed against my ear, and Lon whispered, "Now you're thinking about it, aren't you?"

I tried my best to keep my face expressionless and shrugged. "I have no idea what you're talking about."

He turned away from me, chuckling as he walked a small distance, kicking at the snow as if searching for something. While he was distracted, I scooped a handful of snow to form a ball and lobbed it at him. This time, I hit him right in the ass, and I nearly fell over laughing at the sight of the snow clinging to his perfect butt.

He'd spun on his heel to charge at me, and my laughter quickly turned into squeals. "Don't hurt George! Don't!"

He bypassed George and went straight to me, tackling me in a way that didn't hurt but knocked both of us into the pillowy snow drift, his body firmly pressed against me. His forearms rested on either side of my head so he could lift himself a few inches off me. "If you wanted to smack my ass, you could've used your hands, you know." His dark eyes bored into mine, a mixture of amusement and hunger.

I wasn't sure if my breathlessness was from laughter or

his stare making me wish we were back in our suite, preferably in one of our beds. Or the couch. Or even a nice steamy shower. Like the one we shared earlier that morning. I had to bite back a moan of pleasure as he pressed against me, reminding me of his face between my legs as the water poured down on us in that fantastic bathroom.

Lon grinned again and lifted himself up before rolling to the right. I whimpered quietly at the loss of him, but he simply jumped to his feet and offered me a hand to stand up.

"Aww, young love," a voice behind us cooed. "Remember when we used to be that cute, Bill?" An older woman was smiling fondly at us as her husband worked on creating the base of their snowperson. "How long have you two been dating?"

"Oh, uh," I stammered, because how does one explain to someone who could be their grandma that we weren't dating but met yesterday morning and were now banging each other's brains out.

"Not long, actually," Lon cut in, giving the woman a bright smile. He wrapped his arm around me and pulled me to him. "But, I'd say it's going quite well so far. Don't you think, babe?" He glanced down at me and gave me a little wink.

What the hell was he doing? Obviously, we weren't actually *together*, but my damn heart didn't want to remember that when he said those words.

The woman let out a happy sigh and said, "Well, embrace this stage of it, my dears. If you keep this sort of excitement going, you'll be together even longer than us."

"Sweetheart, leave these two kids alone and help me position this correctly," Bill said in a way that made me think his wife was constantly talking to anyone and everyone around her. It made me long for what they had.

"Oh, alright. Be good, you two, but not *too* good," The woman said to us with a sassy little finger waggle at us.

I managed to say in a slightly strangled voice, "Thanks, Merry Christmas!" I turned to Lon and pressed my face into his shoulder to muffle my giggles at the whole situation. "Oh my God," I said once I had more control over myself. "I want to be that woman one day."

❄

We finally made our way back inside once our noses couldn't stand the cold anymore. My fingers felt frozen inside my damp gloves from playing in the snow for so long, but it was worth it since George looked adorable wearing an extra scarf of Lon's. He might not be award-winning, but he was my favorite snowperson out there.

I gasped at how festive the lobby looked. There'd already been one Christmas tree, but now several more lined the room, twinkling with lights and colorful ornaments. Red and green paper ring garland was strung across the space, and a group of children sat together creating even more with a few adults helping. They had even hung stockings on the large fireplace with all sorts of nutcrackers, Santas, and snowmen on the mantel.

"They still have cookies and hot drinks out," Lon said, gesturing to the other side of the lobby. "Let's grab some and sit by the fire to warm up."

I nodded and started to walk towards the table, when suddenly Lon grabbed my arm and pulled me back to him. My face scrunched in confusion until he leaned down and pressed a tender but full kiss to my mouth. Without thinking, I wrapped my arms around his neck, leaning into the kiss, forgetting that we were in a busy lobby.

A small chorus of catcalls and claps arose, and I bashfully pulled away, simultaneously wanting to hide from the attention but loving it. Lon cheerfully smiled and pointed up above us. "The mistletoe said I had to, and who am I to deny the wishes of the mistletoe?"

"Ah, yes," I nodded sagely. "We wouldn't want to go against the mistletoe. That's, what, like seven years of bad luck?"

"I think that's breaking a mirror, but maybe we should do that again, just in case."

So I grabbed his face and kissed him like we were the only people in the room.

CHAPTER 16

Alonzo Davis
December 24, 5:00 PM
24 Hours Until Christmas Dinner

Supposedly the weather would clear up overnight, and the news predicted the airport would be up and running sometime in the morning. And I found myself hoping that they were wrong, so we'd be stuck here another day.

Knowing my luck, things would clear up perfectly fine, and Mae and I would go our separate ways once we reached St. Louis.

My analytical brain and my heart seemed to be battling as I lounged on the couch, waiting for Mae to finish changing after the shower we shared. Two showers in one day was probably excessive, but we both felt like we needed it after spending a few hours building our snowman. Or George, as Mae insisted his name was. I smiled at that thought and how excited she was the entire time we worked on him despite our lack of snow-appropriate clothing.

That shower was less of a sexual experience and more a means to warm up and get clean after exerting ourselves, and I was perfectly fine with it. I enjoyed every moment I spent with Mae, regardless of what we were doing. I couldn't wait until we joined in on more of the cheesy activities the hotel threw together because it meant doing them with her.

Fuck.

I wanted to keep doing silly and goofy things with her. I wanted to try different restaurants and bars. I wanted to cook for her, watch movies on the couch with my arm around her, fall asleep next to her, and know she'd still be there the next day.

I squeezed my eyes shut and tried to remember that I lived in New York and she lived in St. Louis. There was no logical sense of how we could work; everyone always said long-distance never lasted. Right? I quickly Googled statistics regarding long-distance relationships and let my eyes scan pages as I clicked on link after link. It seemed that about 60% worked out.

Well. More than half was better than nothing.

I closed my laptop, not wanting to see anything else since this tipped it slightly in my favor. A moment later, Mae emerged from her room wearing a black long-sleeved sparkly dress with a short hemline. My eyes didn't know if they should take in her beautiful legs emphasized by a pair of heels, or her mouth painted a sexy shade of red. The answer became clear when she walked across the room, and I saw the dress had an open back that dipped low. My mouth watered with want. Apparently I was into backs. Who knew?

I glanced down at my pair of dark jeans and button-down shirt and frowned. "I don't think I got the dressing up memo."

"It was either this or yoga pants, so I figured I might as well go all out for the hotel Christmas party." She studied me briefly before adding, "I think you look absolutely handsome."

I stood up, shoved my laptop away, and walked to Mae. "Well, good, but I'm nothing compared to how you look." I leaned forward and kissed her gently on the corner of her mouth, careful not to muss her lipstick. "Miss Thompson, may I escort you downstairs to the Christmas Karaoke celebration in the bar?"

"Why, Mr. Davis, I thought you'd never ask."

❄

"Oh my God, how many times do we need to hear a Bing Crosby wannabe sing 'White Christmas'?" I groaned, grateful for the whiskey cocktail sitting in front of me.

"I'd pick that any day over everyone thinking they can hit Mariah Carey's notes," Mae said, grimacing before taking a swig of her drink. "Making this a drinking game was a horrible idea."

"It was your idea."

"That doesn't make it any less horrible," she whined as the next singer took the stage and started singing 'Santa Baby' in an overly sexual baby voice. I shuddered and downed the rest of my drink, assuming that this performance broke one of the excessively complicated rules Mae had created for the game.

A few minutes later, the hotel staff acting as emcee for the night jumped back on stage and grabbed the microphone as we all politely clapped for the last singer. "Alright, next up we have Mae Thompson. She wrote on the card that she picked this song for a special someone tonight. Come on up, Mae!"

She gave me an embarrassed little smile as my mouth dropped open, unsure what to expect. I hadn't seen her sign up.

"Hello, everyone." Mae waved to the crowd in the bar. "I know this isn't exactly how any of us expected to spend Christmas Eve, but I hope you've found ways to celebrate and be happy regardless. I'm pretty damn lucky I met a great guy because of all this. So. This song might not be as upbeat and happy sounding as others, but I think the message is one we can all relate to right now." She glanced over to the emcee, and they turned on the song. As soon as I heard the first slightly melancholy piano notes, I knew exactly what Mae was about to sing: 'Have Yourself A Merry Little Christmas', like we'd talked about earlier when discussing *Meet Me In St. Louis*.

Mae's voice shook with nerves initially, but she sang with confidence and clarity by the time she got to the end of the first verse. A quick glance around the room showed me that she'd grabbed the attention of the whole place. My heart swelled with pride as she hit and held some of the higher notes, and as the song went on, my eyes felt a bit damp. A pang of sadness struck me, not just because of the song, but this was our last night, and I didn't know if or when we'd be together again.

The room went absolutely wild as Mae finished, and she simply smiled before leaving the stage to head to me. I quickly wiped the wetness from my eyes and put on a giant smile for her. I held my arms out for her, and she ran into them, squeezing me tight as I hugged her and kissed the top of her head.

"Damn, girl, I didn't know you could sing like that," I said as we sat back down. "You were amazing."

She shrugged and lowered her eyes to her now empty glass. "I was alright. I figured it was time to mix up the music here. Plus," she looked up at me. "The song seemed fitting after today."

I grabbed her hand and squeezed, unsure of what to say. I wanted to ask about her thoughts on us and staying in contact, but I also didn't want to bring the mood down with a serious chat when we'd been having so much fun all day. So instead, I said, "The song was absolutely perfect."

CHAPTER 17

Mae Thompson
December 24, 8:00 PM
21 Hours Until Christmas Dinner

My phone vibrated on the table, and my mom's name flashed across the screen. I glanced at Lon, who was busy chatting with another hotel guest, so I poked him to grab his attention. "My mom's calling, I'll be right back."

"Sure thing. Don't be gone too long because I think they're announcing the snowperson winners soon."

"Oh, I don't want to miss that." I kissed his cheek and grabbed my phone. I hurried out of the bar to find a quiet spot. "Mom, give me a sec, the hotel has a bunch of holiday activities happening, so it's a bit loud."

"That sounds so fun!" I could barely make out her voice as I stepped into an empty conference room.

"Whew, okay, that's better. How are you?"

"We're all missing you, that's for sure. It's not the same without you here, but I'm glad the hotel is being festive."

I almost felt bad that I thought about my family much for most of the day since I was so busy spending as much time as possible with Lon and taking advantage of the events here. "I miss you guys, too. Are Xander and Jake there with the kids?"

"Yes, thankfully, they were able to make it here last night and decided not to risk the roads and stay with us until after Christmas. It made me feel better knowing they didn't have to drive back and forth in the storm." I could hear all sorts of background sounds through the phone of people laughing and chatting, music playing, and kids shrieking with excitement. "I hope you haven't been too lonely in Detroit, sweetie."

I smiled, thinking about throwing snowballs at Lon and helping some of the kids decorate cookies after I warmed up by the fire. I hadn't been lonely in the slightest. In fact, I'd been having the time of my life. "It's actually been great, Mom. I mean, obviously, I don't like missing time with all of you. But I'm having fun."

"Well, I just wanted to let you know that the airport here will open up sometime tonight, so as soon as the Detroit airport is functioning, you ought to be good."

I groaned at the still unknown airport situation. "Thanks, I appreciate the information. I'll keep you posted tomorrow."

We said our goodbyes and I hurried back to the bar where Lon waited for me. His face lit up when he saw me, and I slid my arm around his waist. "Did I miss it?"

He turned to kiss the top of my head. "Not yet. They're about to announce it now."

"As long as George knows we love him no matter what, it doesn't matter if we win or lose," I said as one of the bartenders made her way to the microphone. "But it would be pretty cool if we won."

"Alright, everyone. It is time for the snowperson competition announcement," The emcee waved a piece of paper and we all went silent as if they were announcing Best Picture. "Mr. and Mrs. Anderson, please come up here."

Bill and his wife made their way to the emcee and I immediately started jumping up and down in excitement. Our George didn't win, but I was totally okay with that.

"Damn," Lon breathed out before turning to me. "I thought we would win."

"The only reason I'm not upset is that we know he's a real winner and because there were some epically detailed snowmen out there. It was like people came prepared with tools or something. We did a fantastic job for not even having proper snow clothes!"

"You know what? You're right." He wrapped his arms around me and pulled me to him. "I'm still a little sad, though. I think you need to give me a kiss to make it better."

I grinned up at him and leaned forward. "I bet I can make you feel better."

❄

"It doesn't matter how many times I've seen it, *Elf* always makes me happy," I said as we stepped out of the elevator later that night and headed to our suite. We stayed downstairs to watch the movie with many other hotel guests, which turned into a sing-along. Some people were still celebrating, but by the end of the movie, I was leaning heavily against Lon with my eyes barely open, so he suggested we head up to our room.

"It's a pretty damn quotable movie, that's for sure," he said, unlocking the door and holding it open for me to enter.

I kicked off my shoes but immediately bent down to pick them up with a groan. "I need to pack. I despise packing."

"Well, how about I help you out so it doesn't take much time and we can hang out? We can watch a movie on TV or talk or…not talk…"

I grabbed his hand and tugged him toward my room. Having him in there felt weird because we'd spent all our time together in his room or outside the suite. I grabbed a couple items of clothing I'd hung up in the wardrobe and laid them on my bed. "Would you unzip me so I can pack this dress up?" I asked, grabbing my hair to put it over my shoulder.

"Now, this is a task I'm definitely more than happy to help with."

CHAPTER 18

Alonzo Davis
December 25, 6:00 AM
11 Hours Until Christmas Dinner

We still hadn't talked about what we were or wanted to be, and time was quickly ticking away. I'd been awake for over an hour, laying in bed with Mae curled up asleep next to me, not wanting to let go of her. I'd checked the weather and airport status about twenty times already. The airport announced they'd worked all night long to clear the runways, and since temperatures had slightly warmed up, they were able to keep them from freezing over again.

Even though we didn't have official confirmation yet, all signs pointed toward us getting out of here today. Soon.

Shit.

"Are you alright?" a half-asleep voice muttered next to me. I knew Mae wanted to wake up early, but after we packed our things last night, we kept each other awake pretty damn late. Neither of us wanted to go to sleep or stop touching each other. It wasn't only about the sex, though. We didn't discuss our situation, but we talked about anything and everything else from our jobs to where we like to travel to our favorite TV shows. I felt like I'd known this woman way longer than two days.

I turned and pulled Mae to me to kiss her good morning. "Truth?"

"Always."

I sighed and plopped down on my back to stare at the ceiling. "The airport is nearly cleared, and I'm not ready to leave you."

She sat up to better look at me, the blanket falling from her still naked body. "Oh, Lon."

I huffed out a dry laugh. "Pathetic, right? I know you only wanted some Christmas fun to get through the blizzard. No strings attached."

"Yeah, it's what we both wanted…" She paused and bit her lip. "But if that makes you pathetic, then I guess I am too. I don't want this to end."

"But it sort of has to. Doesn't it?" I held my breath, hoping she'd tell me that, of course, we could be together. That distance didn't matter as long as we like each other. That we could figure out a way to make it work.

But instead, she grabbed my hand and squeezed. "Yeah, I guess it does. So much of my life is up in the air right now with needing to find a new job. I don't even know if I can afford my apartment much longer. It sucks, though. I like spending time with you."

I sighed deeply, wishing there was something I could do to help relieve her stress from her job and rent. But, a small part of me felt relieved that she also didn't want what we had to end.

Though what we want and what we get aren't always the same things.

We lay there in silence for a few minutes, the melancholy

building between us until I felt nearly suffocated by it. I rubbed my free hand down my face before looking at the clock on the bedside table. I let out a low huff of frustration. "No, I refuse for us to spend the rest of our time together being sad and miserable. If we have to say goodbye, I'd rather cram in as much happiness as possible until then."

A slow smile spread on her face. "Okay, I like the sound of that. What do you have in mind?"

"Well, sex, obviously," I said, giving her my best smirk, and she just laughed and smacked me in the arm, breaking the somber vibe once more.

"Obviously. What else?"

"Oh, you expected more than that? Lord, you're needy." I laughed as she tried to throw a pillow at me. "Okay, okay. After sex, we shower. Then we eat a fancy breakfast in the hotel's restaurant—anything you want. Then we see how we're doing on timing but probably head to the airport and snag seats together on a plane. I promise not to make you spill wine this time."

"And you promise to not spread your legs so much that I'm falling into the aisle again?" She slid on top of me to straddle my hips, and my hands immediately went to her bare ass.

"I make no such promises because I plan to touch you as much as possible on the flight, legs included."

She playfully rolled her eyes but still smiled. "Well, fine. I guess it won't be as obnoxious this time," she said as she slowly stroked my cock with her hand.

My thumb immediately went to her clit and started circling it the way she liked, and I could already feel her wetness against my skin. "Do you have a skirt you can wear on the plane?" I panted out as her hand squeezed harder. "Something with easy access so I can touch you like this without anyone knowing."

She shut her eyes tightly as her breathing quickened. I

grinned at her reaction and said, "Oh, you like the thought of that, don't you? My hand under your skirt, your coat covering your lap so no one can see, and you being forced to keep perfectly still and silent as I tease you until I'm ready to make you come?"

Mae's mouth dropped open with a silent scream as she came as if she was already on that plane with me. "Sweetheart, if I'm going to get you off on the flight, you're going to have to be less obvious than that," I said as I coaxed the last bit of her orgasm out of her.

"Shut up. Condom. Now."

❄

Breakfast went far too quickly, and before we knew it, we were doing sweeps around the suite to ensure everything had been packed. With one last glance, Mae grabbed her purse and suitcase. I slipped my messenger bag over my shoulder and held the door open for her so we could leave the room we'd shared.

"I need to check out and make sure everything's squared away at the front desk, and then we can call a cab," I said, suddenly feeling the weight of our impending goodbyes yet again. As much as we said we'd live up our last moments and enjoy the time we had, reality was forcing its way in quicker than I liked.

Mae let out a small sigh and leaned her head against my shoulder as we rode the elevator down to the lobby. When the door dinged open, I held out my hand for her to grab because the thought of not being able to touch her was too much for me to handle.

"Hello, Mr. Davis and Ms. Thompson. We hope you enjoyed your stay with us." The nice woman, Sierra, from the night we checked in, stood behind the desk waiting to help us.

"Morning, Sierra," I said, pulling my wallet out from my back pocket. "I think we were both pleasantly surprised with how great a time we had." I smiled down at Mae, and her cheeks flushed a hint of pink.

She turned her attention to Sierra and beamed. "You all did an amazing job making everyone feel at home during the blizzard. Thank you so much for everything."

Sierra went over my bill, but honestly, I wasn't even listening to how much I owed. I handed her my card and waited to sign the receipt. "Alright, well, you're all settled. We have a shuttle to the airport right now for our guests, and it looks like they're sitting out front if you want to utilize that."

I glanced at Mae and asked, "Are you ready to head out?"

"No," she said softly with a sad smile. "But we have to. So let's go."

CHAPTER 19

Mae Thompson
December 25, 9:00 AM
8 Hours Until Christmas Dinner

"Hi, we need two tickets to St. Louis, please," Lon said to the man working behind the ticket counter. "We'd been on our way there from New York when the storm diverted us here on the twenty-third." I pulled my original ticket out from my purse and put it next to Lon's on the counter.

We stood in line for a while, and each passing minute made me all the more anxious. I wasn't even sure if I feared there not being space on a plane for us or having to part ways with Lon.

The man looked over our tickets and typed into the computer. "Ah, yes, Flight 356. Let me print you out new tickets. Your flight isn't until 1:30 this afternoon. Do you have any bags to check?"

We both handed our bags over and made our way to

security. "That was...shockingly easier than I expected," I said as we slowly walked through the line. "I was worried we'd have to buy new tickets or something. Wait, we get to still sit next to each other, right?"

"I'll make someone move if we don't," he said before kissing me on the top of my head. He then glanced down at his ticket. "I'm at F25."

I let out a sigh of relief. "Good, I'm G25."

He grinned as he bent down to remove his shoes. "Meanwhile, just a few days ago, you couldn't wait to get away from me on the plane."

"Because you sucked!" I kicked my shoes off, not bothering to untie them, and piled them along with my purse and coat into a container to be scanned.

Lon slipped his suit coat off and carefully folded it to try and avoid wrinkles. "I hope my mom still has a steamer because I hadn't expected to wear this on two flights before needing it." He paused and frowned. "Well, shit, I guess I already missed Christmas Mass, so it doesn't actually matter now."

I reached over and squeezed his hand since I knew he hated disappointing his mom, but at least she knew it was all out of his control. "Regardless, she'll be excited to see you today."

Before I forgot, I quickly texted my family group chat to let them know my flight information and when I was expected to land in St. Louis so someone could pick me up. Within seconds, my phone was bombarded with a stream of incoming texts telling me how excited they were that I was on my way home and that Xander and Jake would happily be at the airport when I landed.

We both made it through security without any incidents, and it was nice having Lon with me since the airport seemed even more crowded than it had when we landed. People were rushing around everywhere to get to their new gates. There were still some cots set up from the people who opted to camp out in the airport for the last two days.

Lon grabbed my hand and said, "Well. We have quite a bit of time to kill. Want to go to one of the restaurants and get Christmas morning tipsy?"

I burst out laughing and nodded. "You know what? Let's do it. I could go for a mimosa right about now."

❄

The flight home was less than two hours long, and I was desperate to make the most of every moment. I would have done pretty much anything to keep us in our happy little bubble longer, but any time I had those thoughts, guilt crept in that I wasn't more upset about being away from my family.

Before I knew it, we had safely landed, and it was time to gather our things to exit the plane. We sat in our seats, waiting for the other passengers to go ahead because we knew that this magical thing between us was over when we stepped foot in the airport.

I kept telling myself I didn't want Lon to see me cry, and as we sat there in silence, I kept chanting in my head, *"You're fine, don't cry. Don't cry. You can cry when you're alone later, but don't cry now."*

As the last passenger passed us, Lon let out a deep sigh. "Well. I don't think we can put this off any longer without pissing off some perfectly nice flight attendants." He stood up and held his hand to help me stand. "Should we head to baggage claim?"

All day I'd had the undeniable need to touch Lon, whether leaning against him, holding his hand, or simply his leg leaning against mine. If I was touching him, all of this was real and meant something. I felt like the moment we were no longer in reach, the last two days would disappear as if they had never happened. So I clung to him as we navigated the busy airport.

We reached baggage claim as the luggage started dropping on the carousel. People around us hurried in every direction, grabbing their bags and rushing toward the exits to head to wherever they needed to be, and I wanted to scream out to all of them, "Don't you understand that my heart is breaking?"

My heart *was* breaking. I knew it didn't make sense, and I knew that starting a brand new relationship when we lived across the country from each other and I didn't have the money to even pretend I could make regular trips to see him made even less sense.

I understood that, but I still hated it.

I hated my company for shutting down and leaving me in a state of uncertainty. I hated the blizzard for ending, so I had to say goodbye. And I hated that Lon wanted nothing to do with St. Louis and would be leaving in a few days.

My eyes were dangerously close to betraying me, so I quickly wiped them and took a few steps forward. "I think I see one of our bags." One of the matching seafoam green suitcases made its way to us, and I grabbed it, noticing it had Lon's luggage tag, so I passed it along to him.

He wrapped his arm around me and pulled me to him, not saying a word. Retrieving our luggage meant we were one step away from goodbye.

A few minutes later, my bag finally dropped into view, and before I could move, Lon grabbed and put it in front of me.

I let out a sigh and said, "Well."

"Yup. Well..."

"I guess we should start walking to the exit?" I asked, unsure what to do in this situation. Part of me wanted to shake him and ask if he felt the same way. If he was as miserable at the idea of this being it as I was? The other part wanted a clean break and run. We pushed through the doors and stepped out into the shockingly bright outdoors. He pulled out his phone and opened the car app to request a ride, and I glanced at my phone and saw a text from my brother saying he was on his way and would be there shortly.

Lon ran a hand through his thick hair and studied me for a moment, his dark eyes overflowing with emotion. "I don't like this."

I gave him a sad smile and said, "Neither do I. But we knew we had a time limit." I leaned up and kissed him, letting my arms wrap around his neck, wishing the crowd of people around us would disappear and leave us alone back in our magical happy place. A single tear finally broke free, and I let out an embarrassed laugh. "Dammit. I didn't want that to happen."

Before I could angrily wipe it away, Lon ran his thumb across my cheek. "You were the best thing I could've hoped for on this trip."

"Thank you for everything. I know you don't expect me to pay you back, even if I could, but I need you to know how absolutely grateful I am that you helped me during this whole mess. I don't know what I would've done."

"Anything for you, Mae." He paused and pressed his lips together in a thin line for a long moment as he seemed to debate something in his head. "Mae, I—"

Just then, a large pickup truck pulled up at the curb a few feet in front of us and let out a loud *beep, beep.* I startled at the sound and immediately was painfully aware of the cold air, the rush of people, and now the tell-tale sound of my incredibly loud niece and nephew screaming my name.

"Aunt Mae! Aunt Mae! You're here!" squealed Erica as she threw herself out of my brother Xander's truck.

Right behind her was Austin, her twin brother, who wasn't quite as high energy as Erica always seemed to be, but close. “Santa came this morning, and you missed it.” he said. I couldn’t tell if he was mad at me or stating a fact.

Erica had already wiggled up the side of my body, so I had no choice but to hold her as I leaned down to kiss Austin on the head. “He did? Did he bring me anything? I’ve been an awfully good girl recently.”

Lon snorted at that, and I shot him a look. He seemed amused at me suddenly being a human jungle gym for the twins. But then his phone dinged, and he frowned down at it and turned to start looking around the pick-up area.

“Miss Maesie Poo!” Xander bellowed in the embarrassing way only an older brother could manage as he hopped out the truck’s passenger side. His husband, Jake, walked around to join him and waved excitedly at me.

“Mae, my ride’s here—” Lon tried to say as Austin began listing each gift he opened that morning, and Erica started singing ‘Jingle Bells’ at the top of her lungs right in my ear.

I turned toward Lon and pleaded with him to wait a moment so I could say goodbye. Austin let go of my arm and declared he wanted to roll my suitcase to the truck, which set Erica off, saying no *she* wanted to, until finally Jake swooped in, grabbed my bag, and loaded it in the back of his truck to stop them from fighting. Of course, this only led to both getting upset with their dad.

“Mae, I need to go, my driver is going to get mad,” I heard Lon say over the chaos of my family.

Xander wrapped me in his arms and gave me a giant bear hug, lifting me off my feet and swinging me around a bit. “Merry Christmas, little sis. I’m glad you finally made it.”

He put me down, and I tried my best to smile at him even though I wanted to scream at them to give me a second. “Thanks. Hold on a second, I need to say bye to a friend.” I turned to where Lon had just been and blinked.

The car wasn’t there anymore. He was gone.

CHAPTER 20

Alonzo Davis
December 25, 3:45
15 Minutes Until Christmas Dinner

I spent the twenty-minute car ride wanting to bang my head against the window in frustration. Everything was totally fucked up now. We'd put off our goodbye for so long that we didn't even get to have one. Before I knew it, the driver pulled up in front of my parents' perfectly average ranch with its sizable yard. I slowly made my way to the front door, never quite sure if I should walk in or ring the doorbell.

The door swung open before I could decide, and my mom threw her arms around me in excitement. "Oh, hell's bells, I was so worried you would miss Christmas. I'm *so* happy you're here, Lonny!"

I melted into her arms, not even flinching at the unfortunate choice of name she always called me, and soaked in the warmth of her embrace. It was as if all the exhaustion and emotion from the last day finally hit me. "Merry Christmas, Mom. It's so good to see you." And despite being heartbroken about leaving Mae, I found it true. I was happy to see her.

"Come inside, you poor thing. It's so cold out here." She dragged me forward with surprising strength for someone nearly a foot shorter than me.

"Did the presents I shipped arrive on time?" I asked. I hadn't wanted to travel with presents, so I shipped them a good week and a half or so ahead of time, but you never knew what delays would come up.

"Of course, sweetie, but we decided to wait for you to be here to open them. Your father is in the living room watching the Christmas football game. You should go in there to say hi."

I rolled my eyes without meaning to and gave my mother a look. "He couldn't at least put on *A Christmas Story* or something? Football, really?"

She brushed me off like it was no big deal, and I supposed to her it wasn't. I kissed her cheek and said, "Okay, I'll say hi to him and then help you with dinner."

"Don't be silly! You're still in your suit, for God's sake. Get washed up and comfortable, and then you can find me."

I begrudgingly entered the living room to see my dad lounged back in his recliner with a beer propped against his stomach. I hated how being around him made me feel like a surly teenager again. "Merry Christmas, Dad," I said simply, leaning against the entryway to the room.

He looked up from the TV and said, "Oh, you're finally here. Good. Your mother's been worrying."

I paused for a moment to see if he'd say Merry Christmas back to me, but that didn't seem to be in the cards. I nodded toward the TV and said, "Any good teams playing today?" My dad had been heartbroken when the local NFL team went to a different city, but that hadn't stopped him from watching the sport any chance he got.

He shrugged and said, "Not particularly, but a game's a game."

Not like your wife couldn't use some help getting dinner ready or anything, but sure, Dad. Honestly, it was better this way because now I could get some nice time by myself with Mom once I was changed. "Well, cool. I'm going to get settled in and then help Mom out."

I grabbed my bag and headed toward my old room. A few years ago they'd finally got rid of most of my high school belongings, and transformed into a general guest room. I removed my suit jacket and grabbed a hanger from the closet to put it away before turning back to my suitcase to find a regular t-shirt to put on.

Before I even unzipped it, I realized something was wrong. This was absolutely not my bag. I finished opening it and saw sweaters, leggings, high heels, and absolutely nothing that belonged to me. I sat on the edge of my bed and proceeded to lose my shit laughing hysterically. How the hell did we manage to do this *twice?*

I touched the luggage tag and considered my options here. I knew Mae headed straight to her parents' house, so the address listed wouldn't be helpful, but it did have her phone number. Without thinking, I grabbed my phone and dialed, anxiously drumming my fingers against my thigh as it rang and rang and—

"Hello?" an incredibly male voice asked on the other side of the line.

I blinked but then remembered she was with family, so maybe one of them answered. "Hello? Is this Mae Thompson's phone?"

There was a short pause that seemed to stretch on for eternity before the man said, "Maybe. Is this the douche in the suit that caused my sister to cry her eyes out for the last hour and traumatize my kids?"

I grimaced at that. "Shit, she cried? Look, that wasn't how I wanted our goodbye to go, and I need to talk to her."

"She's showering right now, so she's not available."

"Also, your husband grabbed my suitcase instead of hers when you all picked her up."

Another long pause occurred until he groaned and said, "Goddamnit, Jake! You grabbed the wrong bag."

"I did? Oh, shit. Who's on the phone?"

"The dickhead."

I squeezed my eyes shut, realizing that Mae's brother would make this incredibly difficult for me. "Look…" I wracked my brain trying to remember his name since I knew Mae had told me in one of our many conversations. "Xander, right? The way we left each other is no one's fault. She was being pulled away by your kids, and I was getting glared at by my Uber driver. It was poor timing, but I still hated it, alright? I need to talk to her to see if I can fix this."

"I don't know, man. I've never seen my sister like this before, and I don't want her to get even more—" There was a rustle through the phone, and I heard Xander shout, "Hey!"

"Alonzo? This is Jake, Mae's brother-in-law. I saw you trying to get her attention, and I know exactly how demanding my twins are, so I feel you, alright? If you need to swap suitcases back, maybe that's the universe's way of saying whatever went on between the two of you isn't over yet. So. Grab a piece of paper, and I'll give you my in-law's address. I expect you to show up tonight while she's still here. Got it?"

"Uh, yeah, thanks, Jake. One sec." There was a desk in the corner of the room so I yanked open a drawer and found a notepad. I pulled the pen open with my teeth and said, "Okay. Tell me it."

CHAPTER 21

Mae Thompson
December 25, 4:30 PM

"Sweetheart, I put your new Christmas pajamas on the bed in your old room. I already washed them, so they're ready for you to wear." My mom called to me through the bathroom door as I brushed my still-damp hair. My parents liked getting the family matching PJs every year, and since the schedule of events got all messed up from the blizzard, they decided we'd wear them for the rest of Christmas instead of getting dressed up for dinner.

"Thanks, Mom," I called back, my voice still feeling raw from all the crying I had done earlier. Once the dam broke, there wasn't anything I could do to stop it. I glanced at my reflection in the mirror and saw two semi-puffy, red-rimmed eyes staring back at me. That wouldn't do at all. I needed some makeup, so maybe my family wouldn't realize how upset I was. I hurried to my old room, still in my towel, so I could change and make myself look a tad more presentable. I gently touched the soft flannel of the PJs and smiled for the first time in what felt like hours. At least I got to spend the rest of the day with my family.

The front door doorbell rang, and I turned my head toward the sound in case I could hear who might be showing up at our house on Christmas afternoon. There was a loud commotion and a chorus of "I'll get it!" ranging from my mom to Xander and, of course, the twins. A few moments later, someone knocked lightly on my bedroom door.

"Mae? You might want to get changed and come down here," Jake's soft, calming voice said through the door.

"Now?" I squeaked, still only in a towel. I shimmied back into the undergarments I'd worn while flying and threw on the pajamas.

"Yeah, it seems pretty important."

I swung the door open, my heart beating with uncertainty. I had no idea what this could possibly be about. Jake gave me a small smile before squeezing my arm gently. "Be nice to him, okay?"

My brows jumped in confusion, and then hope bloomed in my chest. "Oh my God," I breathed out, not wanting to get too excited. "Is it...?"

Jake smiled again and gestured for me to go downstairs. I hurried forward and saw my entire fucking family standing in the entryway in matching outfits staring at a rather rumpled Lon.

He bit his lip and held up his suitcase. "So, funny story," he said as I slowly closed the space between us. "You apparently love stealing my suitcase."

I had no idea if I was laughing or crying at that point, but I was vaguely aware that Mom and Jake were trying their best to clear the area of my incredibly curious and nosy family. Lon dropped the suitcase and wrapped me in his arms, my face burrowing in his chest as I cried tears I didn't know were still in me.

"Don't cry, babe, please don't cry. The moment I got in the car, I knew that wasn't how things were supposed to go. It was never going to be only two nights together for us. I want—no, I need—more than that from you. I just hope you forgive me for not realizing it sooner and saying something."

"I didn't mean to steal your bag again." My voice was muffled in his now soaked shirt. Lon ran his hand through my damp hair and pressed kisses all over my head.

"You didn't technically. Jake did. But I'm thrilled he did. And that you swapped our bags in the first place." He forced me to take a step back so he could fully look at me. "Mae. You're seriously the best thing that's happened to me in a long time, and I love how I feel when I'm with you or talking to you. I don't want to give that up."

"But we live so far away…how would we even do that?"

He shook his head. "I don't know. We figure it out as we go, okay? All I know is I don't need to be back in New York until after the New Year. I can change my tickets to stay here until then if you want me to. No pressure, of course, but I'd love to spend as much time as possible with you. But if you don't want to I—"

"Jesus, man. Take a breath and let her speak!" Xander yelled from down the hall. I glanced over my shoulder and saw Jake grabbing my brother by the arm and yanking him away again.

I blinked rapidly, trying hard to stop my tears as I soaked in all the words Lon said. He wanted me to be in his life. He didn't want us to end. "Does this mean you want to be my New Year's Eve date?"

He grinned, pulling me closer to him again. "Yes. I want that more than anything. And your Valentine's Day date. And your St. Pat's date. And a random Friday night date." His eyes looked above us for a moment before saying, "If I recall, we decided it's bad luck to not kiss under the mistletoe. We can't have that, can we?"

Sure enough, there was mistletoe hanging above our heads which I swore hadn't been there earlier. I looked down the hallway again, and Jake wink before finally leaving us alone. I heard him call, "Hey kids, let's turn on a movie."

Their voices quickly disappeared as Jake herded them to the basement's TV. Down the hall, the opening notes of "Have Yourself a Merry Little Christmas" floated toward us, making my heart swell with happiness and love. Love for my family and this holiday. And love for the man standing in front of me.

I turned back to Lon and threaded my fingers behind his neck before pressing my lips gently to his. "No, we certainly can't risk it."

Not that we needed the good luck. Despite the blizzard, despite the overwhelming travel stresses, Lon was the best Christmas gift I could have wished for. And this was only the beginning.

THE END

ACKNOWLEDGMENTS

Back in Mid-2020 I was let go from my office job and immediately flew into panic mode. My husband said, "why not use this to get serious about your writing?" I cannot believe here we are, two years later, and I am finally not just writing (and re-writing) but am actually publishing my very first book. Thank you to Jeremy for being the most supportive, loving, and amazing husband. Thank you for letting me take this risk and focus on my ultimate passion of writing romance. I love you.

A big shout out and love you to the three other women of this anthology: Erin King, Christina Mitchell, and Meika Usher. I'm so lucky to have you three as such wonderful friends but also writing partners. YES DO!

Thank you to Sarah Estep for always being there for me whether it's to yell at me to write/edit more, talk though characters and plots, or simply unwind and talk about life outside of the books.

Stephanie Kazowz. Whew, what a wild ride the last few years have been, huh? Thanks for being next to me every single step of the indie career that we are both navigating.

Here's to many more books and many more podcast episodes.

And, thank you to my mom. I grew up lucky enough to have a mom who was the absolute best and had no shame for her love of reading romance novels. I love you and miss you and wish you had the chance to read mine. Except I'd tell you to skip the sex scenes because that's just awkward.

Finally, thank you, dear reader. This is just the beginning for me, so if you enjoyed Mae and Lon, I hope you will love all the other couples I have in the works. Here's to 2023 and all that is to come!

ABOUT LIZ

LIZ ZERKEL writes romance filled with humor, heart, and spice. She is also a podcaster with various shows, including Dick of the Week, where she and her co-host discuss everything they love (and sometimes hate) about romance. When not behind the keyboard or microphone, she can be found reading, daydreaming about her next camping trip, or finding her new favorite restaurant to try. She lives in St. Louis with her comedian husband and two black cats, Phantom Cat and Shelley. You can find out more at lizzerkel.com.

9 798201 155148

Printed by Libri Plureos GmbH in Hamburg,
Germany